"In search of mystery, [...]
in inspiring, faith-ba[...]
Carrie Turansky's tim[...]
today's headlines with Victorian England's crusade to rescue
exploited children and provide them with hope and a future
delighted my heart."

Cathy Gohlke, Christy Award Hall of Fame author
of *Ladies of the Lake*

"This stirring dual-timeline tale will grip your heart from the
start and not let you go until you get to the heartwarming ending. A captivating story on an important subject, *A Token of
Love* is Carrie Turansky at her best!"

Roseanna M. White, bestselling, Christy Award–winning
author of THE IMPOSTERS

"Carrie Turansky boldly takes on the issue of human trafficking, a heartbreaking topic as relevant today as it was in
1880s London, in her new novel *A Token of Love*. Courageous
characters, delightful romance, and a compelling plot—hall-
marks of every Turansky novel—are sure to satisfy fans, old
and new."

Michelle Shocklee, award-winning author of *Appalachian
Song* and *Under the Tulip Tree*

"A powerful tale offering a glimpse into the heartbreaking injustice that affects many underserved people; an evil as prevalent
today as in centuries past. Sensitively written, this tender story
addresses the sinfulness of human trafficking, yet there is hope
in the courageous faithful who demand protection for society's
vulnerable. Bravo!"

Kate Breslin, bestselling author of *In Love's Time*

"*A Token of Love* is a powerful story of love, loss, and longing as it sensitively explores the issue of human trafficking with hope and dignity. My new favorite novel from Carrie Turansky."

Carolyn Miller, bestselling author of the REGENCY BRIDES
and REGENCY WALLFLOWERS series

"In *A Token of Love*, Carrie Turansky weaves together the heartwarming stories of two couples in different eras fighting to protect the most vulnerable. A beautiful tale of God at work among His people, this is one novel historical fiction fans won't want to miss."

Karen Barnett, award-winning author
of *When Stone Wings Fly*

A Token of Love

Books by Carrie Turansky

A Token of Love
The Legacy of Longdale Manor
The Governess of Highland Hall
The Daughter of Highland Hall
A Refuge at Highland Hall
Shine Like the Dawn
Across the Blue
No Ocean Too Wide
No Journey Too Far

A Token of Love

CARRIE TURANSKY

BETHANYHOUSE
a division of Baker Publishing Group
Minneapolis, Minnesota

© 2024 by Carrie Turansky

Published by Bethany House Publishers
Minneapolis, Minnesota
BethanyHouse.com

Bethany House Publishers is a division of
Baker Publishing Group, Grand Rapids, Michigan

Printed in the United States of America

Library of Congress Cataloging-in-Publication Data
Names: Turansky, Carrie, author.
Title: A token of love / Carrie Turansky.
Description: Minneapolis, Minnesota : Bethany House, a division of Baker
    Publishing Group, 2024.
Identifiers: LCCN 2024002310 | ISBN 9780764241062 (paper) | ISBN 9780764244049
    (casebound) | ISBN 9781493448142 (ebook)
Subjects: LCGFT: Christian fiction. | Detective and mystery fiction. | Novels.
Classification: LCC PS3620.U7457 T65 2024 | DDC 813/.6—dc23/eng/20240117
LC record available at https://lccn.loc.gov/2024002310

Epigraph Scripture quotation is from The Holy Bible, English Standard Version® (ESV®), copyright © 2001 by Crossway, a publishing ministry of Good News Publishers. Used by permission. All rights reserved. ESV Text Edition: 2016

This book is a work of fiction. Names, characters, places, and incidents are the product of the author's imagination or are used fictitiously. Any resemblance to actual events, locales, or persons, living or dead, is coincidental.

Cover design by Kathleen Lynch, Black Kat Design
Cover image of woman by Malgorzata Maj, Arcangel

Baker Publishing Group publications use paper produced from sustainable forestry practices and postconsumer waste whenever possible.

24   25   26   27   28   29   30   7   6   5   4   3   2   1

To my silver friends,
Lisa and Renee,
and my gold friends,
Cathy, Terri, Cher, and Ann.

"Make new friends, but keep the old.
One is silver and the other gold."
—Joseph Parry

"Is not this the fast that I choose: to loose the bonds of wickedness, to undo the straps of the yoke, to let the oppressed go free, and to break every yoke? Is it not to share your bread with the hungry and bring the homeless poor into your house; when you see the naked, to cover him, and not to hide yourself from your own flesh? Then shall your light break forth like the dawn, and your healing shall spring up speedily; your righteousness shall go before you; the glory of the LORD shall be your rear guard."

Isaiah 58:6–8 ESV

1

Lillian Grace Freemont took up her pen and let her thoughts flow onto the paper. *We must give women more opportunities through education and employment to lift themselves from poverty and shame to positions of respectability and honor. Not only for their own sakes, but for their children, and for the betterment of all society.*

She reread her words, and her throat tightened. Some poor women and girls were cast off and condemned to a life of heartache and pain, with no way out. Why didn't more people speak up for them? Were they too uncomfortable with the subject or simply afraid of what others would think of them if they aligned themselves with their cause? Someone had to take a stand and speak for those who could not speak for themselves.

She rose from her desk and paced across the dark-paneled library of her Eaton Square townhouse. The invitation she'd received to address the Montrose Women's League was an exceptional opportunity. It was the chance to stir the hearts of influential women and motivate them to work for much-needed change.

But could she write a speech worthy of the occasion?

She believed in the cause with all her heart, but she'd never spoken to a large group. For the past few years, she'd focused her attention on serving in her church. But her growing awareness of the needs around her had strengthened her desire to do more.

She'd only voiced her opinion to individuals or in a small circle of friends. But one of those friends had been impressed by what she'd said and passed her name on to the committee leading the League. That had prompted the invitation to present her thoughts at the May meeting. Knowing she would be speaking to a large group on such a challenging topic had made her toss and turn in bed until well after midnight for the last few days. Her fear of public speaking was enough to make her knees quake and her voice falter.

She pulled in a deep breath and closed her eyes. *Please, Lord, help me pull this together. Help me find the right words to make the cause clear and compelling. Give me courage to do what I must!*

Footsteps sounded in the hall, and she opened her eyes.

Her housekeeper, Mrs. Pringle, stepped into view in the open doorway. "A message arrived for you, ma'am."

Lillian eyed the envelope in the housekeeper's hand. "Please, come in. Why didn't Stanford answer the door?"

Mrs. Pringle crossed the room and handed her the envelope. "The young lad who brought the message came to the kitchen door."

"That's odd."

"Yes, but from the look of him, I'd say he's from the East End or some other poor area of town. I suppose he knew he might be turned away if he came to the front door."

Lillian glanced at the envelope. "Is he waiting for a reply?"

"No. He ran off as soon as he handed it to me. He didn't even wait for a sixpence."

"Thank you, Mrs. Pringle."

The housekeeper nodded and left the room.

Lillian tore open the envelope and took out the folded piece of paper. Her eyes darted from her name at the top to the signature at the bottom. *Forever your loving sister, Serena.*

She gasped and sank into the nearest chair. It had been almost nine years since she'd heard from her sister. Serena had run away with a soldier named Robert Dunsmore when she was only seventeen, bringing deep heartache to Lillian and their widowed mother. They had no idea where she'd gone and had only received one brief note five months after she left, announcing the birth of her daughter, Alice.

Painful memories washed over Lillian, bringing a wave of regret. She should have done more to find her sister and bring her home. Gripping the letter, she scanned the words written in a shaky hand.

Dear Lillian,

I know it has been many years since I've written. I am sorry for that, and I ask your forgiveness. I hope you'll come to me now, despite my past mistakes, for I fear I am not long for this world.

Lillian lifted her hand to her heart. How could her little sister be dying? Serena was only twenty-six years old.

There is much I want to explain. But more important than explanations, I need your help to reclaim my daughter, Alice. I had no choice but to turn her over to the Foundling Hospital when she was only three months old. She is now almost eight, and you must reclaim her soon, or I'm afraid she will be sent out to apprentice as a domestic and we'll not be able to find her.

I know I should've reached out to you and Mother sooner, but I was so ashamed of what I've done. I couldn't bear the

11

thought of facing you after the hurt I caused. I told myself Robert would return, and we would collect Alice and be a happy family. But months and then years passed. Robert has not been faithful to me. He left us to fend for ourselves. I had to go into service to support myself and give my darling little daughter away. Hardship and illness have followed me all these years, and I've never been able to reclaim her.

In these last few weeks, my health has taken a bad turn. I've been so ill I'm not able to work or rise from my bed. The money is gone. My few friends have turned away. I am afraid I won't recover. Will you come and let me make amends before it's too late?

I pray you can find it in your heart to visit me. Then I hope you will go to the Foundling Hospital, reclaim Alice, and give her the home and life she deserves. Please come quickly. I live at 237 Miller's Court, second floor, Number 2, White Chapel, London.

Forever your loving sister,
Serena

Tears misted Lillian's vision, blurring the words on the page. *Oh, Serena, how can this be true?*

She stared at her sister's address, her heartache increasing. Serena's choices had taken her down a painful road. But she was not the only one who had suffered in the last nine years. Serena didn't know their mother had passed away not long after Serena left. Nor was she aware that Lillian had become a widow and lost a child . . . a child she could never hope to reclaim.

Two hours later, Lillian's carriage rolled to a stop. She looked out the window, and her heart twisted. The row of decrepit buildings lining the street looked like those poverty-stricken hovels described in a Charles Dickens novel. How could her sister have fallen so low?

Ben Fields, her coachman, stepped into view, wearing a concerned frown. "Are you certain this is the correct place, ma'am?"

She spied the small sign with the number 237 hanging above the doorway. "If this is Miller's Court, then yes, I'm afraid it is."

He opened the carriage door. "Shall I go in with you, ma'am?"

"No, thank you. Please wait here. I'm not sure how long I'll be." She hesitated, then said, "I may need your help."

Surprise flashed in his eyes, but he nodded and offered his hand as she descended from the carriage.

She took one step, and her foot slipped on the slick cobblestone street. The coachman reached out and steadied her. She looked down at the muck smeared on the side of her shoe and grimaced, not wishing to identify the brown sludge. Visiting White Chapel was not for the faint of heart.

She entered the old building, stopped in the hallway, and waited for her eyes to adjust to the dim light. Broken crates, tin cans, and piles of old newspapers lay on the hallway floor. She stepped around them and climbed two flights of creaking stairs to the second floor. When she reached the upper landing, she spied three doors. The number two was scratched into the dark wood of the middle door.

"Give me courage, Lord," she whispered, then approached the door and knocked three times. A few seconds passed, and no one answered. She turned the knob and found the door unlocked. Opening it a few inches, she leaned closer. "Serena, it's Lillian. May I come in?"

"Lillian?" Her sister's voice sounded weak and strained.

"Yes, dear. It's me." She entered and quickly scanned the room. Her sister lay on a narrow bed in the corner, curled up under an old gray blanket. Alarm shot through Lillian as she crossed toward her. Serena's face appeared flushed, and her blond hair lay in stringy locks on the dirty pillow.

Her sister looked up through glassy blue eyes. "I hoped you would come."

Lillian's throat tightened. "I'm glad you sent word. I would've come sooner if I'd known you were ill." She knelt beside the bed and gently brushed her sister's damp hair back from her face. Heat radiated into her fingers. "You have a fever." She spotted a glass of water on the bedside table and offered it to Serena.

Her sister struggled to raise herself enough to drink. Lillian held the glass to her lips, and after a few sips, Serena coughed several times, sounding as if she could barely catch her breath, then she sank back on the pillow.

"Has the doctor come? What did he say?"

She wheezed. "I've no money for a doctor."

Her sister's labored breathing sent fear crawling up Lillian's spine. She quickly scanned the sparse room. A round table, a rickety-looking chair, and two crates were her sister's only furnishings. A small, square window with dirty glass let in little light. There was no fireplace or stove to keep the room warm, although lack of warmth was not her sister's current problem. How could anyone recover from an illness, alone, in a room like this?

Lillian turned to Serena. "I have my carriage waiting downstairs. I'll pack your things, and you can come home with me."

Serena's brow knit. "But what will your husband say? Will he allow it?"

A pang pierced Lillian's heart. "Stephen . . . is no longer with us."

Serena's eyes widened. "What?"

"His ship went down in the North Sea five months after you left."

"Oh, Lillian. I'm so sorry. I didn't know."

Lillian swallowed hard. Although eight years had passed since Stephen's death, mentioning it brought pain to the surface. They had only been married a short time, but she had loved him deeply, and he had loved her. She forced those thoughts away and focused on her sister once more.

"I'll pack your things, then I'll have my coachman come and help you downstairs." Her sister had few belongings. It wouldn't take long to fill the two crates and clear the room.

"I don't deserve your kindness, not after everything I've done." Serena's whispered words sent her into a coughing fit.

Lillian shook her head. "There's no need to think about that now. I'm sure you'll feel quite comfortable in my home, and you'll be well in no time." She forced optimism into her voice.

Within five minutes, she'd collected everything in the room and helped her sister put on a robe.

Serena pulled in a raspy breath. "Please look under the bed. There's a small wooden box."

Lillian knelt and pushed the blanket aside. Reaching under, she searched until she found the box.

"Open it, please," Serena said.

Lillian lifted the hinged lid. Inside lay folded papers, a ribbon, and a few coins.

"Those are Alice's papers from the Foundling Hospital. You'll need them when you go reclaim her."

Lillian's breath caught in her throat as she unfolded the top paper and scanned the words.

Date of entry: 18 September 1877. Female infant. Three months old. Birth name: Alice Catherine Dunsmore. Mother: Serena Faith Crosby.

Lillian stared at the words. The use of Serena's surname confirmed the worst. Her sister had run away with Dunsmore, but she had never married him. She read on.

Father: Robert John Dunsmore, Corporal in the 7th Queen's Own Hussars. Child's date of birth: 14 June 1877. Place of birth: White Chapel, London. Mother left a round golden token with the words Remember My Love *inscribed on the front and tied with a red ribbon through a top center hole.*

A flood of emotion swirled through Lillian as she looked up and met Serena's gaze. How could her sister birth and nurse a child for three months, not counting the months she carried her inside, and then give her up? She tried to restrain her feelings, but it was impossible. "Why didn't you let me help you?"

Serena looked down. "I thought Alice would be safe at the Foundling Hospital until Robert returned. Then we would marry and reclaim her."

"But when you realized he wasn't coming back, you could've come home." Lillian's voice grew more intense. "I don't understand."

Serena shook her head as tears filled her eyes. "How could I come home? I knew you despised me for hurting Mother and bringing shame on our family."

Lillian pulled back as though she'd been struck. "Of course we were hurt and concerned when you disappeared, but I never despised you. I wanted to help. I love you."

Serena's face crumpled. "Truly? You still love me?"

"Yes." Lillian reached for Serena's hand. "I could tell from your letter all was not well. I searched for Robert's family and learned where his military unit was stationed. I wrote to him, and he replied, insisting he didn't know where you were."

Tears overflowed her sister's eyes. "He knew very well where we were. Why would he say that?" She coughed again, then groaned and rolled to her side.

Lillian placed her hand on Serena's shoulder. This was not the time to try and straighten out all that had happened. "We don't need to talk about it now. Let's focus on the present and helping you get well."

Serena sniffed. "Thank you."

Lillian rose. "I'll take a crate downstairs and bring the coachman up to help us."

"Wait. There's one more thing you need to know."

Lillian turned back. "Yes?"

"Before Alice was born, Robert gave me a love token. He had one that matched. I left mine with Alice at the Foundling Hospital. It's mentioned in those papers." She pulled in a shaky breath, sorrow weighing down each word. "Robert sent his back. It's in the bottom of the box."

Lillian lifted the other papers and found the round golden token beneath. She studied the inscription on the front in flowing script. *Remember My Love.* Two small hearts and swirling vines surrounded the words.

She clenched her jaw, fighting off the wave of anger and regret. It seemed Serena had remembered her love for Robert and their daughter, but Robert had abandoned and forgotten those he'd claimed to love.

~

The coachman carried Serena upstairs to Lillian's largest guest room. Lillian helped her settle into a chair and summoned their maid. While the maid gave Serena a sponge bath and rinsed her sister's hair, Lillian wrote a quick note and asked the coachman to deliver it to the doctor. She retrieved a fresh nightgown from her room, then helped Serena slip it on and climb into the feather bed.

Lillian tucked a light blanket around her sister, leaned down, and kissed her forehead. It was still hot, making it clear her fever had not abated.

Serena released a shaky breath and closed her eyes. "Thank you," she said softly.

"Rest now. I'll collect a few things, then come back and sit with you." Lillian waited for Serena to reply, but her sister appeared to have drifted off to sleep. Concern flared in Lillian's chest. The move had been necessary, but it seemed to have drained what little strength Serena had left.

Would her sister recover? She swallowed hard and set off down the hall, a prayer for mercy and healing rising from her heart. She added a plea to know how best to help her sister and niece.

She found Mrs. Pringle and asked her to have the cook prepare some nourishing broth and send up tea. Continuing down the hall, she considered her sister's request that she go to the Foundling Hospital and reclaim her daughter. It was nearly five o'clock, and the doctor was expected soon. She would wait to speak with him, then go to the Foundling Hospital first thing tomorrow morning.

Descending the stairs, she recalled the Foundling Hospital was a respected charity, with a long history of taking in infants whose mothers could not care for them. She'd given several generous donations in the past, never knowing her niece might have benefitted from those gifts.

She entered the library and gathered her Bible, pen, and the speech she'd been writing when her sister's message had arrived. She doubted she could gather her thoughts to continue writing, but she had to try. The meeting was only a few days away.

The front bell rang, and she heard Stanford answer the door. She met the butler and Dr. Frasier in the entry hall.

The doctor nodded to her. "Good evening, Mrs. Freemont."

"Thank you for coming, Doctor." She motioned to the right. "My sister is upstairs in the guest room. If you'll follow me."

They climbed the stairs, and she showed him into her sister's room. "Dr. Frasier, this is my sister, Serena Crosby. She has a fever and cough and is quite weak. I'm not sure how long she's been ill."

Serena didn't stir as the doctor crossed to her bed. He placed his black leather bag on the bedside table, then he gently roused Serena, questioned her, and conducted his examination. Serena spoke softly between coughs, answering his questions in a shaky voice.

Finally, he turned to Lillian. "I believe she has pneumonia, an acute infection of the lungs. She'll need care for some time. Shall I send for a nurse?"

"No. I'll oversee her care myself. Please tell me what's needed."

He nodded. "Give her plenty of liquids, broth, peppermint tea, and soup. Try to calm the cough with warm water, and tea with lemon and honey. She needs to rest as much as possible. Cool her with damp cloths and only cover her with a light blanket." He took out his pocket watch and consulted the time. "I have another call to make, but I'll come back in the morning before ten. If she worsens, send word."

Lillian nodded, trying not to let his final fearful words steal her hope.

He glanced at Serena, then back at Lillian. "Take heart, Mrs. Freemont. With prayer and good nursing, I believe your sister will recover."

"Thank you." Lillian pushed those words past her tight throat.

He sent her a brief smile. "I'll see myself out."

She thanked him again and crossed to her sister's bed. Serena's cheeks were still flushed, but she seemed more peaceful. "Did you hear the doctor? He said you have pneumonia, but he believes you will get better."

Serena's chin trembled. "It's more than I deserve . . . after what I've done."

Lillian knelt and looked into her sister's eyes. "We all have regrets, but there is no need to dwell on them. Seek the Lord's forgiveness and let Him carry them for you."

"How could He forgive me?"

"The same way He forgives us all."

"But if they send Alice out as an apprentice, she'll be lost to me forever!" Shivers shook Serena, and tears traced lines down her cheeks.

Lillian clasped her sister's hand. "Trust me to share this burden with you. I'll go tomorrow and take the token and papers. I'm sure they'll release Alice, and I'll bring her home to you. Then we'll all be together as we should be." She pulled the blanket up around her sister's shoulders. "Now calm yourself and try to get some rest."

"All right." Serena closed her eyes and released a trembling breath. Lillian watched as her sister slowly relaxed, and her breathing became more even.

2

The sound of youthful voices drifted toward Janelle Spencer through her partially open office window. She swiveled her desk chair and looked outside. One floor below, in the park next to the Foundling Museum, six boys raced across the grass, passing and dribbling the football down the field. The tallest one kicked the ball into the goal and scored. His hands shot up in the air, and he danced across the field. His teammates ran toward him, hooting and slapping him on the back.

Memories of Marcus rushed in, and Janelle bit her lip. He loved football—coaching, playing, watching it on television. How many Saturday mornings and Sunday afternoons had she spent cheering for him from the sidelines? But then she'd discovered he'd been involved with his old girlfriend the entire eight months she and Marcus had been dating.

How could she have been so blind? Why had she ignored the signs and forgiven him each time he went silent for a few days and then showed up with a bouquet of flowers and a litany of excuses? She should've known he was lying to her. Was she so desperate to be loved that she refused to see there was something terribly wrong with their relationship?

21

She'd blocked his calls and texts five months ago, but thoughts of him still stung. Pushing those painful memories away, she turned back to her desk. She needed to focus on her work and put Marcus and his deceitful ways behind her.

A knock sounded at her office door, and she called, "Come in."

Iris Williams, director of the museum's guest services, stepped into the office. "I finished the volunteer schedule for June. Amanda is still out. Would you like to look it over?"

Janelle glanced at the clock on the wall. It was nearly four. Amanda Preston, the museum's director, had taken one of their most generous donors to lunch. She should be back by now. Perhaps the lunch had turned into a longer meeting so Amanda could explain the museum's current financial struggles and encourage an extra donation to help them meet their budget.

A ripple of unease traveled through Janelle, but she shook it off. "Sure, I'll take a look."

"Thanks. I need to post this right away. The volunteers always want to switch days and juggle things around before it's official. I need to allow time for that." She passed the two printed pages to Janelle.

She'd just scanned the first few lines when her phone rang. She glanced at her cell screen. "Excuse me."

Iris nodded and turned toward the window.

Janelle tapped on her phone. "Hello?"

"Janelle? It's Amanda." Her words sounded rushed and intense.

Janelle glanced away from Iris. "I'm here. Is everything all right?"

Amanda huffed out a loud breath. "No, it's not. I'm on the way to the hospital. My water broke—I think the babies are coming!"

Janelle pulled in a sharp breath. She had to stay calm for Amanda's sake. "Is Wesley with you?"

"Yes, yes. He's here . . . but it's too early." Her voice rose to a panicked pitch.

"Just try to stay calm. Wesley is there, and I'm sure the doctors will know what to do. You'll be in good hands."

"But the babies will be so small." Amanda's voice trembled. "Would you pray for us?"

Janelle's throat tightened. "Yes, of course. You can count on it." What a surprising change of heart. In the past, whenever Janelle mentioned anything about her faith or prayer, Amanda had turned the conversation in a different direction. But in a time of crisis, people often reached out to those who believed in prayer.

"Thank you," Amanda whispered. "I know I can count on you to handle everything at the museum."

Janelle swallowed hard. The early arrival of Amanda's twins meant she would have to step in as the museum's acting director. She and Amanda had started discussing what would be needed in that role, but there was still so much they hadn't covered. How could she ever fill Amanda's shoes?

In the background, she heard Wesley urging Amanda to end the call.

"We're at the hospital. I've got to go." The phone clicked off.

Questions rushed through Janelle's mind as she lowered the phone.

Iris's eyebrows lifted. "Is Amanda in labor?"

"It sounds like it." Janelle quickly recalled what she'd read about premature babies. Some as young as twenty-two weeks had survived. Amanda was well past that fearful line. But her due date was at least eight weeks away. Breathing or feeding issues were possible. The twins would most likely need to stay in the hospital for several weeks, and Amanda would want to be with them. She lifted a silent plea heavenward for Amanda, Wesley, and their soon-to-be-born twin girls.

Iris sent her a worried look. "Wow, that means you'll be stepping in for her."

Janelle nodded and lowered her gaze to the paper in her hand. Managing without Amanda would be a huge challenge, but she wasn't going to voice that thought. "The best way we can help Amanda is to keep the museum running as smoothly as possible while she's away."

Iris released a deep breath. "I'll do whatever I can to help."

"Thanks." Janelle flipped to the second page, and her stomach quivered. Amanda probably did more than proofread for Iris. The volunteer schedule should be based on the number of visitors expected and any tours or school groups coming through.

She looked up and held out the paper. "This looks fine, but have you checked the reservations?"

Iris sent her a questioning look. "That's how I make the schedule."

"Oh . . . of course. That's good to know."

"Shall I go ahead and post this online, or should we wait for Amanda?"

Energy tingled along Janelle's nerves. The decision was up to her now. She would be in charge until Amanda returned. She rose from her chair. "Go ahead and post it. Let's allow Amanda to focus on her own needs and those of her babies."

Iris gave a brief nod and walked out of the office.

As she passed through the doorway, a man stepped out of her way, then back into view. He looked in at Janelle with a slight smile. "Hello, I'm Jonas Conrad. I'm looking for Amanda Preston."

"Amanda is . . . not available. I'm Janelle Spencer. How can I help?"

He walked into the office. She noted he was at least six feet tall with reddish-brown hair and a neatly trimmed beard and moustache. His steel-gray eyes reflected searching intensity as he glanced around the office and back at her. "I have a four o'clock appointment with Ms. Preston to discuss the fundraising film I'll be making for the Foundling Museum."

Janelle blinked. "A film?"

"Yes, Ms. Preston contacted me last week. We spoke twice on the phone, and she asked me to meet with her today. When will she be back?"

"I'm sorry. Amanda is going to be out of the office for some time. I'll be filling in for her while she's away."

He gave a brief nod. "Okay. I'd be glad to talk to you about it."

Janelle hesitated. "I'm afraid we'll have to postpone that discussion until she returns."

His eyebrows drew down in a V. "Ms. Preston said she needs the film by the first of September so she can show it at the annual fundraising gala."

Janelle's thoughts raced. The gala's venue had been reserved and the caterer selected, but Amanda had said nothing about the program or showing a fundraising film. "I'm sorry. She didn't mention it to me."

"Why don't I show you an example of my work?" He quickly unzipped his black rolling case and pulled out a laptop, then he placed it on the end of her desk and opened the computer. "I'm sure you'll see what a great impact a project like this could have for the museum."

He certainly seemed eager and confident. It would be rude to send him away without seeing his work. She came around the desk and joined him.

He tapped a few keys and opened a video. "We created this film for the British Wildlife Federation. It's been a very successful part of their latest fundraising campaign."

He clicked on the video, and beautiful scenes of rolling hills, pastures, and forests filled the screen, then the voice of the narrator told of the UK's endangered species in need of protection. Amazing images of animals, birds, and reptiles appeared as the narrator continued and made his plea to save those creatures for the benefit of future generations. The creative filming angles, close-ups of the animals, and smooth transitions, along with the narrator's words, were quite compelling.

He tapped the computer to stop the video, then focused on Janelle. "I know I can create a film that will honor the history of the Foundling Hospital and show the importance of supporting the continuing work of the museum."

Janelle bit her lip. As an independent charity, the museum relied on the generosity of individuals, trusts, foundations, and companies to keep their doors open. The need to raise funds put continual pressure on Amanda and all the staff. And the museum's budget had been particularly tight the last few years, especially since the pandemic, when they'd had to close their doors for months on end. Donations had dropped off, and they had not risen back to the pre-pandemic level.

"A fundraising film sounds like a good idea," Janelle continued, "but Amanda is going to be out of the office for some time. I'm not sure if we'll be able to move ahead with this project."

He fixed his intense gaze on her. "Ms. Preston accepted my quote. I cleared my schedule and turned down other work because of our verbal agreement. Our meeting today was to outline her goals so I could begin collecting the background material I need to write the script."

Janelle's eyebrows rose. "Oh . . . she already agreed to the project?"

He glanced away and then back at her. "We didn't iron out all the details, but I was under the impression she wants me to start the project right away."

"I see." Janelle's gaze darted around the room as she debated her reply. He seemed sincere, and there was no reason to doubt he was truthful, but what if he'd misunderstood Amanda's level of commitment? What if Janelle gave him the go-ahead, and that wasn't what Amanda wanted?

"Don't worry. I won't get in your way. I just need a tour of the museum, access to historical records, and information about the museum's current goals and programs. That should be enough for me to work on a rough draft of the script to show Ms. Preston for her approval—or your approval, since you're taking over for her."

"I can't give you the final okay without talking to Amanda."

He frowned. "Can you phone her?"

"Not at the moment."

"I don't understand. Is she ill?"

"No." She glanced toward the hall and then back at him. "She's giving birth to twins, but they're not due for two months."

His eyes widened. "Oh, wow. I hope they'll be okay."

Concern tightened her shoulders. "So do I." She took a deep breath. "I understand you want to get started right away, but I'll have to confirm this with Amanda, and I might also need permission from the board."

He released a slow, deep breath. "I see. Then it seems we're at an impasse."

Janelle tipped her head, acknowledging the truth of his statement.

His eyes lit up. "But since I'm here, maybe you could give me a tour of the museum to get my creative juices flowing. Then I can get started on the script as soon as you hear back from Ms. Preston."

The man's optimism seemed to have no end. "All right. I can show you around."

"Thank you." He closed his laptop, slipped it into the case, and pulled a business card from his jacket pocket. "Here's my contact information. You can text or phone me anytime. When you speak to Ms. Preston, please tell her that if she wants the film ready for the gala in September, I need to get started right away."

Janelle looked up and met his gaze. "I'll do what I can."

⁓

Jonas clenched his jaw as he followed Janelle Spencer out of her office. He could not lose this job, especially not after the disastrous results of his last project. That would sink his fledgling film company and take him and his assistant, Howie, down with it.

Please, Lord. Help me pull this together.

He'd used every persuasive skill he possessed to convince Amanda Preston to hire him to make this film. Now it looked like he'd have to shift his focus and win over her replacement. He watched Janelle's long auburn hair swish across her back as she led the way down the hall. When they passed a window, fiery light shot through her swaying locks.

He swallowed and glanced away. He was single, and there was no reason he shouldn't admire a pretty woman, but he needed to stay focused.

Janelle glanced over her shoulder. "The Foundling Hospital's original name was The Hospital for the Education and Maintenance of Exposed and Deserted Young Children. When the Foundling Hospital first opened its doors to needy children in 1741, the word *hospital* referred to hospitality. We continue that work today in conjunction with Coram, our partner organization, by reaching out to children in care and to vulnerable families." She stopped beside a glass case on the wall to the right.

Light flooded the display of small objects inside. He squinted, uncertain of their significance.

"When the Foundling Hospital opened, the governors decided a record should be kept of anything left with children by their mothers." She motioned toward the display case. "These tokens were given as identifiers, in the hope that if the mother's situation changed, she could return and reclaim her child. The tokens were a part of the official documents and could be easily recognized to prove the identity of an infant."

Jonas glanced at Janelle. "Each one seems different."

"Yes. There are a few coins that are alike, but most of the tokens are unique."

He stepped closer and scanned the metal tags, coins, locks, crosses, keys, necklaces, and other types of jewelry. There were a few objects that surprised him. One looked like a small ivory spyglass, and another was a metal tag with the word *ALE* painted on it. He chuckled and pointed to the tag. "That's a humorous one."

She cocked her eyebrow, making it obvious she took the subject seriously. "Not when you consider that was all the mother had to leave with her child."

He sobered and gave a brief nod. "I see what you mean."

"Literate parents would also leave notes, keeping a copy for themselves, but those who couldn't read or write often left an object they could accurately describe."

"Did many mothers return for their children?"

"Our records show approximately five hundred were reunited."

"Out of how many children?"

She hesitated. "More than twenty-five thousand children came through the Foundling Hospital between 1741 and 1955."

He made a mental note of the number. It was sobering to realize how many children never saw their mothers again. He glanced at the tokens once more and pointed to one in the second row that looked like a slim white fish. "What's the story there?"

"The bone fish is a gambling token. In Jane Austen's novels, she refers to a game called Speculation, which used cards and fish like that one. It was left in 1798 with a boy named John Cox. He was baptized and renamed Nathaniel Lane."

"Were all the children renamed?"

"Yes. Each infant was given a new name to protect the identities of their parents, then they were baptized and sent to the country to stay with a foster family. When they turned five, they returned to the hospital for schooling and training. They remained there until they were old enough to take on apprentice positions."

"At what age would they leave to be apprentices?"

"Some were as young as eight years old. Others stayed until they were fourteen or fifteen. The age of their leaving changed through the years."

Jonas frowned. "Even fifteen seems awfully young to go out to work."

"Working-class families often apprenticed their children at that age or younger. It was typical for the time." Janelle continued down the hall. "Let me show you the Committee Room."

Jonas followed her through the doorway into a large room, where several paintings in gilded frames hung on the wall. Most were of men wearing wigs and clothing that looked like it was from the 1700s. A heavy stone fireplace was centered on the wall to the right, and an impressive chandelier hung from the ceiling. "This room looks older than the rest of the building."

She nodded, looking pleased that he'd noticed the difference. "The original Foundling Hospital building was taken down in the 1960s, but they kept the paintings and furnishings and re-created several of the rooms here in the new museum building." She motioned to the table in the center. "The mothers came to this room to speak to the governors and request to leave their child." She gave him a few more details as he looked around the room, then took him out to the hallway.

He glanced up at the dark wooden staircase leading to the next floor. More paintings hung on the walls and landing.

She motioned toward the stairs. "This staircase is from the west wing of the original hospital building. But the spikes on the railing have been removed."

He shot her a surprised glance. "Spikes?"

"They were added to stop the boys from sliding down the banister after a child fell and died."

He grimaced. No doubt the boy had only been looking for a bit of fun. Had it happened because he hadn't been properly supervised? He quickly dismissed the thought. An accident like that could've happened anywhere, not just in an institution.

They climbed the stairs, past several more portraits and paintings of religious scenes. Janelle led him through another doorway. "This room is a replica of the original picture gallery."

He glanced around the room, which was filled with more paintings and decorative plasterwork. "I enjoy art as much as the next man, but it seems unusual that you have so many paintings here."

Janelle's eyes lit up. "These works of art are an important part of our history. The Foundling Hospital was not only a children's charity home, it was also the first public art gallery in London. Several artists were supporters of the Hospital." She swept her hand in a wide circle. "All of these paintings were donated by the artists, along with the beautiful plasterwork, sculptures, and furnishings you'll see around the museum."

"Hmmm . . . very generous." That might be an angle he could follow for the film. He had read a few articles online to prepare for this meeting, but he needed to know more. "Is there a guidebook that explains the history of the Foundling Hospital and Museum?"

Janelle nodded. "I have several books in my office. You're welcome to look through those or borrow whatever you'd like."

His hopes rose. If she was willing to lend him some books, maybe that meant she was beginning to see the value of the project. "Thanks. That would helpful."

They took the stairs down to the lower level. "We offer educational programs for children, young adults, and families in these rooms, and we hold special events here. This floor also houses our temporary exhibits."

"Tell me about one of those exhibits."

"One I think was especially meaningful was titled *Tiny Traces: African and Asian Children at the Foundling Hospital*. It featured the artifacts and personal stories of more than a dozen children of African and Asian descent."

He nodded. "You've given me a lot of good information. Thank you. I appreciate your time."

She met his gaze. "I hope it was helpful."

"Very helpful. Seeing everything firsthand gives me ideas about where to start my work."

Her brow creased. "Like I said, I still need confirmation from Amanda, and perhaps the board."

"I understand."

"Let's go back to the office, and I'll show you those books."

They climbed the stairs and passed three women headed out the door. Janelle wished them a good evening, making clear they were staff members rather than visitors to the museum.

"What are the museum hours?"

"We're open ten to five, Tuesday through Sunday."

"You work six days a week?"

"I'm usually off Sunday and Monday, but with Amanda away, I may need to adjust my schedule."

They walked down the hall and back to her office. Janelle crossed to the bookshelves, pulled out three books, and handed them to him. "These two will tell you more about the history of the Foundling Hospital, and this one is a biography of Captain Thomas Coram. He worked for seventeen years to gather support and gain a royal charter to open the Foundling Hospital."

He smiled. "Sounds like interesting reading."

She offered a teasing grin. "It is. Captain Coram was a determined man who had a huge heart for children. He wouldn't give up until he gained the support needed."

"I admire a man with determination."

She nodded. "So do I."

He glanced at the book featuring Captain Coram's striking image. If he was going to make films that changed hearts and minds as well as see his company thrive, he would need to match Coram's determination. He just hoped it wouldn't take seventeen years to see his dreams become reality.

3

Lillian stepped down from the carriage and met her coachman, who held an open umbrella.

"Thank you," she said as she accepted the umbrella. "Please wait for me here."

He touched his cap. "Yes, ma'am."

She passed through the Foundling Hospital's front iron gate and followed the path toward the old brick buildings shaped in a large U. She scanned the grass and stone courtyard but saw no one outside on this rainy morning. When she reached the main door, she rang the bell and waited.

The door opened, and a young girl who looked about ten years old with dark brown hair and pale blue eyes looked up at her. She wore a plain brown dress, white pinafore, and white cap. "May I help you, ma'am?"

"Yes. I'd like to speak to the matron, please."

The girl nodded and gave a slight curtsy. "Please come with me."

Lillian glanced around the dim hall as she followed the girl. All was quiet, and the only other person she saw was an old woman mopping the floor near the far end of the long hallway.

The girl stopped before a dark wooden door. "This is the matron's office." She knocked twice, and a woman called for them to enter. The girl opened the door. "Mrs. Stark, there's a lady here to see you."

Lillian stepped into the matron's office.

Mrs. Stark looked up from behind her desk and studied Lillian with a serious expression. She appeared to be in her fifties, with iron gray hair pulled back into a white cap. She wore an unadorned black dress and wire spectacles. "Thank you, Edith. You may go."

"Yes, ma'am." The girl stepped past Lillian and walked down the hall, leaving the door open.

"Come in. I'm Mrs. Stark, the matron. What brings you to the Foundling Hospital?"

"My name is Lillian Freemont. I believe my niece, Alice Dunsmore, has been a resident here since September 1877. Her mother, Serena Crosby, is my sister, and she is living with me now. She would like her daughter returned to her care."

Mrs. Stark pursed her lips, looking displeased. "Why didn't your sister come herself?"

"She isn't well. She asked me to come in her place."

Mrs. Stark clicked her tongue. "This is highly irregular. Do you have the girl's admission papers?"

"Yes." Lillian reached into her reticule. "My sister also gave me this token that matches the one left with Alice." She laid them on the matron's desk.

Mrs. Stark slid her glasses down her sharp nose, picked up the token, and studied it through narrowed eyes. Setting it aside, she unfolded the papers and quickly scanned them. She looked up. "What proof do you have that you are the girl's aunt?"

Lillian blinked. "Proof?"

Mrs. Stark gave an impatient huff. "I can't very well hand over the girl without a signed letter from her mother or other legal papers proving you have a right to claim her."

"I'm sorry. I didn't realize additional proof would be needed."

She took her calling card from her reticule and held it out to the matron. "I have my card."

The woman shook her head, refusing the card. "That could be printed for a shilling at any printer." She rose from her chair, looking as though she was ending the meeting.

Alarm flashed through Lillian. "Please, I assure you, I am Alice's aunt. If you need a letter from my sister, I can bring one back this afternoon."

Mrs. Stark held up her hand to stop Lillian. "The girl may not be here. Let me check our records."

Lillian's heartbeat picked up speed. Was she too late? Had Alice already been sent away?

Mrs. Stark took a leather-bound book from the shelf behind her. "What was the date of her admittance?"

"The eighteenth of September 1877."

The matron opened the book and flipped through. She ran her finger down a page, then shook her head. "There's no need to bring a letter."

Lillian frowned. "No need?"

"It seems Alice Dunsmore died two weeks after her mother left her in our care."

Lillian sucked in a breath. "What?"

"I'm sorry." The matron's flat voice carried no true sympathy. "Your niece passed away from . . ." She consulted the book again. "The measles."

Lillian stared at her. "I don't understand. How could that happen?"

"It's not unusual." The matron sniffed and closed the book. "Childhood diseases take their toll."

"That's all you have to say? A baby dies, and it means nothing to you!"

Mrs. Stark straightened, her gaze piercing. "We do our best to care for the children, but they often come to us in weakened conditions, and that makes them susceptible to illness and death."

Lillian rose from her chair. "My niece was in good health when my sister gave her into your care. It's more likely she was exposed to the disease here and died because of your inadequate nursing."

A thundercloud rolled across the matron's face. "Now, see here! You've no cause to blame us for the child's death."

Hot tears filled Lillian's eyes. "Then who is to blame?"

"Some children never recover from being *abandoned* by their mothers. They are the ones who carry the ultimate responsibility for what happens to their children."

Lillian clenched her jaw. "It is unfair to blame poor, desperate mothers who have no choice in their situation. They give their children over to you, trusting you to cherish them as they do, but I can see now that trust has been misplaced."

Mrs. Stark's expression hardened. "I believe this interview is finished."

"Yes, it is." Lillian turned to go, but when she reached the doorway, she looked back. "I have been a generous supporter of the Foundling Hospital for many years. As of today, you may no longer count on my support."

She strode out the door, with tears misting her vision. Lowering her head, she started down the hall. Without warning, she bumped into the old woman mopping the floor. "Oh, forgive me. I'm sorry. I didn't see you."

The old woman stilled the mop and motioned her closer. "Don't believe what the matron told you," she whispered.

Lillian blinked away her tears. "What did you say?"

"Your little niece isn't dead. I'm sure of it." She shot a quick glance over her shoulder, then moved away from the matron's door and signaled Lillian to join her.

Lillian's heart hammered as she followed her down the hall.

The old woman leaned close and lowered her voice. "I remember your niece. A real pretty little girl with long blond curls and eyes as blue as the sky."

"But the matron said—"

The old woman shook her head. "There's more going on 'round here than meets the eye."

"I don't understand. What do you mean?"

"Your niece is called Mary Graham now. And she was here until about a week ago."

Lillian pulled in a sharp breath. "Are you sure?"

"Yes. That's when she disappeared . . . and she's not the first."

A shiver raced down Lillian's back. "What are you saying?"

The old woman glanced down the hall once more. "I'm saying a few pretty young girls have gone missing, and your niece was the last to disappear."

"You're certain of this?"

The old woman frowned. "I wouldn't lie about something like that."

"I'll speak to the matron." Lillian turned away.

"No!" The old woman grabbed Lillian's arm. "I wouldn't trust Mrs. Stark. You'll have to find someone else to help you find the girl."

Lillian rubbed her forehead, trying to make sense of what she'd been told. "Why would someone take my niece?"

The woman's gray eyes widened, and she whispered, "I'm sorry to say it, but I've heard they take girls and sell them to work belowstairs at brothels."

A dizzy wave washed over Lillian, and she reached for the wall to steady herself. Who would send an eight-year-old girl to such a terrible place?

The old woman shoved her mop into the rolling metal bucket and pushed it down the hall.

"Wait!" Lillian hurried after her.

The old woman looked over her shoulder and shook her head. "That's all I can tell you. Don't ask me anything more."

"But how can I find her? Where should I look?"

The old woman ignored her words, continued down the hall, and disappeared around the corner.

~

Lillian handed her sister a handkerchief and laid a hand on her shoulder. "I know this is frightening news, but we must not lose heart."

Serena clutched the handkerchief and sobbed. "I never should've left her there!"

Lillian gently rubbed her sister's back, silently agreeing. If only Serena would have humbled herself and returned to her family . . . Instead, she'd given up her daughter, and now they were faced with the terrible results of that choice.

Serena wiped her cheeks and lowered the handkerchief. "You must go back and speak to them. Did she die from the measles, or was she snatched away while in their care? They must tell us the truth!"

Lillian shook her head. "It won't do any good to go back now. We don't know who we can trust."

A new round of tears coursed down Serena's cheeks. "Then what can we do?"

Lillian's mind spun. Should she go to the police? Would they believe her or take the word of the matron? Perhaps she should hire a detective to search the city. But she had no idea where to tell him to start. Alice might have been taken away from London. She might even have been sent to the Continent. She swallowed hard, refusing to voice those dreadful thoughts.

Lord, help us!

A wave of courage flowed through Lillian's heart, and she clasped her sister's hand. "This is a heartbreaking situation, but the Lord knows where she is, and it's not beyond His ability to help us find her."

"But how?" Serena demanded.

"I'm not sure of our next step, but if we pray—"

Serena's eyes flashed. "When has praying ever changed anything?" Her throat convulsed. "I prayed and prayed for Robert to come back—for him to love and care for us as he promised. But he never did!"

Lillian's heart twisted. Her sister's hurt was clouding her view. But this was not the time to remind her she had run away with a man who had wooed her and bedded her before they were married. When his actions continued to show his same lack of character and commitment, Serena should not have been surprised, nor should she blame God for the painful outcome of those choices.

Lillian pulled in a steadying breath. "Praying for guidance is always the right response, no matter how desperate we may feel."

"You truly believe He'll show us how to find Alice?" Painful skepticism laced her sister's words.

Lillian knew she must tread carefully. There was no guarantee their prayers would bring the outcome they hoped. "I believe He loves Alice, and He loves us. If she is still alive and in danger, then it stands to reason He wants her to be found and returned to us."

Serena gripped Lillian's arm. "How can He help us find one lost child in a city full of evil people who care nothing for what's good and right?"

Lillian met her sister's gaze. "I don't know. We must ask Him and then follow His lead."

⌣

Lillian straightened her jacket and knocked on the Reverend Benjamin Howell's front door. His sister, Eugenia Howell, answered. She was a plump middle-aged woman with kind blue eyes and a gentle smile.

"Good day. Is Reverend Howell at home?"

"Yes, he is. Come in, Mrs. Freemont. I'll let him know you're here." She turned through a doorway to the left.

A few moments later, Reverend Howell stepped into the entry hall. "Good afternoon, Mrs. Freemont. Welcome." He motioned through the archway toward one of the chairs by the fireplace. She crossed and took a seat.

He sat opposite her. They exchanged a few pleasantries, then he asked, "Is there a particular reason for your visit today?"

"Yes." She hesitated, summoning her courage. "I'm facing a rather difficult family situation, and I'm hoping you might give me your advice."

He nodded. "I'd be glad to listen and offer any assistance I can."

Lillian told him about Serena's illness and the decision to bring her sister home to rest and recover. He nodded, approval in his eyes. Her cheeks warmed as she explained her sister's relationship with Robert Dunsmore, her pregnancy, and her decision to give her daughter into the care of the Foundling Hospital. His expression grew more concerned as she told him about her conversation with the matron.

"She said there was no hope of reclaiming Alice because she died shortly after Serena left her in their care."

The reverend's eyes widened. "I'm so sorry."

Lillian leaned forward. "But when I left her office, a cleaning woman stopped me just outside the matron's door and told me that it wasn't true."

He frowned. "I don't understand."

"She said my niece was in residence until very recently when she . . . disappeared."

Confusion filled the reverend's face. "Disappeared?"

"Yes. And apparently my niece is not the first young girl to go missing from the hospital. The woman believes they were taken to work belowstairs at a . . . brothel." Her face flamed, and she lowered her gaze.

"I see." His brow creased, and he shifted his pained gaze away.

"I don't know if what the matron said is true or if she is lying to cover up what is going on at the Foundling Hospital. If my niece has been taken, then I must find her. But I'm not sure what my next step should be." She clasped her hands. "I thought of going back to the matron, but the cleaning woman warned me not to trust her."

He rose and paced across the room. "This is serious—very serious indeed."

"I considered going to the police, but I have no proof. The records say my niece died, so I'm not sure they would believe me." Lillian sighed. "I thought it best to speak to you first."

He turned toward her. "In all my years serving at Good Shepherd Church, I've never heard anything that would lead me to doubt the integrity of those overseeing the Foundling Hospital. It's always been spoken of as a worthy charity. But it's possible there might be someone on staff who could be bribed to alter records and make it possible for your niece to be taken."

"So, you think the cleaning woman is telling the truth?"

"I don't see any reason for her to lie, but she could be mistaken. Why don't I make some inquiries and speak to the matron under the pretense of confirming your niece's baptismal name and place of burial. That seems like a reasonable request. Perhaps I'll be able to find out something more."

"Thank you." Lillian rose from her chair. "I don't want to believe my niece died as an infant, but the thought that she has been stolen to work in a brothel is too dreadful for words."

"Both are painful to consider. But if she is alive, there is a chance of finding her and returning her to her mother. Let's pray that is the case, then we'll do what we can to discover where she's been taken."

4

2023

Janelle shifted her laptop case and handbag to her other arm while she juggled a shopping bag and tried to push the button to call the lift. There was no way she was carrying this load up three flights of stairs to her flat. Her empty stomach growled, and she released a frustrated breath.

Where was the lift? Tapping her foot, she glanced around the empty lobby. She should pick up her mail, but it had been a long, stressful day at the museum, and all she wanted right now was dinner and a comfy seat on her couch.

The lift bell rang, and the door slid open.

"Thank you, Lord." She stepped in, closed her eyes, and sent off another prayer for Amanda and the twins. She hadn't heard any more since Amanda's frantic phone call around four. She checked her watch and decided she would text Wesley if she didn't hear from him by eight.

The lift door slid open, and she stepped out. There were only three flats on each floor, which usually made her home a peaceful retreat. Janelle lowered the shopping bag and laptop case to the floor, then dug through her handbag for her keys.

The door to 303 opened, and her friend and neighbor Maggie Lewis stepped out. Her face looked pale, and her short dark hair stuck out in odd directions. "Thank goodness you're home!"

Behind Maggie, Janelle could hear loud music from a kids' television program and Maggie's sons, Cole and Caleb, arguing over who could hold the remote.

Janelle unlocked her door. "What's going on?"

Maggie blew out a deep breath, then closed the door to her flat and crossed the landing. "Dan's daughter, Olivia, arrived this afternoon," she whispered and sent Janelle a wide-eyed expectant look. "Her mother is a germaphobe. We haven't seen her in person for more than three years!"

"So, it should be good for her to have some time with her dad," Janelle said.

"Yes, but she's sixteen now. I feel like I don't even know her. She and Dan did weekly FaceTime calls, but that's not the same as having her here with us."

Janelle picked up her laptop case and handbag. Maggie grabbed the shopping bag, then followed Janelle inside and closed the door.

Janelle couldn't help smiling. Maggie didn't even ask if she could come in. Their friendship had grown in the four years since Janelle had moved into the building. Even though Maggie was ten years older, and they were at different life stages, they often spent time together and shared meals, as well as heart-to-heart talks. Maggie had been her greatest support through her breakup with Marcus, and that had deepened their already strong friendship.

Janelle set her handbag and laptop case on the chair. "How long is Olivia staying?"

"We're not sure. Her stepfather is in the hospital with some sort of kidney issue, and her mother is stressed out about it. Olivia could end up staying until September."

"Wow, all summer?"

"Yes." Maggie plopped the bag on the kitchen counter, looking dejected. "This all came up in the last forty-eight hours.

We had no time to prepare. The boys are set to start summer day camp on Monday. I'm working, Dan's working, and I don't know what we're going to do with Olivia."

"She's certainly old enough to stay at home on her own."

"Yes, but she's not happy about being here. If we leave her here alone all week, it might make matters worse."

Janelle nodded. Leaving teens at home with nothing to do all summer could be a problem. "What are her hobbies and interests?"

"She used to play the piano and be into jewelry making and art, but now she just seems glued to her phone."

Janelle frowned. That could really be trouble. She started unloading the shopping bags and setting items on the counter.

Maggie lifted her hands. "I know how to keep Caleb and Cole occupied, but what do teens do in the summer?"

"Spend time with friends? Read? Listen to music? Some of them get jobs."

"She doesn't have any friends here, and I have no idea what kind of books or music she likes. And as far as finding a job, we don't know how long she'll be here, so that's doubtful." Maggie sighed, reached for a glass on the open shelf, and filled it with water.

An idea rose in Janelle's mind. She glanced at her friend's dismal expression and made her decision. "Do you think she'd like to volunteer at the museum?"

Maggie's mouth rounded. "Oh, now that's a good idea."

"We have a few openings for teen volunteers."

"What would she do?"

"She could help at the front desk, greeting guests and selling tickets and items from our gift shop."

"Maybe, but she's a bit of an introvert. I'm not sure she'd like that."

"We're also looking for assistants in kids' art classes."

Maggie nodded. "That sounds more like something she might be willing to do."

Janelle thought a moment more. "And there's the transcription project."

"What's that?"

"Volunteers look through Foundling Hospital records from the 1700s and 1800s and type out what the document says. Some go on to piece together what they find about a particular child and create a new file to save their story."

"Like collecting the clues and solving a mystery."

"Exactly. She'd have to go through an orientation first. I suppose she has basic computer skills?"

"Yes! She's good with computers. How many days a week could she volunteer at the museum?"

"The children's art classes run Tuesday through Thursday. For the transcription project, she would go through orientation, then she could set her own schedule and work at the museum or at home or wherever she likes."

Maggie thought for a moment, then looked back at Janelle. "Dan can work at home on Fridays, and I think I can convince my boss to let me work from home on Mondays. Olivia could help with the transcription project those days. Then she could she go to the museum with you on Tuesday, Wednesday, and Thursday."

Janelle grabbed a container of yogurt and placed it on the top shelf in the fridge. Was she ready to make that commitment on top of all her other responsibilities?

Maggie touched her shoulder. "I know that's a big ask. If it's too much, just say so. I'll still love you . . . but it would really be a huge help and save my sanity."

Janelle turned to Maggie. Her friend looked at her with such a hopeful pleading expression, she couldn't refuse. Taking Olivia to and from the museum three days a week wouldn't be so hard. Once they arrived, she could turn her over to the staff running the volunteer program or give her space in one of the offices to work on transcribing documents.

Maggie and Dan had gone out of their way to help Janelle so many times, making her feel like she was almost part of their family. This was her chance to return their kindness.

She took a deep breath. "Okay. If Olivia is willing to volunteer, I can take her in and bring her home. I'll make sure she's connected with the staff and other volunteers."

"Are you sure it's okay? She doesn't have to fill out an application or something?"

Janelle nodded. "There is an application, but I'll make sure she's accepted . . . since I am the new acting director."

Maggie's eyes widened. "What? When did that happen?"

"Today! Amanda went into labor with her twins."

"Wait, I thought she wasn't due until later this summer."

"She's not, but her water broke this afternoon, and her husband took her to the hospital."

Maggie placed her hand over her heart. "Oh my goodness. That must be so scary."

Janelle's stomach clenched as she recalled Amanda's frantic voice. "She was in a panic when she phoned. She even asked for prayer, and she's never done that before."

Maggie's eyes rounded. "Maybe this will bring her closer to the Lord."

"I hope so." Janelle checked her watch. "I'm going to fix dinner, then I plan to text her husband and see if he can give me an update."

Maggie nodded. "After dinner, why don't you come over and meet Olivia? I picked up some ice cream and a lemon sponge cake. We can talk about the volunteer positions and hopefully get her on board."

Janelle sent a longing glance toward the couch and television.

She'd hoped to have a quiet dinner and catch up on the latest episode of her favorite show, but that could wait. Helping her friend face this new challenge was more important.

～

Janelle took a sip of tea and studied Olivia over the rim of her cup. The girl's dark brown hair hung over her shoulders in soft waves, with hair that partly hid her light blue eyes. Cinnamon-tinted freckles dusted her cheeks and nose, giving her a fresh, wholesome appearance, though Janelle doubted the girl appreciated those freckles. She remembered moaning about her own at that age. Thankfully, most of hers had faded.

Olivia looked up and met Janelle's gaze, then quickly looked away—but that didn't hide the discomfort in her eyes.

Maggie passed Olivia a plate with a slice of cake and scoop of ice cream. "Janelle is stepping in as the director of Foundling Museum, and she was telling me they have some openings for teen volunteers this summer."

Olivia scooped a bite of ice cream into her mouth, ignoring Maggie.

Maggie shot Dan a pointed look as she passed him the next plate.

"What kind of jobs do the volunteers do?" Dan asked as he squirted some whipped cream on top of his cake and ice cream.

"There are a few options." Janelle listed those she'd shared with Maggie, trying to make them sound as interesting as possible, hoping to stir Olivia's curiosity.

Maggie forced a smile as she passed the next plate to Caleb. "Olivia, don't those sound great? Which one do you think would be a good fit for you?"

Olivia shot Maggie a surprised glance. "You want me to volunteer at a museum?"

"We think it would be a good idea for you to have something to do while your dad and I are at work and the boys are at camp. You'd be bored sitting around here all day by yourself."

Olivia frowned. "Staying here sounds better than hanging out at a museum and doing a job that doesn't pay."

Maggie handed Cole the next plate. He looked at it and stuck out his lower lip. "Why did Caleb get more ice cream than me?"

"You both got the same amount." Maggie shifted her gaze to Dan and sent him a pleading look.

He turned to his daughter. "We're glad you're here, and we want you to enjoy your summer. We'll plan some fun activities on the weekends, but during the week, it would be a good idea for you to volunteer at the museum. It might not be a paid position, but you can count it as work experience when you apply to university or when you're looking for a job."

"I worked hard at school all year. I want to relax and sleep in this summer, not waste time at some dusty old museum."

Janelle shifted uncomfortably in her chair. This conversation was not going as she and Maggie had hoped.

Maggie swiped a cloth across the counter, a glint of determination in her eyes. "You can sleep in on the weekend and on Mondays and Fridays when your dad and I will be working from home. On Tuesday, Wednesday, and Thursday, you can go to the museum with Janelle and help with the kids' art classes or pick one of the other volunteer jobs."

Olivia glared at Maggie. "You're not really giving me a choice, are you?"

Dan's face turned ruddy, and he leveled his gaze at her. "You have a choice. You can either decide to have a good attitude and enjoy the summer with us, or you can have a negative attitude and feel miserable. It's up to you."

Olivia's eyes flashed, and she jumped up from the couch. "I knew you'd treat me like this! You don't care how I feel or what

I want! I wish I'd never come!" She spun away, dashed down the hall, and slammed her door.

Dan's jaw clenched as he stared at the empty hallway. Cole and Caleb exchanged wide-eyed looks. Then Dan got up and strode out of the room.

Maggie sighed and rubbed her eyes. "I'm sorry, Janelle. I had no idea she'd react like that."

Janelle blew out a breath. "It's okay. She's got the weekend to cool off. Hopefully by Tuesday she'll be willing to go in with me."

Maggie's expression firmed. "She'll be ready. I'll make sure of it."

Jonas sank into the recliner and put his feet up. The memory of his conversation with Janelle Spencer replayed through his mind as it had a few times since he'd left the Foundling Hospital. She had a winsome way about her. Even though she'd not signed the contract for the film, he'd left feeling hopeful she'd do what she could to move the project forward.

He opened the biography of Thomas Coram and turned to chapter three. The man with the vision for opening the Foundling Hospital was an intriguing character. The plight of the abandoned babies he'd seen on London's streets had grabbed hold of his heart, and he wouldn't give up until he found a way to open a children's home.

A knock sounded at the front door of his flat. He lowered his feet and crossed the room. Checking the peephole, he spotted his friend and assistant, Howie Livingston, staring at the floor with a gloomy expression.

Jonas pulled open the door. "Hey, Howie. Everything okay?"

"No, it's not. Lauren is upset with me. I needed to get out of the house and take a break." He walked past Jonas and into the living room.

Jonas raised his eyebrows. "Come in."

In the five years he'd known Howie and Lauren, he'd admired their relationship and the way they cared for their young son, Liam. But since a drunk driver had slammed into their car eight months ago, he'd noticed rising tension between the couple. Liam had not been injured, but Lauren had sustained significant injuries. Her long recovery and the emotional and financial stress from the accident had put a strain on their relationship.

"You want to talk about it?"

Howie grimaced. "Lauren's worried about money and struggling with the idea of going back to work when she's not fully recovered. But I think it has more to do with her not wanting to be away from Liam so many hours a day."

"And she's upset with you because . . . ?"

Howie sighed. "If I were making more money, she wouldn't have to go back to work. And with the way things have been going for us"—he motioned to Jonas and himself—"she's worried about the future. I tried to tell her everything was going to be okay, that she didn't need to worry, but that just made her more upset."

Jonas stifled a groan. He hated hearing that the results of his impulsive choices were putting pressure on his best friend's marriage. "Oh, mate, I'm sorry."

Howie lifted his hand. "It's okay. We'll get through this."

"Do you want a drink? I've got lemonade."

"Sure." Howie followed Jonas into the kitchen.

Jonas filled a glass with ice and poured Howie a drink. "I'm no expert on solving marriage conflicts, but maybe you could go back and try to listen to her concerns. I think sometimes people just want to be heard. They don't want you to talk them out of their feelings or even fix the problem."

Howie accepted the glass, and they walked back to the living room. "I just wish she'd trust me. We know what we're doing." He took a long drink and lowered himself to the couch.

Jonas sat across from him. "These last few months have been tough for both of you."

Howie leaned back, closed his eyes, and rubbed his forehead. "I thought we were getting past the worst of it—and now this."

"Maybe let things settle tonight and talk it over tomorrow. You can work this out."

Howie sighed. "Yeah, you're probably right. I'll go back and listen and try to see things from her point of view." He shifted on the couch and opened his eyes. "How did it go at the Foundling Museum? Did they sign the contract?"

"Not yet. The director is out on maternity leave with premature twins."

"Whoa, that sounds crazy."

Jonas nodded. "The woman who is stepping in for her didn't even know I was coming."

Howie frowned. "Don't tell me they're going to cancel the project."

"No. She said she'll talk to the director and get back to me."

Howie clicked his tongue. "Bummer. I thought this was a done deal."

"I'm still hopeful." He leaned forward and clasped his hands between his knees. "She gave me a tour of the museum and some books to learn about their history." He pointed to the book on the coffee table. "I've already got some ideas."

"What did you learn on the tour?"

Jonas recalled his interactions with Janelle. She knew her stuff, and she was attractive. He squelched that thought and focused on Howie again. "There's a display case filled with all these little objects. She told me they were tokens left by mothers when they gave up their babies. Each one represents a mother's love and a child's story."

Howie's expression brightened. "That sounds intriguing."

"Yes, and she said the museum's fundraising efforts have been in a slump since the pandemic. They lost a major grant, and they're scrambling to meet expenses."

Howie made a noise in his throat. "That sounds too familiar."

Jonas's gut clenched. The comparison between the museum's financial struggles and those of his film company were surprisingly similar. They'd been working on a documentary for the International Centre for Missing and Exploited Children when the grant they'd been promised was pulled out from under them. Jonas had drained his savings to pay Howie and cover his own bills, hoping and praying they'd be awarded another grant, but it hadn't happened. They'd had to shelve the project after working on it for four months.

"How soon will we know if the museum film is a go?

Jonas blinked and shifted his thoughts back to the present. "We should hear something in a day or two. I'm starting the research and hoping for the best."

Howie lifted an eyebrow. "Let's hope for a better outcome this time."

Jonas sighed. His friend was right. He needed to keep his options open and not sink too much hope or time into this project until he was given a solid green light.

5

1885

Lillian's hands trembled as she laid her speech on the podium. She lifted her eyes and gazed out at the eighty or so women seated in the audience. Most wore colorful day dresses with puffed sleeves and hats with ruffles and ribbons.

Reverend Howell walked into the room and stood at the back, next to a man she didn't recognize. She hadn't spoken to the reverend since visiting his home two days earlier. Had he gone to the Foundling Hospital and spoken to Mrs. Stark? What had he learned about her niece? There was no time to consider those questions now. She must focus her thoughts and give her presentation.

Please, Lord, help me deliver the words you've given to me with strength and conviction.

She pulled in a calming breath and looked out at the audience. "Thank you for your kind invitation. I'm grateful to have this opportunity to speak to you today about the need to improve educational and occupational opportunities for the women of our fair city."

In the front row, two older women exchanged surprised glances, and another woman frowned and whispered something to the lady seated beside her.

Lillian lifted her gaze above their heads and forced herself to continue. "Most of us are blessed to live in comfortable homes surrounded by loving families. We never have to be concerned about our personal safety or wonder if we will have sufficient income to feed and clothe ourselves and our children. But that is not the case for many women in London. Only a few miles from here, there are countless women trapped in painful and difficult circumstances, who feel they have no choice but to follow a dark, degrading path simply to survive."

The stunned expressions of the two older women in the front row nearly buckled Lillian's knees, but she pressed on. "We should not stand by and remain silent when we can follow the example of Jesus, who lifted women from places of obscurity and shame to positions of respectability and honor. His care and actions should inspire us to speak up for those who cannot speak for themselves. His love and concern should prompt us to work for change and provide opportunities for training and honest work that brings sufficient income. We should be the first to understand the plight of these suffering women and offer practical help."

For the next twenty minutes, Lillian gave an impassioned plea for the cause that was so dear to her heart. A few women listened attentively, their open expressions indicating they caught her vision, but others avoided her gaze and shifted in their seats, making it clear they were uncomfortable with the topic.

Lillian glanced down at her final words, then lifted her eyes and scanned the audience once more. "I hope we can work together to provide practical care and opportunities for women who are seeking respectable employment so they can live healthy, honest, and upright lives. Thank you for your attention."

Silence enveloped the room as she picked up her notes and stepped away from the podium. Finally, one woman clapped, and others joined in, but the level of enthusiasm was not nearly as strong as it had been when she was introduced.

With a pounding heart, she returned to her seat, and the meeting was soon adjourned.

Two young women came forward and greeted her. The first introduced herself as Anne Perrone. "Thank you, Mrs. Freemont. Your talk was so inspiring! It brings to mind a speech I heard recently by Josephine Butler. She leads the women's opposition to the Contagious Disease Act. Have you heard her speak?"

"No, I haven't, but I've read excerpts from several of her speeches."

"She is a remarkable woman of faith and such a devoted campaigner! She's quite controversial, but we love her, don't we, Elizabeth?"

"Oh yes. I've been to several meetings where she was the featured speaker. She always moves me to want to do more."

"Excuse me, Mrs. Freemont." An older woman wearing a black bombazine dress and bonnet stepped forward. "Might I have a word?" Her serious expression and tone sent a warning through Lillian.

"Of course." Lillian turned to the two young women. "It was a pleasure to meet you. Thank you for your encouragement."

"You're welcome." Anne sent her a warm smile. "Your speech was like a breath of fresh air. I hope we'll hear from you again soon." She looped her arm through Elizabeth's, and the two young women walked away.

Lillian turned toward the older woman, steeling herself for the expected criticism.

The woman narrowed her eyes. "I must say I was quite surprised by your presentation, and from what I observed, so were many of the women in the audience."

Lillian met the woman's gaze, determined to listen respectfully, even if she disagreed.

"It's not often we hear about the needs of poor and working-class women spoken of with such . . . clarity."

"It is a delicate topic," Lillian admitted, "but I believe there should be a sense of sisterhood among women that allows us to discuss serious matters like these."

The woman leaned closer. "I believe you're right."

Lillian's eyes widened. "You do?"

"Yes, I do." Her expression warmed. "I should have introduced myself. My name is Marion Levinger. I'm the chairwoman of the league."

"I'm pleased to meet you, Mrs. Levinger." Lillian offered her hand, and the woman took it.

"I hope you'll consider becoming a member. We need the addition of fresh young voices like yours."

Lillian hardly considered herself young at thirty-one years of age. But before she could reply, Reverend Howell and the man he'd been standing with approached. The reverend greeted Mrs. Levinger, then turned to Lillian. "Well done, Mrs. Freemont. That was an inspiring message."

"Thank you." Knowing he approved eased her tense shoulders.

Mrs. Levinger turned to Reverend Howell. "Mrs. Freemont may have ruffled a few feathers, but I believe her message was just what we needed to hear. I've grown weary of talks about ornamental gardening and how to set a proper table. It's time we heard more about issues plaguing our society and ways we can take action to improve the lives of those less fortunate." Mrs. Levinger thanked Lillian again, then she excused herself and stepped away.

Reverend Howell motioned toward the man next to him. "Mrs. Freemont, this is Mr. Matthew McGivern. He is a journalist with the *Pall Mall Gazette*."

Lillian offered her hand. "Mr. McGivern, I'm pleased to meet you."

He gave a slight nod, but he ignored her hand. "Mrs. Freemont."

She let her hand drift to her side and studied him more closely. He looked to be in his early thirties and wore a well-cut black suit. But his cravat was askew, and his white shirt appeared to be wrinkled. His dark brown hair, beard, and moustache were all in need of a trim.

Why had Reverend Howell brought a journalist to hear her speak? She hoped he didn't intend to include her remarks in a newspaper article. It was one thing to give a presentation to a group of women, but it would be an entirely different matter to be quoted in the *Gazette*, especially about a sensitive topic that was rarely mentioned in polite society.

Reverend Howell looked around, then lowered his voice. "I spoke to the matron at the Foundling Hospital about your niece yesterday afternoon."

Lillian straightened. Should they discuss this matter in front of Mr. McGivern? Her eagerness to learn what Reverend Howell had discovered overshadowed her caution. "What did she say?"

"She confirmed her baptismal name is Mary Graham."

Lillian's pulse jumped. The cleaning woman had been right about that part of the story.

"But when I asked where the infant was buried," Reverend Howell continued, "she checked her records, then became quite flustered and unable to answer. I pressed her, and she stated she'd only been the matron for six months and didn't know why there was no record of the infant's burial."

Lillian's thoughts raced ahead, raising her hopes.

"That lends credence to the story you heard," he continued. "I don't believe your niece died as an infant, as the matron told you." He turned to Mr. McGivern. "And then last night, by the hand of Providence, I remembered a conversation I recently had with Mr. McGivern."

Lillian glanced at Mr. McGivern, uncertain of the connection.

"He's gathering information for a series of articles he plans to write for the *Gazette*. The more he told me about his investigation of missing young women from the East End, the more certain I felt that he was the man who might help us find your niece."

Lillian turned to Mr. McGivern. "You're searching for young women who've gone missing?"

He nodded, but he looked uncomfortable with the conversation. "It's part of the research I'm doing for a series I'm writing." He motioned toward the stage where Lillian had stood to give her speech. "Like some of the young women you spoke of, we suspect these girls have been abducted and taken by those with evil intentions."

Lillian swallowed, knowing exactly what he meant.

Reverend Howell leaned toward Mr. McGivern. "I sensed the Lord directing me to introduce you to Mrs. Freemont. I'm sure when you consider the young girl's fate if she is not recovered quickly, you'll want to do all you can to assist us in the search."

Mr. McGivern shifted his weight to the other foot, the inner debate obvious in his troubled expression. Finally, he turned to Lillian. "I'm a journalist, not a detective. I can't make any promises."

Her heart lifted. "But you'll help me?"

"I can keep my eyes and ears open and let you know if I learn anything that might be useful."

"Oh, thank you, Mr. McGivern." She reached for his arm. "You don't know how much this means to me."

He lowered his gaze to her hand on his coat sleeve.

Her face warmed, and she slid her hand away.

He pulled a small notebook and pencil from his coat pocket. "Give me a description of the girl."

"Alice, or I suppose she would go by the name Mary Graham,

is eight years old. She has blue eyes and long blond hair she wears in curls. I've never seen her, but the old woman at the Foundling Hospital described her as being very pretty."

"When did she go missing?"

"It's been at least nine days now."

Mr. McGivern closed his notebook. "That's not much to go on."

Lillian tensed. She had to convince him. "Maybe not, but with the Lord's guidance, and your practical knowledge as a journalist, I believe we can find her. How do you suggest we start?"

He sent her a puzzled look. "There is no *we*."

"But I want to help. She's my niece and my responsibility."

He shook his head. "I work alone."

Reverend Howell turned to Lillian. "On our way here, I was telling Mr. McGivern about Mercy House—a home for young women who've come out of brothels, workhouses, or prison. It gives them a safe place to learn a new occupation and have a fresh start as they rebuild their lives. Perhaps the women there might be able to tell you where young girls like your niece end up. That seems like a good place to begin the search."

"That's an excellent idea." Lillian turned to Mr. McGivern. "When do you plan to go?"

"Tomorrow afternoon."

"Wonderful. Shall I meet you there at one o'clock?"

His expression darkened. "I said, I work alone."

Reverend Howell lifted a finger. "Mr. McGivern, I think you might want to reconsider. I believe the women at Mercy House will be much more willing to speak to Mrs. Freemont than they will to you."

Mr. McGivern frowned. "I know how to conduct an interview."

"I'm sure you do, but these women have been mistreated by

men. They may be reticent to give you the information you're seeking for your article or tell you anything that would help in the search for Mrs. Freemont's niece."

Lillian met Mr. McGivern's gaze. "As you heard in my speech, I'm quite sympathetic to the issues these women face. I think I could persuade them to talk to me."

Mr. McGivern's serious expression did not change, but he gave a slight nod. "Very well. You may come. That's a rough area of town—not one a lady like you should travel through alone." Reluctance weighed his every word. "Where shall I call for you at twelve thirty?"

Lillian took her card from her reticule and handed it to him. Her fingers touched his, sending a jolt of awareness through her.

His gaze darted to hers, then just as quickly he looked down at the card.

She suppressed the sensation and lifted her chin. "I live in Eaton Square. That's in Belgravia."

"I know where Eaton Square is." His mouth twisted as he looked her over. "Wear plain clothing, something simple. No jewelry or fancy hat."

She blinked. "Why should it matter how I dress?"

He motioned toward her. "Because dressed as you are today, you'd stand out like a red rose in a rubbish heap. We want to blend in, not draw attention to ourselves."

Her face flamed. "Very well. I'll dress suitably and be ready at twelve thirty."

He gave a brusque nod, then turned and walked away.

A tremor traveled through her as she watched him go. Why was Mr. McGivern so gruff and unsociable? Reverend Howell had rather cornered him with the request to help her search for her niece, but that didn't seem reason enough to account for his disapproving attitude toward her.

Matthew strode down the steps and out the door, muttering under his breath. How had he let them talk him into taking a wealthy, well-dressed woman to a rescue home in White Chapel? It was foolish, if not downright dangerous. But he certainly wouldn't recommend she go there alone. That could lead to disaster.

It was the thought of another defenseless young girl gone missing that had made him finally agree to escort Mrs. Freemont to Mercy House. Why didn't the woman's husband go with her? Then he recalled Reverend Howell had told him she was a widow.

He frowned, pondering the situation. He ought not judge her for being wealthy and attractive. She couldn't help being born into the upper class. What would she think of him if she knew his background? He'd worked hard to put his past behind him, and he'd risen to a respectable position at the *Gazette*. Still, he would never be Mrs. Freemont's equal. The thought irked him, and he pushed it away.

Was there a connection between her niece's disappearance from the Foundling Hospital and the missing girls from White Chapel? Those girls were fourteen to sixteen years of age, while her niece was only eight. He suspected the older girls had been unwillingly taken into brothels. Was the same true of the younger girl?

He lifted his hand and signaled a hansom cab, then directed the driver to take him to the offices of the *Pall Mall Gazette*. It was time to run this new lead past his editor, W. T. Stead.

Twenty minutes later, he climbed down from the cab and paid the driver. With determined steps, he passed the others working in the newsroom and rapped on the editor's door.

"Come in," Stead called in a booming voice.

Matthew pushed open the door and entered the office. The editor, sitting behind his large desk, looked up at him. His cravat was untied, and his bushy silver moustache and beard nearly covered the bottom of his face.

Matthew crossed and stood in front of his desk. "I've come upon an unexpected twist in the search for those missing girls."

Stead pushed his thick glasses up his nose, his eyes bright. "What kind of twist?"

The editor listened with a deepening frown as Matthew relayed his conversation with Reverend Howell and Mrs. Freemont. "I'm surprised to hear it. The Foundling Hospital is a respected charity."

"The cleaning woman told Mrs. Freemont her niece is not the first 'pretty young girl' to disappear. She suspects the girl was taken to work belowstairs at a brothel."

Stead's face turned ruddy. "To use a child like that—it's a crime, a despicable crime."

"Do you think Mrs. Freemont should go to the police?"

"They've been little help to the others who are seeking their missing daughters. There's not enough information to solve those cases, at least that's what they say."

"Perhaps they don't want them solved. Maybe they've been paid off, and they're protecting someone. It wouldn't be the first time we've come across corruption among their ranks."

Stead crossed his arms, glowering as he looked out the window. "It's a wretched business. We must keep pursuing this and expose whoever is behind it."

"Reverend Howell suggested I go to a rescue home in White Chapel and interview women there. He thought they might know something about the missing girls or where that younger girl was taken. Mrs. Freemont wants to go along." He shook his head. "She and Reverend Howell think the women might be more willing to speak to her than to me."

"Yes, that's a good idea. Feed Mrs. Freemont the questions you want answered, then listen well and record those young women's stories."

Matthew shook his head. "I don't like the idea of taking Mrs. Freemont to White Chapel."

Stead chuckled. "If she's as plucky as you say, I think it's a good idea." He paused, thinking. "Find out what took those women to that kind of life and what convinced them to leave it behind. Were some of them taken from their families and forced into it? That will add a human-interest element to the articles and raise readers' sympathy."

Matthew nodded. The *Pall Mall Gazette* was a leader in the new form of investigative journalism. Their goal was to present the truth in a way that swayed public opinion and pushed for change in government policy. Stead had trained Matthew to dig deep and interview as many people as possible.

"We want to shape the articles to stir an outcry and force lawmakers to raise the age of consent. Then the police—at least the ones who are honest—will have the authority to arrest those despicable men who entrap unsuspecting young girls and ruin their lives."

Energy surged through Matthew. Stead was a crusader, and he had passed that zeal on to Matthew.

Stead rapped his knuckles on the desk. "I say follow this lead, see where it takes you, and make the most of it. We need more information if we're going to write a series that will make people sit up, take notice, and bring about changes."

⁓

Lillian slid into the seat of the hansom cab and brushed her hand down the skirt of her plain navy blue day dress. She'd taken Mr. McGivern's recommendation and dressed simply, leaving all her jewelry at home except for the locket with her husband's photograph. She'd slipped it under the bodice of her dress, well out of view. The weather was warm and sunny, so she didn't need a coat, but she had donned a small straw hat with a navy ribbon around the crown. As she was dressed today, she could be mistaken for a teacher or a woman who worked in a shop, rather than a wealthy widow from Eaton Square.

She glanced across at Mr. McGivern. He'd said nothing about her choice of clothing and only offered a brief greeting when he'd come to collect her. He gazed out the side window, focused on his own thoughts. He appeared to be wearing the same black suit and waistcoat he'd worn the day before. But this time his cravat was well tied, and his shirt looked freshly pressed. He might be considered a handsome man with his high forehead, long straight nose, and deep-set blue eyes, if only he would drop his brooding expression and smile occasionally.

His gaze slid to hers.

Her face warmed, and she looked away.

He took his small notebook from his suitcoat pocket. "I have a few questions I'd like you to ask the women."

She'd already formed her own list of questions last night after praying about their visit to Mercy House. Should she abandon those in favor of Mr. McGivern's list? After all, he was a journalist, and she was not. "What would you like me to ask?"

"Begin by questioning them about their background and why they were drawn into . . . the kind of life they were living. Then ask what makes them want to leave that life behind."

She sent him a surprised glance. "The answers to those questions seem obvious. I'm sure most of them felt that they had no choice if they wanted to survive, and now that they do have a choice, they're eager to begin new lives."

"Mrs. Freemont." He tipped his head, looking at her as though he thought she was quite naïve. "Their choices and the reasons behind them may not be as simple as you think."

66

She bristled. "There is no need to be condescending."

He straightened. "That was not my intention."

"I was under the impression the purpose of our visit was to gain information about my niece and the other missing girls."

"It is, but I also want to learn more about the women's personal stories as background for the articles I'm writing."

"Well, I don't believe beginning with such difficult questions is the best way to gain their trust or prompt them to tell us more."

He sent her a pointed look. "The only reason I agreed you could accompany me today was because Reverend Howell believes your presence will encourage the women to give us the information we need. You may ask some of the opening questions, but I will conduct the rest of the interviews."

Irritation flashed through her, and she was about to protest when the cab rolled to a stop. The driver hopped down and opened the door. Matthew stepped out, but rather than turning and offering her his hand, he looked up and scanned the row of buildings. The driver shot him a glance, then held out his hand to Lillian. She took hold and stepped down.

Matthew glanced over his shoulder. "Ready?"

"Yes." She swallowed the rest of what she would've liked to say and followed him up the steps.

He knocked on the door, and a young woman with a cheerful smile answered. She wore a light green dress with ruffles at the neck and hem. Her red curly hair was tied back with a white ribbon. Lillian guessed she was no more than fourteen or fifteen. Surely she wasn't a resident of Mercy House, was she?

"I'm Mr. Matthew McGivern. I believe Mrs. Charles is expecting me."

Lillian looked his way, waiting for him to offer her name, but he didn't. Had he never been taught how to treat a lady, or was he trying to make it clear he was not happy she had accompanied him?

"Please, come in." The girl pulled the door open wider, and they stepped inside. She led them into the sitting room. "Have a seat. I'll let Mrs. Charles know you're here."

Lillian sat in a high-backed chair by the front window, while Mr. McGivern remained standing and glanced around the room. She could almost see the wheels in his mind turning as he took in the modest furniture, full bookcases, and paintings on the wall. Would he include a description of this room in his article?

A slight, middle-aged woman with rosy cheeks and light brown hair threaded with silver walked in. She held out her hand to Lillian. "Welcome to Mercy House. I'm Mrs. Charles."

She rose. "I'm Mrs. Lillian Freemont." She motioned to Mr. McGivern. "And this is Mr. Matthew McGivern. We're friends of Reverend Howell." Lillian wasn't sure if she should mention Mr. McGivern's position with the *Gazette*.

He nodded to Mrs. Charles. "Thank you for seeing us. Reverend Howell told us a little about Mercy House. I'd like to ask you a few questions, and then interview some of the women."

She gave a hesitant nod. "Reverend Howell sent a note. He said you're associated with Mr. Stead at the *Pall Mall Gazette*."

"Yes, Mr. Stead is my editor. He'd like me to include information about Mercy House in a series of articles I'm writing."

Mrs. Charles pressed her lips together, looking as though she was trying to decide how to respond. "We are proud of our girls and the way they are rebuilding their lives, but I must insist they not be named in your article." She lowered her voice. "It's for their own safety."

Mr. McGivern's eyebrows rose. "Of course, if you feel that's best."

"I do. Some of our girls escaped dangerous situations, and their privacy and protection are of the utmost importance."

Lillian studied Mrs. Charles. What exactly did she mean? Why would the women be in danger?

Mrs. Charles sat on the sofa. "Please sit down."

Lillian resumed her seat.

Mr. McGivern sat on the opposite end of the sofa and opened his notebook. "How long has Mercy House been in existence?"

"We opened our door twenty-one years ago, under the patronage of Mrs. Adelaide Grimsley. She was one of the most influential women in England at the time." She leaned toward Mr. McGivern. "And one of the wealthiest. She funded several charitable causes, but she always took a personal interest in all the girls who came to Mercy House. When she passed away, she left an endowment that continues to care for our needs."

Matthew jotted a few lines in his notebook. "What are the ages of the women at Mercy House?

"We accept girls who are fourteen to twenty-one."

Lillian looked up in surprise. She had expected the women would be older.

"What brings them to Mercy House?" Mr. McGivern asked.

"Some of the girls come to us from workhouses, others from prison. A few are orphans who were living on the street. Others are escaping abusive situations."

A pang shot through Lillian's heart. She had suffered the loss of her husband, daughter, and parents, but she'd always had a safe home and more-than-sufficient income to meet her needs. What heartache these girls had experienced, and at such young ages.

"The girls must be recommended by their parish priest, the prison matrons, or another person of influence who believes they have potential and willingness to learn the skills needed to make a new life."

"How many girls reside at Mercy House?" Lillian asked.

Matthew shot her a look. He obviously didn't want her to speak yet, but she sensed a connection with Mrs. Charles and had questions she wanted to ask.

Mrs. Charles sent Lillian a gracious smile. "We have room for fifteen. I wish we had more space. There are so many who need a caring home and training for proper work."

Lillian nodded. "How long do they stay with you?"

"Most are here for at least a year. Some are not able to read or write when they come. It takes time for them to learn those basic skills. Most will go into service, but a few have gifts or talents that allow them to find other positions." She sighed. "But the greater challenge they face is overcoming their painful memories and putting their suffering behind them."

Lillian nodded, sympathy tightening her throat.

"I'd like to speak to the girls now." Mr. McGivern flipped to a new page in his notebook. "One at a time, if you please."

Mrs. Charles studied him for a moment with a slight frown. "I'm not sure they would be comfortable on their own with you. Perhaps if I stay with them, they would be willing to speak to you." She rose and left the room.

Lillian sat quietly while Mr. McGivern wrote several more lines in his notebook.

Mrs. Charles soon returned with a dark-haired girl who looked about sixteen. "This is . . . you may call her Rose. This is Mr. McGivern and Mrs. Freemont."

The girl sent them a shy look and offered a slight curtsy. "Good day, sir, ma'am."

Matthew nodded to Lillian to begin.

Lillian smiled. "We're pleased to meet you, Rose. Mr. McGivern is seeking information for a series of articles he's writing for the newspaper. We're also searching for my eight-year-old niece, who has gone missing from the Foundling Hospital."

We're hoping you might be able to help us learn more about life in London for girls who are facing . . . difficult circumstances."

Rose darted a glance at Mr. McGivern, then looked back at Lillian. "Who's gone missing?"

"My niece, Mary Graham, was in residence at the Foundling Hospital until just a few days ago, but she disappeared, and no one seems to know what happened to her."

Rose's eyes clouded. "I'm sorry to hear that, ma'am."

"She's very pretty with blond hair and blue eyes, and some people believe she might have been taken to work belowstairs at a brothel."

Rose's eyes widened. "Oh, that sounds awful."

"Yes, it does. And we want to do all we can to find her as quickly as possible," Lillian continued. "Before you came to Mercy House, did you work at a brothel?"

Rose quickly shook her head. "No, ma'am. The police nabbed me for begging on the street too many times. They saw a man giving me money and thought I was a fallen woman, but it wasn't true. I never fell that low. Still, they locked me up for more than a year before I came to Mercy House."

Lillian offered a sympathetic nod. "I'm very sorry you were falsely accused. That's a great injustice."

Rose sighed. "It's not just me. Two of the other girls here were locked up for begging. That's all we did, but they don't believe us, no matter what we say."

Lillian swallowed hard. "You've been through some very difficult circumstances. I hope your time at Mercy House will help you put those experiences behind you."

Rose's expression lightened. "Yes, ma'am. This is a good place. I'm learning to be a cook. I can bake bread and puddings. I'll be going out to work soon."

Lillian smiled. "That's wonderful. I'm sure you'll find a good position. There is always a need for skilled cooks."

"I hope so, ma'am. Begging on the street is no life for anyone."

Lillian shifted her gaze to Mr. McGivern.

He returned a slight nod, then looked at Rose. "Have you seen or heard about any young girls who have gone missing?"

Rose's brow creased. "There's lots of girls in White Chapel who disappear. Most were living on the street, begging—and I'm sorry to say, stealing—just to get enough food to eat. Some might have been arrested or got sick and died. It's a hard life."

"Why were those girls living on the street?" he asked.

"Some had no home because their mum and dad died. Others, like me, ran away 'cause it was so bad they don't want to go home."

Lillian's throat tightened as she listened. How had the poor girl survived such a painful life?

Mr. McGivern wrote in his notebook, then looked up. "Thank you, Rose. I think that's all the questions I have for you."

The girl dipped a brief curtsy and left the room.

Mrs. Charles brought in the next girl and introduced her as Amy. She was a slight blond with pale skin and silver-blue eyes. Lillian guessed she might be fifteen, but it was hard to be certain of her age. As soon as she entered, she froze and stared at them as though she thought they would eat her alive.

Mrs. Charles laid her hand on the girl's shoulder. "Amy has only been with us for about a week, but she is doing very well."

Lillian smiled, hoping to put the girl at ease. "Hello, Amy. Thank you for meeting with us. Mr. McGivern is a journalist with the *Pall Mall Gazette*. We're looking for information that will help us find some young girls who've gone missing."

Amy's gaze darted from Lillian to Mrs. Charles.

"We believe my niece, Mary Graham, may have been taken by men who are seeking girls to work in brothels. Have you heard of that happening?"

Amy's eyes widened, and the faint color in her face seemed to drain away. Her throat worked, and she finally said, "Yes, ma'am."

Lillian's pulse jumped.

Mr. McGivern leaned forward. "Tell us what you know." His voice sounded loud and insistent compared to Lillian's.

Amy shrunk back and covered her face with her hands.

Mrs. Charles rose and placed her arm around Amy's shoulders. "It's all right, dear."

"You don't need to be afraid, Amy," Lillian said in a gentle tone. "We are your friends. Nothing you say will cause you any trouble. We're only asking you these questions to help us find my niece and take her out of a dangerous place. You understand what I mean, don't you?"

Amy slowly lowered her hands, revealing tearstained cheeks.

Mrs. Charles shook her head. "I'm afraid this is too upsetting for her. No more questions."

The girl swiped her cheeks with a trembling hand. "No, I want to help them find that girl."

Relief swelled in Lillian's chest. "Thank you, Amy. Why don't you start by telling us your story?"

Amy sniffed and nodded. "I'm the oldest, with eight brothers and sisters. My mum died when I was twelve, and my dad spent most of his earnings at the gin shop. We were hungry all the time. Things got bad with Dad drinking and fighting every night. One day, a man told my dad he needed a maid to work at his house. Dad told me to go with him, so I went. I wasn't afraid to work, and I thought at least I'd have enough to eat. But he didn't want a maid. He took me to the Golden Swan. I was only fourteen. I didn't know anything about men, but I soon learned." She lowered her head. "I only stayed there two weeks, then I ran away. But I got caught, and they put me in prison."

Lillian's heart twisted. What terrible suffering she'd experienced at such a tender age. How would she ever recover from such dreadful treatment?

Mr. McGivern's pencil hovered over his notebook, his gaze riveted on Amy. "Were there any girls younger than you working at the Golden Swan?"

"Not with the men, but they had some little girls belowstairs, cleaning, washing up, and doing laundry. They do that work until they're old enough to work upstairs."

Lillian clenched her jaw, then closed her eyes and forced down the bile rising in her throat.

Lord, help us find Alice before it's too late!

6

2023

On Saturday morning, Janelle picked up her cell phone and tapped in Jonas Conrad's number. His phone rang twice, and he picked up.

"Good morning. This is Janelle Spencer from the Foundling Museum."

"Hi, Janelle." She could hear the hope in his voice.

"I spoke to Amanda this morning, and she gave the go-ahead for the film."

"That's great! Thanks so much." He paused for a moment. "How is she doing? I hope she and the twins are going to be all right."

Janelle smiled. That was thoughtful of him to ask. "Amanda is recovering. The twins are in the NICU, and they will be for quite a while, but they're holding their own."

"That's good to hear."

"Yes, we're all grateful and praying they'll continue to do well."

"I'll add my prayers to yours."

Surprise rippled through her. Jonas Conrad was a praying man?

"I've been reading those books I borrowed from you, and I've spoken to my associate. We're ready to dig into the research, so

I can work on the script. Can I stop by today with the contract for you to sign?"

A funny sensation zinged through her at the thought of seeing him again. She squeezed her eyes shut and reminded herself to remain professional. "Yes. I'll be in the office until five. What time works best for you?"

"How about eleven o'clock?"

She glanced at her watch. It was ten twenty. "You live close enough to be here in forty minutes?"

"Yes. I'm in Soho. I can be there by eleven."

"All right. I see you then."

"Thanks again. I know this film will be a great tool to spread your message and increase support for the museum."

"That's what we need." She tapped off and set her phone aside, then she glanced at the list she'd made while talking to Amanda earlier that morning.

She needed to make sure everyone stayed on track, preparing for the classes and tours, in addition to sending out the next fundraising newsletter and continuing plans for the gala. They were counting on that event to raise the funds needed for the next year. She had to check with Iris about the volunteers' appreciation luncheon and speak to Mark about the items they were borrowing for the next exhibit. Amanda had also asked her to check with Simon about the repairs scheduled to be done on the second-floor windows as well as the annual fire alarm testing. She blew out a deep breath. There was much more to this job than she'd ever realized.

She pulled out her laptop and placed it on her desk. No time like the present to tackle that list.

~

Jonas tucked the signed contract into his rolling case and sent Janelle a warm smile. "Thanks. I'm eager to get to work.

I finished the Thomas Coram biography, and I'd like to look at some of the museum's historical documents."

Janelle sent him a surprised glance. "You must be a speed-reader."

"I am." He grinned. "That's only one of my many exceptional skills."

She laughed softly. "Right up there with humility."

He chuckled. "Touché."

She stood and motioned to her desk and chair. "Have a seat, and I'll show you how to access those documents."

"I don't want to take over your desk."

"It's not a problem. I need to work on some things in Amanda's office next door. You're welcome to work in here today."

"Okay. Thanks." He walked around the desk and placed his laptop case on the chair.

"The team at the London Metropolitan Archives is helping us preserve our records. They've photographed a good portion of them. I can show you how to view those online. We have more than five hundred thousand documents dating back to the 1730s."

He looked up. "Wow, that sounds a little overwhelming."

She nodded. "It can be. The governors and Foundling Hospital staff were meticulous about keeping records. We have general registers, inspection books, committee minutes, petition letters, medical records, and letters from mothers appealing for the return of their children."

He pulled out his laptop and placed it on the desk. She reached for the extra chair and started pulling it toward him.

"Here, let me help." He took over and slid the chair into place next to his. "Here you go."

"Thanks." She took a seat.

He opened his laptop, and she leaned closer. The scent of lavender floated past his nose, and he inhaled deeply. He gave his head a slight shake and refocused on his computer.

It had been more than a year since he'd gone on a date. After he'd renewed his commitment to his faith about eighteen months ago, he'd put dating on the back burner. Instead, he'd focused on his work and gotten involved with a men's Bible study. In the last few months, he'd sensed a longing to connect and prayed about meeting someone who shared his faith and goals in life—someone who would be a good partner.

He glanced at Janelle, and a ripple of awareness passed through him. Maybe he needed to pay attention and see if the Lord was nudging him to get to know her. He smiled at that thought, typed in his password, and unlocked the screen. While he waited for his laptop to connect to WiFi, he glanced around her desk.

A blue ceramic mug held pens and pencils, and an African violet in full bloom in an attractive pot sat on the corner. Next to it stood a framed photo of Janelle with a man and woman and two young boys. Was that her sister and husband with their sons? The man looked Italian, and the woman didn't look anything like her, so he dismissed that idea. He quickly scanned the rest of the room. There were no other family photos or any of Janelle with a husband or boyfriend. She didn't wear a wedding ring. He'd checked the first day they'd met.

"Ready, Jonas?"

He snapped back to the moment "Yes . . . I'm ready."

The corners of her mouth lifted. "All right. Let me show you how to access the transcription project."

She spent the next fifteen minutes explaining that project and showing him how to view the various Foundling Hospital documents. He enjoyed their interactions and asked several questions to keep her talking. It was clear she was not only intelligent and skilled with research, but she was also dedicated to her work and the cause of children in care. All that confirmed the feeling he'd had earlier, and it made him feel certain he wanted to know her more.

"How did you get involved in your work here?"

She sat back, looking a little surprised by the question. An emotion he couldn't quite read flickered across her face. Was it embarrassment or reluctance? He couldn't be sure because it vanished as quickly as it had come. "My parents both struggled with various issues and divorced soon after I was born. I went into care when I was two."

He pulled in a quick breath. "Oh, I'm sorry."

"I was one of the lucky ones. I had a good foster family, and I didn't have to move around from placement to placement as so many children do. I took part in some of the programs here when I was in school, and I became an intern at the museum when I turned twenty. After I graduated from the University of London, I started working here, overseeing art programs for children and adults, and I've had a few different roles since then."

He nodded, impressed with her honesty and drive. "You've accomplished a lot in a short amount of time."

"Thanks. I feel a strong connection to the current programs and those in the past. The Foundling Museum and our fellow organization, Coram, do a tremendous amount of good for young people who are in care or who have phased out and are trying to become established as adults."

He nodded. "That makes sense. Your experiences help you understand those in similar circumstances. You want to help them find what you've found."

She tipped her head and studied his face. "Yes, that's it exactly. We're not just a museum that brings the past to life. We are committed to making a difference for children in care today."

His face lit up, and he pointed at her. "That's brilliant! I think you just gave me the theme for our film."

Her eyes widened. "Really?"

He nodded. "That perspective is just what we need to make

the film relevant and give it the greatest impact." He grabbed a pen and a lined yellow pad from his case and jotted down what she'd said. "Do you have any interns working here this summer?"

"Yes, we have two."

"Could I interview them?"

She nodded. "I can ask them. I think they'd be willing."

"How about kids in care? Do some of them come here for programs or as volunteers?"

"Yes, we have several classes and programs for children and teens. And we have all ages and types of volunteers."

He made a few more notes and looked up. "This is a great angle. If we can weave the past and present together and show the impact on these young people's lives, I know we can make a powerful film."

Janelle smiled. "What else can I do to help?"

"Are there any programs going on today?"

"We're open for tours all day. This afternoon, we have a special tour that includes opportunities to hold objects that are replicas of the tokens and other items related to the children who've stayed at the Foundling Hospital. At two, we have an art class for parents and children."

He glanced at his watch. "Maybe I can get ahold of Howie and have him bring over our camera equipment. We could start filming today." Grabbing his phone from his pocket, he started a text to Howie.

Janelle rose. "Let me check with the artist who is teaching the class. She should be setting up downstairs. I want to make sure she's open to having you film during her class. We'd also need the parents' permission before you film them or their children."

He nodded. "I understand. I have consent forms in my case."

They exchanged a smile. His spirits lifted. He had a good feeling about this project, and the prospect of spending more time with Janelle Spencer made it even more appealing.

7

Lillian carried the tray upstairs, hoping she could convince her sister to take some nourishment. Ever since Serena had learned Alice was missing from the Foundling Hospital, she'd eaten very little. She walked into her sister's room and found Serena lying on the bed, staring toward the window with glassy, red-rimmed eyes.

"I've brought you some chicken soup. It smells delicious."

Serena glanced at the tray, then turned her face away. "I'm not hungry."

Lillian suppressed a sigh. How could her sister recover if she refused to eat? Serena had always been a passionate person who felt things deeply. That often made it difficult for her to control her emotions and think logically. Lillian, on the other hand, had learned to keep a tight hold on her emotions, especially in the last few years.

She set the tray on the bedside table and straightened her sister's blanket. "Let me help you sit up. I'm sure this soup will help you gain some strength."

"What's the use?" Serena's voice wobbled. "My daughter is lost to me, and I'm never going to see her again."

Lillian pulled in a deep breath, determined to be patient. "I know what's happened is painful and upsetting, but we must not give up hope."

Serena tugged the blanket up to her chin. "That's easy for you to say. You've not seen all your hopes and dreams crumble before your very eyes!"

Emotion rushed in, flooding Lillian and breaking through her usual reserve. "That is not true, Serena. I lost my husband, whom I dearly loved. And since John died at sea, there isn't even a grave I can visit. And I was only able to hold my daughter for a few hours before death carried her away. So I *have* seen my hopes and dreams crumble, but even with all that heartache, I refuse to give in to despair."

Tears filled Serena's eyes. "Oh, Lillian, I'm sorry. I never should've said that. What a dreadful sister I am." Her tears overflowed and rolled down her cheeks.

Sympathy softened Lillian's heart. "You're not dreadful. You're weak from your illness and concerned for your daughter. I only mentioned my losses to let you know I understand how difficult this is for you." She nodded toward the tray. "Now, will you please sit up and try the soup?"

Serena's face crumpled. "How can I eat when my darling daughter may be suffering at the hands of evil people?"

Lillian pulled up a chair and took a seat. "Give me your hand."

Serena slowly slid her hand out from under the blanket.

Lillian took hold and gave Serena's fingers a gentle squeeze. "We both have suffered terrible losses. Some we may have brought on ourselves; others happened because we live in a broken world where sin takes a great toll. We can't change what happened to us in the past, but we can learn from it."

Serena sniffed, and her chin trembled. "If only Robert hadn't left us, none of this would've happened. He is the one to blame, not me."

"What he did was wrong, but that is between him and the Lord. You can take responsibility for your part, confess it in prayer, and ask for forgiveness. That's the path toward release from your despair."

Serena lifted her hand and covered her eyes. "How can I ever be forgiven? It's too late."

"As long as you're alive, it is never too late. Remember the thief on the cross next to Jesus? He called out for help on his dying day. Jesus heard him and promised he would be with Him in Paradise."

Serena sniffed and lowered her hand. "I know it's wrong to wallow in regret. But I feel so helpless."

"Your feelings are important, but truth is a much better guide. The Lord offers forgiveness, full and free. But you must ask for it and choose to accept it."

Serena released a shuddering breath. "I do want to be forgiven, but that won't bring my daughter back. What am I to do with this pain in my heart and all my fears? What if we never find her?"

Those questions pierced Lillian's soul. She knew grief tended to magnify emotions. It had taken her many months to release her distressing unanswered questions and rise above the dark clouds after the deaths of her husband and daughter. Some of those painful memories still lingered. Learning to look to the Lord for comfort and strength was an ongoing process.

She focused on her sister. "Offer your pain and fear to the Lord as a sacrifice. Let Him heal your heart. It won't happen all at once, but as you continue turning to Him, He will give you what you need to go on."

Serena bit her lip for several seconds, then slowly seemed to relax. She looked up at Lillian, and her expression softened. "Will you help me sit up?"

"Of course." Lillian tucked the extra pillows behind Serena, and her sister settled back against them. She set the tray on Serena's lap.

Serena slowly lifted a spoonful of soup to her mouth, then sipped another. "Thank you, Lillian."

Lillian's heart lifted. "You're welcome."

She tidied the room while her sister finished the soup. She checked the clock and was surprised to see it was almost three in the afternoon. Mr. McGivern said he would stop by after his visit to the Foundling Hospital.

She glanced at Serena, recalling her sister's tearful reaction when she'd told her what they'd learned at Mercy House. Not wanting to raise her sister's hopes, she hadn't said anything about Mr. McGivern's determination to visit the Foundling Hospital and question the cleaning woman.

Lillian sent Serena a smile. "All finished?"

"Yes. Please thank the cook."

"I will." Lillian lifted the tray. "The doctor said he would stop by around four. Why don't you rest until he comes? I have some things I need to attend to downstairs."

"All right. I'll ring if I need anything." Serena released a soft sigh and closed her eyes.

Lillian carried the tray across the room with light steps.

"Lillian?"

She stopped in the doorway and looked back. "Yes?"

"Thank you for not giving up on me."

A wave of love washed over Lillian, and she sent Serena a gentle smile. "We are sisters, and sisters never give up on each other."

⌒

Matthew looked up and scanned the façade of Lillian Freemont's stately townhouse. Four impressive marble columns spanned the front of the three-story home in the center of Eaton

Square. His stomach tightened. Lillian Freemont had to be one of the wealthiest women he'd ever met.

Reverend Howell told him her husband, John Freemont, had owned a large shipping company, and she had inherited his fortune after his death. She certainly looked much too young to be a widow. Her fair face and dark brown hair and eyes gave her a pleasing appearance. Why hadn't she remarried?

He shook his head, tugged down his waistcoat, and adjusted his cravat. She might be wealthy and attractive, but she wasn't royalty. He should not let the differences between them stop him from following through on his promise to her. He might not be her social equal, but through hard work and determination he had become a respected journalist.

He lifted his hand, intending to knock, then stopped. If all that were true, why did his father's drunken curses and scornful remarks run through his mind at times like this? Eighteen years had passed since his father's death, but the man's disdain still hovered in the back of Matthew's mind. He wasn't a weakling or a coward, no matter what his father had said. He clenched his jaw, forced those thoughts away, and pressed the bell.

A tall middle-aged butler answered the door. "May I help you?"

He straightened his shoulders "Good day. I'm Mr. Matthew McGivern. Mrs. Freemont is expecting me."

The butler gave a solemn nod. "Come in, sir. Please wait here."

Matthew took off his hat as his gaze traveled around the entrance hall. Several portraits in gilded frames hung on the pale blue walls. A large vase of fresh flowers sat on the long wooden table to the right. They gave off a light scent that reminded him of a walk in the park. Straight ahead, at the end of the entrance hall, a wide stairway with an intricately carved banister rose to a landing, then turned and continued up to the next floor. A tall arched window above the landing let in a shaft of late-afternoon light. He glanced back at the brightly colored stained glass in the front door window and sidelights. The room and its furnishings spoke of good taste and wealth, but they didn't seem pretentious.

The butler reappeared. "Mrs. Freemont will see you in the sitting room." He motioned to the left.

Matthew thanked him and walked into the high-ceilinged room with two tall windows that looked out on what appeared to be a private garden.

Mrs. Freemont rose from her chair and offered him a gracious smile. "Mr. McGivern, thank you for coming." Her pleasant voice and the look of welcome in her eyes relieved his apprehension.

He nodded to her, then glanced around the room, taking in the grand piano, deep blue velvet sofa and matching chairs, tall bookshelves on each side of the fireplace, and dark blue draperies at the windows. "You have a fine home."

"Thank you. It has been in my husband's family for many years." She looked around. "I appreciate it even more after hearing the stories told by the girls at Mercy House."

He nodded. The memory of those interviews had made it difficult for him to fall asleep the last two nights. "Their stories have been on my mind as well."

She studied him for a moment. "Were you able to go to the Foundling Hospital?"

"Yes, but I'm afraid I couldn't get past the matron."

Her hopeful expression faded. "Please, have a seat. I'd like to hear what happened." She sat on the sofa.

He took a seat in the chair opposite her. "When I arrived, an older man with a rather surly attitude answered the door. I'm not sure what position he holds there. He didn't introduce himself. I thought I might be able to slip away from him and look for the cleaning woman, but he escorted me directly to the matron's office."

Her eyes widened. "What excuse did you give for being there?"

"I told her the truth—that I was writing a series of articles for the *Gazette*. She seemed pleased that I wanted to interview her, and she answered all my questions. I saw no hint that she wanted to hide any information. She was quite friendly. When we finished the interview, I thanked her and told her I would see myself out, but she insisted on walking me to the front door."

"That's disappointing."

"I decided to look around the outside of the buildings, hoping there might be another entrance I could use, but a grounds-keeper spotted me and sent me packing."

She released a soft sigh. "I'm sorry. It seems I sent you on a wild-goose chase."

"I was able to make note of the layout of the buildings and grounds. A high stone wall surrounds the property, and there are only two gates—one in the rear for deliveries, and the front gate that leads through the courtyard to the main entrance."

Lillian nodded. "That's how I entered on my visit." She thought for a moment. "Do you suppose the staff comes and goes through that back gate?"

"That seems likely."

"What if we stationed ourselves outside that gate? I'm sure I'd be able to identify the cleaning woman if I saw her again."

"We don't know her schedule. That could take hours or even days. And what if she lives on the premises and rarely leaves?"

"She is the only lead we have, and I must find my niece." Lillian clasped her hands. "If you don't want to, I'll go on my own and wait to see if I can spot her."

He frowned and shook his head. "It's not safe to go by yourself.

If someone is abducting girls, then they might harm anyone who tries to stop them."

"I won't try to confront a kidnapper on my own. I'll simply wait in my carriage until I see the cleaning woman come out the gate."

"And what will you say if you do see her?"

"I'll insist she give me more information."

"I doubt that will work."

Her eyes flashed. "Well, I won't sit at home and do nothing. My niece's life is in danger, and I'm going to follow every lead possible until she's found."

The butler stepped into the room. "Excuse me, ma'am. Dr. Frasier is here to see your sister."

Lillian rose. "Please take him upstairs. Tell him I'll join him soon."

The butler nodded and stepped out.

Concern tightened Matthew's chest as he stood. "Is your sister ill?"

"Yes." Lillian's determined expression faded. "She has pneumonia. It's quite serious."

"I'm sorry. This sister—is she Mary Graham's mother?"

"Yes, and I'm afraid the news her daughter is missing has brought her very low. I don't believe she'll recover until her daughter is returned to her."

He clenched his jaw, debating his reply. Finally, he gave a slow nod. "Very well. I'll go with you to watch the back gate. If we do see the cleaning woman, perhaps I can convince her to tell us who is behind this scheme."

Her expression brightened. "Thank you. I'm so grateful. I need to speak to the doctor and my housekeeper to arrange for my sister's care, then I can call for the carriage and be ready to go."

He pulled out his pocket watch and checked the time. It was

almost four. He should return to the office and finish up his work there, but he didn't want to disappoint her. "I suppose we can go directly from here."

A blush stole across her cheeks. "I'm sorry. I shouldn't assume you're free to set off with me at a moment's notice."

"I'll consider it time spent gathering information for my assignment. I can do some preliminary writing while we watch and wait."

"Excellent." Her smile spread wider, and a look of appreciation filled her eyes. "I admire a man who knows how to use his time well. That is an important quality."

Pleasant warmth filled his chest. It had been a long time since he'd heard such affirming words. With the death of his mother, he'd lost the last connection to his family. His closest interactions were with Reverend Howell and a small group of men at church. Even with them, he didn't let down his guard. He'd never told them about his painful childhood or the deeper issues that shadowed his thoughts.

Yet, Lillian Freemont had managed to break through his reserve with a few kind words and a gentle smile. Perhaps it was also the way she seemed to trust him and need his help that drew him toward her.

That thought brought him up short. What was he thinking? He might hold a respectable position at the *Gazette*, but it was very unlikely she would ever consider him anything more than a middle-class journalist, someone who could help her find her niece—certainly not a man worthy of anything more than that. He had better remember all that separated them, or he'd be headed for a painful rejection.

8

2023

On Tuesday morning, Janelle led the way downstairs at the museum. Olivia followed a few steps behind. "Jeremy St. Charles is one of the artists working here this summer. He's leading a printmaking class this morning, along with Lisa Mills. She's one of our summer interns." When Olivia didn't respond, Janelle stopped on the landing.

Olivia's slumped posture and glum expression made her feelings painfully clear.

Janelle studied her with growing concern. "I know this is not how you wanted to spend your day, but if you'll go in with an open mind, I think you might be surprised—and even enjoy yourself."

The girl heaved a sigh and crossed her arms. "I'm only here because Dan and Maggie wouldn't let me stay home."

Hearing Olivia refer to her father as *Dan* didn't bode well. "I understand." How could she get through to this girl and help her change her perspective? A thought struck, and she focused on Olivia. "Your dad is a wise man. He said something important the other night."

Olivia brushed her hair away from her eyes. "What do you mean?"

"You have a choice to make."

Olivia rolled her eyes and sighed. "They didn't give me a choice about volunteering."

"True. But you do get to choose what happens now that you're here. Volunteering can bring some real benefits."

"Like what?"

"Well, I probably wouldn't have this job if I hadn't volunteered here when I was younger. It opened the door for me, and it could be a good opportunity for you too."

The girl's expression didn't change, but she lowered her arms and started down the stairs.

Janelle sent off a silent prayer and continued to the classroom. When they stepped through the doorway, Olivia stopped and looked toward the windows. Sunlight poured through, shining on colorful samples of past art projects that covered the walls and hung from the ceiling.

Lisa crossed the room, a welcoming smile on her face. "Good morning." She wore denim overalls and a bright orange T-shirt. Her long blond hair was braided, and she'd wrapped the braids around the crown of her head. A yellow daisy was tucked over her right ear, and a small silver ring pierced the side of her nose. Unconventional and sunny—that's how Janelle would describe Lisa.

Janelle introduced them, then explained, "This is Olivia's first day as a volunteer, so I hope you'll take her under your wing."

"Of course! I'm glad you're here, Olivia. We're expecting about twenty-five kids ages eight to twelve in about fifteen minutes. Have you done any printmaking before?"

Olivia's eyes widened. "No."

"That's okay. Jeremy is a fantastic teacher. The kids love him. Our job is to pass out supplies and offer lots of encouragement." She glanced at Olivia and seemed to read her apprehension. "You'll be fine. Stick with me, and I'll show you exactly what to do. It'll be fun!"

A wave of gratitude flowed through Janelle. "Thanks, Lisa." She shifted her gaze to Olivia. "Come up to my office after class, and we can have lunch together."

Olivia sent her an uncertain look but mumbled, "Okay."

Grinning, Janelle turned and headed out of the classroom. It was time for Olivia to sink or swim, and she had a feeling Lisa was just the right person to give her swimming lessons.

Jonas strolled down the hall of the museum, his gaze fixed on his phone, scrolling through the photos he'd taken of the tokens on display. He'd spent most of the day looking through documents online, searching for a particularly interesting story. He'd found one that mentioned a mother who'd left a fabric heart token, and he'd gone searching for it in the display case. That had turned out to be a dead end, but he'd seen several other tokens that sparked his interest. Perhaps one of those would lead to an interesting angle for the historical focus of the film.

He pushed open the door to Janelle's office, and someone gasped. His steps stalled, and he lifted his head.

A teenage girl with dark brown hair and pale blue eyes stared at him. She quickly hopped up from Janelle's desk chair. "Who are you?"

He smiled. "I'm Jonas Conrad." This had to be Olivia, the reluctant teen volunteer Janelle had spoken of when they'd connected that morning during a coffee break.

Olivia looked past him. "Where's Janelle?"

"I think she's working in the office next door." He pointed to the left.

Olivia snatched her phone off the desk and started toward the door.

"Wait, are you one of the volunteers?" He knew she was,

but he hoped the question would put her at ease and open a conversation.

She grimaced and stopped. "Yeah."

"Could I ask you a few questions before you go?"

She frowned, and her gaze darted toward the door.

"I'm gathering information for a film I'm making for the museum, and I was hoping to speak to some of the volunteers."

Interest sparked in her eyes. "What kind of film?"

"It's going to highlight the history of Foundling Hospital and show some of the current museum programs."

"Will it be on TV?"

"They're going to show it at the fundraising gala in September, then they'll probably use it on their website and send it to patrons and potential supporters to help raise funds."

She bit her lip, still looking uncertain.

"So . . . would you be willing to answer a few questions?"

She shrugged. "It's only my first day."

"That's all right." He motioned to a chair. "Let's sit down." He grabbed his pen and yellow pad from the desk while she lowered herself into a chair.

"So, what did you do today?"

"I helped in the kids' art class this morning, and I worked on a transcription project this afternoon."

"What kind of art were the kids doing?"

"They made fruit and vegetable prints."

"I've never done that. Tell me about it."

She sighed. "They carve an apple or a potato, dip it in paint, and stamp it on the paper."

He jotted a line and looked at her again. "What did you notice about the kids in the class?"

She frowned. "Notice?"

"You know . . . what were they like? How did they respond to being there?"

She thought for a moment. "Most of them seemed shy at first, like they didn't know how to get started. But then Lisa— she's the intern—and the artist who was teaching the class joked around with them and showed them how to do it."

"Did that help?"

"Yeah. The mood in the room changed. Pretty soon most of the kids were talking and laughing while they worked on their projects. Some of them really got into it and made three or four different prints."

"Why do you think some were hesitant at first?"

She thought for a moment. "Maybe they'd never done it before. Or maybe they didn't want to make a mistake and look stupid."

"So, you think they lacked confidence to try something new?"

"I guess so."

"How did you feel when you started this morning?"

She shot him a surprised glance. "I thought we were talking about the kids."

"And the volunteers."

She shifted her gaze to the bookcase. "I didn't want to be here."

"Why is that?"

"I've never done anything like this. I guess, like the kids, I didn't want to look stupid."

He nodded. "It takes courage to step out of your comfort zone and try something new."

She thought for a moment, then nodded.

"Since this was a new experience for both you and the kids . . . did that help you connect with them?"

Her gaze turned hazy, making it look as though she was recalling the events of the morning. "There was one little girl who just sat there quietly, even after Lisa carved her apple and showed her how to do the stamping. She didn't want to try. But then I sat beside her and talked to her while I carved a potato and made a print. That did the trick."

"That helped her get started?"

Olivia nodded, her lips curving with a hint of a smile. "She didn't say much, but after a few minutes she started copying what I was doing, and she ended up making a nice project."

He grinned. "I bet it felt good to help her like that."

Olivia's slight smile widened. "Yeah, it did."

Janelle stepped into the open doorway. "Oh, here you are." Her gaze shifted from Olivia to Jonas.

"We were just talking about Olivia's first day as a volunteer." He pointed to his pad. "Research for the film." When Olivia glanced away from him, he winked at Janelle.

"Sounds good." Janelle turned to Olivia. "Your dad called. He's on his way to pick you up. He should be here in about five minutes."

Surprise flashed in Olivia's eyes. "My dad's coming?"

Janelle smiled. "Yes. Why don't you grab your backpack and wait in the lobby? You can see him pull up from there."

"Okay." She stepped behind the desk, picked up her dark green backpack, then strode out the door. "See you tomorrow."

When she disappeared around the corner, Janelle crossed toward him. "What did she say about her first day?"

"It sounds like the art class was a positive experience. She could relate to the kids who were hesitant to try something new."

Janelle looked relieved. "That's good to hear. How was your afternoon?"

He chuckled. "Besides eyestrain from trying to decipher eighteenth-century handwriting on all those documents, I'd say it went pretty well."

"Find anything helpful?"

"What I saw today helped me create the framework, but I didn't find the focal point. Not yet."

"Well . . . there's always tomorrow."

He glanced at his watch. It was ten past five. The museum was closed. Would Janelle stay and work longer or . . . ? "I'm going to pick up some Chinese food. Would you like to join me?"

She met his gaze, questions in her pretty blue eyes.

He waited, hoping she'd say yes.

A smile softened the corners of her mouth. "I love Chinese. Where's the restaurant?"

"I usually take the tube to Tottenham Court Road and stop by a little restaurant called Chopstix. Then I walk over to Soho Square Garden and find a bench in the sunshine."

Her eyes twinkled. "That sounds good. I just need to pack up my laptop, and I'll be ready to go."

9

Lillian looked out the side window as the carriage rolled to a stop. Before she and Mr. McGivern had left her home, she'd asked her coachman to take them to the Foundling Hospital and park in the rear of the property, a short distance from the back gate.

She scanned the empty tree-lined lane. "There's not a soul in sight now."

Mr. McGivern shifted to the left. "I can't see the gate from this side. May I sit next to you?"

"Of course." She slid toward the window to give him as much room as possible.

He sat beside her, then moved closer, his arm brushing hers. The fragrance of his shaving soap wafted toward her. She pulled in a deep breath, enjoying the fresh evergreen scent. It had been a long time since she'd been this close to a handsome man.

She silently scolded herself. There was nothing suggestive behind his request to sit beside her. They had parked in this secluded spot to look for the cleaning woman, not for a romantic interlude.

"Your coachman chose a good location." Mr. McGivern focused out the window. "We're far enough away that we won't attract attention, but close enough to see anyone coming or going." His serious tone indicated he wasn't the least bit affected by her nearness.

She pulled in a calming breath and shifted her gaze away from him. How silly to let his nearness ruffle her. Why had her thoughts even taken her in that direction?

He took out his pocket watch. "If some of the staff go home for dinner, they should be leaving soon."

Her stomach contracted at the mention of dinner. Why hadn't she thought to bring something for them to eat while they waited? Maybe bringing a picnic basket would've made this seem like a friendly outing, rather than one with a much more serious purpose. Still, she was sorry she hadn't thought to bring some fruit, cheese, or bread for them to share.

A loud squeak sounded above her shoulder, and the carriage jostled slightly.

Mr. McGivern turned. "Perhaps we should give your coachman leave to find a pub and have his evening meal while we wait."

She swallowed. If her coachman left, she would be alone with Mr. McGivern, and she'd have no way of getting home if the need arose. "I'm not sure that's wise."

He looked her way, his gaze sincere. "You've no cause to worry, Mrs. Freemont. You are safe with me."

Her face flushed. Did he mean he would protect her if needed, or that she shouldn't fear any improper advances from him? Either way, she appreciated his reply and let go of her apprehension. "Very well."

"I'll speak to him. What is the coachman's name?"

"Ben Fields."

He opened the door and climbed down. "Mr. Fields, I expect we'll be here for at least an hour or two. You're free to look for a pub and find some dinner. But do be quick about it."

"Thank you, sir. I won't be long." Her coachman climbed down, and his footsteps faded off down the lane.

Mr. McGivern climbed back inside and resumed his seat.

Silence hung between them for a few seconds. She might as well use the time to learn something more about him. "What made you want to become a journalist?"

He continued studying the view out the window, and she wondered if he would ignore her question.

Finally, he turned toward her, and a mixture of emotions she couldn't quite read flickered across his face. "I started selling newspapers when I was a young boy to help support my widowed mother. Soon after I turned twelve, I began cleaning the offices of the *Gazette*. One evening, Mr. Stead caught me sitting in the corner of the newsroom reading the latest issue rather than sweeping the floor. I thought he'd sack me for sure. Instead, he became my benefactor as well as my editor."

"You became a journalist at twelve?"

Mr. McGivern's eyes lit up, and he chuckled. The change it brought to his face was quite remarkable, and she smiled in response.

"No, I mean he took an interest in me and made it possible for me to attend school. He said if I did well, he'd help me attend the University of London. I worked hard at the *Gazette* and my studies, and he covered some of my expenses. When I graduated, he offered me a position, and I've been there ever since."

So, Matthew was a self-made man who had risen through his own efforts rather than inheriting wealth or position. Some might be put off by that knowledge, but she admired him for it. "How long have you worked as a journalist at the *Gazette*?"

"It will be ten years in July."

She nodded, estimating that he was in his early thirties, as she had suspected.

"I'm not sure what would've happened to me if Mr. Stead hadn't caught me reading that night and decided to give me those opportunities."

"It sounds as though Providence as well as Mr. Stead has been guiding your life."

He studied her for a moment, keen interest in his eyes. "Yes, I believe that's true. And I've sensed it even more these last few months."

She tipped her head, inviting him to say more.

"My mother had a strong faith. For years, she urged me to read the Bible and attend church with her, but I was always too busy. At least that's what I told her. About a year ago, her health began to fail. The doctors told us there was no cure. Her trust in the Lord and hope of heaven were a great inspiration for me. I took her encouragement to heart and renewed my faith, and that has made all the difference."

Lillian nodded, her appreciation for him growing. "Painful times tend to highlight our need for faith and a strong relationship with the Lord."

"Yes, they do." The light dimmed in his eyes. "My mother passed away last November."

Lillian's heart clenched. "I'm very sorry for your loss."

"Thank you."

"I know how difficult it is to lose those you love. Both my parents have passed away."

His gaze met hers. "Reverend Howell told me you also lost your husband."

She stilled, surprised they had discussed her widowhood. "Yes, my husband, John, died eight years ago. We'd been married less than two years when his ship went down in the North Sea."

"You have my sympathies. I've never been married, but I imagine that would be a deeper kind of loss than losing a parent."

"Both are painful. I don't know how people can go through losses like those without faith to sustain them."

Understanding shone in his eyes, and he gave a slow nod.

Suddenly, he shifted and focused out the window again. "Two women just passed through the gate."

She turned and scanned the lane, spotting the women.

He lowered his voice. "Do you recognize either of them?"

She leaned toward the window and searched the women's faces as they came closer. One was a young redhead. The other was a tall, thin, middle-aged woman. Lillian's spirit deflated, and she shook her head. "Neither one is the woman who spoke to me, but they might know something."

He nodded, opened the carriage door, and stepped down.

Lillian followed him into the lane. "Excuse me, do you ladies have a moment?"

The women stopped a few feet from the carriage and exchanged apprehensive glances. The middle-aged woman lifted her chin. "What do you want?"

Lillian smiled, hoping to put them at ease. "My name is Lillian Freemont. I'm wondering if you know an older woman who does cleaning at the Foundling Hospital. She's heavyset and looks about sixty or perhaps a bit older."

The redhead narrowed her eyes. "Why do you ask?"

"I spoke to her a few days ago. She gave me some information about my niece, who has been in the care of the Foundling Hospital for almost eight years. But there seems to be some confusion about what has happened to her."

The two women exchanged glances, and the redhead said, "You should speak to the matron."

Lillian shot a glance at Mr. McGivern.

He gave a slight nod and turned to the women. "Ladies, I'm Matthew McGivern, a journalist with the *Pall Mall Gazette*. I'm looking into the disappearance of several young women. We believe they may have been taken against their will to work in brothels. We want to find them and be sure those who abducted them are arrested."

The redhead's eyes went wide. "We don't know anything about that!" She grabbed the other woman's arm and tugged her away.

"Wait!" Lillian called. But the women scurried down the lane without looking back. She sighed and glanced at Mr. Mc-Givern. "They certainly didn't want to help."

He watched the women with a brooding frown. "No, but I suspect they may know more than they were willing to say." He opened the carriage door and offered her his hand.

They climbed in and waited another thirty minutes, but no one else passed through the back gate.

Lillian leaned toward the window and scanned the lane once more. The sun had dipped lower, and the shadows of the trees darkened her view. "It seems no one else is coming out. Why don't we go in and see if we can find someone who will speak to us?"

He cocked one eyebrow. "That sounds rather daring."

"I think it's worth the risk. I'm not afraid."

He glanced down the lane. "Very well." They climbed out and walked toward the back gate. As they drew closer, he held out his hand and whispered, "Stay behind me."

She nodded and followed him through the open gateway. They stepped off the path and onto the grass to avoid the sound of walking on the gravel. She searched the back courtyard. A broom leaned against the wall near the back door, next to three large metal milk cans and a few gardening tools. Several wooden crates were stacked by the milk cans.

Mr. McGivern approached the sturdy wooden door and tested the handle. The door opened. He nodded to her, and she passed through ahead of him. They entered a hallway with a high arched ceiling. A gas lantern on the wall gave off just enough dim light for them to see their way.

He glanced around, then started down the hall. She tiptoed

after him. Halfway down the hall, a door opened on the right, and a young woman stepped out, carrying a tray of dirty dishes. Her eyes rounded. She gasped, and her gaze darted from Lillian to Mr. McGivern. "Who are you?"

Mr. McGivern lifted his hand. "Sorry. We didn't mean to startle you. We're looking for one of the women who works here." He turned to Lillian.

She softened her tone. "She is an older woman in her sixties, heavyset with gray hair. She does the mopping."

Her face lit up. "Oh, you mean Betsy?"

Lillian had no idea if that was the woman's name, but she nodded. "Is she working this evening? We'd like to speak to her."

The young woman's expression saddened, and she shook her head. "Mr. Parker sacked her yesterday for no reason at all. Now I must do all the sweeping and mopping."

Mr. McGivern straightened. "Can you describe Mr. Parker?"

The girl glanced over her shoulder and lowered her voice. "He's bald with a big red nose, and he never says a kind word to anyone. He'd just as soon give you a black eye as say good morning. He's real mean-spirited. We all try to stay far out of his way." Her eyes went wide, and she covered her mouth. "I shouldn't have said that. You won't tell him, will you?"

Lillian held out her hand. "Don't worry. What you said is safe with us."

"Do you know Betsy's surname?" Mr. McGivern asked.

"No, sir. I'm sorry. I don't."

Lillian's thoughts raced ahead. "Do you know where she lives?"

The young woman shook her head. "She used to live here, but I'm not sure where she went after he sacked her. I don't believe she has any family, except a niece in Glasgow. Maybe she went there."

A door slammed above them, and heavy footsteps sounded on the stairs. "Rachel? Where are you?"

The girl gasped. "That's Mr. Parker!"

Mr. McGivern grabbed Lillian's arm and tugged her into an alcove, behind a partially open door. He slipped his arm around her waist and pulled her tight to his side.

Lillian's heart pounded, and she held her breath.

"I'm down here, Mr. Parker," the young woman called, moving away from them.

The man's footsteps came closer, then stopped a few feet away. "What is taking you so long?"

"Sorry. I just need to drop these off in the kitchen. Then I'll go back for the rest."

Mr. Parker huffed and strode past the alcove. "Why is the back gate still open?"

"I don't know, sir."

Keys jingled as his footsteps traveled down the hall, away from them.

Lillian's heart lodged in her throat. She looked up at Mr. McGivern. He returned a calm look, one that seemed to say not to worry, everything was under control. She hoped he was right, but how would they get out if that man locked the gate, cutting off their means of escape?

Matthew slowed his breathing and strained to listen. At least two minutes had passed since Mr. Parker walked by a second time, then climbed the stairs and slammed the door above. He loosened his hold on Mrs. Freemont and whispered, "Let's go."

She sucked in a breath. "Are you sure he's gone?"

"Yes, and there's nothing more we can do here now." He guided her out of their hiding place.

She stepped into the hall and looked both ways. Her anxious

expression tugged at his conscience, and a surge of protective instinct rushed through him. "We'll be all right." He placed his hand lightly on her back and guided her down the hall. When they reached the door, he tested the handle and found it locked.

Mrs. Freemont shot him a fearful glance.

"Just a moment." He fiddled with the handle and finally managed to release the lock. They slipped outside, and he quietly shut the door behind them.

"Wait here. Let me check." He stepped out and looked around. The sun had set, and the sky glowed golden orange above the trees beyond the high stone wall surrounding the property. He didn't see a night watchman or anyone else. He turned and signaled her to join him.

She crept forward, and they slipped down the gravel path, but as the gate came into view, they both slowed. A heavy lock and chain had been placed around the center bars of the tall iron gate.

Mrs. Freemont stifled a gasp. "How will we get out?"

He glanced toward the corner of the building. "We could go around front, but I suspect that gate is also locked by this time of night." Lifting his gaze, he studied the stone wall. It stood at least eight feet high and was partially covered with vines and moss. There were a few small footholds, but it wouldn't be an easy climb. "We'll have to go up and over."

She lifted her eyes toward the wall. "How?"

He turned and searched the back courtyard. They needed a ladder, but he didn't see one. An idea clicked, and he pointed toward the building. "Let's use those crates."

She offered a hesitant nod. They returned and collected two crates each, then carried them to the wall.

He placed his larger crate on the ground, then stacked the slightly smaller crate on top. "That should give us enough height so we can pull ourselves up to the top of the wall. You go first."

"Me? Why should I go first?"

He leaned closer and lowered his voice. "I can steady you as you climb. Then I want you to sit on top and wait for me to join you. I'll lower myself to the ground on the other side, and I can help you down."

She glanced at the rickety crates. "If I'd known I'd have to scale a wall I might have dressed differently."

He studied her dark green dress with its full skirt, high lace neck, and formfitting top. It wasn't ideal for climbing over a wall, but it certainly showed off her feminine curves nicely. His face heated, and he looked away. "I'm sure you'll be fine."

Even in the fading light he could see her cheeks glowed pink. "Very well, but you must turn your head when I step up on those crates."

He huffed. "Don't worry, I'm more focused on getting away without being caught than catching a glimpse of your ankles."

She shot him a heated glance, then spun around and stepped up on the first crate. It jiggled, and he grabbed hold of her waist to steady her.

She sucked in a breath. "I'm fine!"

He dropped his hands, suppressing a grin. She stepped up to the next crate, swayed, then spread her arms and found her center. He lifted his hands, ready to catch her if she lost her balance.

She rose on her tiptoes and slowly reached up, but her hands were still several inches below the top of the wall. "I'm not high enough."

"I'll boost you up."

"You'll do no such thing!"

"Stop fussing!" He quickly stacked his two crates next to hers and climbed to the top. Cupping his hands, he leaned toward her. "Put your foot here, and I'll lift you up."

She scowled at his hands for a second, then grimaced. "Oh,

very well." Lifting her skirt a few inches, she placed her foot in his joined hands. He slowly raised her higher. She grabbed hold of the wall and hauled herself up, all the while her skirt brushed against his shoulders and face, blocking his line of vision.

He felt her foot leave his hand. Leaning back, he looked up and nearly fell off his crate. With a gasp, he grabbed the wall and pulled himself higher. It took quite a scramble, but he finally reached the top and claimed a spot next to her. Panting, he looked her way with a triumphant grin.

She returned a broad smile. "We made it."

"At least we're halfway." He glanced down. It looked farther than eight feet. But surely he could lower himself over the side and drop to the ground without too much trouble.

"What about the crates? Won't someone see them?"

"There's nothing we can do about that now." He shifted to the left a few inches. "I'm going to turn and drop down, then you can do the same."

She sent him a wide-eyed look. "You make it sound like a walk in the park."

"Don't worry. I'll catch you."

She lifted her eyes toward heaven. "Wonderful."

"Do you have another idea?"

"Not really."

He twisted, then backed over the side. His arms burned as he held on to the top of the wall and slowly lowered himself. When his arms were fully extended, he held his breath and let go. A second later, he landed safely on the soft, spongy grass. Relief rushed through him, and he looked up. "All is well. Your turn."

Worry shadowed her expression as she looked down, then she set her mouth in a determined line. With her skirts ruffling in the breeze, she turned and slowly lowered herself over the side. One foot swung across the wall, searching for a toehold. "Oh, I don't like this," she muttered.

He reached up. "You don't need to like it. Just lower yourself as far as you can, then let go. I'll catch you." He glanced away for a moment, then turned back and focused on her shoes. "That's the way," he called softly. "Just a bit farther."

Suddenly, she yelped, slipped from the wall, and fell into his arms. He grabbed hold, but the speed and weight of her sent them tumbling to the ground.

Sputtering and flailing, she scrambled off him. "I'm so sorry. Did I hurt you?" She brushed the hair from her eyes and hovered over him, searching his face. "Speak to me, Mr. McGivern. Are you well?"

He coughed a few times and looked up at her. "Other than a few broken ribs, I'm fine."

Her eyes flashed wide. "Truly, I broke your ribs?"

He grinned. "No, Mrs. Freemont, I'm teasing. You just knocked the air out of me, that's all." He huffed and sat up. She'd lost her hat, and a streak of dirt traced a dark line down her cheek, but she'd never looked prettier.

Her bewildered expression melted into a smile. "I think after this escapade you've earned the right to call me Lillian."

He nodded. "All right. Then you must call me Matthew."

"Very well, Matthew. Would you like some assistance?" She held out her hand.

"I would." He grabbed hold and rose to his feet, enjoying the feeling of her small, warm hand in his.

She let go, then brushed the grass and leaves from her dress. With a quick dip, she scooped her hat from the ground. "Goodness, I must look frightful."

He shook his head. "Not at all. I'd say you look like you've been on quite an adventure."

She sent him a teasing smile. "At least we made it out alive."

He chuckled as they started down the lane together. "Yes, we did."

When they'd first met, he'd realized she was well-spoken and passionate about social issues. But he'd assumed her wealth and position in society would make her aloof. He'd never imagined she'd bravely partner with him, be willing to climb over a high wall, and then laugh about her tumbled appearance. And she'd been more than willing to put herself in danger to search for her young niece.

He'd been wrong about Lillian Freemont. She was much more than he'd ever expected.

10

Janelle settled on the park bench next to Jonas. Across the lawn, she could see the statue of King Charles II and a small black-and-white Tudor-style building. A few people strolled past, some with dogs on leashes and others with children in tow. It was a peaceful spot with tall trees, curving paths, and a gentle breeze.

She took her container of Chinese food from the bag and opened the top. The mingled scents of vegetable noodles and lemon chicken rose. "Mmm, this smells delicious."

"Wait until you try the teriyaki beef." He opened his container, then glanced at her. "Do you mind if I say a prayer before we eat?"

Her heart warmed. "I'd like that." She lowered her head and closed her eyes.

"Father, thank you for this day and this food. We pray for Amanda and the twins and ask you to watch over them at the hospital. Thank you for Janelle and her work at the Foundling Museum. Please guide her and give her wisdom as she leads her staff and carries on all that's needed while Amanda is away. And please help me make this film the most effective tool possible. Thanks for this food. We pray in Jesus's name. Amen."

Gratitude flooded her heart as she lifted her head. "Thank

you. That was kind of you to pray for Amanda and for me. I definitely need God's wisdom to try and fill Amanda's shoes."

"From what I can see, you're doing a great job."

She smiled and dipped her chopsticks into her lemon chicken. "Thanks. I never realized all that's involved, especially staying on budget. That's the only way our staff can hold on to their jobs and we can continue offering our programs for kids in care."

He sent her an understanding nod. "I'm sure it's a challenge."

They ate in companionable silence for a couple minutes, then she said, "Now that you know how to access the museum's records, I suppose you'll go back to working at your office?"

He shifted on the bench and looked her way. "My office is actually the spare bedroom in my flat."

She blinked and glanced at him. She'd imagined him working in a modern office with a receptionist out front and a production studio, as well as an assistant or two.

"You look surprised."

"Oh, no . . . it's just that I thought . . ."

"It's okay. We're a young company, and it's just me and Howie right now, so working from home makes sense. But you won't find anyone more committed to making an impact than we are. That's why we took the name Vision Impact Films."

She nodded. "The Bible says we shouldn't despise the day of small things."

Interest sparked in his eyes. "Right. And Jesus said the one who is faithful with a little will be given more." He grinned. "That gives me hope."

Delight swirled through her. He not only prayed—he knew his Bible. "Being faithful with what you've been given is an important principle."

They both took a few more bites of their food, and she could tell he was as pleased with her comments as she was with his.

She took a sip from her water bottle. "Tell me about some of the other films you've made."

"You saw part of the one we did for the British Wildlife Federation."

She nodded, recalling the beautiful images of the countryside, birds, and animals.

"And I've done a few for a youth theater group called Rising Stars. Then I filmed one for a manor house in Berkshire that's owned by the National Trust."

"Oh, I love visiting National Trust sites. Anything else?"

He nodded. "Last year we started working on a documentary for the International Centre for Missing and Exploited Children, but the grant for the funding fell through. We had to stop work and shelve the project." He huffed and shook his head.

"Sounds like that was disappointing."

He grimaced. "It was painful. I probably shouldn't have invested so much time in the project without being certain we'd secured that grant, but the need is so great."

"That is an important cause."

"It is, and it's personal for me."

She sent him a questioning look.

"When I was fifteen, there was a girl who lived two houses down from me. Her name was Sarah. We'd known each other since we were six. I used to walk to and from school with her and her older brother. But one day, I got in trouble and had to stay after school. Her brother had football practice, so she walked home alone, and that's when she was taken."

Janelle stilled. "I'm so sorry. Was she . . . found?"

"She escaped seven days later." He stared off across the park. "That was the longest week of my life. I barely slept. Couldn't eat. I kept thinking if I'd been with her, it wouldn't have happened."

Janelle's throat tightened. "You were only fifteen. It wasn't your fault."

"That's what everyone said, but I knew it wasn't true. If the two of us had been together, that man would've driven on by. But on her own like that, she was an easy target."

"Thank goodness she got away."

"Yes, but it was traumatic for her. Ever since then, I've looked for ways to support efforts against human trafficking. Then last year, I met a man who works for the International Centre for Missing and Exploited Children. When I heard about their programs to educate kids and help find missing children, I knew I wanted to make a documentary to help get the word out. I applied for two grants, and I felt certain I'd get at least one of them." He shook his head. "But it didn't happen."

"How far were you into the project?"

Jonas blew out a deep breath. "We'd gotten the script written and started filming, but there was a lot more that needed to be done."

Janelle shook her head. "That must be frustrating to have to stop in the middle of something that was so important to you."

"Yeah, it was. But it's helped me learn more about trusting the Lord's timing, even when there are delays or canceled projects."

Janelle nodded, her admiration for him growing. How many times had she struggled and complained when her plans changed or her hopes were delayed? "I need to take that thought to heart."

His smile returned. "Maybe we can remind each other."

⁓

Jonas lowered himself onto the couch and scrolled through the photos he'd taken at the museum. When he reached the photos of the tokens, he slowed and studied them once more.

Each one had been left by a mother who felt desperate to retain some connection with her child. Every token represented a story of love and loss, heartache and sacrifice. How could he do justice to those children and their mothers in a fifteen-minute film? Maybe he could stretch it to twenty, but even then, it didn't seem like enough time to tell the full story.

Howie squinted and rubbed his eyes. "I'm getting eyestrain trying to read these old documents." He shifted on the other end of the couch and turned toward Jonas. "What do you think about focusing on the story of a mum who was reunited with her child? I read a couple of those."

Jonas tapped his fingers on the armrest. "That could work, but that wasn't the usual outcome. Most of those kids never saw their mums again."

"Yeah, but that's so harsh. Don't we want to make this film upbeat and show the positive side of things? After all, we're trying to raise money for the museum."

Jonas's thoughts spun back through the children's stories he'd read in the last week. They were often unsettling and sad, but those children probably would've died if their mothers had not turned them over to the care of the Foundling Hospital. In the 1700s and 1800s, when a woman had an illegitimate child, she became a social outcast, and it was nearly impossible for her to find a position to support herself and her child.

Their stories tugged at his conscience, and he shook his head. "I've been thinking about doing a longer film, a true documentary that could tell more of the history."

Howie sent him a puzzled look. "Do you think they'd pay us to do that?"

Jonas grimaced. "Probably not, but we're doing all this research. Why not use it twice—once for the fundraising film and then an extended version that tells the rest of the story?" An idea rose in his mind, and he straightened. "We could enter it in the British Documentary Film Festival. They have a category for historical pieces. If we won that award, it could really boost our reputation."

Howie scratched his chin. "Winning is a long shot."

"We're good at what we do. This is just the opportunity we need." Jonas typed in the film festival and checked the dates. "Yes! The deadline for entering is November third. That gives us plenty of time. We can fit it in around our other work."

Howie cocked an eyebrow.

"Or I should say, *I* can fit it in."

Howie's mouth tipped up on one side. "I'll help. Half the battle is finding a good topic that will grip the judges, and this could work if we find the right angle."

Jonas nodded, appreciation for his friend lifting his spirits. "Thanks, Howie."

Howie grabbed his notepad from the coffee table. "Why don't I look for some other sources besides the Foundling Hospital documents—maybe we'll find something else online."

Jonas nodded. "Go for it." He'd done a brief search after his first phone conversation with Amanda Preston, but there were probably more articles that could inspire themes for their films.

Howie lowered his head and typed on his laptop. "The Foundling Hospital is listed in a lot of articles. I'll scroll through and see if there's anything interesting."

"Sounds good." Jonas rose, walked into the kitchen, and filled his electric kettle. Maybe a cup of tea would give him a new wave of energy. He liked the contemporary angle Janelle had suggested, but he needed a solid idea that would have an emotional impact for the historical portion of the film—one that could be expanded for the documentary.

"Hey, come and see this," Howie called.

Jonas returned to the living room and stood behind Howie's chair. "What did you find?"

"It's a blog post with excerpts from an article in the *Pall Mall Gazette*. Look at the headline—'Child Snatched from Foundling Hospital. How Girls Are Bought and Ruined.'"

"What?" Jonas leaned closer and scanned the first few lines quoted from the newspaper article. "That's crazy. Send me the link."

Howie nodded, and Jonas returned to his chair and picked up his laptop. The tea could wait. Howie's email appeared, and Jonas followed the link to the article. His heartbeat picked up speed as he continued reading.

This excerpt is taken from the series The Maiden Tribute to Modern Babylon, *which exposes the sale, purchase, and violation of children in London and the international slave trade of girls.*

Jonas stared at those words. He glanced at the date of the article, and his eyebrows rose. He'd thought human trafficking was a modern problem, but this article was published in 1885.

Howie looked up. "Check the fourth paragraph. That's where they mention the Foundling Hospital."

Jonas skimmed down and read aloud, "'Through a careful investigation, we learned that girls in residence at the Foundling Hospital, as young as eight years old, have disappeared from that institution and been secretly sold to brothel owners in White Chapel.'"

Howie made a frustrated noise in his throat. "How could they sell little girls to a brothel?"

Jonas shook his head. "I have no idea." He read further, and disgust turned his stomach. Everything Janelle had told him about the history of the Foundling Hospital had made him believe it was a reputable children's home. How could this have happened?

Howie frowned. "Do you think this was an isolated incident or something that went on for a long time?"

"I don't know." Jonas leaned back and stared toward the ceiling. Did Janelle know the Foundling Museum had this kind of skeleton in its closet?

"Have you seen anything about this at the museum?"

Jonas sat up. "No. I've spoken to the acting director several times, and she never mentioned it. I can't imagine she would try to hide something like this. Maybe she doesn't know."

"You better ask her."

Jonas glanced at his laptop once more. "We need to find out if this is true."

"How are you going to do that? This article is one hundred and fifty years old."

"If this really happened, there has to be more written about it."

Howie sent him a doubtful look. "Maybe, maybe not. We don't know what kind of newspaper the *Gazette* was. Maybe it was written by some journalist who was trying to sell more copies by stirring up a scandal."

Jonas nodded, but he couldn't deny the uneasy feeling sweeping over him. He'd told Janelle how committed he was to fighting human trafficking. She wouldn't keep this kind of information from him on purpose, would she?

11

1885

"Well, Matthew, give me an update." W. T. Stead leaned forward and sent him an expectant look. "How close are you to showing me that first article for the series?"

Matthew's neck heated, and he shifted his weight to the other foot. He should have something more to show his editor by now. "I've interviewed several people and collected quite a bit of information. The last few days I've been focused on the disappearance of Mrs. Freemont's niece from the Foundling Hospital."

Stead frowned. "That's one lead, but it's not the full story. What about the girls at Mercy House? What did you learn there?"

"I interviewed four girls. Their experiences were . . . quite gripping. I could use those for the first article, but I haven't had time to follow up on what I learned there."

Stead's bushy eyebrows rose. "Haven't had time? That was four days ago."

"What I mean is, looking for information about Mrs. Freemont's niece seemed more pressing."

"Watch yourself, Matthew. Don't let this become a personal issue. You need to keep your perspective and remain impartial.

I don't mind you sharing information with Mrs. Freemont. I want her niece found and returned to her family as much as you do, but we've got to push ahead with our original plan for the series."

Matthew's gut twisted, and he fingered the note in his pocket from Lillian. How could he stay impartial when he knew how anxious she was to find her missing niece? She was willing to do whatever was needed. How could he do anything less?

Mr. Stead slapped his hand on the desk, jolting Matthew back to the moment. "Get back out there. Scour the city. Find out who is behind the abductions of those girls from White Chapel! We need to get these articles in print and put a stop to this!"

"Yes, sir."

"I want to see that first article on my desk by Thursday afternoon." Stead motioned toward the door.

"Very good, sir." Matthew strode out of Mr. Stead's office and headed for the newsroom. The scent of cigar smoke and printer's ink hung in the air. Several reporters hunched over their desks, scribbling away on their stories, while a few others had gathered in the corner, discussing their assignments.

He sank down at his desk and pulled Lillian's note from his pocket. She'd written his name in flowing script on the front of the envelope that had been hand-delivered by her coachman earlier that morning.

Dear Matthew,

My sister Serena and I want to thank you for the gallant way you have stepped forward to help us in the search for Alice. You have given us hope that we will find her and that she will be returned to us very soon.

Though we didn't locate the cleaning woman at Found-ling Hospital, I am remembering those events with a light heart. Thank you for going there with me and for making sure we were able to get away safely without being seen. That was quite an adventure—one I'm sure I'll never forget.

I've spoken to Reverend Howell and my sister, and we have an idea for the next step in our search. We'd like to discuss it with you and ask for your thoughts as well as your help. I will be home all day. If you are able, please come at your convenience.

Sincerely,
Lillian

The content of the note tugged at his conscience. Knowing she appreciated his efforts and was counting on his continued help sent a rush of determination through him. But he couldn't ignore his editor's stern words. He had to focus on finishing that first article by Thursday. He'd already reviewed his notes from the visit to Mercy House and had an idea how he might shape the article, but he had to make sure everything he included could be corroborated.

His gaze dropped to Lillian's note once more, and he set his jaw. Even if he had to work from six in the morning until midnight, he would find a way to meet that deadline and fulfill Lillian's request.

~

Lillian poured a cup of tea for Reverend Howell and glanced at the clock on the sitting room mantel. Matthew's note said he would arrive by six, but it was almost six thirty. She passed the cup to Reverend Howell. "I wonder why Mr. McGivern is late."

He sent her an understanding look. "I'm sure he has a good reason for the delay. I've gotten to know Matthew quite well in the last year, and he's proven himself to be a man of his word."

She had sensed that about him as well and was glad to hear the reverend confirm it.

He took his watch from his vest pocket. "I'm afraid I'll have to leave soon. I have a meeting at the church at seven o'clock."

She rose. "I wouldn't want you to miss your meeting. I can pass on our ideas to Mr. McGivern when he arrives."

He set his cup on the low table in front of the sofa. "I would stay longer, but it's the missions committee, and we're discussing several new candidates who have asked for our support."

She nodded. "I understand."

Stanford stepped into the doorway. "Mr. McGivern has arrived, ma'am."

Relief flowed through her. "Please show him in."

The butler nodded and stepped away.

A moment later, Matthew entered, and his gaze went directly to Lillian. "I apologize for my late arrival. There was a fire near the offices of the *Gazette*, and a snarl of carriages blocked our way. We had to drive quite a distance to find a path around the crowd and the fire wagons."

Concern lined Reverend Howell's face. "I hope no one was injured."

"I saw some of the *Gazette* reporters on the scene. I'm sure we'll read the details in the paper tomorrow morning."

Reverend Howell explained his need to leave for the missions meeting, and Matthew apologized again for being late. Reverend Howell shook his hand and bid them good night. Stanford saw him out.

Lillian motioned toward the sofa. "Please have a seat."

"Thank you." Matthew sat at one end.

She settled at the opposite end. "Thank you for coming. I hope my note didn't seem too presumptuous. After I sent it, I realized it might have sounded as though I expected you to drop whatever you were doing and come right away."

He shook his head, sincerity in his eyes. "No need to apologize. I'm glad you feel you can call on me."

She offered him a cup of tea.

He accepted it and took a sip. "You had an idea about the search for you niece?"

"Yes. Reverend Howell and I were discussing what you and I learned at Mercy House, especially our interview with that young woman, Amy. She mentioned there were younger girls working belowstairs at the Golden Swan." She paused. "I think that's the next lead we should follow."

His eyebrows rose. "What are you suggesting?"

Her cheeks heated, and she shifted on the sofa. Going to a brothel was not a topic she could easily discuss, but it was necessary. "I'm sure there are many . . . establishments like the Golden Swan in London. My niece may not be working there, but I want to pay a visit and see for myself."

He frowned. "The Golden Swan is no place for a woman like you."

She straightened. "It's no place for an eight-year-old girl either."

He rose and paced across the room, clearly unhappy with her idea.

"I want to speak to the people in charge and learn if she's there."

He turned and studied her with a dubious look. "If she is there, which is highly unlikely, I don't believe they would tell you the truth or turn her over willingly."

"What should we do, then—go to the police?"

His frown deepened. "I've spoken to them twice about the missing girls from White Chapel. They say they're investigating the disappearances, but so far none of those girls have been found." He shook his head. "I don't like to say it, but I suspect they may have been paid off by someone who doesn't want those girls found."

She stifled a gasp. "You don't think they would search for Alice?"

"They might listen to you and file a report, then they'd speak to the matron and close the case." He crossed his arms, looking deep in thought. "I believe our best option is to continue the search ourselves, at least for now."

Lillian's heart lifted. "So you'll go to the Golden Swan?"

"I'm not sure how I can get in. I'll have to think of some kind of ruse."

"I don't want to lie."

His eyebrows dipped. "Don't worry. You won't have to. You're not going with me."

She set her jaw and rose from the sofa. "I went with you to the Foundling Hospital. We snuck in and out without too much trouble."

He closed his eyes, obviously restraining himself. "It's not the same. Going into the Golden Swan will be much more dangerous."

"That may be true." Her voice grew more intense. "But I must find Alice. I'm responsible. None of this would've happened if I had been more . . ." Her throat tightened, cutting off her words.

His brow creased. "What are you saying?"

She swallowed hard. "I knew my sister was becoming enamored with Robert Dunsmore. I should have cautioned her to guard her affections until she was certain of his character and commitment. But John and I had only been married for a short time. I was so focused on my own happiness that I ignored the danger signs."

He shook his head. "Your sister made her own choices. What happened to her is not your fault."

"But she was only seventeen—so young and naïve. If I'd not been so wrapped up in my own life, I could've seen what was coming and prevented all this heartache."

There was no censure in his expression, only an understanding look that encouraged her to tell him more.

"A few months after she ran away with him, she wrote and told us she was expecting a child. I made a few inquiries, but then my husband's ship went down, and I lost . . ." She pressed her lips tight, unable to say the rest. How could she tell him the dear child she'd so longed for had only lived a few hours? She pulled in a deep breath, reining in her emotions. "I lost hope and gave up the search."

Eight years had passed, but she still felt the weight of her failure to protect her sister almost as deeply as she grieved the loss of her husband and child. "I'm sorry. I don't mean to pour out all my troubles on you. But now you must see how important it is that I find my niece."

"Lillian, as much as you love your sister, you can't right all the wrongs in her life." His voice softened, and his gaze held steady.

It was kind of him to try and ease the burden she felt, but he didn't understand the depth of regret she carried for everything that had happened to Serena and Alice. "Please, I want to go with you and do what I can."

He released a deep breath, looking as though he might be softening to her idea.

"We know there are young girls trapped at the Golden Swan," she said. "Maybe my niece is there, maybe not. Either way, I believe the Lord gave us that information for a reason. Let's go there together and see what we can do to help them."

Conflicting emotions crossed his face. "I'll find some way to get in and try to speak to the girls, but I can't allow you to go with me."

She crossed her arms and held his gaze as the mantel clock

ticked off the seconds. She needed his help, so she would have to concede. "All right. How will you get in?"

He stared into the fireplace for a few seconds, then turned to her. "I'll go as a deliveryman, maybe take some vegetables to the kitchen. If I arrive early in the morning, it shouldn't be too busy. That way I might catch the girls belowstairs on their own."

"If you do find my niece, do you think she'll leave with you—a man she doesn't even know?"

He studied her for a moment, obviously still conflicted. "I suppose you could ride along in the carriage. If your niece is there, and she's reluctant to leave with me, I could bring you to her."

Relief rushed through Lillian. She still wished she could accompany him into the building from the start, but she could tell this was the only compromise he would offer. She would ride along, pray for his safety and success, and be on hand if needed.

Considering the risks, she should be grateful, but she couldn't push away the feeling she should do more.

12

Janelle stirred the pasta sauce into the beef, and the tantalizing scent of basil and oregano filled the kitchen. Red and white tortellini was one of her favorite recipes from childhood. Even though it would probably give her carb overload, it was exactly what she wanted to ease the strain of the day.

Every time she'd turned around, one of the staff members at the museum was upset about some trivial problem. How did Amanda do it? She knew taking over as director would be challenging, but she hadn't expected this level of disagreements and stress.

A knock sounded, and her front door opened. Maggie walked in and strode toward the kitchen. "Oh, we are in trouble now."

Janelle set aside her wooden spoon. "What's wrong?"

Maggie plopped down on a stool at the counter and sent Janelle a frazzled look. "We told Olivia she has to leave her phone out in the living room to charge at night, but she's been sneaking out there and taking it back to her room so she can talk to some boy named Tony for hours!"

Janelle smiled. "Aww, don't you remember talking on the phone for hours when you were a teenager? That's not really a problem, is it?"

126

Maggie's eyes went wide. "Well, it might not be if she'd told the truth, but when we confronted her, she lied about it."

Janelle's smile faded. "Oh, that's not good."

"No, it's not."

Janelle swiveled toward the range and turned off the burner. "So, what are you going to do?"

"I don't know! We need some kind of consequence and a better plan for the phone."

Janelle faced Maggie again. "The issue with the phone is important, but lying about it sounds like a bigger problem. Maybe you could talk to her about the importance of honesty and trust."

"Right now, she's not talking to us about anything."

"Sorry." Janelle sighed. "What do you think her mum would say? Maybe Dan should talk to her so you can act as a united front."

Maggie shook her head. "Dan says he doesn't want to bother Diane because she's too stressed about her husband's illness. But I think the real problem is he doesn't want to admit that he's having trouble handling Olivia."

"I can see how that would be hard." Janelle picked up the wooden spoon. "How did you find out Olivia was sneaking her phone back to her room?"

"Last night I couldn't sleep, so I got up to get a snack." Maggie waved her hand. "I know, eating at night is terrible for you, but this time I'm glad I gave in to the urge. When I walked through the living room, I noticed her phone was missing. So, I tiptoed down the hall and listened at her door."

"Eavesdropping, eh?"

"That's a parent's right—or I should say a stepparent's right."

"What did you hear?"

"She was laughing, and then she said, 'Oh, Tony, you're so

funny.' I'm thinking, who is Tony, and why is she talking to him at two in the morning?"

"Did you go in and confront her?"

"No, I decided to wait and talk to Dan. First thing this morning, I told him what I heard, but Olivia was still asleep, and he had to leave for work. We decided to wait until he got home to talk to her." Maggie huffed out a breath. "Why would she lie to us?"

"Maybe she felt cornered and just gave in to the temptation. Or maybe that's how she gets out of trouble with her mom and stepdad."

Maggie held up her finger. "Well, that's not going to work with us."

"What did Dan say when he talked to her?"

"He told her we knew she took her phone back into her room last night. Of course, she said she didn't. Then he said I overheard her talking to a boy. She denied it and said I was making it up to get her into trouble! I about blew my top at that, but somehow, I managed to control myself."

"Good for you."

"Dan didn't back down. He told her, we pay for the phone and if she wanted to continue using it, then she needed to stick to our rules, let him check her calls, and leave it in the living room each night. Obviously, she was not happy about that."

"Did she hand over the phone?"

"Eventually, but first she said we don't love her or trust her, then she added a few more choice words before she threw her phone down and ran out of the room. The last thing we heard was—you guessed it—her door slamming."

"Wow, that's tough." Janelle stirred the sauce, trying to think of some way to help Maggie. "I wonder why Tony wants to talk to her at two in the morning."

"We asked her the same thing, but she wouldn't say much about him."

A prickle of unease traveled through Janelle. "He doesn't sound like a good influence."

"No, he doesn't." Maggie slid off the stool and walked around the counter and into the kitchen. "So . . . I was wondering, has she mentioned Tony or any of her other friends?"

Janelle turned. "Not really. We talk a little on our way to and from the museum, but we're just getting to know each other."

"Could you maybe . . . ask her about him?"

"What makes you think she'd tell me?"

"She likes you."

Janelle sent her a doubtful glance. "Why would you say that?"

"When she first started volunteering at the museum, she was dragging her feet each morning, but these last few days I haven't had to prod her to get ready. She's up and dressed before I am."

"Just from that you think she likes me?"

"Well, she doesn't seem to hate you as much as she hates us. Maybe she'll confide in you, and you can . . . you know . . . pass on anything important that you learn."

Janelle put the lid on the sauce and turned down the burner. "I'm sorry she's giving you and Dan such a hard time, but I doubt she's going to tell me her deepest secrets."

Maggie clasped her hands. "Could you just test the water and see if she'll open up?"

Janelle pulled in a deep breath. It might be awkward, but she cared about Olivia, and Maggie was her best friend. She couldn't let her fight this battle alone. "Okay. I'll talk to her and see what I can learn, but don't let that be your only hope for working through these issues with Olivia."

"Oh, thank you!" Maggie gave her a tight hug. "Dan and I will keep working on it from our side, I promise."

Janelle carried her lunch tray toward the booth in the back corner of the café and glanced over her shoulder at Olivia. She'd invited her out to lunch, hoping to strengthen their connection and see if she could learn anything that might reduce the conflict with Maggie and Dan.

She slid her tray onto the table. "This looks like a good spot."

Olivia placed her tray across from Janelle and took a seat.

A shiver of anticipation traveled down Janelle's back as she settled into the chair. She sent off a silent prayer, asking the Lord to soften Olivia's heart and give her wisdom for their conversation. But first, she decided to follow Jonas's example. "Mind if I say a prayer and thank the Lord for our meal?"

Olivia sent her a curious look, then shrugged.

Janelle held back a smile and lowered her head. "Father, thank you for this day and for this food. We're grateful we can take a break and enjoy it together. Please guide our conversation and help us remember how much you love us. In Jesus's name, amen."

Olivia raised her head. "You're not embarrassed to pray out loud?"

Janelle shook her head. "I might get a few odd looks, but that doesn't bother me. Praying before a meal reminds me God is the one who provides everything I need, and it gives me a chance to say thank-you."

Olivia quirked her eyebrow. "You sound like Maggie."

Janelle smiled, pleased Olivia would connect their shared faith. "Maggie and I do have a lot in common, including our belief that prayer helps us connect with God."

Olivia took a sip of her drink and ripped open the bag of crisps.

Janelle poured the dressing over her salad. "How did the art class go this morning?"

"It went okay. But some of the kids were my age, so that was a little strange."

"Why is that?"

"All the kids in the other classes were younger than me. Today, they were my age or older. Most of them were better artists than I am."

"So how did you handle it?"

She munched on a crisp. "Lisa said all I needed to do was hand out supplies and offer encouragement. It was a little weird, but I guess it was all right. I just walked around and told them what I liked about their project. Some of them ignored me, but most of them seemed happy when I said something nice about their work."

Janelle nodded. "I'm glad you found a way to help. The kids in that class all live with foster parents, so they need all the encouragement you can give."

Olivia gave a slow nod. "There's a girl at my school who lives with a foster family. I don't know why she stays with them instead of her real parents."

"There are all kinds of reasons kids go into care." Janelle debated what to say next, then decided to plunge ahead, hoping it might encourage Olivia to open up. "I was in care from the time I was two until I turned eighteen."

Interest sparked in Olivia's eyes. "Really? How come?"

It was still tough to admit her parents' issues, but she'd been through enough counseling to realize their problems were their responsibility, not hers. "My parents struggled with drugs and alcohol, so they couldn't take care of me."

"Wow, that must have been tough."

"I don't remember much about those first two years of my life. After that, I was placed with foster parents. They were kind and treated me well, almost like I was born into their family. They were older, and they've since passed away, but I'm grateful for the time we had together and the loving home they provided."

Olivia studied her with new interest.

"Every child in care has a unique story, but they're not so different than you. They go through some of same things you're facing."

Olivia chewed on her sandwich, looking thoughtful. "Yeah, going back and forth to live with one parent and then the other isn't easy. I didn't want to come to London this summer. But my stepdad is sick."

"How's he doing now?"

"He's still in the hospital, and my mum hates hospitals. It's really hard for her." Olivia sighed. "I guess I get why she sent me to stay with my dad for now."

Janelle nodded and took a sip of her water. "So how is it going with Dan and Maggie? Have you settled into a good routine?"

Olivia's expression clouded. "Not really. They're so strict I feel like I'm in jail."

Janelle determined not to react or defend Maggie and Dan. "I'm sure it's not easy when you haven't seen them for three years."

"Their rules are totally different than my mum's. She trusts me and gives me a lot more freedom."

Janelle nodded to encourage Olivia and keep the conversation going. "How are their rules different?"

"They limit TV and computer time, and with Cole and Caleb there, I never get to choose what we watch."

"I imagine it is different having two brothers to deal with."

"Half brothers." Olivia grimaced. "And Dan and Maggie make me charge my phone in the living room at night. They don't give it back until after breakfast."

"That sounds like a change for you."

"Yes! My mum's not strict about my phone. But Maggie and Dan check it every day to look at all my calls and texts. They're just waiting for me to step over the line so they can take the phone away permanently."

"Their rules may be different than your mum's, but parking your phone in the living room at night makes sense." Janelle lightened her tone. "Everyone benefits from a good night's sleep, especially a growing teenage girl who needs her beauty rest."

Olivia scowled. "So, you're siding with them?"

"No, I'm not siding with anyone. I just think it might help to try and understand their perspective as well as your own."

Olivia dumped the rest of the crisps onto her tray. "They've been grilling me about my friends."

Janelle straightened. Here was the opening she'd been praying for. "You mean the people you're calling?"

"Yes! Why should they care who I phone? It's not hurting them. The bill is the same if I phone one person or twenty."

"I don't think money is the issue."

Olivia sent her a confused glance. "Then what's their problem?"

Janelle pulled in a deep breath, hoping she wasn't making a mistake. "Maggie mentioned you were talking to a boy named Tony the other night."

Olivia's face flushed. "She told you that?"

"Yes. She and your dad don't know Tony, so that's a concern."

"We just talk on the phone. I'm not going out with him. He doesn't even live in London."

"How did you meet him?"

She sighed. "We met online playing *League of Legends*. We talked about the game for a few weeks, then we connected on Instagram."

Janelle enjoyed scrolling through Instagram and sharing photos and videos with friends, but she'd never heard of *League of Legends*.

"He's my age," Olivia continued. "We have a lot in common."

"Like what?"

"His parents are divorced, so he gets what that's like. He's funny and caring. We like the same games, shows, and music, so we always have something to talk about. He's a great listener, and he never puts me down or makes me feel dumb. I can tell him anything, and he understands. I've never met anyone like him." Her voice warmed and grew softer with each description.

Warning bells went off in Janelle's head. This guy sounded too good to be true. "Even with all those things in common, you still need to be careful."

"Why? What are you worried about?"

She thought for a moment, trying to put her finger on what was bothering her. Tony sounded like the kind of boyfriend every girl wanted, but for some reason, Janelle wasn't convinced. "Just don't give him your personal information, like your last name or where you live."

Olivia rolled her eyes. "Why? You think he's a stalker?" Her sarcastic tone made it clear she didn't appreciate Janelle's advice.

"I don't know who or what he is . . . but neither do you, not really."

Olivia started to protest, but Janelle held up her hand. "All you know is what he's told you."

She huffed. "I checked his Instagram account. He looks exactly like he described himself."

Janelle slowly stirred her straw in her drink, trying to think of some way to get through to Olivia. She looked up and met the girl's heated gaze. "I care about you, Olivia. And I wouldn't want anyone to hurt you."

Olivia frowned. "Tony would never hurt me. He's not like that."

She gentled her tone. "I hope you're right."

"I know I am."

Janelle took a sip of her water, praying for the best way to end this part of the conversation. "Can I share one more thing?"

Olivia shrugged. "I guess."

"Your dad and Maggie love you, and even though their rules are different than your mum's, they want what's best for you."

Olivia gave her head a slight shake. "Yeah, right."

Janelle looked down at her half-eaten salad. Had she just made things worse? Olivia obviously wasn't happy Maggie had told her about Tony and the late-night calls. Would she carry that resentment home and pour it out on Maggie and Dan?

13

1885

Matthew tugged down the brim of his flat plaid cap and glanced across the carriage at Lillian. "I'll be back as soon as I can. This shouldn't take long." He grabbed the wooden crate of vegetables and climbed down. Dressed in old work clothes, he hoped to pass down the street unnoticed. He pressed his shoulder against the carriage door and closed it tight.

Lillian looked out the window. Her forehead creased, and emotion flickered in her eyes. "Please be careful."

He nodded, touched by her concern. Then he looked up at the coachman. "Stay with the carriage. Mrs. Freemont will be waiting here."

The coachman nodded. "Very good, sir."

Matthew turned and strode down the narrow side street, toting the crate of carrots, potatoes, and onions. Few people were out this early in the morning. An old man in a tattered hat and coat drove past in a rickety horse-drawn cart. An elderly woman swept the area in front of a small tailor's shop, but no one else ventured into his path.

He rounded the corner of Commercial Road and slowed his pace, studying the buildings. Three doors down, the sign for the Golden Swan hung on a wrought-iron bar above the front window. When they'd driven by in the carriage, he'd spotted steps going down to a lower-level entrance just past the front door. He shot off a silent prayer and continued down the street.

With a quick glance over his shoulder, he took the stone steps down and stopped before an old wooden door. He hefted the crate onto one arm, gave a brisk knock, and waited. No one answered, so he knocked again.

His heartbeat pounded in his ears as he strained to listen for any sounds inside. Finally, the door creaked open a few inches.

A young girl looked out. She had bright blue eyes and a mess of red curls falling from her white cap. "Yes, sir?"

"Good morning. I have a delivery." He nodded to the crate.

She sent him a surprised glance. "Where's Harry?"

"I'm the one delivering today."

She bit her lip and glanced over her shoulder. "Mrs. Crocker isn't down yet."

"That's all right. I can just drop these off in the kitchen."

She nodded and opened the door wider. "This way."

He stepped inside and followed the barefoot girl. She couldn't be more than ten years old and wore a ragged blue dress with a stained white apron over the top. "My name's Matthew. What's your name?"

She glanced at him with a worried look. "Why do you ask?"

He smiled. "Just being friendly."

A flash of fear crossed her face, and she stepped back. She'd probably met too many men who wanted to be *friendly*.

He softened his voice. "Please, don't worry about me. I mean you no harm. I'll just drop these off and be on my way."

She sighed, looking tired, and motioned to the open doorway across the hall. "You can put the vegetables in there."

"Thank you." He stepped into the kitchen. The long rectangular room was lit by a row of windows near the ceiling. A big wooden worktable filled the center of the room. Shelves and cupboards lined the walls around the sink, and a big cookstove stood to the left. The girl followed him in but kept her distance.

Another small girl with long blond hair stood on an overturned crate, cracking eggs into a bowl. She wore a loose green dress and dirty yellow apron. She was also barefoot.

His heart lurched. Was she Mary Graham?

She looked up, fearful questions reflected in her brown eyes.

Disappointment coursed through him. Mary Graham had blue eyes. This was not the girl they were seeking. He pushed that thought aside. "Good day." He added a cheerful lilt to his voice, hoping to calm their suspicions. "I have some nice fresh vegetables for you."

The blonde shot a quizzical glance at the girl who had answered the door. "Nancy, why'd you let him in?"

She shrugged. "I couldn't very well turn him away. Mrs. Crocker wouldn't like that."

"We can't pay you," the blonde said.

"That's all right. I'm sure the Golden Swan has an account."

She pointed to the table. "You can leave them there."

He lowered the crate. "Mrs. Crocker is the cook?"

Nancy nodded. "That's right, but she won't be down for a while."

He glanced around the kitchen, noting the stack of dirty pots and pans on the counter. "You girls look awfully young to be working here. How old are you?"

The blonde shot Nancy an uneasy look.

He raised his hand. "Don't worry. I won't cause you any trouble."

They said nothing, so he continued. "Did either of you live at the Foundling Hospital before you came here?"

Nancy shook her head. "I stayed at the workhouse with my granny, but she died. Mr. Bradbury brought me here." She glanced at the blonde. "Jane's always lived here."

138

He made a mental note of Mr. Bradbury's name and glanced at Jane. "This has always been your home?"

Jane nodded. "My mum used to work upstairs, but she got sick and died. Mr. Bradbury said I could stay on as long as I do what Mrs. Crocker says."

"It's just you two helping Mrs. Crocker and doing all the work? No other girls?"

They glanced at each other.

He cocked his eyebrows. "Is there someone else?"

Nancy bit her lip, then said, "There's Ellen."

Jane flashed a heated glance at Nancy. "Don't say anything else!"

"Why not? Maybe he can help her."

"Mr. Bradbury will skin you alive if you don't hush up," Jane whispered.

Nancy lifted her chin. "Ellen needs to see a doctor."

A jolt of concern shot through him. "She's ill?"

Nancy squirmed. "Not exactly ill . . . just roughed up and hurting."

He stiffened. "I can take her to the doctor."

Both girls' eyes widened, and they exchanged anxious glances.

"She can't leave," Jane insisted. "We're not allowed."

"Who roughed her up?"

Jane clamped her mouth closed and looked away, obviously refusing to say.

He shifted his gaze to Nancy. "I know a kind doctor who would be glad to help her. I can take her there now."

Nancy hurried over to Jane and tugged her down from the crate. She leaned in and whispered in Jane's ear. Jane shook her head and said something back, but their voices were so low he couldn't hear their words. The whispered argument continued a few more seconds. Finally, Nancy turned toward him. "Come with me."

He followed her out of the kitchen and down the hall. She walked quietly, her feet barely making a sound on the rough wooden floorboards. She opened a door on the right and motioned him inside. He stepped into a dark musty room that smelled of dirty bedding and unwashed bodies. A lantern turned low sat on a table by the narrow bed in the corner. A ragged brown blanket covered a small, still form.

Nancy crossed to the bed. "Ellen?"

The girl on the bed didn't move.

Nancy turned the blanket down and touched Ellen's shoulder.

Matthew took a few steps closer. The girl's face was covered with a tangle of dark hair.

Nancy leaned down and whispered, "Ellen, there's a man here who wants to help you. He says he can take you to see the doctor."

"What?" Ellen's voice sounded weak and scratchy.

Nancy gently brushed the hair away from Ellen's face.

He sucked in a breath and clenched his jaw. The girl's cheek was badly bruised, and one eye was swollen shut. Her lower lip was cut and puffy.

He squatted next to her bed. "Hello, Ellen. I'm Matthew. I'm sorry someone hurt you. I'd like to take you to see my friend who is a doctor. I'm sure he'll help you feel better."

Ellen's eyelashes fluttered, and she sent him a fearful glance. "I can't leave. Mr. Bradbury would kill me for sure."

"I'll make sure that doesn't happen." He turned to Nancy. "Does Ellen have a coat or shawl?"

Nancy darted to the peg on the wall and retrieved a brown wool shawl. "She can have mine."

"That's kind of you." He focused on Ellen. "Can you sit up?"

Nancy reached down and helped her friend, lifting her and wrapping the shawl around her shoulders. She looked up at Matthew. "I don't think she can walk very far."

"Ellen, I'd like to carry you. Is that all right?"

She sent him a confused look, as though she was surprised he would ask her permission. Clutching the shawl tightly, she nodded.

He wrapped the blanket around the frail girl and lifted her into his arms. She weighed much less than he'd expected. He looked down at Nancy. "Check the hall and see if anyone's there."

She nodded, then darted to the door. A second later, she looked back at him. "All clear."

He carried Ellen down the hall, past the kitchen. Jane watched from the kitchen doorway with her hand over her mouth and a fearful look in her eyes.

"Don't worry. She's safe with me. I promise." He kept his voice low and his head down, holding Ellen close to his chest.

Nancy ran ahead and opened the outer door for him.

"Thank you." He wished he could take all three girls. But right now, Ellen was the one most in need of help.

⁓

Lillian leaned toward the open carriage window and looked out. Her stomach tensed. Where was Matthew? At least fifteen minutes had passed since he'd gone into the Golden Swan. She'd agreed to wait in the carriage, but she'd never imagined it would take this long. What if someone had realized he wasn't a deliveryman? What would they do to him?

She thrust open the carriage door.

The coachman turned in his seat. "Mrs. Freemont, did you need something?"

"I'm just going to walk to the corner and look down the street."

"But Mr. McGivern said you're to wait here."

"I'll be fine." She set off down the narrow side street, scanning the buildings and view ahead. When she reached the corner, she glanced both ways. A few men walked past the shops and businesses lining Commercial Road, but Matthew was not among them.

She couldn't leave him on his own to face whatever had happened at the Golden Swan. She started down the street in the direction of the brothel.

Two policemen walked toward her. She lowered her head, intending to pass them on the left, but one of them stepped into her path and stopped her. "Where are you going, missy?"

She pulled in a startled breath and looked up.

The taller policeman with muttonchop sideburns and a thick, dark moustache looked her over with a steely-eyed gaze. "What are you doing out so early in the morning?"

She lifted her chin and kept her gaze steady. "I'm going to meet a friend. Now, if you'll excuse me." She stepped to the right, attempting to go around him.

The other policeman blocked her way. "Not so fast."

Her heartbeat sped up, and she took a step back. Her gaze darted from one policeman to the other. "I've done nothing wrong. You have no reason to stop me."

"Who is this *friend*, and where are you meeting him?" His suggestive tone made it sound as though she was headed for an illicit rendezvous.

She swallowed, debating her answer. She couldn't very well tell him she was going to the Golden Swan. That would only make them more suspicious. She straightened her shoulders. "I can assure you, there is nothing improper about my friend or our meeting." She stepped to the left.

The taller policeman grabbed her arm. "We have orders to arrest women walking the streets."

Lillian gasped. "I am not a woman of the street!"

"We'll see about that." The shorter policeman took hold of

her other arm, and the two began tugging her across the road, away from the Golden Swan.

"You are mistaken!" Lillian's thoughts flashed back to her visit to Mercy House and what the girls had said about being misunderstood and arrested. She tried to jerk out of their grasp, but it was impossible. "You've no cause to arrest me! I am a respectable woman!"

"That's what they all say," the taller policeman muttered, tightening his hold.

"Please, you don't understand. I've come here to help—"

"Stop!" a man shouted behind them.

Lillian looked over her shoulder, and her heart surged. Matthew jogged down the street after them. In his arms he carried a girl wrapped in a blanket. Had he found her niece? "Matthew!"

The policemen turned, dragging Lillian around with them.

Matthew caught up, his gaze darting from Lillian to the policemen. "What's going on?" He shifted the girl in his arms, revealing her bruised face and swollen eye. "Where are you taking Mrs. Freemont?"

The taller policeman tipped his head toward Lillian. "You know her?"

"Yes. Mrs. Freemont and I are intent on helping young girls who've been forced to work in *establishments* such as these." He glanced toward the Golden Swan, making his meaning clear.

The taller policeman's gaze dropped to the girl in Matthew's arms. His serious expression eased, and a hint of sympathy crossed his face. "That's one of the girls?"

"Yes, and she needs a doctor's care. Mrs. Freemont's carriage is just around the corner."

Lillian noted the girl's hair was dark brown, not blond. He hadn't found Alice, but from the bruises on the girl's face and her swollen mouth, she was in desperate need of rescue.

The two policemen exchanged glances and let go of Lillian's

arms. "You're free to go, but don't get caught walking around here on your own. The Contagious Disease Act is still in effect. We're supposed to bring in any women we suspect of—"

"I understand," Lillian quickly replied. She turned to Matthew. He shot her an exasperated look, then tilted his head in the direction of the carriage.

She gave a quick nod, and they set off, leaving the policemen behind.

"What were you thinking?" He lowered his voice, but it didn't hide his anger.

"I was thinking you'd been gone much longer than I expected, and I was concerned."

"I told you to wait in the carriage."

"I did wait, but when so much time passed, I thought something might have happened to you."

"So you ignored your promise to me, came out on your own, and almost got yourself arrested!"

"Don't scold me. I left the carriage because I thought you might need my help."

His stormy expression remained unchanged. "We'll discuss this later. Right now, we've got to get this girl to a doctor."

The little girl had snuggled down in the blanket, leaving only the top of her head showing. Lillian's heart seized. The poor child appeared to be in dreadful condition. Who could've done such a terrible thing to a defenseless little girl?

They rounded the corner, and the carriage came into view. Relief rushed through Lillian. "Let's take her to my home. I can send for Dr. Frasier."

"I can take her to Reverend Howell's. You're already caring for your sister."

Lillian's throat swelled, and she touched his arm. "Please, let me care for her."

He studied her a moment more. "Very well."

Her coachman jumped down as soon as he saw them coming and jerked open the carriage door.

"Hold her while I get in." Matthew passed the little girl to the coachman, then climbed in. The man carefully handed her to Matthew. He sat back and settled the girl on his lap, adjusting the blanket so her face was revealed once more.

Lillian's coachman offered his hand, and she climbed in and sat opposite Matthew. The girl lay still and quiet, her swollen face pressed against his chest. Had she fallen asleep, or had she lost consciousness from her injuries? Her heart clenched again, and she lifted a silent prayer for mercy.

Lillian followed Matthew up the stairs. Mrs. Pringle and her maid, Bessie, had gone ahead and down the hall toward the second bedroom.

As Lillian passed Serena's open door, her sister called out, "Lillian, who is that?"

Lillian stepped back to her sister's doorway. "That's Mr. McGivern, the journalist from the *Gazette*."

Serena's eyes widened, and she rose on one elbow. "The child in his arms—is it Alice?"

Lillian's throat tightened. "No, dear, it's not Alice. It's a young girl named Ellen who needs our help."

"What happened? Where did you find her?"

"I need to get her settled. I'll come back and explain everything as soon as I can."

Serena rose to a sitting position. "Please, tell me now."

Lillian glanced down the hall as Matthew stepped into the next bedroom. It would only take a moment to calm Serena. Mrs. Pringle and Bessie would know how to begin helping Ellen.

She turned to Serena. "We heard there might be some young girls working at a brothel called the Golden Swan in White

Chapel. We thought there was a possibility Alice had been taken there. Mr. McGivern went in this morning disguised as a deliveryman. He didn't find Alice, but he spoke to two girls, and they told him about Ellen. I'm afraid she has been badly beaten."

Serena lifted her hand to her mouth. "Oh my goodness. Who would beat a child?"

"I don't know. It seems impossible to me as well. I've sent for Doctor Frasier."

"Please let me know what he says after he sees her."

"I will. Rest now, and I'll give you a full report when we know more."

Serena nodded and slowly lay back on her pillows.

Lillian left Serena and entered the next bedroom. Matthew stood to the side, watching as Bessie and Mrs. Pringle unwrapped the blanket from around Ellen. The girl's eyes remained closed, and her limbs hung limp. A shot of fear coursed through Lillian. Were they too late?

The girl moaned, and relief rushed through Lillian. There was still hope.

Lillian spoke to Bessie as she crossed to the bed. "Please bring up some hot water and towels. Then fetch one of the nightgowns from my room." It would be huge on the girl, but that was the best they could offer at present.

"Yes, ma'am." The maid hurried out of the room.

Lillian turned to Matthew, knowing she needed to release him so he could return to his work at the *Gazette* or whatever else he had planned for the day. "Thank you for bringing us home—and for everything."

Matthew's gaze darted from the girl to Lillian. "I'd like to stay until we hear what the doctor says."

A rush of gratitude filled Lillian. "There is a bench in the hall if you'd like to wait there. Or would you prefer to wait downstairs in the sitting room?"

"No, I'll wait up here, if you don't mind."

"Not at all. It will be a comfort to know you're near." As soon as the words left her mouth, heat flooded her cheeks.

A flash of surprise crossed his face, then a slight smile lifted one side of his mouth. "I'll be right outside in the hall if you need anything." He gave a brief nod, then walked out.

Lillian shook her head. Why had she said that? She wasn't trying to be flirtatious. But it was true. She appreciated Matthew's strength and wisdom, and she felt safe when he was near.

But a small vine of worry wove around her heart. She must be more careful about expressing her thoughts and feelings. She didn't want to give him the wrong impression. They were partners in the search and had become friends, but anything more was not possible. The risks were too great—too painful—to consider. Love and loss always went hand in hand. And her heart could not bear more devastating grief.

Matthew paced down the hall, then turned and made his way back to the bench. He pulled his watch from his pocket and checked the time. Dr. Frasier had been with the girl for more than twenty minutes. It was almost ten, well past time that he should report in at the *Gazette*.

He was nearly finished with the article that was due on his editor's desk tomorrow morning, but he needed to continue confirming the facts and polishing what he'd written. It was a lengthy piece that he hoped would stir readers to action. He glanced at the closed bedroom door once more. He couldn't leave, not until he was sure Ellen was going to recover.

The bedroom door opened, and Lillian and Dr. Frasier stepped into the hall. Matthew rose and joined them.

Lillian motioned to Matthew. "Doctor Frasier, this is Matthew

McGivern. He's a journalist with the *Pall Mall Gazette*. He's the one who discovered Ellen at the Golden Swan."

The doctor met his gaze with shining eyes. "It's a good thing you found that little girl when you did. She's severely dehydrated and weakened from lack of food and ill treatment. I'm not sure how much longer she would've lasted without your intervention."

Matthew straightened. "She will recover, won't she?"

"I believe so. Her face is badly bruised and swollen, and she appears to have a broken rib, but there don't seem to be any other injuries. With rest, nourishing food, and good care, she should regain her health. Overcoming the emotional wounds from her poor treatment may take longer than her physical healing."

Matthew clenched his jaw and nodded. No child should ever be treated as Ellen had.

The doctor glanced at Lillian. "She and your sister have much in common."

A question lit Lillian's eyes.

"They both need healing for their body and their spirit." The doctor shifted his gaze to Matthew. "I'm glad to meet you, Mr. McGivern. Thank you for what you did for Ellen. I hope to see you again." He extended his hand.

Matthew shook it. "Thank you."

Dr. Frasier turned to Lillian. "I'll stop by tomorrow morning before ten to look in on Ellen, and I'll see your sister then as well. Send word if Ellen worsens in any way."

"I will. Thank you, Doctor."

"No need to come down. I know the way." Dr. Frasier nodded to them, then started down the stairs.

Matthew turned to Lillian. "I'm relieved to hear his report."

"Yes." She looked up at him, sincerity shining in her expression. "You saved a life today."

"*We* saved a life." His heart lifted as he held her gaze. "I know I resisted your idea of going to the Golden Swan, but I believe Providence guided us there."

Lillian nodded. "He saw Ellen's need and sent us there to rescue her."

He turned his cap in his hand, thinking through what he needed to say. Finally, he met her gaze. "I'm sorry for the way I reacted when I saw those policemen hauling you away. I shouldn't have spoken so harshly."

"It's all right. I was so stunned by their assumptions. I didn't handle it well." She hesitated, then added, "I should've waited in the carriage as you asked. I'm sorry."

He gave a slight nod, pleased she'd also offered that apology. Seeing those two beefy policemen dragging her across the street had shaken him even more than seeing Ellen's bruised and battered face.

"Lillian?" Serena called from her room.

"Yes?" Lillian walked down the hall and looked through the open doorway. Matthew followed and stopped beside Lillian.

Lillian's sister sat up in bed, several pillows behind her back. She wore a blue robe and held an open book in her lap. Her wavy blond hair hung in a single braid over her shoulder. She looked from Matthew to Lillian. "Please, come in. What did the doctor say?"

Matthew and Lillian entered, but he waited by the door while Lillian crossed to the bed. He wasn't in the habit of visiting women in their bedrooms, but he supposed with both sisters there, it wasn't improper.

Lillian relayed Dr. Frasier's report and instructions for Ellen's care.

Sympathy filled Serena's eyes as she listened. "Oh, the poor girl. Who would do such a thing?"

"I don't know, but someone at the Golden Swan has a very hard heart."

Serena's gaze moved to the doorway. "I hate to think of her alone in that room. Why don't you move her in here with me? I'd be glad to watch over her."

Lillian hesitated. "But you're still recovering, and you need your rest."

"How can I rest knowing she is all by herself?"

"Bessie and I will take turns caring for her. She won't be alone until she's much stronger."

"I want to help. It will do me good to have someone to think about other than myself."

Lillian laid her hand on her sister's shoulder. "Let's see how she's doing tomorrow."

Serena looked his way. "Mr. McGivern, don't you think it would be a comfort for the girl to stay in here with me?"

He darted a glance at Lillian. "I'm sure you and your sister can work out what is best for everyone concerned."

Serena lay back with a sigh. "Very well, but if she improves tomorrow, I hope you'll move her in here. We could be good company for each other."

Matthew slipped his hand in his pocket, feeling his watch, then glanced at Lillian. "My first article for the series is due tomorrow. I should be going."

"Of course." She motioned to the door. "I'll see you out." They left Serena's room and walked downstairs.

When they reached the entry hall, he stopped and turned to Lillian. The light from the stained-glass window spread a rainbow of color over her dark hair and fair face. She was beautiful, and the trusting look in her eyes sent a ripple of surprise through him. He shifted his gaze away. He should not let his thoughts take him down a hopeless road.

He cleared his throat. "I'll speak to Reverend Howell about Ellen. Perhaps he'll know someone who might be willing to take her in when she's a bit stronger."

"Let's not make plans to move her." Her words sounded like a gentle appeal.

"Are you certain?"

She nodded. "I am."

He shifted his weight, suddenly reluctant to leave her. He squelched that thought with a silent reprimand. He had an article to finish. There was no reason to stay any longer.

"Thank you . . . for all you did today." Her voice softened, and she looked up at him expectantly.

The warmth and appreciation in her voice melted his resistance, and he stepped toward her. "I'm glad we could take Ellen out of that dreadful place. . . . I'm just sorry we didn't find Alice."

The light in her eyes faded, and the sorrow returned.

He wanted to reach out, touch her arm, and tell her everything would be all right, but he couldn't make that promise, nor could he express his feelings for her in such a personal way. It wouldn't be right.

He pulled in a deep breath. "I'll keep looking while I'm working on the articles. I'll let you know what I learn."

She nodded, but he could tell the weight of concern for her sister and niece had returned, dampening her spirits. "I don't want to keep you. I know you have work to do."

"Yes, I do." He broke eye contact and forced himself to turn away. "Good-bye, Lillian."

She opened the door, and he stepped out into the midday sun and descended the steps.

What was he thinking? When he'd seen that look of openness and trust in her eyes, he'd almost crossed a line and shown her his true feelings. Were her actions just an emotional response to all they'd experienced that morning, or did they mean something more?

He shook his head. He had better be careful. He was becoming much too attached to Lillian Freemont.

14

2023

Jonas strode down the museum hallway and looked into Janelle's office. He didn't find her working at her desk, so he walked next door and knocked.

"Come in," Janelle called.

Unease tightened his stomach as he opened the door and stepped inside. He'd been putting off this conversation, but he couldn't wait any longer.

Janelle looked up and greeted him with a smile. "Hi. I didn't expect to see you this morning. I thought you had an appointment."

He nodded, feeling the weight of his concern. "I did, but I postponed it. I need to talk to you."

Her smile dimmed. "Is something wrong?"

"I want to discuss some information we found when we were researching the history of the Foundling Hospital."

"Of course. Please, sit down."

He took a seat. "The other night, Howie and I were looking online, and we found excerpts from an old newspaper article that stated an eight-year-old girl disappeared from the Foundling Hospital. Later, it was discovered she'd been sold to work in a brothel."

Janelle's eyes widened. "What? Where did you read that?"

"It was part of a series published in the *Pall Mall Gazette* in 1885 to expose the abduction and trafficking of girls and young women in Victorian London."

"Trafficking of girls . . . from the Foundling Hospital?"

"Yes . . . I take it you're not aware of it?"

She started to answer, then frowned and bit her lip. "A few months ago, there was an archivist here from Canada. I overheard her talking to Amanda about an incident in the late 1800s when a young girl disappeared."

"How did Amanda explain it?"

"She said the girl ran away, and she was later found and returned to her family."

Jonas studied her a moment more. "That's all?"

"Yes. She didn't say anything about her being sold or taken to a brothel. That's dreadful. How could anyone on our staff do such a terrible thing?"

"We're not talking about the current staff. This happened more than one hundred years ago. Still, I'd like to know if those responsible for selling the girls were held accountable and brought to justice."

She stared at him.

"So you've never heard anything else about this?" He couldn't keep the doubt out of his voice.

Hurt flashed across her face. "No, I promise you, I haven't."

He eased back. She was obviously telling the truth and deeply disturbed by what he'd told her.

Janelle shook her head. "The Foundling Hospital has always been a refuge for vulnerable children. How could this be true?"

A pang of regret shot through him. What if he was wrong about this? "There is a possibility it might not have happened as it was reported, but we won't know until we do some more research."

"Maybe the *Gazette* was one of those newspapers that published sensational stories that were more fiction than fact."

"That's what Howie said too." He tapped on his phone and opened his email. "I'll send you the link so you can read the excerpts yourself."

Her laptop dinged. She opened the message, and her gaze darted across the screen. Emotion flickered in her eyes, and her expression grew more intense. "This is . . . unbelievable."

He slipped his phone in his pocket. "It doesn't seem to fit with the rest of the Foundling Hospital's history."

She looked up and met his gaze. "It's my responsibility to understand our history and portray it honestly. If this is true, I can't sweep it under the rug."

"We won't know until we do some more research."

She sent him a questioning look. "You want to help me?"

"I'm curious to know the rest of the story. It might impact the film."

She gave a thoughtful nod. "Someone at the London Metropolitan Archives might be able to help us find more information." She reached for her phone. "Let me talk to them and see if we can arrange to meet with one of the archivists who is familiar with our records."

"Could you ask if they have copies of the *Pall Mall Gazette* from 1885? I'd like to read the rest of that article and the others in the series."

She nodded. "I'll ask."

He watched her as she scrolled through her contacts and tapped in the number. Determination glinted in her blue eyes. She was obviously taking his concerns seriously. That was a relief. What would she do if they discovered the *Gazette* article was based on facts, and the Foundling Hospital did have such a dark chapter in its past?

Janelle leaned closer to the computer, scanning the words of the second *Pall Mall Gazette* article. She pulled in a breath through clenched teeth. How could this have happened? She'd thought such horrors only occurred in contemporary times, but it seemed evil people had been carrying out those same schemes in the Victorian era.

"We'll be closing in ten minutes." Martha Fitzgerald, a sixty-something archivist at the London Metropolitan Archives, stepped up beside Jonas. "Can I help you with anything else before you go?"

Jonas glanced at his watch. "I didn't realize the time."

They'd spent the last two hours looking at 1885 Foundling Hospital records and then reading the first two articles in the series *The Maiden Tribute to Modern Babylon*.

Janelle had been surprised to see the initial article covered six pages. What she'd read had stirred her disgust and anger, and she could only imagine how it must have shocked readers in the Victorian era, when morality and propriety were highly held virtues. Had Queen Victoria and members of her court read the series? If so, how had they responded when they learned what was happening only a few miles from the palace?

Janelle turned to Martha. "Can you tell us if the *Gazette* was a respected periodical? I know some newspapers liked to embellish their stories. Should we believe what they reported?"

Martha thought for a moment. "I believe the *Gazette* was a reputable and influential newspaper. It was one of the first to use investigative journalism techniques to confront the social issues of the day. Their coverage helped change the course of society and law."

Janelle released a deep breath. So much for the idea they had fabricated the story to boost circulation. With such lengthy articles and impassioned reporting, she'd suspected the information was most likely accurate.

She looked up at Martha. "The article said the young women and girls mentioned were given fictitious names. Is there any way to find out who they were and learn more about them?"

Jonas turned in his chair. "We'd like to confirm if any of them were taken from the Foundling Hospital."

Janelle cringed, wishing he hadn't given that bit of information. Protecting the reputation of the Foundling Hospital and museum was important, but she supposed they had to be honest if they were going to find the answers they were seeking.

Martha's brow creased. "I can speak to one of my colleagues. Charles Knowles is familiar with the Foundling Hospital records. Perhaps he can find what you're looking for."

"We appreciate your help. Thank you." Janelle reached in her handbag and took out her card. "That has my contact information at the museum. You or Mr. Knowles can phone, text, or email me there."

Martha nodded. "Charles loves a good mystery. This is just the type of inquiry he enjoys. It may take some time, but I'll ask him to get back to you with whatever he learns."

Jonas took out his card. "I'd like to be informed as well. We're eager to learn more about the connection between the Foundling Hospital and this series in the *Gazette*."

Janelle swallowed, hoping she'd made the right choice bringing Jonas and telling the archivist why they were seeking the information.

Martha nodded. "Of course. I'll let him know you'd both like that information."

Jonas turned to Martha. "We know there were at least four articles in this series, maybe more. But I only see the first two listed in your system. Is there some way to access the others?"

"I can check on that as well."

"Thanks. Is it possible for us to download these two articles?"

"Yes. You can copy the link, then sign in and access or download them whenever you'd like."

Janelle rose and thanked Martha while Jonas took a photo of the link with his phone. Then he stood and turned to Janelle. "Ready to go?"

She nodded and picked up her handbag. A slight headache throbbed at her temple, and she rubbed her forehead.

He studied her for a moment. "Are you all right?"

She sighed. "I've got a headache."

He sent her a compassionate glance. "Sorry. I know those articles weren't easy reading."

"No, they weren't. At least they didn't mention the Foundling Hospital in the first two articles, but reading all that was going on and knowing some of our girls might have been taken breaks my heart."

He slipped his arm around her shoulders and gave her a gentle squeeze. "I admire you for being willing to look into it."

She nodded, but she couldn't stop the painful wave of disappointment rising from her heart. "I've always believed the Foundling Hospital saved children's lives. I've been proud of our history and what we've accomplished. But if it's true that members of our staff sold young girls into such horrible situations . . . what does that say about the museum and my work there? Am I promoting an organization that victimized children?" She shuddered and crossed her arms.

"Hey, that was a long time ago. Let's hope the people responsible were arrested and jailed."

"I hope you're right. But I won't stop looking until I know all the facts."

"Are you going to speak to Amanda?"

A thread of worry tugged at her heart. Did her boss know the full story? If she did, had she purposely hidden the facts from that visiting curator? She shifted her gaze back to Jonas. "I'd like to read the rest of those articles before I talk to Amanda."

He turned toward her. "Even if it's true, that doesn't negate the good that was done for thousands of other children—in the past or the present."

She nodded, hoping Jonas was right. She shouldn't expect the Foundling Hospital history to be spotless with no hint of selfishness or sin. They lived in a broken world, and God had given people free will. They could choose to follow Him and live a life guided by His principles of love and justice, or they could chase after their own sinful and selfish desires.

Still, she couldn't help wondering how many girls had been hurt by the irresponsible actions of Foundling Hospital staff and how widespread the impact might be. She must find out what had happened to those girls.

⌒

Janelle turned her office chair toward the window as she listened to Amanda's update from the hospital. The twins were eighteen days old and still in the NICU, with multiple issues arising every day.

"Chloe gained two ounces, but Sophia is not gaining." Anxiety filled Amanda's voice. "She's tiny . . . and I'm just so worried about her."

"I'm sorry, Amanda. That must feel like you're riding a roller coaster the way their condition changes from day to day."

"It actually changes from hour to hour." She released a weary sigh.

Concern tightened Janelle's shoulders, and she shifted the phone to her other ear. This was not the time to ask Amanda what she knew about the girls who had been taken from the Foundling Hospital in 1885. Once the twins improved and she and Jonas had more information, she'd speak to Amanda and let her know what they'd found.

Janelle pulled in a deep breath. "How are you feeling? I hope you're still able to get some rest."

"I spend most of every day at the hospital, watching over one baby and then the other. There are only a few things they let me do to help care for them. Still, I want to be there as much as possible. When we go home at night, we grab something to eat and then fall into bed, but it's hard to sleep. I keep thinking about the girls and wondering what's happening at the hospital. I hate being separated from them. The next morning, we shower, dress, grab breakfast, and head back to the NICU."

"How's Wesley holding up?"

"He's been my rock. I don't know how I could go through something like this without him. You should see him hovering over the girls. He talks to them and sings. It makes my heart melt."

Janelle smiled. It was hard to imagine Wesley, a studious editor for a scientific journal, singing to his premature twin daughters, but knowing that he did warmed her heart.

Amanda yawned. "How is everything there?"

"Here?" Janelle shifted in her chair, debating her answer. The museum was open, and the programs were up and running. She wouldn't mention Iris was upset with Claudine for not telling her about an extra tour that had been added at the last minute yesterday, leaving her without enough volunteers to cover the welcome desk. Or that Michael had requested more time off to help his mother move, which put them behind schedule on setting up the next exhibit. Those were matters Janelle could handle.

She forced confidence into her voice. "Everything is rolling along."

"Have you heard anything from the man who's making the film for the gala?"

Janelle paused, considering her answer. "Yes, he's been at the museum several times. I showed him how to access our historical records. He's been looking through those and photographing some of the artifacts. He has some solid ideas for the contemporary portion of the film, but he's still searching for the best way to weave in our history."

"Has he started filming?"

"He and his assistant filmed a couple of the children's art classes."

"I hope they got permission from the parents and guardians."

"Yes, I made sure they did."

"Good." Amanda was quiet for a few seconds. "This project is a big investment. It had better pay off."

"I think it will."

"I hope so. If we don't see an increase in donations by the end of the year, we may have to consider cutting some staff positions and programs."

Janelle's stomach plunged. That was the last thing she wanted to do. "I don't think it will come to that. Jonas showed me some of the other films he's made. They all look very impressive."

"Oh . . . It's Jonas, is it?"

Janelle could hear the lift in Amanda's voice, and her cheeks warmed.

"Is there something you want to tell me about . . . Jonas? I know he's single. Has he asked you out?"

"Amanda!"

"What? I told you how things progressed when Wesley and I were dating."

Janelle thought for a moment. "Well . . . we've shared a couple dinners after working on historical research for the film, but I wouldn't say we've gone on a date."

"Sharing dinners sounds very close to dating. Keep me in the loop. That's just what I need to take my mind off what's happening in the NICU."

Janelle shook her head. "You must be desperate for a distraction if you think my sorry love life is going to keep your mind occupied."

Amanda paused. "Don't let what happened with that dreadful guy Marcus discourage you." She softened her voice. "The right man will come your way in time. Maybe he already has. You just need to be patient and keep an open mind."

Heat flooded Janelle's face. She'd enjoyed the time she'd spent with Jonas, but she'd held back, not wanting to misjudge his actions and make another mistake. Was he truly interested in her, or did he only consider her someone to share dinner with so he didn't have to eat alone?

He had slipped his arm around her shoulders after they read those dreadful articles at the London Metropolitan Archives, and he'd prayed for her when they'd shared Chinese food at the park. Those seemed to be the actions of a caring friend. Was that all she wanted, or was she ready to risk her heart once more?

Maybe it was time she let go of the past and looked to the future with an open mind . . . and an open heart.

15

1885

Lillian folded down the blanket over Ellen's shoulders and gently smoothed back her hair. "Are you comfortable, dear?"

"Yes, ma'am. This bed is soft." Ellen looked around the room, then settled her gaze on Serena. "You're Miss Lillian's sister?"

Serena smiled. "That's right. You may call me Serena."

"Why are you in bed?"

"I'm recovering from pneumonia. That's an infection of the lungs."

Questions flickered in the girl's eyes. "How long have you been ill?"

"Quite a while. But I'm much better than I was. The doctor said I may get up and dress tomorrow. I'll have to take it slow, but I'm grateful to be improving."

"That's good." Ellen sent Serena a weak smile.

Lillian took a seat on the chair between their two beds. She'd agreed to bring Ellen into Serena's room that morning. The doctor felt it would help them both, and her sister seemed eager to encourage the young girl.

Lillian turned to Ellen. "Now that you're feeling a little better, we hope you'll tell us more about yourself." What she really wanted to ask was how she had ended up at the Golden Swan, but she wanted to gain the girl's trust first.

Ellen's brow puckered. "What do you want to know?"

Serena turned toward Ellen. "How long did you work at the Golden Swan?"

Lillian's gaze darted to Serena, but her sister was focused on Ellen and didn't see Lillian's warning to go slow and give the girl time.

Ellen plucked at a loose thread on the sheet, then finally said, "About a year."

"And before that," Lillian asked, "did you live with your family?"

Ellen shook her head. "Never knew my real mum or dad."

Sympathy flooded Serena's expression. "I'm so sorry."

"My mum left me at the Foundling Hospital when I was just a wee babe."

Lillian's pulse surged, and she stared at Ellen. "You grew up at the Foundling Hospital?"

Ellen nodded. "Well, I lived out in the country with the Mc-Neil family from the time I was a month old until I was almost six. Then they had to take me back to hospital. I didn't want to go, and they didn't want to send me, but they said that was the way it had to be."

Lillian's nerves tingled, and she leaned forward. "How did you get from the Foundling Hospital to the Golden Swan?"

"Most of the girls go out to work."

Lillian nodded. "That's what we've been told."

"After I turned eight Mr. Parker pulled me aside and told me he found a position for me and that I'd be leaving that night."

Serena frowned. "At night? That seems odd."

Ellen nodded. "Most girls had a nice send-off with their friends telling them good-bye and giving them little gifts when they went out to work. But not all of us. A few left without saying good-bye."

Serena's gaze darted to Lillian, and they exchanged a knowing look. She focused on Ellen again. "So, you left that night?"

Ellen nodded. "Mr. Parker told me not to take anything or tell anyone I was going. He said they'd be jealous and angry with me for getting such a good position." Her lips puckered as if she'd tasted something sour. "But he lied, that's for sure and certain."

Goosebumps raced down Lillian's arms. "He took you to the Golden Swan that night?"

"Yes, and I've been scrubbing floors, washing pots, and caring for the fires ever since." Ellen shook her head. "It's a bad place. Mr. Bradbury is mean, and Mrs. Crocker is not much better. I never want to go back there."

Lillian laid her hand on Ellen's shoulder. "You'll never have to go back. We'll make sure of it."

Serena shifted on her bed so she could face Ellen. "You left the Foundling Hospital a year ago?"

"Yes, ma'am."

"Did you know a young girl there named Alice Dunsmore? She would be a year younger than you."

"What does she look like?"

Serena's voice softened. "She has blond hair and blue eyes, and they say she's very pretty."

"She went by the name Mary Graham," Lillian added.

Ellen's eyes lit up. "Mary Graham? I remember her. When she came to the hospital after staying with her country family, she cried herself to sleep almost every night. A lot of the little girls cry. I could tell she missed her country mum and dad and her brothers and sisters."

Tears flooded Serena's eyes. "Oh, my poor child."

Ellen looked from Serena to Lillian. "Do you know Mary?"

Serena sniffed and brushed a tear from her cheek. "I'm her mother. We tried to reclaim her, but the matron told us she'd died from the measles."

Ellen frowned. "Why did she say that? Mary was fine, at least when I was there."

Lillian passed a handkerchief to Serena, then turned back to Ellen. "We believe Mary was taken to work somewhere like the Golden Swan, but we're not sure. Mr. McGivern was looking for her when he found you."

"You were trying to find Mary, but you found me instead?"

"Yes. I'm sure the Lord sent us to intervene on your behalf."

Ellen sent her a confused look.

"What I mean is, God saw how you were being mistreated, and He sent us there to help you."

Her eyes lit with understanding. "I prayed to God, but I didn't know if He heard me."

Lillian placed her hand on Ellen's shoulder. "I believe He heard your prayers—and ours."

Ellen met Lillian's gaze. "Then we must keep praying for Mary."

Matthew straightened his shoulders and knocked on Mr. Stead's office door.

"Come in." The editor's booming voice filled the hallway.

Matthew pulled open the door and walked into the office.

Mr. Stead sat at his desk with stacks of files and folded newspapers covering the surface. He raised his head and looked at Matthew over the top of his glasses. "Do you have the article?"

"Yes, sir." Matthew passed him several sheets of paper.

"Do you realize what time it is? I was just about to leave for the day." He nodded to Matthew. "Sit down. I'll look this over."

He lowered himself into the chair and rubbed his damp

hands on his pants legs. What was wrong with him? Why did he doubt himself? He was a good writer, and he'd spent hours polishing this story. Surely Mr. Stead would be pleased.

The editor's gaze skimmed across the first page. His brow creased, and he shook his head. "We can't use this."

Matthew sucked in a breath. "What? Why not?"

"This is like giving the answer before you've stated the problem."

Matthew frowned. "I don't understand."

"We can't start the series by telling how those young women at Mercy House are being transformed so they can lead new lives. You've got to start with the problem, grip your readers with the horror of what sent those girls down that dark path."

"But I thought writing about the young women at Mercy House would capture readers' attention and make them want to read the rest of the series."

He lifted his hand. "We can't lead with that!"

Matthew blew out a breath. "If you don't want to start there, what do you want?"

"Tell me how those girls ended up in such dire circumstances. What's the connection between their stories and the girls who are missing in White Chapel? Explain the danger young women face. Write an article that will make me weep and cry out for justice!"

"You want me to go back to Mercy House and do more in-depth interviews?"

Mr. Stead leaned back in his chair and ran his hand down his beard. "The best angle would be to find one girl and focus on her story, from start to finish. Describe her experiences in detail and show how painful and unjust her life has been."

"Just one girl?"

"You can add information about others so readers will understand the full scope of the problem, but keep the focus on that one girl for the first article." Mr. Stead lowered his gaze and scanned a few more lines. He made an unhappy noise in his throat. "I'm not sure you've got a girl at Mercy House who fits the bill."

Matthew huffed. "Well, I can't just pull a victim out of thin air."

"No, the story must be factual." Mr. Stead glared at him. "I've trained you to be an investigative journalist. Find one of those missing girls from White Chapel! Get the real story!"

Matthew rubbed his forehead, his thoughts swirling. He had a list of six girls who'd gone missing, plus Lillian's niece. He suspected one might have eloped against her family's wishes, but the other five appeared to be victims of abductions. He'd interviewed family members and friends and spoken to contacts in the seedier side of London. Word around White Chapel was that the girls had been taken to brothels or stolen away to the Continent.

Matthew met the editor's gaze. "I could focus on the search for Mary Graham, the girl who is missing from the Foundling Hospital."

Mr. Stead scowled. "Casting a negative light on the Foundling Hospital would not be the best choice, especially for the lead article. The men on the board of governors are respectable peers who have great influence. We want them as our friends, not our enemies."

Matthew clenched his jaw. Where did that leave him?

Mr. Stead thrust Matthew's article back. "Hold on to this for later. It's not a bad article. It's just not the right one to begin the series." He thought a moment more. "Take a lesson from that novelist Charles Dickens. Write each article with a suspenseful ending, so readers will be begging to read the next."

Matthew accepted the papers with a grimace. "How much time do I have?"

Mr. Stead crossed his arms. "You've got a week—ten days at the most. Get back out there and do what I'm paying you to do!"

Matthew rose from his chair. "Yes, sir."

Mr. Stead leaned forward. "Stop looking so glum. You're not sacked. I'm just redirecting your efforts so these articles will make the greatest impact."

"I understand." But Mr. Stead's rejection felt like a bitter blow. He'd done his best, researching and writing that article. Still, it wasn't good enough. He wasn't good enough. His father's scowling image rose in his mind, and he forced it away.

Mr. Stead stood and grabbed his hat from the shelf behind him. He strode around the desk and placed his hand on Matthew's shoulder. "You've got good instincts and determination. You'll find the right path forward."

Matthew thanked him and walked out of the office as the editor's words replayed in his mind. How was he going to find one of those missing girls and write a story that would satisfy Mr. Stead as well as grip the hearts and minds of readers across London?

He headed down the hallway and sent off a prayer. *There is no way I can do this without your help, Lord. Show me the way. Guide me toward the story you want me to tell.*

Lillian replaced the hymnal in the rack and remained standing as Reverend Howell rose and faced the congregation.

His gentle gaze traveled over the sanctuary, and he lifted his hand to pronounce the final blessing. "May the Lord bless you and keep you. May He lift up His countenance upon you and give you peace. Amen."

The congregation responded with a soft chorus of amens. Around her, people gathered their belongings and began moving out of the pews.

Lillian picked up her reticule and scanned the sanctuary. Where was Matthew? She'd sent him a note the day before and asked him to meet her after the Sunday morning service at Good Shepherd Church.

When she reached the rear door where Reverend Howell waited, she greeted him and offered her hand. "Thank you for your message. It was very meaningful."

He smiled and nodded. "I appreciate your kind words."

She leaned toward him and lowered her voice. "Have you seen Mr. McGivern? I learned something important I want to pass on to him."

"He was seated in the rear of the sanctuary and was one of the first to leave."

"Thank you. I'll look for him outside." She quickly crossed the nave and descended the stone steps to the churchyard. Several groups of people stood on the grass or walkway, engaged in conversations. Off to the left, near the path leading around the church, she spotted Matthew.

Their gazes connected.

Her heart fluttered, and a sense of connection flowed through her. She looked away and suppressed her response. She had asked him to meet her after church so she could tell him what she'd learned from Ellen. But she couldn't deny how many times she'd thought of him or how much she'd looked forward to seeing him again. He had given no hint that he was aware of her growing feelings, or what he thought of her, but she determined to watch him closely and see if he might reveal anything.

He lifted his hat and smiled. "Good morning, Lillian."

She returned a smile and greeted him.

"How is your sister? And Ellen? I hope they're improving."

"They are both much better. They're sharing a room now, and that has lifted Serena's spirits. She has been reading aloud to Ellen and teaching her how to embroider."

"I'm glad to hear it." He paused and glanced around the churchyard, then he took a step closer.

Her breath caught, and she looked up at him.

"You said in your note that you had something to tell me?"

Her hopes deflated. "Yes. Now that Ellen is recovering, we encouraged her to tell us more about her life and how she ended up at the Golden Swan."

His eyes lit with interest. "What did she say?"

"She told us she was in the care of the Foundling Hospital before she was taken there."

His eyebrows rose. "When was this?"

"She's nine years old and had been at the Golden Swan for about a year."

"Did she say who took her there?"

Lillian nodded. "It was Mr. Parker—that same man who locked the gate when we went there looking for the cleaning woman."

Matthew paused, considering her words. "I suspected that man might be involved. What else did she say?"

Lillian relayed the other details Ellen had shared with her. "Now that we have Ellen's story and know Mr. Parker was behind her abduction, and possibly Alice's as well, do you think it's time we go to the police?"

Matthew rubbed his jaw. "I went to the police station yesterday, hoping for an update on their investigation of the missing girls from White Chapel. They had nothing to report."

"But if Ellen told them what happened to her, surely they'd see the connection to my niece's disappearance and force Mr. Parker to tell them where she was taken."

"No one can force him to admit what he's done. If they question him, he'll just deny it."

Lillian sighed. "Then what can we do?"

Matthew thought for a moment, then his frown eased. "I'll speak to Mr. Parker and see what I can learn."

"I thought you said he wouldn't admit what he's done."

"Yes, but if I go there posing as someone who wants to buy a girl—"

Lillian gasped. "You think Mr. Parker is actually *selling* the girls?"

"That's the only reason I can imagine he'd take such a risk."

A shiver raced down Lillian's arms. "That's terrible. The man must have no conscience."

"Oh, he has a conscience, but I'm sure he stopped listening to it long ago."

"What will you say?"

"I'll use what I learned at the Golden Swan and what Ellen told us. That should make my story credible. I'll try to get him talking and see what I can learn."

She gripped her reticule, fighting off a growing sense of uneasiness. "Matthew, this sounds awfully dangerous."

"Don't worry. I can take care of myself."

"But if he discovers who you really are and why you're there, there's no telling what he might do."

Matthew reached for her hand. "I'll be careful. I promise."

She held tight to his warm, strong hand, and gratefulness flooded her heart. "Thank you, Matthew. What can I do to help?"

He gave her hand a gentle squeeze, then let go. "I'd like to speak to Ellen and learn as much as possible from her before I have to face Mr. Parker."

"Would you like to have lunch with us today? I have my carriage here." It was a bold invitation. She had invited other friends from church to join her for lunch, but not other single men. "That is, if you don't have other plans."

He sent her a pleased smile. "I'm free, and I'd enjoy having lunch with you . . . and speaking to Ellen, of course."

Her cheeks warmed, and she looked down, but she felt certain that didn't hide her smile.

~

Matthew followed Lillian, Serena, and Ellen out to the rear terrace after lunch. The view below opened to a peaceful private garden with a tall cedar tree, manicured flowerbeds, and lush green lawn—a hidden sanctuary in the middle of a bustling city.

Serena took a seat on the wicker settee to his left, glanced at Ellen, and patted the cushion beside her. The girl sat next to Serena and leaned against her side.

Lillian motioned to a wicker chair with a plump cushion. "Please have a seat, Matthew."

"Thank you." He lowered himself into the chair, and she sat across from him. He glanced around the terrace and then back at Lillian. "It must be nice to have a quiet spot like this where you can retreat from the world."

Lillian surveyed the garden with a winsome expression. "It is a peaceful spot. I especially love to come out here to hear the birds and watch the sun set."

He nodded, then shifted his gaze to Ellen. The swelling in her face had gone down, and most of her bruises had faded from purple to light blue and green. Lillian had asked him to wait until after their meal to question Ellen. She wanted the girl to feel comfortable with him rather than being ambushed with questions from someone she barely knew. He'd agreed to wait and had tried to engage her in conversation during the meal. But now he was eager to speak to her and learn as much as possible.

He gentled his voice. "Ellen, Mrs. Freemont told me you lived at the Foundling Hospital before you were sent to work at the Golden Swan."

Ellen shot an apprehensive glance at Lillian.

"It's all right, dear. Mr. McGivern is a trusted friend. You may speak openly with him."

Ellen slowly nodded. "Yes, sir. I was at the Foundling Hospital until I turned eight."

"I understand Mr. Parker is the one who took you to the Golden Swan?"

A shadow crossed her face at the mention of the man's name, and her lips turned down. "Yes, sir."

"What is Mr. Parker's position?"

She looked down and clasped her hands in her lap. "I don't know."

He would need to speak in simpler terms. "What does he do at the Foundling Hospital?"

She thought for a moment. "He oversees the boys, and he talks to the matron a lot. I think he orders food for the cook."

"Is he the one who finds places for the children to go out to work?"

She nodded. "Yes, sir. He found positions for us."

Matthew leaned forward. "Does he have an office there?"

"Yes, sir. Belowstairs, near the kitchen."

"Can you tell me how he looks, and how he acts toward the children?"

She bit her lip. "All the girls are afraid of him, and most of the boys are too. He has dark eyes and a big nose, but he doesn't have any hair on top of his head. Just a bushy beard and moustache."

Matthew straightened. That was a good description of the man who'd met him at the door the day he'd gone there and spoken to the matron. He recalled the man's abrupt manner and his unwillingness to let Matthew out of his sight.

Lillian leaned forward slightly. "Mr. McGivern is going to speak to Mr. Parker and try to learn where he's taken Mary. Is there anything else you can tell us that might be helpful?"

She thought for a moment. "Mary is a nice girl. I hope you find her."

Serena pressed her lips together and turned her face away.

Lillian reached over and laid her hand on Ellen's arm. "Don't worry, dear. We won't give up until we do."

He clenched his jaw. *Lord, help me. I've got to find that little girl.*

Ellen's gaze darted back to meet his. "Do you remember my friends, Nancy and Jane at the Golden Swan?"

He nodded, recalling their bare feet and their stained and ragged clothes.

"They don't like working there, but they've got no family. No one to help them get out."

Matthew's chest tightened. He regretted leaving them behind, but Ellen's situation had been so dire, he'd focused on helping her. But it wasn't too late to help the others. Surely, he could do something for them. "I'll speak to Reverend Howell and ask for his advice."

"They're good girls, but Mrs. Crocker makes them work real hard, and sometimes Mr. Bradbury is rough on them, like he was to me."

Sympathy filled Lillian's expression, and she sent him an imploring look, then she turned to Ellen. "We'll see what we can do."

A look of relief crossed Ellen's face. "I know they'd be grateful to get away from there."

Matthew shifted his gaze toward the garden, considering the situation. If he returned to the Golden Swan and posed as a deliveryman again, would the girls be willing to leave with him? Before he tried that idea, he'd have to find a safe place for them to stay and someone who would help them recover and secure better positions.

Lillian turned to him, and some unnamed emotion flickered in her eyes. "Would you like me to show you the garden?"

His pulse sped up. He hadn't expected to have time alone with Lillian. "Yes, I'd like that."

She turned to Serena. "Would you like to join us?"

Serena shifted her gaze from Matthew to Lillian with a slight smile. "Thank you, but I'm a bit tired. Why don't you two go ahead?"

"Very well." Lillian led him inside and down the back steps. They walked out the rear door and entered the quiet garden.

"My husband's mother was a devoted gardener," Lillian said as she started down the grass path between the curving flowerbeds. "She chose these plants so there is always something blooming from late March through mid-November."

His gaze traveled over the waves of bright spring flowers filling the beds. He'd admired flowers in public gardens and shops, but he didn't know much about them. He bent and took a closer look at the clumps of small blue flowers scattered between the taller blooms. Each stem looked like an upside-down bunch of grapes. "What do you call these?"

"Grape hyacinth." She plucked a stem and handed one to him. "They're bulb plants that come back each spring. They've always been one of my favorites."

He twirled the stem in his fingers, admiring their bright blue color and compact design.

She continued down the path, then stepped into the shade of a cedar tree and turned toward him. "Thank you for waiting until after luncheon to speak to Ellen. I appreciate your patience and the kindness you showed when you asked her those questions." The sincerity of her words filled him with pleasure.

"I'm glad you approve."

Her brown eyes glowed, and dimples creased her cheeks. "I'm

grateful for all you've done for Ellen, and your willingness to speak to Reverend Howell about the other girls."

"I'm glad to see how much she's improving. Have you thought about what to do when she's fully recovered?"

"We haven't said anything to her yet, but Serena and I have spoken. We'd like her to stay here with us and attend school in the autumn."

"That's generous of you."

She glanced toward the house and lifted her eyes to the terrace. "I've lived alone in this beautiful home ever since . . ." Her voice faltered. "Well, for a very long time." She shifted her gaze to him. "It's time I open my door and my life to whatever the Lord has for me."

He stilled and searched her eyes. Was she speaking of Ellen and the girls from the Golden Swan, or did her words carry a deeper meaning?

Her gaze warmed and lingered, and he sensed she was offering him a new level of openness and trust.

A rush of emotion swept through him, bolstering his courage. "Lillian, your kindness as well as your brave heart and strong faith have made a deep impression on me. I've come to think of you as more than a friend, and I hope you feel the same."

Her eyes widened. "Matthew . . . I . . . I'm not sure what to say."

Regret punched him in the gut. What a fool he was to voice his thoughts without being more certain of her feelings. Even if their family background and social standing were equal, he was not worthy of her. "I'm sorry. I shouldn't have assumed you meant—"

"Please don't apologize. I do admire you and appreciate all you've done—"

He grimaced. "You don't need to explain."

"But I do." She closed her eyes. "Let me think for a moment how to say this."

His shoulders tensed as he studied her pensive expression. Finally, she looked up at him. "I've been a widow for eight years. John was the first man who called on me, and from that day, I knew he was the man I would marry."

Matthew clenched his jaw and steeled himself. There was no way he could ever compare to John Freemont, a wealthy business owner who had won her heart on the day they met.

"I was young, and I loved him dearly," Lillian continued. "Losing him as I did was . . . very painful. And then, a short time later, I lost . . . our newborn daughter." Her voice choked off, and she looked down.

He froze, struck by the pain in her voice. "I'm so sorry," he whispered.

She lifted her gaze, and tears glittered in her eyes. "Her name was Ann Marie. She only lived a few hours, but she was the most beautiful baby I've ever seen."

He longed to pull her into his arms and comfort her, but he didn't have that right. Instead, he stood attentively, ready to listen to all she had to say.

Her throat worked. "So, you see, it's difficult for me to consider opening my heart and risking that kind of loss again."

He paused, praying for the right words, then he reached for her hand. "It is a risk, but I'm not asking for a commitment—just a chance to come alongside you and see where our friendship might take us."

She thought for a moment, then met his gaze. "I appreciate your honesty. I need time to consider what you've said. I don't want to lead you on or hurt you with false hopes."

He pressed down his disappointment and offered a slow nod. "I understand. You are worth the wait . . . and so much more."

A pink blush filled her cheeks, and she looked down, but her lips turned up at the corners with a trembling smile. "Thank you," she whispered.

16

Lillian stared into the sitting room fireplace, watching the golden flames flicker and dance. Serena had gone upstairs to tuck Ellen into bed, leaving Lillian alone with her thoughts. She pulled her shawl more tightly around her shoulders and leaned her head back against the chair.

Memories of her walk in the garden that afternoon with Matthew filled her mind. Why had she been surprised by his statement that he would like to be more than a friend? She had sensed a growing closeness between them. Wasn't this the logical next step?

If she agreed to what he was suggesting, it could change the course of her life. It might eventually lead to love and marriage—but it could also lead to heartache and loss. Was she ready to open her heart to those possibilities? The prospect both thrilled and frightened her.

If she refused him, she'd hurt him deeply. He might continue to search for her niece, but she would lose their growing connection. And that might mean she'd spend the rest of her life as an unmarried widow. Why did she struggle so to find the answer? He wasn't asking her to marry him. But he did want to know if she was open to that possibility in the future.

She was almost thirty-two. If she didn't marry within the

next few years, there would be no chance of bearing another child that she could love and raise. But even if she did marry, there was no guarantee she'd be blessed a second time and not lose that child as well.

She closed her eyes against the burning sting. Did she have the courage to accept those risks? Could she move forward and offer her heart again, knowing grief and loss could be right around the corner?

Help me, Lord. I don't know what to do.

Her thoughts drifted back to the first time Reverend Howell had introduced her to Matthew. He'd seemed uninterested and even been a bit rude. But as she'd gotten to know him, she'd realized he was focused and determined to do his job well. She admired him now, and she especially appreciated his commitment to finding her niece. He'd gone to great lengths and put himself in danger, proving his integrity. But there was something else about him—a vulnerability behind his brusque exterior that made her curious. If she accepted his offer to deepen their friendship, she could learn more and see what was truly in his heart.

A thought struck, and she sat up straighter. Had the Lord brought Matthew into her life not only to rescue her niece, but to bless her with another opportunity for love, marriage, and a family? Did He have another rescue in mind—that of her heart?

Serena walked back into the sitting room and sank into the chair across from Lillian's. "Ellen finally fell asleep."

Lillian shifted on the chair and focused on her sister. "It's good of you to spend so much time with her."

Serena's slight smile didn't outweigh the sadness in her eyes. "Helping Ellen makes me feel as though I can make up for some of the time I've missed with Alice."

Lillian's throat tightened, and she nodded. "I was thinking about Ellen's two friends at the Golden Swan. If Matthew can bring them out, I'm open to having them stay here with us."

Serena locked gazes with Lillian. "You want to take in all three girls?"

Lillian nodded. "But we must consider the commitment. They'll need a great deal of help with basic skills so they can be ready to attend school."

Serena's expression brightened. "Ellen reads a little, but she had no opportunity to continue her studies once she was taken to the Golden Swan. I'm sure I could teach her and the other girls."

"Reverend Howell suggested they might go to Mercy House, but they are too young. And even if they were older, there's no room for them there now. We could offer them a loving home where they could regain their strength and confidence as well as learn those basic skills."

Serena nodded. "I think it's a wonderful idea. I'm glad to do whatever I can."

Lillian leaned back in the chair, letting her thoughts drift again. What would Matthew think of her bringing those girls into her home?

She turned that thought over in her mind. It would take a true shift in her thinking if their relationship continued to progress into a courtship. She would need to partner with him and keep his thoughts and wishes in mind. And if they married, her inheritance, home, and all she owned would be shared with him.

Was she ready to give up her independence? She covered her eyes and moaned softly.

"What's wrong?" Serena asked.

Lillian lowered her hand. "Matthew spoke to me today. He's hoping we can be more than friends."

Serena gasped. "Oh, Lillian, that's wonderful! I knew it! I'm so happy for you!"

Lillian tipped her head. "I didn't agree."

"What?" Serena's eyes widened. "How could you turn him down?"

"I didn't turn him down. . . . I simply said I need time to consider it."

"Why, for heaven's sake? He's respectable and ever so handsome, and the way he's helped us search for Alice shows he is an honorable man with a good heart—unlike some men who I've no wish to name or ever see again!"

Lillian sent her sister a sympathetic look.

Tears filled Serena's eyes. "Oh, Lillian, this is a wonderful opportunity. Surely you want to say yes."

"I do care for him, but there's much more to consider. I can't make this decision based on my feelings."

Serena huffed and crossed her arms. "You're always so practical! For once in your life, can't you put aside your doubts and follow your heart?"

Lillian pressed her lips together, holding back the urge to remind Serena where following her heart had taken her and her daughter. "I'm going to pray and wait for the Lord's direction."

Serena rolled her eyes. "All right, but don't blame the Lord if it's truly fear that holds you back from all He wants to give you."

Lillian's breath caught in her throat. Was that what she was doing—giving fear the upper hand and ignoring the Lord's leading?

She rose from her chair. "Good night, Serena." Without waiting for her sister's reply, she strode from the room.

⌇

Matthew shot off a prayer, walked through the rear door of the Foundling Hospital, and glanced down the long corridor. He didn't see anyone, but he heard voices and the clatter of dishes farther down and off to the right.

"Bring me the potatoes," a woman's voice rang out. "Not those! I want the ones in the storage room."

A boy who looked about ten dashed into the hallway and started toward him. When he caught sight of Matthew, his steps stalled. "Can I help you, sir?"

"Yes, I'm looking for Mr. Parker."

The boy pointed over his shoulder. "He's in his office. Down the hall, on the right, past the kitchen."

"Thank you." He nodded to the boy and sent off another silent prayer, asking the Lord to lead the conversation. He had a general idea how he would approach the man, but he was uncertain how to convince Mr. Parker to divulge where he'd taken Alice.

He passed the kitchen, then he straightened his shoulders and knocked on the next door.

"Come in."

Matthew opened the door and looked in. The hunched older man sat behind his desk in the dimly lit room. Filing cabinets and shelves stacked with boxes lined the walls. There were no windows in the office. The only light came from a lamp on the corner of his desk.

"Good day. My name is Matthew McGivern. Are you Mr. Parker?" He had decided to use his real name and be as truthful as possible during their meeting.

Parker gave a slight nod, but his wary expression didn't change. "What brings you here?"

"I understand you handle the placement of girls who need a position."

"That's right." He narrowed his eyes and scanned Matthew. "I've seen you before. Aren't you the reporter from the *Gazette* who spoke to the matron a few weeks ago?"

Heat radiated up Matthew's neck. He'd hoped the man wouldn't recall his visit. Now that he did, Matthew would need to be even more careful. He put on a slight smile. "Well, that's what I told the matron."

Parker arched an eyebrow. "So you're not a reporter?"

His mind spun as he searched for an answer. "My purpose that day was to learn all I could." He lowered his voice. "You see, I'm interested in . . . obtaining a girl for one of my clients."

Parker studied him a moment more. "What do you mean?"

"I understand from Mr. Bradbury at the Golden Swan that, for a price, you might be willing to . . . provide a girl for a similar purpose."

Parker's expression darkened. He rose, crossed the office, and closed his door. Then he turned and faced Matthew. "I might be able to help you—if your client can pay. What exactly are you looking for?"

"The word in town is that you supplied a pretty young blonde with blue eyes a few weeks ago and sent her to . . ." Matthew lifted his eyebrows, hoping Parker would supply the name of the brothel.

Parker returned to his desk. "I'm surprised Bradbury would give you my name."

"Most men are willing to talk if the price is right . . . and my client can afford to pay for what he wants."

Mr. Parker took a pen from the ink stand and wrote on a piece of paper, then slid it across his desk. "Can he pay this price?"

Matthew read the figure, and a chill traveled through him. It was a huge sum, but there was no need to negotiate. He didn't really intend to buy a girl. Still, he needed to follow through and play the game. "That's more than we expected."

"Well, you're asking me to take a big risk."

He paused, trying to think of a way to bring the conversation back to where Alice had been sent. "I want to confirm you're the one who supplied the blonde. We're looking for a similar girl between the ages of eight and ten. She must be in good health and have a friendly, outgoing manner."

Parker huffed. "You're not asking for much."

"Those are my client's requirements." He waited while Parker pondered his request. It seemed he needed a little more motivation. "Perhaps those who took that blonde might be willing to sell her to my client for a higher price."

Parker pulled back, looking irritated. "I doubt Jackson would be willing to sell her."

"You mean Jackson at the Ruby Palace?"

Parker shook his head. "No, he's at the Lady's Slipper." He quickly shifted his gaze away, as though he realized he'd said more than he intended.

Energy zinged along Matthew's nerves, but he needed to stay focused and reassure Parker. "If you can supply what's needed, then I'm sure my client would be happy to deal with you rather than try to negotiate with Jackson."

Parker leaned forward and placed his arms on the desk. "Who is this client of yours?"

"I'm not at liberty to say."

"Then I'm not sure I can help you."

Their gazes locked, and a few seconds ticked by. Matthew lifted his chin. "If you can give us what we want, then we're not talking about only a one-time purchase. We'll continue to do business with you."

Parker leaned back in his chair, looking satisfied. "All right. But I'll need a few days to make the arrangements."

"How long?"

"Two days, maybe three. How shall I contact you when everything is ready?"

Matthew took his private calling card from his pocket and handed it to Parker. "Send word to my flat."

Parker rose from his chair. "I'll be in touch."

"Very good." Matthew rose and held out his hand.

Parker hesitated, but then reached out and shook. His hand was rough and as cold as the man's expression.

"Until then." Matthew nodded to him and walked out the door. Relief poured through him as he strode down the hallway and out the back door. *Thank you, Lord!*

He couldn't wait to tell Lillian and Serena that he knew where Alice had been taken. Then all he had to do was find a way to steal her out from under the nose of Mr. Jackson at the Lady's Slipper.

Lillian paced across the sitting room, stopped at the front window, and looked out. Glancing down the street, she searched for Matthew, but she didn't see him. What could be taking so long? She had expected him to return more than an hour ago. She hoped he hadn't run into trouble at the Foundling Hospital.

She turned away from the window and glanced at Serena and Ellen, who were nestled together on the sofa. Releasing a sigh, she sank into the chair across from them and picked up her knitting.

Serena glanced up from the book she was reading aloud with a silent question in her eyes. Lillian shook her head, then tried to focus on the story as her sister continued reading.

Serena had just turned to the next page when the butler opened the sitting room door. "The Reverend Howell and Mr. McGivern are here to see you, ma'am."

Relief flooded Lillian, and she rose. "Please show them in."

Serena closed the book and slid her arm around Ellen's shoulder. The girl's gaze darted from Lillian to Serena, apprehension in her eyes.

Matthew and Reverend Howell entered.

"I'm so glad to see you," Lillian said. "I was starting to worry."

Matthew crossed toward her. "I'm sorry to keep you waiting. I stopped to speak to Reverend Howell on the way back. I asked him to come with me."

A prickle of unease flowed through Lillian. Why had he asked Reverend Howell to come?

Serena stood, anxious lines creasing her forehead. "Oh, please, don't tell me you're bringing bad news."

Matthew's eyebrows lifted. "No, I'm sorry. I didn't mean to alarm you. My trip to the Foundling Hospital went well—better than expected."

Lillian lifted her hand to her heart. "Please tell us more."

"Mr. Parker believed my story, and he admitted he was the one who sold Alice to a brothel in White Chapel called the Lady's Slipper."

Serena gasped and sank back on the sofa. "She's truly at a brothel?"

Lillian sat at her side. "I know that sounds frightening, but now that we know where she is, we'll find a way to get her out."

Serena looked up at Matthew. "Oh, this is dreadful." She clasped her hands. "Mr. McGivern, please tell me you'll find a way to rescue Alice. No child should be held in such a wicked place!"

Lillian laid her hand on her sister's arm. "Please be calm, Serena. Let him speak."

Matthew motioned to the reverend. "We believe if I go there disguised as a deliveryman, as I did at the Golden Swan, I might be able to bring her out."

Lillian nodded, and relief flowed through her. "Could you go tomorrow?"

He thought for a moment, then he nodded. "I can collect what's needed this afternoon and be ready to leave at six in the morning. If she is willing to leave with me, I think it would be a comfort for her to see a lady in the carriage. Can you come with me?"

A wave of gratitude filled Lillian's heart. "Yes, of course."

Serena rose. "I want to go as well."

Lillian tensed. Serena's health had improved, and she seemed stronger emotionally since Ellen had come to stay with them. But was she ready to return to White Chapel? How would she handle the outcome if they were not able to rescue Alice?

"Please, I want to be there." Serena's voice rang with sincerity. "She is my daughter."

Lillian glanced at Matthew, deferring the answer to him.

He gave a slight nod. "It's fine with me if Serena would like to come as well."

Reverend Howell looked around the circle. "This is an important endeavor. I'd like to pray with you all."

"Yes, please," Lillian said. "We'll need the Lord's guidance and protection."

Lillian, Matthew, and Reverend Howell settled in chairs, and Serena returned to the sofa with Ellen.

Reverend Howell looked from Lillian to Serena. "What Matthew learned today is important information. Mr. Parker needs to be stopped so that no more children can be taken from the Foundling Hospital. As soon as Alice is safely in your care, we intend to go to the police and see that Mr. Parker is arrested."

Lillian tensed and glanced from Reverend Howell to Matthew. "Should we go to the police now?"

Matthew met her gaze. "We don't have proof that money was exchanged when Ellen was sent to the Golden Swan. But once Alice is freed, we'll have her story as well as Ellen's, plus what Mr. Parker told me. I intend to include it all in my articles. With that much evidence, the police will have to listen."

"What about Jane and Nancy?" Ellen asked. "When will you get them out of the Golden Swan?"

Lillian sent Matthew a look she hoped would encourage him to answer gently.

"We'll get them out as soon as we can."

Lillian could not mistake the sincerity in his voice. He did not make promises lightly, and she was confident he would keep his word. Her heart lifted and filled with admiration for him.

The truth shone through like a bright morning sunrise. The Lord had brought Matthew into her life to help her and her sister through this difficult time. He was strong, dependable, and committed—a man who took action to live out his faith despite the danger.

Loving Matthew would be well worth the risk to her heart.

17

Janelle grabbed her empty shopping bags and took her list off the counter. She needed to go to the store to pick up a few items for the dinner she was making for Jonas that evening. She smiled, remembering how her invitation had surprised him. Then his expression had changed to a look of pure pleasure. He'd offered to bring dessert, and she'd gladly accepted.

Cooking was not one of her best skills, but she'd watched the video explaining how to make chicken piccata, then made a list of all the ingredients she'd need. She lifted her keys off the hook by the door and stepped out to the landing.

The door to Maggie and Dan's flat opened, and Maggie looked out. "Where are you going?" she whispered.

"I'm headed to the supermarket. Can I pick up anything for you?"

Maggie's eyes widened. "I'm coming with you." She leaned back into her flat. "Dan, I'm going to the supermarket with Janelle. I'll be back in a while."

"Okay," Dan called over the sound of the boys shouting in the background.

Maggie quickly pulled the door closed.

"Need a break?" Janelle asked with a grin.

"Definitely."

189

"Let's take the stairs. I need the exercise." Janelle pushed open the heavy metal door and trotted down the steps.

Maggie followed. "I was wondering . . . have you had a chance to talk to Olivia?"

Janelle had put off telling Maggie about that conversation since it only seemed to irritate Olivia. "I tried. I took her to lunch, hoping to build more of a connection."

"How did it go? Did she tell you anything I need to know?"

They reached the main floor, and Janelle opened the door to the lobby. "I asked her about Tony, and she said they met online playing a game called *League of Legends*. Then they connected on Instagram."

Maggie groaned as they crossed the lobby. "I was hoping he was someone from her school. At least she'd know a little more about him."

Janelle held the door for Maggie and then followed her outside. "Olivia said they have a lot in common. She seems convinced he's Mr. Wonderful."

Maggie shook her head as they started down the street in the direction of the supermarket. "Why aren't his parents taking his phone away at night? That's so irresponsible to let him phone a girl at two in the morning!"

"They probably don't know."

Maggie lifted her hands. "Great! They're clueless. That makes me even more sure he's not the kind of boy we want calling her. I hope he doesn't show up at our door, hoping to see her."

"She said he doesn't live in London, so it sounds like it's just an online friendship." They reached the corner, and Janelle pushed the crossing button.

"I hope so." Maggie tapped her foot as she watched the traffic and waited for the light to change. "Tomorrow night is our anniversary. Our regular babysitter was scheduled to come over, but she canceled. Now Dan wants to leave Olivia in charge of the boys, but I'm not sure that's a good idea."

Janelle shot Maggie a questioning glance. Leaving Olivia in charge of Cole and Caleb, especially when she'd ignored Dan and Maggie's rules about her phone, didn't seem like a good idea. She pulled in a deep breath. "I could come over and spend the evening with Olivia and the boys."

Maggie turned toward her. "Would you? Oh, that would be great!"

"Sure. I don't mind. You and Dan deserve a night out by yourselves."

Maggie hugged her. "Thank you, Janelle. I owe you big time for this!"

Janelle returned the hug, along with a pat on the back. "You don't owe me anything. I'm glad to stay with the kids." The light changed, and they crossed the road.

Maggie's steps seemed lighter, and she wore a more hopeful expression as they entered their neighborhood supermarket. "Maybe I'll get some strawberries and ice cream. The kids would love that." She grabbed a container of berries and placed them in her basket. "What do you need?"

Janelle checked the list on her phone. "Chicken breasts, garlic, lemons, parmesan cheese, some crusty bread, and capers."

"Capers? Wow, that sounds special. What are you making?"

Janelle tossed three lemons in her basket. "Chicken piccata. Jonas is coming over for dinner."

Maggie gasped. "Jonas—handsome filmmaker Jonas?"

Janelle couldn't hold back her smile. "Yes, that Jonas."

"Oh, that's great! What are you going to wear?"

Janelle's grin faded. "I don't know."

"Oh, you have to wear something special." Maggie thought for a moment, then her eyes lit up. "I know, how about that pretty blue dress you wore to Marie's engagement party? It looks great on you, and it makes your eyes stand out. That's sure to set the mood for a romantic evening."

Heat rushed into Janelle's face, and she waved off Maggie's words. "It's just dinner."

"Then why are you blushing?"

Janelle picked up her pace. "I'm not blushing!"

"Yes, your cheeks are all rosy."

"Well . . . I don't want to lure Jonas into a romance by the way I dress."

Maggie shoved her arm. "Girl, there is nothing wrong with dressing up and setting the mood. It shows you think he's special . . . and that's how you feel, right?"

Janelle added two heads of garlic to her basket. "I like Jonas. He's smart and creative, and his faith is important to him."

"Then what's the problem?"

"I don't know. I guess I'm worried what he'll think."

Maggie sent her a confused look. "What do you mean?"

"Inviting him over was my idea, but now I'm second-guessing myself. I'm not sure if I'm ready to jump into a relationship again after what happened with Marcus." Her voice faded off as the wave of painful memories returned.

"Forget about Marcus. He doesn't deserve one more minute of your thoughts."

Janelle nodded. "You're right."

"Inviting Jonas over for dinner and making it a special evening is not jumping into a relationship. It just says you want to get to know him."

"Right. That's what it means." But she couldn't deny the nervous fluttering in her stomach. She pulled in a deep breath and lifted her chin. She'd made the invitation, and he'd accepted. There was no turning back. "I can do this."

"Yes, you can. And it's going to be a wonderful evening."

Janelle picked up a package of chicken breasts and placed

it into her basket. She needed to listen to her friend and put Marcus out of her mind. He had betrayed her and broken her heart, but that didn't mean Jonas would do the same. This was a new friendship with a different person. She could take what she'd learned from her past mistakes and make new and better choices this time. She'd give herself time to get to know him and make sure he was trustworthy before she gave away her heart.

⁓

Jonas smoothed his hand down the front of his shirt, then rang Janelle's doorbell. Her invitation to come over for dinner had been a pleasant surprise. He'd invited her out to dinner twice, but those had been casual takeout meals they'd shared at the park, not real dates. He'd enjoyed those conversations and their time together, and he hoped for more. But he'd sensed she was hesitant to respond to his interest for some reason.

Since their visit to the London Metropolitan Archives, she seemed to be softening toward him. Then she'd invited him to come over for a homemade meal, raising his hopes. Now, if he could just handle the evening well, it might open the door for a closer relationship.

He glanced down at the container holding the banoffee pie. It was one of his family's favorites. He'd called his mum that morning to ask for her recipe, then he dashed out to the shop to buy what was needed. Back at his flat, he'd taken more than two hours to prepare the pie. It didn't look quite as nice as those his mum made for special dinners, but he hoped Janelle would like it.

The door opened, and Janelle greeted him with a warm smile and shining blue eyes. She wore a light blue dress that flowed over her feminine curves in an appealing fashion. "Wow, you look nice."

"Thanks." She glanced away, seeming a little embarrassed by his compliment, then pulled the door open wider. "Please, come in."

He walked into her flat and glanced around the living room. Tall windows to the left let in golden light from the sunset. A navy blue couch and loveseat sat opposite each other with a fireplace and built-in bookshelves filling the far wall. Plants, pillows, and lots of books gave the room a homey, comfortable feeling. "I like your place. It looks like you."

She smiled. "Thanks. I've had fun decorating. Most of the pieces are from estate sales or charity shops. A few things are new, like the coffee table and the lamps."

He nodded. She was thrifty, but she also had an eye for style and beauty. More to appreciate about her. He held out the pie. "I hope you like banoffee pie. My mum always serves it on special occasions, so I thought I'd give it a try."

Janelle's eyebrows rose. "You made the pie?"

He grinned. "I did. You said you were making chicken piccata, so I wanted to make something special to go with it."

She accepted the pie. "Well, I'm impressed."

He chuckled. "You better wait until you taste it before you offer more compliments."

She led him into the kitchen and placed the pie on the counter. Then she lifted the lid on a pan and checked on the chicken. They shared lighthearted conversation while he set the table, and she chopped vegetables to add to the salad. When the food was ready, they took seats at the small dining table, and he offered a prayer over the meal.

She looked up and sent him a warm smile. "Thank you. Please help yourself."

He spooned rice on his plate, then topped it with the chicken and a good helping of sauce.

She watched expectantly as he took his first bite.

The chicken was tender and flavorful, and the sauce was creamy with a hint of parmesan. The lemon and garlic burst on his tongue. "Wow, this is really good," he said.

A look of relief crossed her face. "I'm so glad. I've never made it before."

"Really? Well, I'd say you definitely mastered the recipe."

She took a bite, looking pleased, then said, "Tell me about your family."

He explained he was the oldest, with two younger brothers and a sister, and that he'd always taken on a protective role with his siblings. She asked him a few more questions about his parents and where his family had lived. He spent the next few minutes telling her about his younger years in Berkshire.

"How about you?" he asked. "Do you have brothers and sisters?"

She hesitated and glanced away. "I've thought of looking online to see what I could learn about my birth family, but something holds me back."

He stifled a groan. How could he have forgotten she'd told him she'd been raised by a foster family? "I'm sorry. That was . . . insensitive of me."

"No, it's all right." But he could tell it was still a point of pain or at least discomfort for her.

He shifted to a new subject and asked her about her time at university and then about her hobbies and interests away from work. She relaxed and was soon smiling again as she talked about how she loved to visit antique shops and tour properties held by the National Trust. She collected classic books with beautiful bindings, and she grew an assortment of herbs and flowers on her balcony.

After they'd finished eating, he helped clear the table and volunteered to dry the dishes while she washed. "I've always thought the person who cooked shouldn't have to clean up alone."

She squirted washing up liquid into the sink. "I don't mind."

"I'd rather help because the sooner we finish washing up, the sooner we can try my pie."

She laughed, then handed him a tea towel. "All right. Here you go."

Ten minutes later, she sliced the pie and dished up a piece for him. "Let's sit out in the living room."

He carried his pie and cup of tea out of the kitchen and took a seat on the couch. She sat next to him—not too close, but not too far away either. He nodded to her. "You go first."

She dipped her fork into the pie and then brought it to her mouth. Closing her eyes, she tasted the first bite. Her eyes popped open. "Mmm, this is delicious!"

"Glad you like it. I'll be sure to tell my mum." He scooped up a bite and let the sweet caramel and whipped cream melt in his mouth. The soft slices of banana and sweet biscuit crumb crust added just the right contrast.

He took a sip of tea, hoping what he was going to say next wouldn't dampen the growing closeness he'd sensed that evening. "I checked my email before I left home, and I saw a message from Martha Fitzgerald at the archives. She emailed both of us."

Janelle's eyes widened. "Really? What did she say?"

"I didn't read it yet. I thought I'd wait so we could look at it together."

"Okay. I'll get my laptop." She rose, walked down the hall, and disappeared into a room on the right. A few seconds later, she returned and sat beside him, closer this time.

She opened her email and scrolled to the message. Skipping the greeting, she read aloud, "'We found more information about the series *The Maiden Tribute to Modern Babylon*, published in the *Pall Mall Gazette*. The entire series has six articles and was published in a booklet later that year. A copy is available for you to view at the British Library. Charles Knowles is still looking for information that might connect the Foundling Hospital and the articles above. He's particularly looking into the identities of the girls mentioned in the series. He hopes to have more information for you soon. I trust you'll find the booklet helpful. I wish you the best in your search. Sincerely, Martha Fitzgerald, the London Metropolitan Archives.'" Janelle looked up and met his gaze. "It sounds like we need to pay a visit to the British Library."

"Do you think they're open on Sunday?"

"Maybe. Let me check."

She typed *the British Library* into the search bar and scrolled down to view their open hours. "They're open from eleven to five tomorrow."

He nodded, considering his plans for the following day.

She looked his way. "I'm going to church at St. Mark's tomorrow morning, but I'm free in the afternoon."

He usually attended Hope Church in Soho on Sunday mornings, but he'd be glad to change his plans if it meant he could share the day with Janelle. "Why don't I join you for church in the morning. After, we can go to lunch and then the library. How does that sound?"

Her eyes lit up. "I'd like that."

A rush of hope flowed through him. Attending church, sharing lunch, and teaming up to continue their research at the library would give him another chance to show Janelle how much he enjoyed spending time with her.

18

1885

Matthew looked out the carriage window as they bumped along the nearly deserted street in White Chapel. A foggy mist hung in the air, casting a gray stillness over the scene. A milkman unloaded cans from his wooden cart parked at the side of the street, but no one else seemed to be up and about at that early hour.

Across from him, Lillian and Serena sat side by side, gazing out the opposite carriage window.

Serena looked up at the decrepit buildings, and a shadow crossed her features. "This is very near where I used to live. If only I'd known Alice was just a few streets away!" Her voice choked off, and she shook her head.

The stench from the dirty streets flowed through the open window. He grimaced and held his breath.

Serena raised a hand and covered her mouth. "I think I'm going to be sick."

Lillian scooted closer to her sister. "Close your eyes and take a few shallow breaths. You'll be all right."

Matthew looked out his window again. Up ahead, he spotted the sign for the Lady's Slipper. His nerves tingled, and he straightened. So many details had come together for them to reach this moment. Now he needed courage to follow through with the plan to rescue Alice and bring her into the loving arms of her mother and aunt.

"There's the Lady's Slipper." He scanned the front of the building, noting the brothel was located on a corner. The carriage slowed and pulled to a stop. He had instructed the coachman to park a short distance away, but close enough to keep the building in sight.

Lillian slid across the seat and looked out his window. "There's a side entrance with steps that lead downstairs."

He nodded. "That's probably the entrance to the kitchen. I'll try to go in that way."

She looked at him with a mixture of concern and hope in her eyes.

He held her gaze a moment more. "Pray for me."

"I will." The warmth and trust in her expression sent a surge of courage through him.

He opened the carriage door and climbed down. Lillian slid the crate of vegetables toward him. He grabbed hold of the crate, then closed the door. "I'll be back as soon as I can. Please stay here." He firmed his voice to make his wishes clear.

Lillian's mouth tipped up at the corners. "I will . . . unless the Lord tells me to go."

"If you feel the urge, make sure it's the Lord."

She grinned and nodded.

Hoisting the crate, he turned and strode down the street. *Guide my steps, Lord. Help me find Alice and bring her out safely.* It was a simple prayer, but it came from his heart, and he was confident the Lord heard and was with him.

When he reached the corner, he glanced back. Lillian watched him from the carriage window, and he had no doubt she was praying for his safety and success.

He descended the stairs and knocked on the door. No one answered. He tested the handle, found it unlocked, and pushed the door open. He stepped into the dim hallway, leaving the door ajar behind him to give added light.

The floor looked wet, and halfway down the hall he spotted a girl on her hands and knees, scrubbing the tiles. She wore a white cap covering her hair, and a dark green dress and white apron. She dipped her scrub brush into a pail of water, then looked up. Her light blue eyes went wide. "Who are you?"

"I have some vegetables for you."

She sent him a confused look, then brushed a blond curl back from her cheek.

"Are you Mary Graham?"

Fear flashed across her face. "How do you know my name?"

A shot of joy pulsed through him. "I'm a friend." He softened his voice. "I want to help you leave this place."

She shook her head. "I don't know you."

"No, but I know your mother and your aunt, and they're eager to see you."

She straightened to her knees, searching his face with a look of wonder. "You know my mother?"

Voices and footsteps sounded in the distance.

"Yes." He shifted the crate to one arm and held out his hand. "Come with me—now."

Frozen, she stared at him.

The footsteps grew louder, and two men descended the steps just beyond Mary. Both were middle-aged and dressed in work clothes. One was taller, with red hair and a beard. The other was shorter, heavyset, and balding.

The taller man scowled at him. "What are you doing down here?"

"I'm delivering these vegetables."

The balding man narrowed his eyes. "I didn't order any vegetables. Where are they from?"

"The greengrocer on Pearl Street."

200

The two men exchanged doubtful looks, and the bald man stepped around Mary, blocking Matthew's view of her. "We get all our groceries from Crawford's. I don't take deliveries here. You either came to the wrong place, or you're up to no good." He looked over his shoulder. "Get her out of here."

The other man grabbed Mary's arm. She cried out as he hauled her off down the hallway, away from Matthew.

Matthew's stomach twisted, and his thoughts spun. "Sorry. I must be in the wrong place." He turned to go.

But the bald man hustled around him and blocked his path. He cocked his eyebrow. "You can leave the vegetables."

Matthew held his gaze steady. "If you didn't order them, I should take them back."

The man's glare deepened. "I said leave them—and count yourself lucky to get out of here in one piece."

Matthew held tight to the crate for another second, then shoved it at the man, knocking him off his feet. He jumped around the man and ran for the door.

The man shouted curses as he scrambled up from the floor. "Don't come back, or I'll black your eyes!"

Matthew dashed up the steps and ran down the street, anger and regret tearing through him. Nearing the carriage, he called up to the coachman, "Take us back to Mrs. Freemont's."

The man nodded to Matthew and lifted the reins.

Matthew jerked open the door, shoved the crate of vegetables inside, and climbed aboard. The carriage immediately rolled down the street.

Lillian gripped the edge of the seat, her gaze intense. "What happened?"

Serena stared at him, wide-eyed. "Where is Alice?"

Matthew sank down across from them and shook his head. "I spoke to her. She was scrubbing the floor, but two men came downstairs and caught us talking. They knew I wasn't supposed to be there. They took Mary away and ran me off."

Serena burst into tears. "Oh, my poor girl." She reached for Lillian, buried her face in her sister's shoulder, and wept.

"I'm sorry." Pain twisted Matthew's chest as he watched the tearful sisters. "We'll have to think of a new plan."

"I know you did what you could." Lillian's voice carried no condemnation, but he read the disappointment in her eyes. Lillian held her sister as the carriage rocked and swayed down the street.

He clenched his hands, forcing down his anger. He'd been so close. If he'd only had a few more seconds, he could've gotten her out. He closed his eyes and laid his head back. The sting of failure pierced him like a burning arrow in his chest. *What do we do now, Lord?*

⁓

Matthew sidestepped a large puddle and hurried down the street as rain drizzled around him. He'd sent Lillian a note and asked her to meet him at the Cheshire tea shop that afternoon at two. Checking his pocket watch, he picked up his pace, determined to arrive on time and not keep her waiting. He glanced down the street to the tea shop, glad it was only a short walk from the *Gazette*.

The disastrous results of his attempt to free Lillian's niece from the Lady's Slipper the day before had kept him awake until after midnight. He'd met with Reverend Howell that morning to come up with a new plan, then sent word to Lillian, asking for a meeting.

He pushed open the door to the tea shop, and the bell overhead jingled, announcing his arrival. He pulled in a deep breath of cinnamon-scented air and glanced around. In the corner, at a table for two, Lillian looked up and met his gaze. He crossed the room and joined her.

She smiled as he approached, but he noted the touch of sadness in her eyes and the slight slope of her shoulders.

He pushed down a stab of guilt and sat in the chair opposite her. "Thank you for coming."

"I was glad to receive your note. I've been debating what to do next. There must be some way to free Alice." She opened her mouth, looking as though she was about to say more, but the waitress approached the table. She greeted them and took their order for tea and scones.

"I spoke to Reverend Howell, and we have an idea," Matthew said.

Her eyes lit up. "What is it?"

He glanced around, then lowered his voice. "I received a message from Mr. Parker. He has selected a girl and is ready for me to pick her up at the Foundling Hospital."

Her forehead creased. "I thought you said that was just a ruse to get him to tell us where he'd taken Alice."

"It was, but I believe buying the girl will provide the proof to secure Parker's arrest and give the police the information they need to remove Alice from the Lady's Slipper."

"I see." But the explanation didn't ease Lillian's concerned expression.

The waitress returned with a small teapot, two cups, and a plate stacked with four scones. Lillian poured the tea, and Matthew helped himself to a scone.

"There's one problem with this plan." He shifted in his chair, wishing he didn't have to ask for her help. But there seemed no way around it. "The amount of money required to buy the girl is more than Reverend Howell or I have on hand. We wondered if you . . ." He glanced away, unable to finish the sentence. How could he ask her for money? It would only remind her of the difference in their financial standing.

"How much is he asking?" Her tone was gentle.

He looked up and named the amount.

She blinked and dropped her gaze. "Well, that is a high sum."

"I know it's a lot to ask."

"But the money would be returned after Mr. Parker is arrested?"

"Yes, it may take some time, but I assure you, I'll see to it that all money is paid back."

"When do you need it?"

"Parker asked me to meet him at the Foundling Hospital tomorrow night."

"Very well. I'll speak to my banker today and withdraw the funds."

He finished his cup of tea, grateful that part of the conversation was past. "Reverend Howell is going with me tomorrow night, and I thought your presence might make the girl more comfortable."

"Of course. Shall we take my carriage?"

"That would be helpful."

"What time shall I come for you?" she asked.

"Come at eight, then we can stop at the reverend's on our way."

"After you make the exchange, where will you take the girl?"

"Reverend Howell and his sister have offered to care for her."

Lillian nodded. "They are very kind. She'll be well cared for there."

"After we go to the police and Mr. Parker is arrested, she'll be returned to the Foundling Hospital."

The waitress stopped by their table. "May I bring you anything else?"

He glanced at Lillian, and she shook her head. "Nothing else, thank you."

When the waitress stepped away, she asked, "How is the work going with your articles?"

"I found a solid lead on one of the missing girls from White Chapel, and I was able to confirm the information."

She gave a slight nod.

"Have you seen today's edition of the *Gazette?*" He took a folded section of the newspaper from his coat pocket.

"No. Did they publish your first article?"

"Not yet. It should be in Monday's edition. But they printed this warning today."

She sent him a questioning glance. "A warning?"

He slid the front page toward her and pointed to the box in the lower right corner. "It's already caused quite a stir."

Lillian's gaze returned to the newspaper, and she read the warning aloud. "'All those who are squeamish, and all who prefer to live in a fool's paradise of imaginary innocence, selfishly oblivious of the horrible realities that torment those whose lives are passed in the inferno of London, will do well not to read the *Pall Mall Gazette* of Monday and the following days.'" She looked up. "My goodness. That makes your articles sound . . . quite sensational."

"Mr. Stead felt the warning was needed, but he's also intent on raising circulation. He hopes the series will cause a great outcry and pressure Parliament to pass the Criminal Law Amendment Act."

She gave a slow nod. "The law that will raise the age of consent."

"Yes, it will give the authorities more power to arrest men like Mr. Parker and others who entrap underage girls."

She placed her cup on the table. "These are controversial topics. I hope you're handling them . . . as sensitively as possible."

"I'm trying, but I don't have the final word. Mr. Stead is quite heavy-handed when he edits. In fact, he often makes so many changes I'm surprised he doesn't give himself the byline."

She offered a sympathetic look.

He leaned back in his chair. "It's all right. He's taught me a lot. I don't begrudge him editing my work."

"Well, I don't want to keep you. I'm sure you need to get back to the *Gazette*. And I should return home to Serena and Ellen."

He did need to look over his article once more and gather his notes for the next, but he didn't want to miss the opportunity to hear her answer to the question he'd posed in her garden more than a week ago. He reached across the table and laid his hand over hers. "Stay a little longer if you can."

She looked at his hand, but she didn't pull hers away. A gentle smile lifted her lips. "All right."

He smiled. "Another cup of tea?"

"Yes. Thank you."

He poured her a cup and spent the next thirty minutes enjoying her company and conversation. She didn't give a direct answer to his question, but he sensed a stronger bond, which gave him hope.

～

Lillian glanced at her bedroom mirror and ran her hand down her skirt. She had chosen a simple navy blue dress for that evening's journey to the Foundling Hospital, but she had taken extra time styling her hair. She turned to the right and left, checking the results in the mirror. Would Matthew notice?

She cast that thought away. He had never commented on her dress or appearance except for the first time they'd met, when he'd scowled and told her she needed to dress simply or else she would look like a rose in a rubbish heap when they visited Mercy House.

A smile touched her lips. He'd been so gruff that day, unhappy that Reverend Howell had surprised him with the request to help her find her missing niece. How much had changed. Her heart swelled as she recalled all he'd said and done for her and the way he'd taken on the quest to bring Alice home and made it his own.

She pinned on her small straw hat with the navy ribbon around the crown, took one final glance in the mirror, and left the room. Stopping at Serena's door, she knocked softly.

Her sister opened the door and slipped out. "Ellen just fell asleep," she whispered.

Lillian nodded. "I'm leaving now."

"Please be careful. And wake me up when you return, no matter how late it is."

"I will." Lillian kissed Serena's cheek, descended the stairs, and called for her carriage. As soon as her coachman pulled up out front, she climbed aboard and set off for Matthew's flat.

Settling back on the seat, she clasped her hands in her lap and tried not to worry. But as the carriage rolled along, her thoughts darted from one possibility to the next. She closed her eyes and shifted her anxious thoughts to a prayer.

Please, Lord, watch over Matthew and keep him safe. Let him make the exchange easily and give us the evidence we need to ensure Mr. Parker's arrest. And please let his arrest bring us closer to Alice's rescue.

The carriage slowed to a stop, and her coachman hopped down. "Shall I go to the door for Mr. McGivern?"

"Yes, please. His flat is number three."

Two minutes later, Matthew emerged and joined her. "Good evening, Lillian." The light from the gas streetlamp shone through the window, highlighting Matthew's handsome features. His gaze traveled over her with warmth and approval in his eyes.

"Good evening." She hesitated, unsure what to say next. His unanswered request to deepen their friendship filled her mind, tying her tongue.

He studied her closely. "Are you all right?"

"Yes, of course." She looked down and adjusted her skirt. This was not the time to discuss their relationship or how it might impact the future.

He cleared his throat. "Do you have the funds?"

"Yes." She opened her reticule and withdrew a long white envelope.

He accepted it and met her gaze. "Thank you for trusting me with this."

"It's a worthy cause."

"I'll see that it's returned to you."

"I know you will."

He glanced toward the window for a moment, then looked back at her. "I don't expect my meeting with Parker will last long. As soon as we have the girl safely in the carriage, we'll take her to Reverend Howell's. After she is settled, I'll return home, write out a statement, then take it to the police first thing in the morning."

Lillian nodded. "Should I go with you to the station and explain what we know about Alice?"

He frowned slightly. "I'd welcome your company, but I don't know how long it will take. I'll make sure they understand Parker's connection with Alice and the need to free her from the Lady's Slipper."

She nodded. "Very well. I'll wait to hear from you, but I hope you'll let me know their response as soon as you're able."

Gentle understanding filled his eyes. "I know how important this is to you. I'll come directly to your home after things are settled with the police."

"Thank you."

They stopped at Reverend Howell's, and he joined them. The two men briefly reviewed the plan for the exchange and what would follow, then they rode in silence, the carriage darkening and then briefly lighting as they passed streetlamps.

Matthew focused out the window, his expression serious.

Finally, the carriage slowed and halted. Lillian looked out the window. Across the road, the dark silhouette of the Foundling Hospital rose against the silvery gray clouds in the night sky. Her stomach tensed, and she turned to Matthew.

He met her gaze, reassurance in his eyes. "Wait here. I'll be back as soon as I have the girl."

19

Matthew climbed down from the carriage and looked up at the coachman. "I should only be a few minutes. Please stay with the carriage and watch over Mrs. Freemont and Reverend Howell."

The coachman touched his cap. "Yes, sir."

Matthew strode across the road to the Foundling Hospital's back gate, his thoughts focused on his upcoming conversation with Parker. The most important point was to maintain his story and get the girl safely away.

The gate had been left open, and one gas lamp glowed near the back door, lighting his path. Matthew approached and knocked four times as he'd been instructed in Parker's note.

Only a few seconds passed before the door opened a few inches, and Parker looked out. He narrowed his eyes and scanned the path behind Matthew. "You're alone?"

Matthew nodded.

"You have the money for the girl?" It was odd that Parker didn't bother lowering his voice. But no one else seemed to be around.

"I'd like to see her first."

Parker scowled. "Don't trust me, eh?"

"I'd like to be sure of what I'm paying for."

Parker turned and pulled a young blond girl around in front of him. Fear filled her eyes, and her chin trembled as she looked up at Matthew.

His gut clenched, and his anger simmered. He forced down his response, reached into his suitcoat pocket, and pulled out the envelope. "Here's the money."

Parker took the envelope and leafed through the stack of bills inside, his lips moving as he counted. He looked up and nodded. "You can take her."

Matthew held out his hand, but the girl didn't move.

"Go on, Susan." Parker pushed the girl forward.

"No!" The girl's voice rose in a frightened cry.

Matthew placed his arm around her shoulder and guided her down the path, away from Parker. "It's all right," he whispered. "You've nothing to fear. You'll be well cared for."

They'd only gone a few steps when he heard tramping feet beyond the gate. A second later, several men burst from behind the wall and poured through the open gateway. He tightened his arm around the girl's shoulder.

"Stop right there!" one man shouted, lifting a lantern.

Matthew squinted against the bright light and lifted his hand to shade his eyes. "What is going on?"

Two men rushed forward. "Drop your hold on the girl!"

Matthew sucked in a breath. They were policemen!

"You're under arrest!" One of them hustled forward and grabbed the girl away from Matthew. She cried out, then whimpered.

"Put your hands in the air!" A tall officer strode toward Matthew. He raised his lamp, and light flickered off the silver buttons on his uniform.

Matthew shook his head. "You've got the wrong man." He pointed over his shoulder toward the building. "Parker is the one you want. He's been selling young girls to brothels."

211

The policeman glared at him. "Is that right?" His mocking tone was filled with disgust.

"Yes! I'm a journalist from the *Pall Mall Gazette*. I'm writing a series about the disappearance of several girls."

The policeman huffed out a scornful laugh. "Put your hands behind your back."

"I'm telling the truth! Parker sold several girls, and I intend to expose what he's been doing."

"Save your story for the judge."

Matthew clenched his jaw as cold steel clamped around his wrists. The officer took hold of his upper arm and hustled him toward the gate.

A fearful cry pierced the night.

The hair rose on Lillian's neck. She gripped the seat and leaned toward the carriage window. "What was that?"

"I don't know." Reverend Howell joined her.

Lillian scanned the dark road near the Foundling Hospital's back gate. A glowing lantern appeared, and several dark forms moved through the open gateway. She gasped. "Are those policemen?"

Reverend Howell reached for the door handle. "I'll go see what's happened."

"I'm coming with you." Lillian followed him out of the carriage.

Ben Fields jumped down from the driver's seat and pointed toward the stone wall. "Look, there's a police wagon parked down the road behind those trees."

Lillian grabbed up her skirt and started across the road. Just then, two policemen strode out the gateway, hauling Matthew between them.

Fear shot through her. "Matthew!" She ran toward him, followed by Reverend Howell.

"Stay back!" One of the policemen holding Matthew lifted his lantern higher. "This man is under arrest."

Lillian froze in the middle of the road, her heart pounding. This couldn't be happening!

"You've made a mistake!" Reverend Howell called. "Release him at once. Mr. McGivern has done nothing wrong!"

"Procuring an underage girl is a crime."

"That's not what he's doing!" Reverend Howell continued. "He is a journalist with the *Gazette*, covering a story."

The policeman shook his head, and the two officers holding Matthew started down the road toward the police wagon.

Lillian shot Reverend Howell a panicked glance. They had to stop them! She couldn't let them arrest Matthew for a crime he didn't commit.

"I'm Reverend Benjamin Howell from Good Shepherd Church. I can vouch for Mr. McGivern's good character. This was all done to prove Mr. Parker is selling young girls to anyone willing to pay, no matter what their intentions might be. Mr. McGivern is exposing evil, not perpetrating it!"

"That's the truth!" Lillian insisted. "I assure you, Mr. McGivern's intentions are honorable."

Please, Lord! Make them listen and realize Matthew is innocent!

Matthew and the policemen reached the wagon. They opened the back door and lowered a step. "In you go." They pushed him toward the wagon, and he mounted the step and climbed inside.

Lillian's heart sank as they closed and locked the door. "Oh, Matthew!"

He looked out the barred window, with a grave, hollow-eyed

stare. "Go to my editor, Mr. Stead. Tell him what's happened." The wagon lurched, then rolled down the road.

"You're in the right," Reverend Howell called. "We'll see that you're freed!"

Lillian stared after them, frozen to the spot. "I don't understand. How could this happen? No one knew what we'd planned."

Reverend Howell turned toward her. "No one except Mr. Parker. He must have informed the police."

Lillian's pulse surged. "He must have planned this to take the focus off himself!"

Reverend Howell gave a grim nod. "It appears so."

Lillian spun toward the Foundling Hospital. "We've got to stop him."

She'd only gone two steps before Reverend Howell pulled her back. "He's a clever man and very dangerous. We shouldn't try to deal with him on our own."

"But we can't let him get away with this."

"Our best course is to do as Matthew asked—go to his editor and seek his help to straighten this out."

A surge of anger blazed through Lillian, heating her face and tightening her throat. Matthew shouldn't have been arrested. Mr. Parker and all those dreadful men who bought and sold girls for evil purposes ought to be the ones behind bars—not the gallant and brave man she loved!

The realization echoed through her heart, ringing true. No matter the risk or challenges ahead, she loved him, and she would not let him fight this battle alone. He didn't deserve such dreadful treatment. She would not rest until she had done all she could for him. Her thoughts spun as she strode back to the carriage.

Ben Fields opened the door for her. "Home, madam?"

"No. Take us to the office of the *Pall Mall Gazette* on Fleet Street."

Reverend Howell shot her a surprised glance. "Do you think there will be anyone there at this late hour?"

"I believe they print the morning edition at night. Perhaps we can find someone there who can tell us how to contact the editor."

Thirty minutes later, the carriage arrived at the front door of the *Gazette*. Lillian looked out at the building, and her spirits sank. The windows were dark, and it looked as though everyone had gone home for the night.

Reverend Howell leaned out the window. "Mr. Fields, drive around the building and see if there is a side or back entrance." He turned toward Lillian. "Perhaps the pressroom is in the rear."

Lillian nodded and watched out the window as the carriage rounded the corner. Light shone through several windows near a loading dock at the back of the building. "Look, there's an open door!"

The coachman pulled the carriage to the side of the street, and Reverend Howell and Lillian climbed out. A loud mechanical sound filled the air as they mounted the steps and approached the rear entrance. Inside, massive presses roared as newspapers shot through the huge machines.

A tall, thin man wearing a stained apron over his clothes strode toward them, shaking his head. He motioned to the door, urging them back outside. The noise of the presses was so loud there was no possibility of speaking to him, so they did as he indicated.

He followed them out and closed the door. "No one is allowed in the pressroom. It's not safe."

"We understand," Reverend Howell said. "But there is an emergency, and we need to contact Mr. Stead."

The pressman frowned. "What kind of emergency?"

"One of the *Gazette* journalists is in trouble, and he asked us to contact Mr. Stead."

The man rubbed his chin. "Which journalist? Who are you talking about?"

Reverend Howell turned to Lillian, a look of uncertainty in his eyes.

Lillian stepped forward. "Please, sir, we must deliver the message to Mr. Stead tonight. It's an urgent matter. Would you kindly tell us where he lives?" She used her sweetest tone. "We'd be ever so grateful, and so will Mr. Stead when he receives the message."

His expression softened. "Well, I suppose I can find out for you."

"Oh, thank you so much. You're very kind."

The man's face turned ruddy. He nodded and quickly walked back inside.

Less than three minutes later, the pressman returned and handed Lillian a folded piece of paper. "Here you go."

Lillian nodded. "Thank you."

"Yes, thank you," Reverend Howell added.

Lillian and Reverend Howell quickly descended the steps and crossed to the carriage. She handed the paper to her coachman. "Can you take us to this location?"

He read the note and scratched his chin. "I think I know the street." He held the door for her as she climbed in and took a seat.

Reverend Howell joined her and checked his pocket watch. "It's past eleven o'clock. Perhaps we should wait until morning."

"Matthew asked us to contact his editor. I believe the sooner we do so, the better."

But as the carriage rumbled down the dark street, her head

throbbed, and her stomach swirled. Would Mr. Stead answer his door at this time of night, or was this journey a fool's errand?

⁓

Faint candlelight glowed from the front windows of Mr. Stead's townhouse on St. Margaret Street. Lillian released a shaky breath and turned to Reverend Howell. "It looks as though he might still be awake."

"It's worth a try." They left the carriage, and Reverend Howell knocked on the front door.

Seconds later, the door creaked open a few inches, and an older man carrying a candle and wearing a nightcap and robe looked out. "It's nearly midnight. Who are you? What do you want?"

"We are sorry to disturb you, sir. I'm Reverend Benjamin Howell, and this is Mrs. Lillian Freemont. We're here to bring a message from Matthew McGivern."

Mr. Stead straightened. "A message from Matthew? What happened?"

Reverend Howell glanced at Lillian.

She turned to the editor. "I'm afraid Matthew has been arrested."

Mr. Stead pulled the door open wider. "Come in and explain yourselves."

Reverend Howell and Lillian entered. Mr. Stead muttered under his breath as he led them into his sitting room. A lantern on the side table spread a little light, and flickering flames in the fireplace added a bit more.

Mr. Stead turned to them, his expression grim. "Sit down and tell me what Matthew has done."

Reverend Howell lowered himself into the nearest chair. "Let me begin by assuring you Matthew has been falsely accused."

"He must have done something, or he wouldn't have been

arrested," Mr. Stead huffed, plopping into the overstuffed chair opposite Reverend Howell.

Lillian sat on the sofa. "Matthew went to the Foundling Hospital hoping to prove a man employed there is selling girls to work in brothels, but the man turned the tables on Matthew. . . ." She poured out the rest of the story, detailing all that had happened that evening and ending with Matthew being taken away by the police.

Mr. Stead narrowed his eyes, looking at her more closely. "So you're the woman whose niece has gone missing from the Foundling Hospital."

"Yes, sir. Matthew has been a great help in the search. In fact, in an earlier conversation, he convinced Mr. Parker to divulge who purchased my niece and where she's been taken."

Stead shifted on his chair. "He knows where she is?"

"Yes. He went there disguised as a deliveryman a few days ago, hoping to free her, but two men who work there threatened him and chased him away."

Mr. Stead rose, clasped his hands behind his back, and paced across the room. "I knew he was searching for the girl, but I didn't realize he'd actually found her."

"He did, sir. She told him her name, confirming her identity."

"She's still at the brothel?"

"Yes, sir, belowstairs at the Lady's Slipper in White Chapel."

Mr. Stead nodded, and his grim expression eased. "This might turn out for the best after all."

Lillian stared at him. "What do you mean?"

"When Matthew writes about this, it will cause a firestorm! And the sooner the better!"

Lillian sent him an uncertain look. "You want Matthew to write while he's in jail?"

"Of course. He's a journalist! Being wrongly accused in his efforts to free a young girl from a brothel can be the focus of his next article! It will show how far we're willing to go to confront evil! It's sure to gain sympathy and bring even more attention to the series."

An uneasy look crossed Reverend Howell's face. "But Matthew's been falsely accused. He must be exonerated."

"Of course, of course. The *Gazette* keeps a barrister on retainer for legal matters. I'll speak to him first thing in the morning and see what can be done. While we wait, Matthew can continue writing the series from his jail cell." Mr. Stead gazed into the fire. "This might be the stroke of luck we need."

Lillian stared at him. How could he say that? She'd seen Matthew's face as he'd been hauled away by those policemen. Being arrested for a crime he did not commit was not only unfair, but also deeply distressing.

Bile rose and singed her throat. Would Mr. Stead do all he could to free Matthew, or would he take his time, hoping the story of Matthew's unjust arrest would sell more newspapers? He seemed more interested in creating a sensation and swaying public opinion than in clearing Matthew's name and securing his release.

20

2023

Janelle wove her way through the crowded tube station and followed Jonas toward the exit. He reached back and took her hand. She slid her fingers through his, and her heart swelled. His kind gesture offered an extra sense of care and protection. The crowd thinned as they reached the stairs, but he didn't let go of her hand. A smile rose to her lips as they climbed the steps to the street level.

"The library is just a short walk." He nodded to the right, and they set off, still walking hand in hand.

It was only midafternoon, and this had already been such a wonderful day. Jonas had been waiting for her in the lobby when she arrived at St. Mark's for the ten o'clock worship service. They'd found seats together, two rows from the front. He'd joined in singing with her and easily found his way to the book of Ephesians to follow along with Pastor Scott Brown's message.

When the service ended, she introduced him to the pastor and Maggie and Dan and their boys. Then Jonas greeted Olivia. Maggie and Dan asked him a few questions. He'd handled it all graciously, even when Dan teased her for not telling them Jonas was joining her that morning. Maggie had rolled her eyes and elbowed her husband.

After church, Janelle and Jonas stopped at the Sunflower

Café and ate lunch outside under a bright yellow umbrella. They talked about the message and the similarities and differences between St. Mark's and Hope Church. Then they'd taken a crowded ride on the tube to King's Cross Station, which was only an eight-minute walk from the British Library. Each experience and conversation made her feel closer to Jonas and gave her more reasons to appreciate him.

When they reached the library, he pulled open the front door. "After you."

She returned his smile. "Thanks."

They stopped at the main reference desk, and the librarian sent them to the second floor. They rode the lift, then crossed to the periodical reference desk.

The gentleman behind the desk looked up. "May I help you?"

Janelle nodded. "We're looking for a booklet titled *The Maiden Tribute to Modern Babylon*. It's a compilation of a series of articles that was published in the *Pall Mall Gazette* in the summer of 1885."

The man turned to his computer and typed in their request. A few seconds later, he met her gaze. "We have an original copy." He rose from his chair. "I'll get that for you."

"Would we be able to check it out?" Janelle asked.

"I'm sorry. It's classified as internal reference and only available to view here at the library."

Janelle nodded. "Okay. Thanks."

The librarian stepped out from behind the desk and disappeared between the stacks.

Jonas turned to her. "It should be interesting to see what's included in the other articles."

Janelle nodded, but her stomach tensed. If one of them confirmed the Foundling Hospital's involvement in the scheme to sell young girls to brothels, she'd have some very serious decisions to make.

The librarian returned and handed her the booklet. "Here you go. Please handle it carefully."

"We will." She carried it to a nearby table and took a seat. Jonas sat next to her. She opened to the table of contents and skimmed down to the third article in the series, "Falsely Accused and Jailed in Pursuit of the Truth." With a light touch, she turned the pages and settled in to read.

Jonas leaned closer, and they silently began reading the first page.

Janelle gasped and pointed to the fourth paragraph. "Can you believe the writer set up the man on staff at the Foundling Hospital?"

"Let's keep reading. It sounds as though he had good motives and was trying to expose what was going on."

She read the next section, and her head began to throb. The writer, a Mr. Matthew McGivern, accused an unnamed man at the Foundling Hospital of selling at least two young girls to brothels in White Chapel, and suggested there might have been more. It wasn't clear if the man behind the scheme had been caught and prosecuted, at least not in that article.

Jonas glanced her way. "Wow, the journalist ended up being arrested. That's a twist I didn't expect."

Janelle nodded and found her place in the article to continue reading.

A few minutes later, they finished making notes on that section, then turned the page to read the next. But Janelle found herself staring at the interior of the back cover. She ran her finger down the center fold. "Someone tore out the other pages! Who would do that?"

Jonas huffed and rose, taking the booklet with him. "Let me check with the librarian. Maybe they have another copy that's not the original."

As he left, Janelle made a few more notes. The accusations

against the Foundling Hospital were painfully clear and left a bitter taste in her mouth. Why hadn't she heard these details before? She'd always believed the Foundling Hospital's full history had been shared in exhibits and articles with honesty and integrity.

They had never tried to hide questionable issues connected with their care and treatment of the children. A recent exhibit, *Feeding the 400*, had shed light on the Great Milk Scandal of the late eighteenth and early nineteenth centuries. A guest curator had looked back at the records and discovered the cream had been skimmed from the whole milk before it was delivered to the Foundling Hospital. That meant, for years, the children drank milk that lacked the calories and nourishment needed. Amanda hadn't hidden that discovery. She'd called in an independent group to investigate and clarify what had happened.

But this scandal was much more serious, and making it known would need to be handled with great care. It was time to discuss what she'd learned with Amanda, but she dreaded the thought.

If Amanda knew the truth and had kept it all under wraps, that would put Janelle in an even more difficult position.

⁓

Jonas walked back toward the table where Janelle waited. He could tell she was discouraged by her weary expression. The article had confirmed her worst fears. Now she would have to deal with what they had uncovered.

She looked up as he approached. "Does he have another copy of the booklet?"

"No, but there's another one at a library in Essex. He sent a request and said he'd let me know when it arrives."

Janelle released a resigned sigh. "It's probably for the best. I've read just about all I want to take in today."

He sat down beside her. "I'm sorry. I know this is disheartening, but it's probably better that you discovered the truth rather than someone else reporting this and blindsiding you."

She offered a slow nod, then glanced at her watch and reached for her handbag. "I need to head home. Maggie and Dan are going out for dinner for their anniversary. I promised to spend the evening with Olivia and the boys."

He didn't like sending her off on this gloomy note. "Why don't I come with you?"

She cocked her eyebrow. "You really want to spend the evening with Olivia, Cole, and Caleb?"

"If that's what you're doing, then yes, I would."

Her smile returned, along with a look of relief. "If you're sure you don't mind."

"Not at all."

⤙

Janelle padded softly down the hall in Maggie and Dan's flat. Cole and Caleb were finally settled in their room for the night, listening to an audiobook with the lights turned down low. She heard Olivia talking to Jonas in the living room, which was interesting. Olivia hadn't said more than five words to them since they'd arrived.

She and Jonas had spent the evening playing a board game with Cole and Caleb. They'd invited Olivia to join them, but she'd said no, then fixed her eyes on her phone, scrolling through social media and texting the whole time. Janelle had been disappointed, but at least Olivia had stayed in the living room with them.

Jonas looked up as Janelle walked in. "I was just thinking, since Olivia is familiar with the museum transcription project, she might be able to help with our research."

Janelle sat down next to him. "What would she be looking for?"

"Maybe she could check the records in 1885 and see if she can find anything . . . interesting." He sent her a pointed look, and she caught his meaning.

Was it wise to tell Olivia about the *Gazette* articles and the girls who'd been taken from the Foundling Hospital? She debated a moment more, then turned to Olivia. "Would you like to help with some extra research? You'd need to keep what you learn confidential."

Olivia shrugged. "Sure. Who am I going to tell?"

Tony's name came to mind, but Janelle wasn't going to mention him, not after the way Olivia reacted the last time she'd brought Tony into the conversation.

Janelle focused on Olivia again. "Okay. Here's what we're working on. We've found a series of old newspaper articles that say some young girls were taken from the Foundling Hospital and sold to brothels."

Olivia's eyes widened. "Whoa, that's not cool."

"No, it's not. The writer of the articles used fictitious names for the girls to protect them. We'd like to find out who they were and learn what happened to them."

Interest flickered in Olivia's eyes. "So, this is sort of like solving a mystery."

Janelle nodded. "That's right."

"Can I read the articles?"

Jonas frowned and glanced at Janelle. "It's a pretty serious topic. Do you think Maggie and Dan would be okay with that?"

Olivia huffed. "I'm sixteen. That's certainly old enough to read the newspaper."

"I think it's okay," Janelle added. "But I'll make sure to mention it to them."

He took out his phone and handed it to Olivia. "Text me your number, and I'll send you the link to the first two articles.

We took some photos of the third article, but we're still searching for the last three in the series."

Olivia's fingers flew as she texted Jonas her number, then handed his phone back. He sent her the link and photos. She tapped on the link, then fixed her gaze on her phone. A few seconds later, she wrinkled her nose. "This article should definitely be rated for mature audiences only."

Janelle tensed. "If you're not comfortable reading it, you don't have to."

Olivia lifted her hand. "No. It's okay." She read a little longer, then looked up. "You're trying to find out the names of these girls?"

Janelle nodded. "Especially those who were taken from the Foundling Hospital. We also want to know what happened to them and who was behind it."

Olivia scrolled back to the top of the article. "Did you Google it?"

Janelle nodded. "We tried a few different searches, but we didn't find any direct links to the information we need."

"Did you look through Wikipedia? That's where I usually start when I'm writing a paper for school."

Janelle frowned. "I'm not sure Wikipedia is a credible source."

"No offense, but you shouldn't be a research snob. It's a great place to start." Olivia scanned the article once more. She typed something into her phone, scrolled for a few seconds, and her eyes lit up. "Here you go."

Janelle's pulse jumped. "What did you find?"

"I typed *Pall Mall Gazette* and the name of the series, and this website came up." She clicked through, and her eyes darted over the screen. "It looks like the guy who wrote the series worked for a famous editor named W. T. Stead. The website is about him." She read on for a few seconds. "It says the journalist was arrested and sent to jail for buying a girl from the Foundling Hospital."

"Yes, that's what we read in a booklet at the library today." Janelle glanced at Jonas.

He sat forward. "Does it identify the girls who were taken?"

Olivia kept reading. "The girl he bought was called Eliza Armstrong in the article. But he was arrested before he got away with her. Her real name was Susan Peterson, and she was returned to the Foundling Hospital." Olivia looked up. "Is that the girl you're looking for?"

Janelle leaned closer to Olivia, trying to read her phone. "The third article mentioned two girls who were taken from the Foundling Hospital and sold to work belowstairs at brothels. It happened quite a while before the incident when the writer was arrested. Those are the girls we want to identify."

Olivia nodded, then looked down at her phone and kept reading.

"Why don't I go get my laptop?" Janelle stood. "Then we can all take a look at the website."

Jonas nodded. "Good idea."

She went over to her flat, retrieved her laptop, and rejoined Olivia and Jonas. Olivia emailed her the link, and Janelle opened the page. Her gaze darted over the information, and she sat back. Most of it related to the editor's life, work, and influence on society. There was a brief mention of the series, and it gave a few excerpts from the articles.

"Look at the bottom of the page." Olivia nodded to Janelle. "It has a list of other websites and books that have more information about the editor. One of those might help you find the answers to your questions."

Jonas nodded. "Thanks, Olivia."

Olivia grinned. "I told you to check Wikipedia."

Jonas chuckled, then winked at Janelle. For the next half

hour, they hovered over her laptop, following links and making notes to help continue their search.

Jonas pointed to the list of references and external links at the bottom of the Wikipedia webpage. "Maybe we should see if we can find some of these books."

Janelle studied the titles. "I'll check the British Library online catalog." She quickly brought up the British Library website and typed in the first title. "They've got that book. Let me see if they have any of the others." She typed in four more titles, but only one of those was listed. She showed him what she'd found.

He nodded, looking pleased. "We'll pick them up tomorrow."

The way he'd said *we* warmed her heart. Turning back to her laptop, she quickly reserved the books.

Jonas leaned back on the sofa. "That was a good lead. Thanks, Olivia."

The girl was grinning from ear to ear, but she didn't seem to hear Jonas. Her gaze was glued to the phone.

Janelle leaned forward. "Olivia, did you hear Jonas?"

"Hmmm?" Olivia turned to Janelle. "What?"

Jonas chuckled. "Who are you texting?"

Olivia's cheeks flushed beneath her freckles, and she looked away. "A friend."

Janelle's happy mood deflated. No doubt she had been exchanging messages with Tony.

Jonas grinned. "Is it your boyfriend?"

Olivia shook her head. "He's just a friend."

"So, he's a boy, and he's your friend, but he's not your boyfriend?"

Olivia huffed. "You're worse than Maggie and Dan."

"Oh, come on," Jonas continued in a humorous tone. "You can tell us."

Olivia shot up off the couch. "Why are you asking me all these questions?"

Jonas held up his hands. "Hey, I'm sorry. I was just teasing."

The front door opened, and Maggie and Dan walked in. Maggie's gaze darted from Olivia to Janelle. "Is everything okay?"

Janelle met Maggie's gaze. "Yes. We've had a good evening. Olivia helped us find some information we've been looking for."

Maggie placed her handbag on the side table. "What kind of information?"

Olivia crossed her arms and shot an irritated glance at Maggie. "Don't worry. It was just some old newspaper articles about the museum's history. Why do you always think I'm doing something wrong?"

Maggie's eyes widened. "I don't think that."

"Yeah, right."

Dan frowned. "Olivia, don't use that tone with Maggie. She just asked you a simple question."

Hurt glittered in Olivia's eyes. "You always take her side. You never stand up for me."

"I'm not taking anyone's side."

Janelle sent Jonas a worried glance, and he returned an uncomfortable look.

Olivia spun away and started down the hall.

"Olivia," Dan called.

Maggie reached for Dan's arm. "Let her go. She needs time to cool down."

"It's past nine. She needs to turn over her phone."

"Let's give her a few minutes before we have to fight that battle." She turned to Janelle. "Sorry. I hope she wasn't like this all night."

Janelle sent Maggie a sympathetic look. "No, she was fine."

Dan shoved his hands in his pockets. "We appreciate you both coming over. It was a nice break for us."

Jonas nodded. "Glad to do it."

Janelle agreed and gave Maggie a hug. "I hope you two had a nice evening. Happy anniversary."

Dan slipped his arm around Maggie's shoulder and sent them a weary smile. "Thanks."

Janelle gathered her belongings, and she and Jonas said good night, then stepped out to the landing and crossed to her door.

"Why do you think Olivia reacted like that?" Jonas asked. "I hope it won't spoil Maggie and Dan's evening."

"I think they'll be all right." Janelle looked up at him. "I enjoyed today."

Humor lit his expression. "Even the board game with the boys and Olivia's teenage angst?"

She smiled. "Yes, even that. Having you there made it all . . . special."

His eyes glowed as he took a step closer. "Thanks. I enjoyed it too." His gaze slowly traveled over her face, as though he was taking in each feature.

Her heartbeat sped up. Was he going to kiss her good night? Did she want him to? Memories of the way he'd sung with her that morning at church, how he'd reached for her hand and guided her through the tube station, his playful laughter during the game with the boys, and the silent looks they'd exchanged that evening, communicating their thoughts without needing any words, all flowed through her mind.

He waited, holding her gaze, silently asking her permission. She lifted her face toward his as he dipped his head. Her eyes slid closed just as his lips met hers with a kiss so soft and tender it melted her heart. It only lasted a few seconds, but it was long enough to make her senses spin with delight.

He stepped back, grinning. "Thank you."

"You're welcome." Goodness, she could hardly catch her breath.

"We'll have to do this again . . . soon."

She laughed softly. "Yes, it was a lovely day."

He leaned in and kissed her forehead. "Good night, Janelle."

"Good night."

He pushed open the door to the stairs, looked back with a smile, then started down the steps.

Janelle released a soft sigh as she opened her door. Jonas's kiss and all he'd done today had made her feel special and cherished. It was a good feeling, easing away her worries from the past and giving her a fresh wave of hope for the future.

21

1885

Matthew lay on the hard cot and stared at water stains on the ceiling of his jail cell. Cold air seeped in through the thin wool blanket covering him, and he shivered. The weight of worry had kept him awake most of the night, leaving him with a headache and gritty eyes.

Faint light filtered through the small dirty window above, alerting him that morning had arrived. They'd taken away his pocket watch, so he had no idea of the actual time. He rolled to his side and closed his eyes against the pounding in his head.

What now, Lord? I tried to do what's right and look where it's taken me. I don't understand.

He pondered that thought a few minutes, and the stories from the Bible of John the Baptist and the apostle Paul came to mind. They were good men who served the Lord, yet they were unjustly treated and had to spend time in prison. Should he expect anything less? Commitment to Christ and doing His will did not mean the road would always be smooth and he would never face trouble. He had taken a stand against evil, and that came at a great cost.

"McGivern, you've got visitors." The guard's gruff voice stirred him from his somber thoughts.

He sat up and glanced at the guard. "Who is it?"

"Your legal counsel and some other man. Come with me."

Matthew rose as the guard unlocked the cell. He straightened his shirt and brushed off his rumpled pants, then followed the guard down the hall. The guard opened a door and ushered him into a small room. Mr. Stead and Mr. Baldwin, the barrister on retainer for the *Gazette*, sat on the far side of a wooden table in the center of the room. They looked up and met his gaze as he entered. Mr. Baldwin's thoughtful expression reflected concern, while Mr. Stead narrowed his eyes and searched Matthew's face.

The guard nodded toward the table. "Take a seat. You have thirty minutes." He stepped back, but he remained in the room, beside the door.

Matthew sat across from Mr. Baldwin and Mr. Stead. "Thank you for coming."

Mr. Stead rested his arms on the table. "Well, Matthew, I heard a brief explanation from your friends last night. I've passed that on to Mr. Baldwin, but I'd like you to explain how you got yourself into this situation."

"Of course." Matthew recapped all that had happened since he'd realized Mr. Parker was the man selling girls to brothel owners. "But last night when I followed through with my plan to expose him, I was arrested instead."

"How did the police realize what you were doing?" Mr. Baldwin asked.

Matthew squinted toward the window. He'd spent a good part of last night trying to piece together how that had happened. "Mr. Parker must have contacted them. As soon as I gave him the money and started to leave with the girl, the police charged in and arrested me."

Mr. Stead drummed his fingers on the table. "Why did you put yourself in a situation like that? You should have spoken to me before trying something so . . . I don't know if I should call it daring or foolish."

Matthew lifted his hands. "You told me to get out there and find the story! That's what I was doing."

Mr. Stead grimaced. "I didn't think you'd try something that would get you arrested!" He turned to the barrister. "Mr. Baldwin, can you straighten this out?"

The barrister's mouth turned down. "I'm afraid this is more complicated than I expected." He focused on Matthew. "You actually gave Mr. Parker money and accepted the girl?"

"Yes, but I took her no more than four steps before the police stopped me."

"You may have had honorable intentions, but technically, when you paid for that girl, you broke the law by procuring an underage child."

Frustration rose, and Matthew tightened his fists. "But I would never harm her. Reverend Howell and Mrs. Freemont were waiting in the carriage. They'll back up my story. I planned to turn the girl over to the reverend's care until Parker was arrested and the girl could safely return to the Foundling Hospital."

"Their statements may help, but it doesn't erase the fact you made the arrangement, paid for the girl, and took her into your custody."

Matthew closed his eyes and rubbed his forehead. "I did it to prove Parker was behind this scheme."

Mr. Baldwin nodded. "I understand, and I'll speak to those overseeing your case. Perhaps they'll release you on bond until your trial."

Matthew dropped his hand, his senses reeling. "There's going to be a trial?"

"I'm afraid so."

Matthew groaned. "I don't believe this. Why can't they see it's all a misunderstanding? And what about Parker? He's the one who should be arrested."

Mr. Stead huffed. "I doubt he's still in town."

Matthew's gut clenched. What had happened to Lillian's money? Had Parker turned it over to the police, or had he fled with all or part of it? How would Matthew repay Lillian? He'd failed to free her niece, and his plan to have Parker arrested had backfired and landed him in jail with a shameful accusation attached to his name. But worst of all, those evil men who bought and sold girls were still out there, plaguing the city and ruining young lives.

His father's scornful words rose and filled his mind. *"You're a coward and a weakling. You'll never amount to anything."* Maybe what his father had said was true. He clenched his jaw as painful regret seared his soul. There was no hope for a future with Lillian now. He would never be worthy of her.

Mr. Stead pulled a sheaf of paper from his leather case and laid it on the table with a pen and bottle of ink. "Even though you're locked up here, you still need to finish writing those articles."

Matthew raised his eyebrows. "You're not sacking me?"

"No, of course not! Your actions may have been impulsive, but I suppose when I was your age, I might have done the same thing."

Matthew straightened, a flicker of hope returning. He thought he'd ruined his career and would lose his position, but it seemed Mr. Stead was willing to give him another chance.

"The first article ran this morning. It's already causing a commotion. I have the draft of your second back at the office. I'll revise that so it's ready for the next edition. Then I'll be back here tomorrow, and I expect you to have finished the next article. Write about what happened at the Foundling Hospital! Stir up the debate and let them hear your side of the story."

"Yes, sir. I'll start working on it right away."

Mr. Baldwin rose. "I'll see what I can do, and I'll keep you informed."

"Thank you." Matthew shook hands with the barrister, then turned to his editor. "I appreciate your support, sir."

Mr. Stead clamped his hand on Matthew's shoulder. "You're a good man, Matthew. We'll see this through. When your motives become clear, I believe things will be set right."

Matthew's throat tightened, and he nodded his thanks.

⌣

Lillian clutched her reticule, trying to tamp down her anxiety as she walked down the hallway of the central police station with Reverend Howell. Their request to see Matthew had been denied, so they'd pressed on with their decision to ask the police to rescue Alice from the Lady's Slipper. Lillian glanced to the right and left as they passed several offices where policemen and detectives worked at their desks.

The officer leading the way stopped and knocked on a door. The name *Detective Charles Wright* was painted on the frosted window. A deep male voice called for them to enter.

The officer who had guided them down the hall opened the door. "There is a man and a woman here who say they have information about a missing girl."

"Bring them in." Detective Wright rose from behind his desk as Lillian and Reverend Howell entered. He looked them over with a serious expression. "Your names, please."

"I'm Reverend Benjamin Howell from Good Shepherd Church. And this is Mrs. Lillian Freemont of Eaton Square. We've come today about Mrs. Freemont's missing niece, Alice Dunsmore. She was also known as Mary Graham when she was at the Foundling Hospital."

The detective's forehead creased, and he motioned to the two chairs facing his desk. "Have a seat." They sat, and he focused on Lillian. "Your niece was in residence at the Foundling Hospital?"

"Yes, sir. My sister was unable to care for her daughter when she was an infant, so she placed her in the care of the Foundling Hospital. Alice is eight now. My sister recently came to live with me, so I went to the Foundling Hospital, hoping to reclaim her daughter, but the matron told me Alice had died as an infant." She hesitated, trying to think of how to explain the rest.

"I'm sorry for your loss."

"The matron was not telling the truth, or she is mistaken, because another member of the staff told us Alice had been there until very recently and then disappeared."

He frowned. "Who told you she disappeared?"

Lillian relayed the cleaning woman's story, giving every detail she remembered.

Detective Wright cocked an eyebrow, looking doubtful.

"It's all true. We've done our own investigation, and we know my niece was sold to work at the Lady's Slipper in White Chapel."

He steepled his fingers and sent her a pitying look. "Mrs. Freemont, I know it must be distressing to learn your niece has passed away, but—"

Heat flashed into her face. "My niece is not dead! She is very much alive and trapped in that terrible place. Please, you must believe me. A man named Mr. Neil Parker at the Foundling Hospital is the one who sold her to whoever is in charge at the Lady's Slipper."

The detective studied them with a skeptical look.

Reverend Howell leaned forward. "Detective, are you aware of an incident at the Foundling Hospital last night?"

"No, I'm not."

Reverend Howell pulled in a deep breath. "One of our friends, Mr. Matthew McGivern, who is a journalist with the *Pall Mall Gazette*, went there, gathering information for the series of articles he—"

The detective lifted his hand. "You mean the man behind that scandalous article on the front page of this morning's edition?"

Reverend Howell sent Lillian a surprised glance, then turned back to Detective Wright. "Yes, he's the one writing the series."

Detective Wright glared at them. "That article is a pack of lies! We've followed every lead we've been given trying to find those missing girls. How dare he imply we've neglected our duty!"

Lillian's stomach plunged, and she swallowed hard.

"I only briefly scanned the article," Reverend Howell continued in a calm tone. "I'm not certain what he said about the police. But the point of our visit today is to ask you to rescue Mrs. Freemont's niece from the Lady's Slipper."

The detective jerked open his desk drawer and pulled out a pad of paper. "What's the girl's name?"

"Alice Dunsmore," Lillian said. "But the Foundling Hospital gives each child a new name, so she is known as Mary Graham." Lillian gave him the rest of the information they had collected. But she could tell by his grim expression that their association with Matthew had cast even more doubt on their story. Her spirits deflated as she watched him jot a few brief notes on the pad.

He set down his pen. "I have the information I need. We'll look into it, and I'll be in touch."

That was all he was going to say? Lillian glanced at Reverend Howell. How could they leave knowing the detective doubted their story?

Reverend Howell rose. "Thank you, Detective Wright. We appreciate your time."

Lillian stood. "I hope you'll do all you can to free my niece and return her to us."

The detective gave a brief nod, but he made no promise.

Hot tears burned Lillian's eyes as she followed Reverend Howell out of the office and continued down the hall. She suspected that Detective Wright hadn't promised his help because he didn't intend to put anything more than minimal effort into the case.

If her niece was going to be set free from that brothel, Lillian would have to find another way.

～

Lillian and Serena strolled down the oval path around the outskirts of Eaton Square Garden. Ellen walked ahead of them, twirling a small yellow flower between her fingers. Lillian had suggested a walk in the private garden across from her townhouse, hoping it would calm her anxious thoughts.

There had been no word from the police, Matthew, or his editor, though she'd asked Mr. Stead to keep her informed. Since she was not allowed to visit Matthew, she might not hear anything until he was released, or until his trial. A shiver raced down her back, though it was a warm, sunny afternoon. *Please, Lord, let the truth come to light.*

Serena turned toward her. "Lillian, did you hear me?"

"I'm sorry. What did you say?"

Serena sent her an understanding look. "I asked if you think it's time to see about some new clothes for Ellen." Serena glanced away. "I thought we might wait until Alice comes, but I'm not sure how long that will be."

Pain twisted Lillian's heart. "Hopefully, it won't be much longer." She pressed down a surge of frustration as she recalled Detective Wright's response to their visit. She had kept most of those details from Serena and simply told her the police had been informed and said they would follow up.

She glanced at her sister. "I'll send a message to the dressmaker and ask when she can come to the house."

Serena nodded. "I'm sure Ellen will enjoy having some new clothes."

"Mrs. Freemont, hello!" A young blond woman in a stylish blue day dress and matching hat walked toward them. "I'm Anne Perrone. We met the day you gave a speech at the Montrose Women's League."

"Yes, of course. I remember you and your friend Elizabeth. It's nice to see you again."

"Thank you. I didn't realize you lived in Eaton Square. I'm visiting my brother George and his family. They live at number forty-two."

"We're at 124, just across the street."

Ellen wandered across the grass a few feet away, following a butterfly. Lillian kept an eye on her while listening to her friend.

Anne glanced around, then leaned toward Lillian. "Did you read the lead article in the *Gazette* this morning?" She raised her hand to her throat. "The situation in White Chapel is simply dreadful!"

Lillian's pulse surged as she recalled the contents of the article. She had purchased a copy of the *Gazette* on her way back from the police station and read the first part in the carriage. She'd shown it to Serena as soon as she'd arrived home, and they'd read all six pages. "It is heartbreaking to think of those who are suffering at the hands of evil men."

Anne shook her head. "Those poor women! That article read very much like one of Josephine Butler's speeches. I'm sure she will be up in arms about this. I hope it will make people realize how dreadful the situation truly is and convince the authorities to wake up and take action."

Serena turned to Anne. "You're speaking of finding the young girls who have been reported missing?"

"Yes, that's exactly what I'm talking about. Those poor girls!"

"My daughter is one of those missing girls."

Anne's eyes widened. "Oh no! How could that happen?"

Serena explained how Alice had been taken from the Foundling Hospital and that Matthew had gone to the Lady's Slipper but had been unable to free her daughter.

"My goodness! I'm terribly sorry. I hope she'll be returned to you very soon. If there is anything I can do to help, please let me know. I'll be staying with my brother for another week."

"Thank you." Serena took out a handkerchief and wiped her damp eyes.

Anne reached for Serena and gave her a gentle hug. "I'll be praying for her and for you."

They said their good-byes, and Anne walked in the direction of her brother's house.

Serena turned to Lillian. "She is very kind."

"Yes, I felt a kinship with her the first time we met. Let's invite her for tea soon."

Ellen rejoined them, and they continued down the path a short distance. Lillian and Serena took a seat on one of the benches while Ellen knelt and looked for four-leaf clovers among the grass.

Lillian gazed across the park, contemplating Anne's comments about Josephine Butler. She'd never heard her speak in person, but she had read a few articles that summarized her inspiring talks. She was a woman of deep faith who courageously took a stand for the protection of women and girls, even though she knew she would face harsh criticism and sometimes even physical danger.

Perhaps it was time they took a lesson from Josephine Butler.

Matthew stared at the note from Mr. Baldwin, then read it again. His trial was set for the middle of June. He would not be released on bail before that time. He sighed, leaned back against the wall, and closed his eyes. *Why, Lord? I feel like I'm being hit with one blow after another.*

He'd spent most of the previous day writing an account of the search for Lillian's niece and the incidents at the Foundling Hospital, giving Alice and her family fictitious names. He'd kept his article as factual as possible, but he felt certain he'd made his disgust clear that the true criminal had gotten away. He hadn't named Parker, but those familiar with the Foundling Hospital staff would know who he was describing.

Would the article finally motivate the police to investigate the situation and arrest Parker—if he was still in town? He hoped that would be the result, but doubts flooded his mind as he recalled the reaction of the detectives when he'd been questioned. No matter how many times he explained the situation, they didn't seem to believe what he said. In fact, they acted as if he was lying and deserved to be prosecuted for procuring an underage girl. He shook his head and pushed those troublesome thoughts away.

Mr. Stead had stopped by that morning and dropped off the latest issue of the *Gazette*. His second article in the series was featured on the front page and continued on page three.

He had not been allowed a visit with Mr. Stead. Instead, his editor had to pass the newspaper through the bars of his cell, then Matthew handed him the next article. He supposed he should be grateful they allowed that much. But it was hard to be thankful when the situation seemed so unjust.

He'd also given Mr. Stead a note for Lillian and asked him to make sure it was delivered as soon as possible. He prayed she would accept it and believe he was truly sorry for all that had happened. He told her he would repay the money and make things right as soon as he was able. But he had no idea when that might be.

Matthew scanned the brief note from Mr. Baldwin again, then rose and paced the short distance across his cell. Being confined and cut off from everyone was maddening. There was no way of knowing what Lillian was thinking or if she would ever speak to him again. His articles were finally published, but he had no idea if they were pushing those in power toward needed change, or if his words were simply tossed in the rubbish bin.

He lowered himself to his cot and rubbed his forehead. He had to keep working on his next articles. Pouring his thoughts into his writing seemed to be the only way to stay sane in these frustrating circumstances.

Help me, Lord. I know you have a message you want to get across. Give me the words you want me to say.

He picked up the paper and pen and began to write.

22

1885

Lillian tucked her arm through Serena's and started down the street with the group of about forty ladies from the Montrose Women's League. Josephine Butler and Anne Perrone led the way, walking a few feet in front of Lillian and Serena.

A man wearing a bloodstained apron stepped out of his butcher shop as the women passed. "Look at the flock of lady birds!" he called in a taunting voice.

An old man with a long white beard leaned out an upstairs window. "Whooee, where are you ladies headed?"

Another man dressed in a business suit and derby hat strolled toward them. He nodded to Lillian with a leering look. "What's your name, sweetheart?"

Josephine glanced over her shoulder. "Ignore them. We are about the Lord's business."

Lillian nodded and focused straight ahead, closing her ears to more calls and whistles as their group moved down the street. Dressed in their finest day dresses, they looked out of place on this street in White Chapel, but they had come on a mission and would not be deterred from reaching their goal.

The last forty-eight hours had passed in a whirlwind since Lillian, Serena, and Anne had called on Mrs. Josephine Butler and asked for her advice and help. Josephine was deeply moved when she heard how Alice had disappeared from the Foundling Hospital and been sold to the Lady's Slipper. She agreed to join forces with them, and the four women had spent that afternoon planning their strategy.

They composed and sent a notice to all the members of the Montrose Women's League and several other female friends, asking them to attend a public meeting on Friday in front of the Lady's Slipper. They also contacted Mr. Stead at the *Gazette*, informing him of the meeting and inviting him to send a reporter to cover the event.

Lillian imagined Mr. Stead and all the journalists at the *Gazette* had been extremely busy for the past several days. The response to Matthew's articles had been explosive, and several protests and meetings had sprung up around the city in support of tightening laws to protect women and girls from exploitation.

The *Gazette* had sold out each day, and extra newsprint had to be purchased so more copies could be printed for those who wanted to read the series. Just as Matthew had hoped, people's hearts had been stirred to action when they'd learned about the missing girls from White Chapel and the Foundling Hospital.

As the women gathered in front of the Lady's Slipper, Serena leaned closer to Lillian and whispered, "Do you really think this will work?"

Lillian glanced around the group and then up at the three-story building. Curtains covered the windows, and no one looked out. Her stomach tensed. She didn't even want to think about what went on in those rooms. "The Lord is on our side. We just need to do our part and trust Him with the outcome."

Serena nodded, determination filling her expression. "Yes, He knows what's needed." But her chin trembled as she scanned the building and then shifted her gaze to the group.

Anne climbed the front steps of the Lady's Slipper and turned to face the women. "Thank you for coming. We're grateful for your willingness to join us here today. As we said in the notice you received, we are here on a mission . . . and that mission is to free the underaged girls who are trapped in the Lady's Slipper. And we will not leave until they are released!"

The women applauded, and a few added amens.

"Now, I'd like to introduce a woman who bravely speaks out for the protection of women and girls. She is someone I deeply admire, and I'm confident when you hear her speak, she will win a place in your hearts as well. Please welcome Mrs. Josephine Butler." Anne clapped as she stepped aside, and the other ladies joined in with polite applause.

Josephine mounted the steps and faced the group. Her face glowed with vitality that made her appear younger than her fifty-seven years. Dressed in a modest dark green suit and hat, she gazed out at them with an intense but sincere expression. "Thank you for your warm welcome. I can see that you are a dedicated and courageous group of women, and that is exactly what is needed here today.

"We have come to be a voice for the voiceless, for the forgotten women and girls who are subjected to exploitation and injustice. It is our sacred duty to protect them, to champion their rights, and to restore their dignity."

Several women clapped, and Josephine paused and nodded to them.

"We must do all we can to build a society where every woman and girl can thrive, where their dreams and aspirations are nurtured, and where their worth is recognized. Working together, we can forge a future where freedom reigns for generations to come."

More applause rose from the group.

"But this will not happen without sacrifices," Josephine

continued. "We must be willing to take a stand against evil and speak up for what is true and right." She lifted her hand and motioned toward the building behind her. "Trapped in this den of iniquity are girls as young as eight years old who were sold here against their will. They should be enjoying their childhood in peace and safety, but that is not the case for these poor girls. This is a crime that cannot be ignored any longer. They must be released and returned to the care of their families and friends."

"Yes, let the girls go!" one woman called, and other voices rose in agreement.

Serena clutched Lillian's arms, her eyes shining.

"We can no longer turn a blind eye to the suffering of these children. We must smash the chains of oppression, uphold the principles of justice, and rise to challenge the systems that perpetuate their oppression, forging a new path of freedom and dignity for these girls and for others who are also chained. Joining our hands and hearts, we can be the guardians of hope for those who have been silenced, and the defenders of dignity for those who have been stripped of their worth."

She turned and faced the front door of the Lady's Slipper. Raising her fist, she knocked firmly three times. "Let the children go!" Josephine called, her voice loud and impassioned.

"Yes! Let them go!" Serena called. Other women's voices rose around them, calling out for the girls' release.

The curtain moved in one of the first-floor windows, and a young woman looked out. Her gaze traveled over the crowd with a stunned expression, then a firm hand pulled her away, and the curtain fell back in place.

Josephine turned toward the women once more. "Let's lift our voices in a hymn, and let it be our prayer as well as our cry for freedom. Join me in singing 'I Think When I Read That Sweet Story of Old.'"

Josephine's voice rang out true and clear as she sang the first line, and the other women joined in.

> I think when I read that sweet story of old,
> When Jesus was here among men,
> How He called little children as lambs to His fold,
> I should like to have been with them then.
> I wish that His hands had been placed on my head,
> That His arms had been thrown around me,
> And that I might have seen His kind look when He said,
> "Let the little ones come unto me."

Memories of Lillian's own dear daughter flooded her mind, and tears flowed down her cheeks as she sang the beloved hymn. Ann Marie was safe in the Savior's care, but oh, how she missed her and all that could have been. Now she lifted the song for her niece, praying she would be released and soon come home.

Serena slipped her arm around Lillian's back, and their voices blended in harmony.

The door of the Lady's Slipper opened, and a tall man with dark hair and a beard stepped out. He wore a gold vest and black pants, with his white shirtsleeves rolled up to his elbows. He scanned the group as their voices fell silent. "You ladies need to move on. This is private property." His voice was as hard and cold as his expression.

Josephine straightened her shoulders but remained on the top step.

His frown deepened. "I'm talking to you, woman! Get away from my door."

Anne stepped up beside Josephine, and Lillian and Serena climbed the steps and stood on her other side.

He huffed. "You've got no business here. You need to leave!"

"We would be happy to go," Josephine said, "as soon as you release the underage girls working here."

He shook his head. "I don't have any underage girls here."

A murmur passed through the crowd.

Heat surged into Lillian's face. "We know you have a girl here who is only eight years old. Her name is Mary Graham, and she was abducted from the Foundling Hospital."

He scowled. "There's no Mary Graham here! Now, get off my steps and take your songs and speeches where someone wants to hear them."

Josephine lifted her chin. "We know the girl is here, and we demand her release."

His mouth lifted in a mocking smile. "You demand, do you? I can call out my men to remove you, or you can go peacefully. Which is it going to be?"

Josephine's expression firmed. "We are not leaving without Mary Graham."

"Then I warn you there will be consequences." The man stepped inside and slammed the door.

Lillian's heart pounded, and she turned to Josephine. "Do you think he'll truly send men to remove us?"

"I believe he's bluffing, but we must be on our guard." Josephine straightened and turned to the group. "Ladies, let's gather in closer for a time of prayer."

Most of the women responded by tightening the circle, but a few women on the edge turned and walked away.

"I will lead in an opening prayer, then others may add their requests and petitions. Please bow your head and join me."

Lillian held tight to Serena's hand and lowered her head, a silent cry rising from her heart.

"Father in heaven, please come to the aid of your daughters who have gathered here to speak for those who are held captive and cannot speak for themselves. We ask you to break through to the hearts and minds of those responsible for their captivity and prompt them to release those girls today. We know you love all the girls and women at the Lady's Slipper, and you hear our prayer on their behalf. We call on you to right this wrong and show your great power and love by freeing them."

A holy silence settled over the group, then another woman's voice rose as she called out to the Lord for the girls' release. A third and then a fourth woman prayed aloud, asking for mercy, justice, and protection for the girls.

The sound of wagon wheels rolling down the street reached Lillian. She lifted her head and gasped. The wagon's driver whipped the horses, sending them rushing forward. "Look out!" she yelled.

⌒

Matthew lay on his jail cell cot with his hands behind his head and his eyes closed. The time between lunch and dinner always seemed to drag and pull his spirits lower. He'd already finished his next article and written a note to Reverend Howell. Now the hours stretched out before him with nothing but unanswered questions to fill his mind.

What was Lillian doing right now? Why hadn't she answered his note? Was it because her money had been lost, and she blamed him? Or was it his arrest on such a humiliating charge that had convinced her to distance herself? He grimaced and stifled a groan. He didn't blame her. He'd held on to his position at the *Gazette*, but the situation would have lasting consequences to his reputation.

The sound of keys jingling roused him from his thoughts, and he opened his eyes.

The guard unlocked his cell door and pushed it open. "Get up, McGivern. Grab your jacket. It's time to go."

"Go? What do you mean?"

"You can pick up your belongings at the front desk on your way out."

Matthew sat up. "I don't understand."

"Your barrister is out there with a couple other men. He'll explain it."

Matthew rose, stuffed his arms in his jacket, and followed the guard down the hall and out to the front room of the police station. Reverend Howell, Mr. Stead, and Mr. Baldwin waited for him by the front desk.

Reverend Howell stepped forward and grasped Matthew's hand. "Good to see you, Matthew."

"Thank you. I'm glad to see you too." He shook the reverend's hand, then turned to Mr. Baldwin. "How did you convince them to let me out on bail?"

The barrister's eyes lit up. "You're not out on bail. All the charges against you have been dropped."

Matthew's jaw dropped. "I'm free to go? There won't be a trial?"

"That's right." Mr. Baldwin nodded. "Your series of articles caused such a protest across London that the police pushed on with their investigation. It took them a few days, but they found Mr. Parker, even though he'd disappeared from the Foundling Hospital. When they questioned him, he said he knew you were a reporter, not someone intent on buying the girl for immoral purposes. He thought alerting the police to arrest you would create a distraction and give him time to get away. He confessed to selling five girls to brothels in the last year and a half, including Mrs. Freemont's niece."

Matthew stared at Mr. Baldwin, hardly able to process his words. Parker had been arrested and had confessed. Matthew's name was cleared. A wave of relief poured through him. He lifted his hand and rubbed his stinging eyes. *Thank you, Lord.*

Mr. Stead clamped his hand on Matthew's shoulder. "And not a day too soon."

Matthew lowered his hand and met his editor's gaze.

"You're free just in time to cover what may be your biggest story yet," Mr. Stead continued, "and the perfect way to tie up the series."

"What are you talking about?"

"Lillian Freemont has organized a public meeting and invited Josephine Butler to be the speaker."

Matthew's eyebrows rose. "Isn't Josephine Butler the woman calling for the repeal of the Contagious Disease Act?"

"Yes, that and other causes. She always creates quite a bit of controversy whenever she speaks. The meeting is set for this afternoon in front of the Lady's Slipper to demand the release of Mrs. Freemont's niece."

A surge of fear shot through Matthew. He knew Lillian was determined to rescue Alice, but he had no idea she'd try to confront those men at the Lady's Slipper. "What time is the meeting?"

"Three o'clock." Mr. Stead glanced toward the large clock on the wall behind the front desk. "If we hurry, we might get there in time to hear Josephine Butler speak and see how those running the Lady's Slipper will respond."

Matthew recalled the hostile attitude of the two men who had chased him out of the Lady's Slipper the day he'd tried to rescue Alice, and his chest tightened. What would they do to Lillian and the other women who gathered there to seek Alice's release?

Reverend Howell seemed to read Matthew's distress. "Don't worry. We've alerted the police. I expect they're already on the way."

He clenched his jaw, and determination coursed through him. "We've no time to waste. Let's go."

Mr. Stead passed him a small notebook and pencil as they strode out the door. "You'll need these."

Matthew tucked them in his jacket pocket and quickened his steps. He'd cover the meeting and write the article, but not until he made sure Lillian was safe.

⌇

Lillian rushed down the front steps of the Lady's Slipper. Women screamed and dashed out of the street as the wagon raced closer. An older woman tripped on her dress, and another woman pulled her away from the street just before the wagon thundered past.

Lillian ran to her side and reached out her hand. "Are you hurt?"

The woman took hold and shook her head. "No, just shaken." She rose and brushed off her skirt.

The driver of the wagon shouted to the horses, and they slowed to a stop a short distance down the street. He and another man jumped down and started toward the women.

Lillian's breath snagged in her throat. She turned and looked for Serena. Her sister, Anne, and Josephine hurried toward her.

"Mr. Jackson told you to leave!" the tall, muscular driver called, scowling at them as he moved closer. He wore dirty work clothes and carried a long piece of wood that looked like a heavy broom handle. The other man was short and lean, but he bore an equally threatening expression.

Serena linked arms with Lillian, and Anne and Josephine stepped up on the other side. The other women moved behind them.

The two men stopped a few feet away. The driver glared at Lillian and her friends in the front line. "You need to clear out!"

Lillian swallowed hard and met his gaze. "We are not leaving without Mary Graham and the other underage girls."

The driver shook his head. "No! You have to go—now!"

Lillian lifted her chin. "We have as much right to be on this public street as you do."

"Don't sass me, girl! You're blocking the road! Get moving!"

Josephine narrowed her eyes. "You're breaking the law by keeping underage girls at a brothel."

"We know one was stolen from the Foundling Hospital!" Serena added, her voice indignant.

The driver's face turned ruddy. "Your time's up! Leave now, or we'll make sure they'll have to carry you away!" He raised the broom handle and began striking his palm—once, twice, three times—as he moved nearer.

Lillian tightened her hold on Serena's arm, and an urgent prayer rose from her heart.

Galloping horses sounded in the distance. She turned as a carriage rolled around the corner. The door flew open, and a man jumped out, followed by three other men.

Lillian stared in disbelief, and her heart leaped. *Matthew!*

"Lillian!" Matthew ran toward her, and the crowd of women parted.

Reverend Howell, Mr. Stead, and another man she didn't recognize dashed after him.

Matthew's gaze darted from her to the two men. He gave her a quick determined nod, then stepped in front of her. Facing the men, he pulled his notebook and pencil from his pocket. "Your name, sir?"

The tall man shot him a confused look. "What?"

"Your name, please." Matthew's tone remained calm and steady. "I need it for the article I'm writing for the *Pall Mall Gazette*."

The man pulled back and shook his head. "I'm not giving you my name." He pointed to the women. "They're causing a disturbance and blocking the way to our door."

"You're employed by Mr. Jackson, owner of the Lady's Slipper?"

The man's eyes flashed. "I didn't say that!"

Matthew cocked an eyebrow and lowered his voice. "I didn't name Mr. Jackson or the Lady's Slipper in my last article, but I may have to add that information to the next."

The shorter man glared at Matthew. "I wouldn't advise it."

"Would you like to make a statement about what happened here today?" Matthew poised the pencil over his notebook and sent them an expectant look.

The tall man growled, "I'm not telling you anything!"

"All right." Matthew slipped the notebook and pencil in his pocket. "Then I have something I'd like you to tell Mr. Jackson. We know he has underage girls working here. The police have been informed and are on their way as we speak. If he wants to avoid arrest, he needs to release Mary Graham and any other underage girls he's holding here."

The driver struck the ground with his stick. "I don't believe you! The police don't care what happens here."

Matthew took his watch from his pocket and looked at it. "I'd say you have less than ten minutes. If the girls are released by the time the police arrive, Mr. Jackson might avoid arrest." Matthew lifted his head. "I can't promise it, but that's his best option at this point."

The driver speared Matthew with a glaring look, then spit on the street. "If you're lying, we'll know where to find you."

Matthew stood tall and steady, unmoved by the man's threat.

The two men exchanged wary looks, then the tall one jerked his head toward the wagon. "Let's go." They turned, swaggered down the street, and climbed aboard the wagon.

Lillian sagged with relief as they drove away.

Matthew turned to Lillian and searched her face. "Are you all right?"

She nodded, emotion tightening her throat. "When were you released? How did you know . . . ?" Her voice wobbled, and tears stung her eyes.

He sent her an endearing smile. "They arrested Parker and dropped the charges against me."

Her heart soared. "Oh, Matthew, I'm so glad."

"So you're not angry with me?"

She shook her head, surprised by his question. "No, of course not."

A look of relief flashed across his face, and he reached for her.

She stepped into his arms and closed her eyes. Resting her head against his solid chest, she soaked in the protection of his arms around her. He held her close, and she wished the moment didn't have to end.

"Let's gather the women." Josephine's words reminded Lillian she and Matthew were not alone.

She stepped back and looked up at Matthew. "Thank you."

He nodded, his eyes shining. "There's more to say, but it can wait." He scanned the front of the Lady's Slipper, and his expression sobered. "Let's hope they take my message to Mr. Jackson, and he's inclined to believe it."

Reverend Howell spoke to the women across the street and encouraged them to rejoin the others. The women gathered in a tighter circle. Lillian introduced Josephine to Matthew, Reverend Howell, and Mr. Stead. The editor introduced Mr. Baldwin.

Josephine sent a serious glance around the group. "I suggest we close ranks and block any customers from entering the building, in the hope that will motivate them to release the girls."

The front door of the Lady's Slipper opened, and Mr. Jackson stepped into view. He looked out and scanned the group. "I don't take kindly to people disrupting my business."

Lillian's pulse surged, and she gripped Matthew's hand.

Jackson narrowed his eyes in a hateful glare directed at Matthew and spat a curse. "Take the three girls and leave." He stepped inside and disappeared.

Serena tugged Lillian toward the bottom of the steps.

A middle-aged woman in a flimsy red robe stepped into the doorway and pushed the first girl outside. She looked about ten and wore a plain green dress and white apron. Her light brown hair had been braided, and the long plait hung over her shoulder. She froze and stared out at them with wide brown eyes.

The woman in the red robe pushed out a second girl, who looked younger. She wore a dirty white cap over her black curly hair and had large brown eyes. She gripped the first girl's hand, bit her lip, and looked down at her bare feet.

Lillian slipped her arm around Serena's back.

The woman grabbed a third girl and pushed her out to the top step, then stepped back and closed the door. The little girl brushed a long lock of wavy blond hair from her face and stared at them with sky-blue eyes.

Serena gasped. "It's Alice! I know it is!"

Lillian held tight to her sister's hand. "Wait. You must be calm. She's already frightened."

Alice huddled with the other two girls, her anxious gaze darting from one face to the next.

Josephine nodded to Serena. "Come with me."

Lillian released Serena's hand and followed her up the steps.

Josephine knelt in front of them. "Hello, girls. My name is Josephine. I would like to take you to a safe place where you'll be well cared for. Can you tell me your names?"

The girls exchanged hesitant glances.

"It's all right," Josephine continued in a gentle voice. "We're here to help you."

The first girl slowly raised her head. "I'm Cathy Newman, and this is Daisy Simmons." She pointed to the second girl.

Josephine smiled. "I'm glad to meet you." She turned to the blonde. "What about you, my dear? What's your name?"

Lillian held her breath, her heart pounding in her throat.

The little blonde looked at Josephine with a trembling chin. "Mary . . . my name is Mary Graham."

Serena stifled a gasp and knelt in front of Mary. The girl's eyes widened, and she pulled back.

Lillian laid her hand on her sister's shoulder, then directed her gaze to her niece. "We're glad to see you, Mary, and to meet your friends. We've been looking for you since you left the Foundling Hospital."

Mary sent her a curious glance, but the mention of the Foundling Hospital seemed to calm her.

Serena held out her hand to Mary. "Come with us. We have a carriage waiting down the street."

Mary slowly reached out and took hold of Serena's hand. Joy burst across Serena's face, and tears ran down her cheeks. Anne took charge of the other two girls, and they followed Serena and Mary down the steps.

Josephine's face glowed as she lifted her hand and called the women closer. "Thank you, ladies. Your fervent prayers and courageous stand have helped secure freedom for these three girls. Well done! As you return home to the warmth and safety of your own hearth, remember the women and girls who were not blessed with freedom today and pray for them. I hope you'll also consider joining me as we continue working toward liberation and safety for all women and girls who are caught in such painful circumstances."

The women applauded, and several came forward to thank Josephine.

Matthew met Lillian at the bottom of the stairs, his eyes shining. "You found your niece and reunited her with her mother."

"*We* found her."

He grinned. "Yes, we did."

Her throat tightened as she looked up at him. "I'm grateful, Matthew, for everything you've done, especially for your articles. They've made a great impact." She glanced down the street. Serena and Alice still held hands as they walked toward the corner where their carriage waited.

His gaze followed hers. "I should let you go. Your sister and niece need you."

"Yes." But she hesitated, wishing she didn't have to leave. "When can I see you?"

A tender longing filled his eyes. "I'd go with you now if I could, but I must speak to Mrs. Butler and get a quote from her speech, and I should interview a few others. Mr. Stead wants this article right away. He's holding off printing tomorrow's issue so we can include what happened here."

Pushing aside her hesitations, she spoke from her heart. "Can you come tomorrow? There's so much I want to say."

He reached for her hand. "Yes."

She wove her fingers through his. "Would you like to join us for breakfast at eight? Is that too early?" Her cheeks warmed. She sounded so eager.

He grinned. "Eight sounds perfect, and I'll bring you a copy of the *Gazette*."

"Wonderful. I'll look forward to it."

He gave her hand a gentle squeeze. "Take care. I'll see you then."

23

Janelle reread the last few lines of the final *Gazette* article, then leaned back in her office chair. Neil Parker, the matron's assistant, had been arrested and confessed to selling five young girls to brothel owners. All those girls had been freed, and the men who had purchased them had been jailed and would stand trial along with Parker.

Relief flowed through Janelle, and she closed her eyes. *Thank you, Lord.*

Three of the girls had been rescued in a most amazing fashion by a group of women, including the mother and aunt of one of the girls. The women had staged a protest in front of the brothel to demand the release of all the underage girls being held there.

Janelle wished she could've been there to see those brave women take their stand. Josephine Butler had been instrumental in leading the protest. Reading her impassioned speech quoted in the article had sent goosebumps down Janelle's arms. She was obviously a woman of deep faith and strong convictions. Janelle would have to look her up and see what else she could learn about her.

A knock sounded at her office door, and she called, "Come in."

Jonas stepped into the office, looking handsome and eager to see her. He held up a small leather-bound book, one they had reserved and picked up at the library yesterday. "I read the first two chapters on the way. It's amazing."

Janelle's heart thumped. She rose and quickly stepped around her desk. She'd taken the other book and skimmed the first half without finding anything helpful.

He crossed to her side and opened *A Foundling's Tale: Lost, Sold, and Redeemed.* "Look at these chapter titles. I think they make it clear the author, Mary Alice, is one of the girls we're looking for." He turned to the table of contents.

Janelle's gaze skimmed down the list. *Loved but Born into Poverty; Life with My Country Family; Return to the Foundling Hospital; A Day in the Life of a Foundling; Stolen Away in the Night; Sold to the Lady's Slipper; The Drudgery of a Brothel Scullery Maid; Valiant Protest in the Street; Rescued to a New Life* . . .

He met her gaze with a triumphant smile. "See what I mean?"

Janelle nodded. "I've spent the last hour online reading the other articles in the series. Those chapter titles fit the story perfectly."

"This is a really amazing piece of history." He reached for her hand, a sincere look in his eyes. "I've been thinking . . . this story would make a great focus for a documentary."

Janelle's mind spun. "You mean the gala film?"

"No. This would be a separate project, a longer film that could show the full story of what happened to Mary Alice and the other girls."

Anxiety tightened Janelle's stomach, and she bit her lip.

"Trust me, Janelle." He wove his fingers through hers. "I can handle it in a way that shows Neil Parker is the true villain of this story, not the Foundling Hospital."

She slipped her hand from his and turned toward the window. How could he suggest featuring one of the darkest chapters in the Foundling Hospital's history in a documentary? What would people think if they admitted girls in their care had been sold to work in brothels?

Jonas stepped up next to her. "A documentary about human trafficking with a personal focus like this could really grab people's hearts and make a powerful impact."

Janelle crossed her arms. "It could also cast the museum in a very negative light. We're barely holding on financially. If we lose any more support, we'll have to cut staff and programs. We might even have to close our doors."

His excitement dimmed, and he was quiet for a few seconds. "I know it sounds risky, but I'm sure I can write the script in a way that vindicates the rest of the staff and focuses on how the girls were rescued and went on to lead productive lives. I can even end by weaving in the museum's important work with youth today." He laid his hand on her shoulder. "If I don't do it, someone else might find this information and question why it hasn't been acknowledged by the museum. Let me tell the story, and I'll shape it in a way that puts the Foundling Hospital and the museum in the best light possible."

Janelle rubbed her arms, wishing she had the ability to see into the future and know how the public would respond to seeing the story played out in a film.

He slipped his arm around her shoulders. "Why don't I outline the script and show you my ideas? I won't move forward with it until we talk again."

Before she could reply, the office door opened, and Olivia walked in. As soon as she saw them, her eyes widened, and her steps stalled. "Oh, sorry."

Jonas pulled his arm away and stepped to the side.

Janelle's face warmed. "It's all right. Come in."

"I was just coming to get my lunch from my backpack." She started across the office.

Jonas reached for *A Foundling's Tale*. "We got a copy of the book that was written by one of the girls who was taken from the Foundling Hospital back in 1885."

Olivia paused and sent him a curious look. "A girl wrote it?"

He nodded. "When she was older."

"Oh, I get it." She pulled out her lunch sack.

"Now that we know her name," Jonas said, "would you like to look for information about her while you're working on the transcription project?"

"I guess I could."

"Thanks. That would be great." Janelle crossed to her desk. "Let me write down her name and the dates we have. That should help in the search." She checked the book, wrote the information on a sticky note, and handed it to Olivia.

She read the note aloud. "'Alice Catherine Dunsmore, born 14 June 1877. Baptismal name: Mary Graham. Admitted to the Foundling Hospital 18 September 1877.'"

"Check the general register for the year she was admitted," Janelle advised, "and then look and see if there is an appeal letter from her mother. Maybe check the medical records too."

"I'll work on it after lunch. I'm going to eat downstairs with Lisa."

Janelle nodded. "Okay. Thanks."

Olivia returned a slight smile, then walked out of the office, her lunch and sticky note in hand.

⌒

Later that afternoon, a knock sounded at Janelle's office door. She looked up and called, "Come in."

Olivia sauntered in and returned the sticky note, new information scribbled on the front and back. "I found Alice Dunsmore's records. It said her token was returned to her aunt to give to her mother. But then there was another note that said she donated the token to the museum in 1927."

Janelle blinked. "She gave her token back?"

Olivia nodded.

"Did the records say why?"

"She sent it with a letter and a copy of her book." Olivia glanced at the small leather-bound book on Janelle's desk.

Janelle followed her gaze and sucked in a breath. "We have a copy of her book in our collection?"

Olivia nodded. "That's what the records say. Her letter explains everything. The link is on there." She nodded to the sticky note.

"Thanks. I'll take a look." She spent the next half hour reading those records and the letter. The last item on the corner of the sticky note read *Token #942*.

Janelle left her office and took the stairs down to the cool and cavernous archive room. She walked down the aisle, scanning the cabinet numbers, then stopped and pulled open one of the drawers. Rows of small, clear glass boxes filled the shallow felt-lined space. Each one held an artifact from the Foundling Hospital's history. Some would be put on display in exhibits, while others remained safely tucked away, holding their stories until someone needed them in the future. She carefully ran her finger down the row, searching for number 942.

She spotted the box, and her heart pinged. She placed it on the table and lifted the lid. A round metal disk with a hole drilled at the top lay inside. A faded red ribbon looped through the hole. The words *Remember My Love* were etched on the face of the token and surrounded by two hearts and swirling vines.

She studied the intricate design, remembering what she'd read about Mary Alice's mother and aunt. Their love for her had never wavered. They'd refused to give up the search until she was found and returned to their care. That was love well worth remembering.

24

2023

Janelle crossed the lobby of her building and pushed the button to call the lift. She turned to Jonas. "Is it okay if we stop by Maggie and Dan's for a minute? I want to thank Olivia and show her the photo of Mary Alice's token."

He nodded. "Good idea. I think she'd like to see it."

The lift door slid open, and Jonas held it back so Janelle could go first.

She stepped in, grateful he'd suggested picking up dinner and sharing it at her flat while they read more of Mary Alice's story.

They stepped out on the third floor and crossed the landing to Maggie and Dan's door. She knocked and waited a few seconds.

The door slowly opened, and Cole looked out.

"Is your mum home?" Janelle asked.

He nodded and pulled the door open wider. "She's in the living room."

Janelle stepped inside, followed by Jonas.

Dan, Maggie, and Olivia turned toward them. Maggie's face was flushed, and Dan's dark eyes snapped. Olivia stared at her dad with rigid shoulders and glittering eyes.

Janelle swallowed. They had obviously walked into the middle of something. Jonas sent her a questioning glance, silently asking if they should stay or go.

"Sorry." Janelle turned to Maggie. "Should we come back later?"

Maggie sighed. "No, it's all right. What can we do for you?"

"Jonas and I just wanted to stop by and thank Olivia for her help today."

No one said anything for a few seconds, then Dan huffed and motioned toward Olivia. "She helped you with something?"

Olivia crossed her arms and glared toward the windows, anger and hurt flickering in her eyes.

"Yes," Janelle continued. "She has good research skills, and she used them to help us find some important records today."

Maggie nodded. "I'm glad she's been helpful."

Janelle turned to Olivia. "With the information you gave me, I was able to locate Mary Alice's letter and token as well as her book. I took some photos." She pulled out her phone and crossed the room toward the girl.

Olivia looked down at Janelle's screen. Her hardened expression eased as she viewed the image of the round metal token with the words *Remember My Love* etched on the front. "Her mum left this with her?"

"Yes. Jonas and I are going to read more of her story tonight."

"Her mum must have really loved her." She sniffed and lifted her gaze to Dan. "Unlike some parents."

Dan sighed. "Olivia, you know we love you. How many times do we have to say it before you believe us?"

"If you loved me, then you wouldn't take away my phone."

"If you'd stick to the rules, we wouldn't have to."

"Oh, you and your rules! That's all you care about!"

Dan shook his head. "That's not true. Maggie and I are trying to do what we think is best. And right now, you're showing us you're not able to handle your phone as you should."

"You just don't want me to talk to my friends."

"We told you—you can talk to them during the day, but not at night."

"But Tony works during the day. The only time he can talk is at night."

"You have the phone until nine. There must be some time he can phone before that."

She glared at Dan. "There isn't! And now he thinks I don't care!"

Dan closed his eyes, obviously trying to control his temper. "Olivia, you have to follow the rules if you want to keep your phone."

"You don't understand. You're ruining my life!"

Dan's eyes flashed. "That's enough. Go to your room. And don't come out until you settle down and can talk to us in a respectful tone of voice."

"Fine!" Olivia marched down the hall, and two seconds later, her door slammed.

Maggie lifted her eyes to the ceiling. "Lord, help us. What are we going to do with that girl!"

Janelle sent her a sympathetic look and whispered, "What happened?"

Maggie lowered her voice. "She snuck out here again last night to talk to Tony. When we confronted her, she said she's tired of Dan checking her calls and texts, so she cleared her whole history."

Dan held up her phone. "That's why I'm taking it away."

Janelle swallowed. No wonder Olivia was upset. That phone was her social lifeline. But she could understand why Dan and Maggie needed to give Olivia consequences for her actions.

Jonas caught Janelle's eye and looked toward the door.

Janelle returned a slight nod. "We should give you time to work this out."

Maggie walked them to the door and rubbed her forehead. "I never realized having teenagers could be this hard."

Janelle gave her a hug. "I'll pray for you, and hopefully tomorrow will be a better day."

"You're still taking her to the museum tomorrow morning, right?"

"Yes. I'll pick her up at eight thirty."

Maggie heaved a sigh. "Thanks. I hope she'll be in better spirits by then."

Janelle smiled and nodded. "See you tomorrow."

Jonas settled on the couch next to Janelle, resting his shoulder against hers. The more time he spent with her, the more certain he felt about pursuing their relationship. Janelle had a depth and sincerity he admired. Their shared faith was also a plus, and he couldn't deny the attraction he felt whenever they were together. She was special and well worth the pursuit.

They'd finished their dinner of fish and chips and were enjoying a bowl of fresh strawberries while they talked about what they'd discovered that day. He'd steered away from discussing the documentary. No need to pressure her. He had time to convince her that it was a worthy project. Instead, he decided to focus on his plans for the fundraising film.

"I'd like to use some child actors in the historical part of the film. Do any of the museum staff have kids who are six to ten years old? Using volunteers rather than paid actors would help us stay on budget."

Janelle nodded. "That's a good idea, and we have costumes at the museum you could use." She thought for a moment. "Ruth has identical twin daughters who are eight, and Peter has two boys in that age range." She smiled. "Maybe Maggie and Dan would let Cole and Caleb take part."

"Those two have a lot of energy. They'd probably be great in front of a camera."

"Do you need any teenagers? Maybe we could involve Olivia. Acting in a film might help her take her mind off Tony."

He gave a slow nod, his thoughts traveling back to the argument between Olivia, Dan, and Maggie. "Olivia seems obsessed with that boy. What do you know about him?"

Janelle relayed what Olivia had told her about Tony the day they'd had lunch together, along with what Maggie had said.

Jonas's shoulders tensed as he listened. "She's never met him in person?"

"No. He doesn't live in London."

He shook his head. "That doesn't sound good—especially the way she describes him liking everything she likes and being so sympathetic about her parents' divorce."

"Why is that a problem?"

"It sounds off, and it makes me wonder if he's really a sixteen-year-old boy . . . or someone older."

Janelle's brow creased. "Really?"

He nodded. "When I was doing research on the film for the International Centre for Missing and Exploited Children, I watched a few videos they use to teach online safety to teens. Some of the warning signs they show in those videos fit the situation with Olivia and Tony."

Janelle sent him a doubtful look. "I know she spends a lot of time texting and talking to him, but don't all teenagers do that?"

"Maybe, but the way Olivia is reacting to Dan and Maggie about him seems out of proportion. It's like he's got an emotional hold on her. The term they use in the training is *groomed*. We should probably mention it to Dan and Maggie."

Janelle grimaced. "I hate to bring more conflict into their relationship."

"If Tony has bad intentions, then Olivia needs to be protected."

Janelle clicked her tongue and sent him a doubtful glance. "Are you sure? I remember what you told me about your friend Sarah. I understand it's a sensitive subject for you."

He stiffened. "I know what I'm talking about. And not just because of what happened to Sarah. I did a lot of research about human trafficking, and I know how teens are targeted and taken. It's a serious problem, Janelle."

She studied him a moment more, then gave a slow nod. "Okay."

He shifted his gaze away and took a drink of lemonade. Janelle didn't seem convinced Olivia might truly be in danger, but he couldn't let this go. If he was right about Tony, the potential consequences were too steep. He'd have to talk to Maggie and Dan. If he ignored it and something happened to Olivia, he'd never forgive himself.

~

Janelle glanced at the file on her desk containing the research she and Jonas had collected, then shifted her gaze to the photo of Mary Alice's token on her laptop screen. After reading the *Gazette* articles and Mary Alice's book, she had the full story of what had happened to those girls in 1885, and what they'd suffered had gripped her heart.

That morning, Jonas had shown her his outline for the script of the documentary he wanted to make. He wanted her approval and support to move forward with the project and enter it into a film festival, using the information they'd found about Mary Alice and her family.

Her stomach tensed. She had to speak to Amanda, but she dreaded confronting her boss. Was Amanda aware of what had happened back in 1885? What would she say when she learned Jonas wanted to make a documentary including that information?

She closed her eyes. *Lord, I need courage. In my heart, I believe Jonas is right. We need to be honest. But if Amanda knows and has been hiding it . . .*

She blew out a breath. Worrying ahead of time was not going to solve the problem. She had to face it head-on and trust the Lord to guide her conversation with Amanda.

She tapped in Amanda's number and lifted the phone to her ear. Amanda answered, they exchanged greetings, and Janelle listened to Amanda's update on the twins, who were still in the NICU.

At a lull in the conversation, Janelle shifted in her chair. "There's something we need to talk about."

"Oh dear. That doesn't sound good. Is someone on staff giving you a hard time?" Amanda's voice carried a light, humorous tone.

"No. This is something more significant."

"Okay. What is it?"

Janelle steeled herself. "When Jonas and I were researching Foundling Hospital history for the gala film, we came across some information that's quite . . . surprising."

"What did you find?" Her tone was totally serious now.

Janelle gave a short summary, then held her breath, waiting for Amanda's reply.

"Are you sure this is true?" Amanda sounded genuinely surprised.

"Yes. We found the same information in a few different sources, including a firsthand account from one of the girls who was sold. When she was an adult, she wrote a book about her life. What she wrote matched what we read in the *Gazette* articles."

Silence buzzed along the phone line for a few seconds, then Janelle forged ahead. "I remember there was a guest archivist here from Canada a few months ago. She asked you about an incident in 1885. You told her a girl ran away, but she was later found and returned to her family."

"Yes, I remember."

"I think that girl was the one who was sold to a brothel."

Amanda pulled in a sharp breath. "Are you serious?"

"Yes, very serious."

"I had no idea."

Janelle sank back into her chair. "Thank goodness."

"Wait! Did you think I knew about this and was trying to keep it hidden?"

"I didn't know what to think. You're the expert on Foundling Hospital history. It seemed odd that you wouldn't be aware of it."

Amanda sighed. "Some children *did* run away. We have records of that, but I never knew any of them were sold into such terrible situations."

"How could we have never heard about this?"

"I'm not sure. Maybe it was purposely hidden by the staff, or they hoped it would be forgotten."

That made sense. No doubt the staff regretted what had happened to those girls and wished it would fade from everyone's minds.

"Do you remember how shocking it was when we discovered the milk scandal in 2015?" Amanda's tone grew more intense.

"I wasn't working at the museum then, but I heard about it."

"We had to call in a private research group. The cost was outrageous. The media blew the story out of proportion, and there was a huge drop in donations. Even though it happened more than a century ago, it gave a negative impression of our work."

Janelle swallowed. "Now that we know what happened in 1885, we have to decide how to handle it."

"There's no need to do anything about this right now."

Janelle swiveled toward the window, praying for courage. "Jonas wants to include what we learned in a documentary."

Amanda gasped. "No! Absolutely not! It would shock our donors and cast a permanent dark cloud over the museum."

"I'm not talking about the fundraising film he's making for the gala. He wants to make a separate, longer film that would focus on Mary Alice's story."

"That is out of the question. We are not paying for a documentary, especially not one that would damage our reputation."

"He's not asking us to fund the documentary."

She huffed. "Good, because we can't afford it. And I'm not about to give approval for a project like that."

Janelle braced herself. "He doesn't really need our approval or permission. The information is available to the public online and in the British Library and National Archives. Anyone could find it and use it however they want."

Amanda made a frustrated noise in her throat.

"I'm sorry. I know this is hard to hear with everything else you have going on."

"You have to convince him to drop the idea. We can't risk this getting out, not when our budget is strained to the breaking point."

Janelle's thoughts scrambled. "What if someone else discovers what happened and releases it in a damaging way?"

"I'll be back in a few months. Let me handle it then."

"Can we risk waiting? Wouldn't it be better to work with Jonas? He says he can show this in a balanced way and make it clear we're committed to honestly portraying our history rather than hiding the negative parts of our past."

"And you believe that?" Amanda's high-pitched voice conveyed her rising frustration.

Janelle pulled in a calming breath. "I believe he can make

a documentary that's honest yet still gain sympathy and support."

"Janelle, human trafficking is a hot-button issue! Announcing our involvement, even if it was in the past, will hurt us. I'm sure of it."

"But if we try to hide this, and it becomes known, won't that cast even more doubt in everyone's mind?"

"I can't make the decision right now!" Amanda's harsh tone made it clear the discussion was over.

Janelle closed her eyes. Was it Amanda's decision to make, or was it hers? Did she have the courage to ask that question? She might be the acting director, but Amanda would eventually return. And when she did, Janelle's response to this situation could determine her future at the museum.

25

The evening of the rescue, Lillian descended the back stairs to the kitchen. It was after nine, and her cook, maid, and housekeeper had retreated to their own rooms for the night. She was hoping for tea and something sweet, but she didn't want to bother any of the staff at that late hour.

She filled the kettle and put it on the stove, then opened the cupboard and scanned the shelves. She spied a biscuit tin and popped off the lid. The scent of cinnamon and ginger tickled her nose. Ginger biscuits, her favorite. She placed the tin on the worktable and took a teacup from the cabinet.

Leaning back against the counter, she pondered the events of the day with a sense of awe. *Thank you, Lord, for all the answered prayers!*

As soon as they'd arrived home, Serena had pulled Lillian aside. "I want to tell Alice I'm her mother, but I don't want to overwhelm her."

Lillian leaned closer. "So much has happened today. Let's wait and see how she adjusts to all the changes. I'm sure the Lord will make it clear when the time is right."

Serena gave Lillian a hug. "It won't be easy to wait, but I believe you're right."

They gave the girls a simple dinner, then with the help of Mrs. Pringle and Bessie, they bathed the girls and helped them change into borrowed nightgowns. Serena and Lillian decided to let them all stay together, hoping it would ease their fears. They moved another bed into Serena's room, so Mary could sleep with Ellen, and Cathy and Daisy could share the other bed. As the sun set, they'd tucked the girls into their beds, said prayers, and kissed each one good night. Serena had insisted on staying with them until they all fell asleep.

A wave of gratitude flowed through Lillian as she considered the progress Serena had made since coming to stay with her. Her health had been restored, and her faith had been renewed. She seemed ready to leave much of her sorrow behind and step into her role as mother now that she had the support needed to love and care for her daughter. Together, she and Serena would forge new lives for the girls.

It wasn't only Serena who had been transformed in the past few months. Bringing her sister home and searching for Alice had given Lillian a new focus. That had led to meeting Matthew and rescuing Ellen and the other girls. How good God was to lead her in this new direction, help heal her heart, and give her hope and a future. Tears misted her eyes, and she offered a heartfelt prayer of thanks.

The teakettle whistled, and she prepared her cup of tea.

Serena walked into the kitchen. "I thought you might be down here." She studied Lillian's face. "Is everything all right?"

"Yes, these are happy tears." Lillian brushed the moisture from her cheek. "Would you like some tea?"

"That sounds perfect." Serena took a cup from the cupboard, and Lillian poured the hot water into her sister's cup.

Serena sank onto a stool at the worktable in the center of the kitchen. "You should see them snuggled up in their beds. They look like little angels."

Lillian slid the tin of ginger biscuits toward Serena. All children looked like angels when they were fast asleep. But she didn't want to say anything that would dampen Serena's joy. "I'm glad they're settled for the night."

"I know what you're thinking."

Lillian sent her an innocent look. "What is that?"

"Caring for them won't always be as easy as it was tonight. I'm sure the hardships they've suffered will make their adjustment here a challenge. But Alice is home with me at last, and that's what matters most."

"I'm happy for you, Serena."

"I know I can't make up for the time we've lost, but I pray that being together will bring healing to her heart and mine." Serena took a sip of tea. "What do you think about calling her Mary Alice? That way she could keep both names."

"That's a lovely idea, but I think you should ask her and be sure she's comfortable with both names."

"Perhaps when I tell her she is my daughter and explain some of the story, that might be the time to talk about her name. I'm content to call her Mary for now."

"Yes, there's no need to rush."

Serena's eyes filled. "For eight years I've grieved the loss of my daughter and longed to bring her home from the Foundling Hospital. With the upheaval and uncertainty of my life, I couldn't imagine how it could ever happen . . . but you made it possible."

Lillian's throat tightened. "I'm very glad she's here with us."

"How can I ever repay you? Your kindness and forgiveness have given my daughter back to me."

Lillian shook her head. "Seeing you and Alice together is all the repayment I want."

Serena's eyes glowed as she looked at Lillian. "I'll never forget what you've done for me and my daughter. No sister has ever shown more love."

Lillian reached for Serena and gave her a hug. "We're blessed to have each other, and now these dear girls. Together we'll love and guide them toward a brighter future."

~

Matthew stopped at the open doorway to Lillian's dining room while the butler announced his arrival.

Lillian's gaze darted to meet his, and she smiled as she rose. "Good morning, Matthew. Please come and join us."

He nodded and returned a smile just for her, then glanced around the table. "Morning, everyone."

Serena and Ellen said hello, while the other three girls sent him curious looks.

"Girls," Serena said, "this is Mr. Matthew McGivern. He is our good friend and a journalist with the *Pall Mall Gazette*. When someone greets you, it's polite to respond in like manner. Let's say, 'Good morning, Mr. McGivern.'"

The four girls responded in unison, with some giggles.

He grinned. "What a pleasure to see you all looking so well and enjoying such a fine breakfast."

Smiles lit the girls' faces.

Lillian led him to the buffet. Matthew's gaze traveled over the silver serving dishes displaying various breakfast items, and his mouth watered.

She offered him a plate. "Please choose whatever you'd like."

"Thank you." He handed her a folded copy of the *Gazette* and accepted the plate. "The events of yesterday are featured front and center."

She opened the newspaper and read the headline, "'Three Underaged Girls Saved from White Chapel Brothel.'" Her eyes skimmed the page.

He waited, eager to see her reaction to the article.

Finally, she looked up. "This is brilliant, Matthew."

"Thank you. Mr. Stead said he'll publish the article on Mercy House tomorrow, then he wants one more article to conclude the series."

"One more?"

"Yes. He wants me to return to the Foundling Hospital and write an article that will help restore their reputation."

Lillian glanced away with a slight frown.

"I know you have reason to doubt the staff's intentions after the way you were treated by the matron, but Parker told the police he worked alone to alter the records and make the arrangements to sell the girls."

"No one else was involved?"

"Not according to Parker." Matthew added a slice of bacon to his plate. "Mr. Stead is personal friends with some of the men on the Foundling Hospital's board of governors. He doesn't want to make it difficult for them to raise the funds they need to care for the children."

Lillian gave a slow nod. "I understand. I suppose if the matron and the rest of the staff were not aware of what was happening, then we shouldn't hold it against them." She lifted the lid on the serving dish of the eggs so he could help himself. "I'd like to go with you to the Foundling Hospital."

He nodded, pleased with her request. He'd wanted to invite her but was hesitant to ask her to leave her sister and the girls on their first full day together. "I was planning to go later this morning. Would that fit into your plans for the day?"

She thought for a moment. "Yes. I'm sure Serena and Bessie can handle things here." She ushered him to the empty seat next to hers. They both sat down and enjoyed breakfast with Serena and the girls. The conversation ranged from those who liked eggs and those who didn't, to who kicked more in their sleep, and when they might go out and explore Lillian's private garden. Cathy seemed to be the most talkative, while Mary and

Daisy were quieter. Ellen joined with the girls' conversation as though she'd been their friend all along.

After breakfast, Lillian called for the carriage, and they rode to the Foundling Hospital. A young woman greeted them at the door and ushered them to the matron's office.

As soon as Mrs. Stark recognized Matthew, her expression grew stony. She narrowed her eyes and shifted her gaze to Lillian. "And you are?"

"Mrs. Lillian Freemont."

Recognition flashed in the matron's eyes, and she looked away.

"I spoke to you in April to ask about my niece, Alice Dunsmore, who was renamed Mary Graham. You told me she'd died as an infant, but I learned that wasn't true."

Mrs. Stark gave a solemn nod. "Yes, I remember meeting you." She shifted her stern gaze to Matthew. "You are the author of that . . . scandalous series of articles in the *Gazette*."

"I wouldn't call my articles scandalous. I'd say they've raised awareness of a serious issue and exposed men who needed to be arrested for their crimes."

Her mouth puckered as though she'd tasted a lemon. "Mr. Parker is no longer associated with this institution. That man is a thief and a deceiver. I'm sorry I didn't realize what he was doing sooner. I never would have allowed it to continue."

Matthew nodded. "I understand. We've spoken to the police, and Mr. Parker confirmed no one else on staff knew he was altering records and selling girls to brothels."

"Of course we didn't know!" Mrs. Stark raised her hand to her chest. "It's shocking. I don't know how we'll ever recover from such a disgrace."

"That's why I've come," Matthew continued in a calm and steady voice. "My editor, W. T. Stead, wants to make sure our readers understand that one man with evil intentions does not represent the entire staff of the Foundling Hospital. He asked me to interview you and write an article that will highlight the good work you're doing to help restore the hospital's reputation."

Mrs. Stark blinked. "Oh, well . . . that would be very much appreciated."

Matthew nodded. "We know the Foundling Hospital has a long history of exceptional care for children in need, and we want to support you in that work."

"Very well." The color returned to Mrs. Stark's face. "I'd be happy to answer your questions." She nodded to Matthew. "How can I help?"

Matthew asked her a series of questions and jotted her answers in his notebook. When they were finished, Mrs. Stark turned to Lillian. "I apologize for the misinformation I gave you about your niece. I can imagine how upsetting that must have been." Her tone and expression sounded sincere. "I'm glad to know she has been found and returned to her mother."

Lillian hesitated, the struggle to release her resentment toward the matron clear. She pulled in a deep breath and met Mrs. Stark's gaze. "We're very glad she has been rescued and is safely home."

Mrs. Stark rose. "There's something I'd like to give you." She turned to the shelf behind her desk and ran her finger across the row of ledgers. She pulled out one and turned several pages. "When your sister left her daughter with us, she left a token."

Lillian straightened. "Yes, that's right."

Mrs. Stark returned the ledger and pulled out a box from a lower shelf. "They made a note of it in your niece's records." She opened the box and thumbed through several folded packets. "Here it is."

Lillian leaned forward as Mrs. Stark unfolded the paper and took out a round golden disk with a slim red ribbon looped through the hole. The matron held it out toward them.

Matthew scanned the writing on the token. *Remember My Love* was written across the front, along with two small hearts and a few flourishes. Matthew glanced at Lillian. Had she seen it before?

Lillian nodded, and moisture glittered in her eyes. "My sister has one that matches."

The matron handed her the token. "Please return it to your sister and her daughter with my good wishes."

Lillian held it in her open hand, a look of wonder in her eyes. "I'm sure she'll be grateful to have it. Thank you."

"You're welcome." The matron cleared her throat, obviously touched by the exchange. "Now, is there anything else I can do for you? Any other questions?"

Matthew picked up his pencil again. "Are there any final words you'd like me to include in the article?"

Mrs. Stark thought for a moment, then said, "Our goal has always been to care for vulnerable young children and give them a safe and stable place to live and receive the training they need to become healthy, productive adults. We look forward to continuing that work with the faithful support of our many friends and benefactors. We are grateful for their trust as we endeavor to do all we can for the children."

Matthew nodded. "Very well said." He rose. "This article should appear in the *Gazette* the day after tomorrow."

Lillian slipped the token into her reticule and stood beside him. "Thank you, Mrs. Stark."

"You're most welcome. Thank you for coming and for giving us an opportunity to restore our good name."

Lillian gazed out the carriage window as the coachman passed through the gate into Regent's Park. She turned to Matthew. "Did you tell the coachman to take us through the park?"

He grinned, a mischievous look in his eyes. "I was hoping we might have time to stop and take a stroll through the gardens."

"What about your article?"

"It's already half written in my mind. It shouldn't take more than an hour or two to get it down on paper."

How thoughtful he was to plan this stop for them. "A stroll in the park sounds lovely."

He lifted his hand and rapped twice on the side of the carriage. The coachman slowed and pulled to the side of the road. Matthew opened the door and helped Lillian down.

He looked up at Mr. Fields. "Would you please return for us in one hour?"

"Yes, sir." He nodded and touched his cap, then the carriage rolled away.

Lillian glanced across the park, admiring the tree-lined paths, manicured lawns, and flower beds filled with colorful summer blooms. "Oh, it's beautiful. I haven't been here in ages."

Matthew offered her his arm. "Shall we?"

She slipped her arm through his. Walking side by side, they set off down the path. Up ahead, a plume of water rose above a large fountain. The soothing sounds of splashing water and birds singing in the trees calmed her spirit. They'd been through so much in the past few days, it was a pleasure to put it aside and soak in the beauty of nature.

She looked up at him. "I'm very glad you thought of this."

"I was hoping it might give us time to talk."

Her cheeks warmed as she thought about what she needed to say. "I've wanted to speak to you as well."

He sent her an earnest look. "Lillian, I know that you—"

"Please, may I go first?"

He sent her a concerned look but nodded. "Of course."

She paused to organize her thoughts. "I've been thinking about what you said to me the day we spoke in my garden."

"About my wanting to be more than a friend?"

"Yes. And I wanted you to know the reason why I asked for more time to consider my answer."

He gave a hesitant nod.

"It's not because there is anything lacking in your character or behavior toward me. You've shown true loyalty and kindness in many ways. I've had time to consider my reaction, and I realize I've let pain from the past and fear of the future cloud my thoughts."

Understanding filled his eyes.

"But I don't want pain or fear to guide my life any longer. I know there are risks involved in opening my heart to you." She looked up at him. "But you've proven you're a caring and wise man. So, if it's not too late, my answer is yes. I hope we can be much more than friends."

His eyes danced. "Too late? Never!" He held tight to her hand, and they stepped off the path and into a shady alcove of trees.

Lillian's heartbeat sped up.

Matthew faced her and took both her hands in his. "Lillian, from the first day we met, I realized you were someone very special. I didn't acknowledge my attraction to you because I doubted there was any possibility you could ever care for me. But as I've gotten to know you, I've learned you are a warmhearted and generous woman who would not judge me for my past. Your kindness and courage, as well as your trust in the Lord, shine through in all you do, and that makes me eager to spend more time with you and see where the Lord will lead us."

Lillian's throat tightened. "I don't know that I deserve any of those beautiful compliments."

He gazed into her eyes. "You do. And I look forward to pointing out those qualities in the days ahead, so you'll see them too." He lifted her hand to his lips and kissed her fingers.

She stepped toward him, and he encircled her in his arms and held her close. She rested against his chest with a deep sigh of contentment. Matthew was a gift from God—her second chance to love and be loved.

26

Jonas popped the lid off his lunch, and the spicy scent of chicken curry filled the air. Janelle had called in the order so they could eat together in the museum staff lunchroom. He smiled across the table at her. "What did you order?"

"The same as you." She didn't look up.

He studied her a moment. "Janelle, is something wrong?"

She glanced around the lunchroom, then lowered her voice. "I spoke to Amanda. She said she'd never heard the details of what happened to Mary Alice and the other girls."

"Good. I'm glad she wasn't trying to keep it under wraps."

Janelle nodded, but something was obviously still bothering her. "She's upset, and she's concerned about the information getting out. When I told her you wanted to include it in a documentary . . ." She clenched her teeth and shook her head.

His gut twisted. "What exactly did she say?"

"She's convinced it would paint the museum in a negative light and hurt us financially. And we can't take another hit to our donations. Our budget is stretched to the limit now."

Jonas stared at her. "She's not canceling the contract for the gala film, is she?"

"No, but you can't include anything about Mary Alice or the other girls who were sold."

286

Jonas sat back, disappointment coursing through him. He'd been tossing around the idea of adding a short scene to the gala film that would mention Mary Alice, but that was out of the question now.

He focused on Janelle. "I see her point about not wanting it in the gala film. But a longer documentary could make it clear the museum wasn't withholding this information and that you're committed to honestly portraying the past."

Janelle lifted her hands. "I believe you, and I tried to explain that, but she wasn't convinced."

Jonas's thoughts spun. His work on the gala film was moving ahead without a hitch. In the last two days, he'd shifted his focus to revising the documentary script. He'd hoped to get started filming soon. This was a story that needed to be told, and not just for the chance to win a prize. He wanted to support ongoing efforts against human trafficking and make sure what happened to those girls was not forgotten.

He met her gaze. "I want to make this documentary."

"I know, but Amanda is totally against it."

"You're the museum's acting director. Shouldn't you be the one who decides if you'll offer the support of the museum?"

She sent him a pained look. "You want me to go against Amanda?"

What happened to those girls was important, but he couldn't let it damage his relationship with Janelle. "I'm sorry. I know this puts you in an awkward position."

"If I offer the museum's support, Amanda will be furious. But if I don't, I'll be letting you down—and not just you, everyone who supports the museum and trusts us to accurately portray our history."

His heart clenched, and he reached for her hand. "I know there's no easy answer. We've got time. Let's pray about it and wait for the Lord to show us the best path forward."

She tightened her hold on his hand, still looking uncertain. "I've always said I believe God guides us when we pray, but . . . this is hard."

He hated causing the worry he saw in her eyes. His thoughts shifted to Matthew McGivern, the journalist who'd been arrested and jailed for his efforts to prevent any more girls from being sold to brothels. He'd shown great courage in taking a stand for what was right, penning those articles, and rescuing those girls.

The challenge stirred his soul, and an idea rose in his mind. He turned it over for a few seconds, then shifted his gaze to Janelle. "Maybe we should pay Amanda a visit and present a wise appeal."

"A what?"

"A wise appeal—it's something Pastor Jack from Hope Church teaches based on the story of Daniel."

She tipped her head, her interest obviously piqued.

"Remember how Daniel was taken away as a captive and sent to Babylon?"

"Yes."

"The king wanted him to eat a certain diet, but Daniel wasn't comfortable with that."

"What does that have to do with talking to Amanda about the documentary?"

He grinned. "Daniel appealed by letting them know he understood the king's point of view, then he explained what he wanted in a gracious way. Since he had such a good attitude and expressed himself so well, they gave Daniel permission to eat the food he thought was best."

"So you think if we speak to Amanda in person and explain your ideas, she might change her mind?"

He nodded. "We have the right motives and a good plan. Let's lay that out for her. Maybe she'll catch the vision and offer her support."

"Do you really think it will work?"

"We won't know unless we try."

Janelle released a slow, deep breath. "No matter how wise we make our appeal, we better back this up with a lot of prayer. He's the one who has to change her mind."

Jonas grinned and nodded. "Now you're talking."

~

Later that afternoon, Janelle and Jonas walked through the lobby of the University College Hospital and took the lift to the neonatal unit. They had called Amanda, and she'd agreed to meet with them. They stepped out of the lift and pressed the buzzer to enter the unit.

They approached the nurses' station, gave their names, and asked to see Amanda.

The nurse nodded. "She said you were coming. Wash your hands, and you can go in." She motioned to the sink behind them.

As they washed their hands, Jonas asked, "Do you think we'll see the twins?"

"I hope so, but I suppose it depends on how they're doing and how Amanda feels after our meeting."

Jonas sent her a serious look. "Right."

Footsteps sounded down the hall, and Janelle glanced over her shoulder.

Amanda approached and greeted them.

Janelle tossed the paper towels in the waste bin. "It's good to see you, Amanda. How are the twins today?"

"They're doing all right. Wes is with them now, so we have time to talk."

Janelle motioned to Jonas. "This is Jonas Conrad from Vision Impact Films."

Amanda nodded. "I'd shake hands, but it looks like you just washed them."

He smiled. "I'm glad to meet you, Ms. Preston. Thanks for seeing us today and taking time away from your daughters."

"It's good to have a break." She motioned to the left. "Let's go to the parents' lounge. We can talk there."

Janelle's stomach tightened as she walked down the hall with Amanda and Jonas. She sent off a silent prayer as they entered the lounge.

Amanda settled on one end of the couch. "How is the film coming for the gala?"

Jonas smiled. "We're making good progress. The script is finished, and we've done about half the filming. Janelle has been a great help."

"Good. We're behind on our fundraising goal this year, so we have a lot riding on the gala."

Jonas gave a firm nod. "I understand, and I'm committed to giving you an inspiring film that will raise the needed funds."

Amanda's tense expression didn't ease.

Janelle leaned forward. "I've read the script, and we've discussed the film at length. I'm confident our donors will be impressed and want to support our work at the museum."

Jonas focused on Amanda with a serious gaze. "The Foundling Hospital has a fascinating history. And I believe we can inspire a wider audience with a documentary that tells Mary Alice's story. That's why we wanted to talk to you today."

Amanda shot a heated glance at Jonas and then Janelle. "I thought I already made it clear I don't want that information released in a documentary."

"I understand why you might feel apprehensive," Jonas continued in a calm tone. "You want to guard the museum's reputation, and you're concerned showing Mary Alice's story could have a negative impact on donations."

Amanda sent him a pointed look. "Exactly. If people find out the Foundling Hospital was involved in selling girls into prostitution, they'll blame us for not protecting those children. That's going to send any potential donors running the other way, and they'll take their checkbooks with them."

"I hear what you're saying, and I understand your concerns," Jonas continued. "But only one man on staff was involved in selling the girls. The others knew nothing about it. After he was caught and arrested, they put extra provisions in place to protect the children. I'll make sure that's clear."

Amanda's pursed lips made it obvious she wasn't convinced yet.

Jonas rested his forearms on his thighs and clasped his hands. "I can show Mary Alice's story in a way that touches people emotionally and will make them sympathetic toward her and toward all the children who have been rescued and given new lives through the Foundling Hospital."

Janelle added, "When Mary Alice was older, she wrote a book about her experiences. That gave us the details of her story, and more importantly, it showed how grateful she was for the care she received at the Foundling Hospital. She donated a copy of her book to the museum, along with the token her mother left with her when she was first admitted. They could be the focal point of a new exhibit we could open in conjunction with the release of the documentary."

Amanda's expression eased slightly as she looked from Janelle to Jonas. "So . . . how would you tell the story?"

Jonas reached for his case. "I brought a rough draft of the script. Let me show you what we have in mind. I think you'll see it's a worthy project."

Amanda tipped her head. "I suppose I can take a look."

Jonas pulled out the script, then shifted his chair over next to Amanda. Janelle moved closer on her other side. For the next fifteen minutes, Jonas read aloud several scenes and explained the images he had in mind.

Janelle smiled as she watched his animated expressions. He had obviously spent a good deal of time thinking through the project, and he communicated his vision with ease. She shifted her gaze to Amanda, and her hopes rose. Keen interest shone in Amanda's eyes, as though she could picture what Jonas was describing.

Finally, Jonas lowered the script. "Do you have any questions?"

Amanda hesitated a moment more. "I see where you want to go with this. It's a risk, but if we open an exhibit at the same time, I think it might work."

Janelle's heart soared, and she beamed Jonas a smile.

He returned the same and turned to Amanda. "Thank you. I'll look forward to giving you an early screening and hope you'll offer your endorsement."

Amanda lifted her hand. "We'll see when the time comes. For now, I hope you'll focus on the gala film. September is not that far away. We're counting on you and that film to boost our donations."

Jonas gave a confident nod. "We'll be ready."

Amanda shifted her gaze to Janelle. "Would you like to see the twins?"

"Yes, I'd love that!"

"How about you, Jonas? Would you like to see them too?"

"Yes, thanks. We've been praying for them."

Amanda's eyebrows rose. "Well . . . that's good to know." She stood. "Come with me."

Janelle squeezed Jonas's hand as they walked down the hall. He grinned and sent her a wink, making it clear how pleased he was with the outcome of their meeting.

⌒

Jonas arrived at the museum the next morning just after ten. With Howie's help, he brought in the load of equipment he'd need to continue filming. Using the key Janelle had given him, he rolled the large black case into one of the classrooms on the lower level. Howie followed him in, carrying their two cameras and a sack of cinnamon buns. Jonas took a swig of his coffee, then opened the case and pulled out two extension cords and the light stand.

Janelle walked into the classroom. "Good morning."

He watched her approach, wishing Howie wasn't standing next to him so he could greet her with a kiss. "Morning."

Her eyes twinkled, sending a sweet private greeting, then she glanced around the room. "What's the plan for today?"

He shook off those distracting thoughts and focused on what he hoped to accomplish. "We want to film several rooms in the museum, and then shoot some of the paintings and historical artifacts." He picked up his iPad and scanned the list. "I'd also like to film Mary Alice's book and token."

She nodded and glanced at her watch. "I'm expecting the caterer to phone and confirm the gala menu. Then I'll let them know we have one hundred and seventy-two so far."

"That's great."

"I'd love to have two hundred."

He nodded. "Is Olivia busy? We could use her help."

Janelle glanced at the clock on the wall. "She's helping in a class until noon, but she should be free after that. I'm sure she'd love to help."

"Okay. Thanks." He glanced around the room. "Is it all right if we leave our equipment here for a few days?"

Janelle nodded. "I cleared the schedule. There's nothing going on in this room for at least a week."

"Great. Thanks. It will be a lot easier if we don't have to haul everything in and out each day." He lowered his iPad. "Did you have a chance to speak to Ruth about her daughters acting in the film?"

"Yes. She loves the idea, and she's sure her daughters would be happy to be involved. Peter liked the idea too. He said you can count on his boys. When do you want them to come in?"

"Maybe tomorrow. Let's see how it goes today. I'll let you know by four."

"Okay." Her phone rang. She glanced at the screen and sent him an apologetic look. "That's the caterer. I better take this."

"No worries." He leaned down and kissed her cheek.

She sent him a surprised smile, then walked out of the room with her phone to her ear.

He watched her go, admiring the swish of her auburn hair against her shoulders, her slim figure, and her shapely legs. He shook his head and turned around.

Howie was grinning from ear to ear. "Looks like there's more going on between you two than just making a film."

Jonas lifted his hands and smiled. "What can I say . . . she likes me."

Howie guffawed and punched him in the arm. "Yeah, right."

⁓

Janelle finished her conversation with the caterer, confirming the number of guests and the menu, then set the phone on her desk. She opened a file on her computer and added a note about the dessert choices.

A knock sounded at her door, and Lisa walked in, leaving the door open. "Janelle, do you know what time Olivia is coming back?"

Janelle shot her a surprised look. "What do you mean?"

"She helped with the eleven o'clock class, and then she said she was going to meet a friend."

Janelle's heart lurched. "You mean she left the museum?"

"I think so. She was supposed to help me set up for the one o'clock class, but she's not back yet."

Jonas walked in and glanced from Lisa to Janelle. His cheerful expression faded. "What's going on?"

Janelle met his gaze. "Lisa can't find Olivia."

Jonas glanced toward the door. "Do you want me to go look for her?"

Lisa sent him a worried glance. "I already checked every room in the museum."

He frowned. "Did she take her backpack?"

"Yes, she grabbed it on the way out of the classroom. That's when she told me she was going to meet a friend."

Janelle's heartbeat surged. "I'll try calling her." She swiped her phone off the desk and scrolled through her contacts. How could she have let this happen? Maggie trusted her to keep Olivia safe, and now she'd taken off to who knows where.

Olivia's phone rang three times, then went to voice mail. "She's not answering. I'm calling Maggie."

Jonas crossed to her desk. "I thought you said Olivia didn't have any friends in London."

Janelle tapped in Maggie's number. "That's what Maggie told me."

"Then who is she—" He stilled. "You don't think she's meeting Tony, do you?"

Janelle's stomach dropped. If that was true, Maggie was going to kill her.

Jonas rubbed his forehead. "I should've talked to them."

Maggie's phone rang three times before she picked up. "Hi, Janelle."

"Brace yourself. One of the interns just told me Olivia left the museum to meet a friend."

"What?" Maggie's voice rose.

Janelle winced and pulled the phone away from her ear. She turned to Lisa. "When did you last see Olivia?"

Lisa glanced at her watch. "About 12:10. I'm sorry. I didn't know she wasn't supposed to leave, or I would've said something right away."

Maggie must have heard Lisa's comments because she moaned.

Janelle pulled in a calming breath. "Maggie, why don't you try calling Olivia and see if she'll answer. If you find out where she is, Jonas and I will go there and bring her back."

Jonas stepped closer, a serious frown etched across his face.

"She doesn't have her phone! We took it away after that last argument."

Panic cinched Janelle's chest tight, and she glanced at Jonas. "She doesn't have her phone." He leaned in, and she tapped on the speaker button. "Has she made any new friends? Someone you could phone?"

"No! That's one of her biggest complaints—she has no friends here!"

Janelle hated to suggest it, but she had no choice. "What about Tony? Do you think she might have made plans to meet him?"

"Oh, if that's true, Dan is going to have a heart attack!"

Jonas spoke into the phone. "Maggie, are you at home or the office?"

"I'm home. Cole had a dentist appointment this morning."

"Does Olivia have access to a laptop or a tablet at your flat?"

"She has a laptop in her room." Maggie sniffed, her voice sounding tearful.

"Check and see if you can access a message app or some other way she might have connected with Tony or another friend."

Janelle sent Jonas a grateful look.

"I'll go look." A few seconds later, Maggie said, "I'm opening her laptop."

Janelle bit her lip, counting off the seconds.

"She has a message app!" Maggie's voice rang out. "We had no idea. Let me check. . . ."

Janelle leaned on the table and closed her eyes. *Please, Lord. Watch over Olivia.*

"Oh no! She was talking to Tony for hours last night!"

Janelle gulped in a breath. "Do you see anything about them meeting today?"

"Just a minute. . . ."

Janelle shot Jonas an anxious glance, and he returned an equally uneasy look. If Jonas's suspicions about Tony were true, this was a much more dangerous situation than just leaving the museum to meet a friend.

Maggie gasped. "They're meeting today at one thirty, in front of the Royal Opera House on Bow Street in Covent Garden."

Janelle checked her watch. It was ten to one. It would take at least thirty minutes to reach the Opera House, maybe longer if they had to wait for the tube.

"Dan has our car! He's supposed to pick up Caleb after camp. What am I going to do?"

Janelle looked at Jonas, and he nodded. "We'll go to the Opera House and see if we can find her."

"I'll phone Dan. He's working at his office in Kensington. Maybe he can get there before you."

Janelle rose. "Okay. We'll phone as soon as we know anything."

"I'll get an Uber," Jonas said, pulling out his phone. "That should get us there faster than the tube."

Janelle grabbed her sweater and handbag while Jonas ordered an Uber. Then she and Jonas walked out to the front lobby.

He pushed open the door, his gaze on his phone. "The driver should be here in about three minutes."

"Thanks." Janelle pulled in a deep breath, trying to calm her racing heart. "Do you think we can get there by one thirty?"

He glanced at his phone again. "We've got thirty-five minutes. That should be enough time, unless we hit a lot of traffic."

"What was Olivia thinking, taking off like this to meet some boy she doesn't really know?"

Jonas shook his head. "If he really is a *boy*, I'll be surprised."

A shiver raced down Janelle's back. *Please, Lord, help us get there in time to head off any trouble.*

The Uber driver arrived, and Janelle and Jonas piled in the back seat.

Jonas leaned forward. "Take us to the Royal Opera House on Bow Street, and please hurry."

The driver nodded and sped off around the corner. They made good time through the city, but Janelle bit her lip and checked her watch at every red light. Twenty minutes later, the driver turned onto Bow Street, but a barricade blocked the road. Several police officers and a large crowd had gathered in front of the barricade.

The driver looked over his shoulder. "Sorry, I can't get you any closer. You'll have to walk from here."

"That's okay. Thanks." Jonas opened the passenger door and climbed out.

Janelle followed and scanned the scene. "What's going on?"

"I don't know. Let's see if we can get around this crowd. The Opera House is just down the street." He reached for her hand, and they wove through the crowd toward the barricade.

Jonas caught the attention of a police officer. "Can we go through?"

He shook his head. "Not unless you have an invitation."

"What's the event?"

"The Prince and Princess of Wales are arriving at Paul Hamlyn Hall."

"Is that near the Royal Opera House?" Janelle asked.

Several photographers and reporters with microphones were

scattered among the people gathered there. The Prince and Princess of Wales always drew a crowd of onlookers and paparazzi wherever they went.

The policeman nodded and pointed down the street. "It's that big glass conservatory."

"We're supposed to meet someone in front of the Opera House."

The officer motioned to the side street. "Go down Russell, then take a right at James, and another right at Floral. That will take you around to Bow. You can access the entrance to the Opera House from that side."

Jonas thanked the officer, took Janelle's hand, and started down the street again. "This shouldn't take too long. Keep an eye out. Olivia might have been stopped here too."

Janelle scanned the faces of those they passed, but she didn't see Olivia.

As they turned down a narrow street, he let go of her hand and pulled out his phone. "I'll check the route and be sure we can find our way through this maze."

A few motorcycles were parked to the right, but this small side street was nearly deserted. They reached the next corner and turned right again as they circled the block.

Janelle glanced at her watch, and her heart lurched. It was already 1:25, and they still had to make their way back to Bow Street. "We've only got five minutes."

Jonas picked up his pace, and Janelle hurried along beside him. They finally reached the corner and turned onto Bow. The impressive Royal Opera House came into view with its six tall classic columns spanning the façade above the main entrance.

Janelle scanned the pavement in front of the building. Up ahead, by the entrance to the Paul Hamlyn Hall, another crowd lined up on the other side of the barricade with additional police, reporters, and photographers. Her gaze darted back to the Opera House, and her breath caught. At the far corner of the building, Olivia stood in the shadows, watching the cars that passed.

Janelle gasped and pointed. "There she is!"

A white van pulled up across the street. The side door slid open, and a stocky middle-aged man with dark hair climbed out. He looked both ways, then strode toward the Opera House.

Jonas and Janelle broke into a run, but the man reached Olivia first and slipped his arm around her shoulders. She looked up at him with a confused expression. He quickly guided her toward the street. She shook her head and tried to pull away. He tightened his hold, tugging her in the direction of the van with the open side door.

"Hey! Let go of her!" Jonas yelled as he dashed down the pavement, still several meters away.

Olivia screamed. A few people on the edge of the crowd turned around. The man spotted Jonas in pursuit and tried pulling Olivia in the opposite direction.

"Olivia!" Dan ran past Janelle, racing toward his daughter.

"Dad!" Olivia yelled, trying to free herself from the man's grip.

Jonas rammed into the man, knocking him off balance. The man's arms flew out, freeing Olivia.

Dan reached them a split second later and swung his fist at the man. Ducking and cursing, the man spun away and dashed across the street. "Go, go, go!" he yelled as he jumped into the van.

The van's engine roared, and tires squealed as the van whipped a U-turn. Two police officers jogged toward Olivia, Dan, and Jonas.

Olivia burst into tears. Janelle ran to her side and pulled her into her arms. "It's all right, Olivia. He's gone. You're okay."

Olivia leaned into Janelle, shaking and crying. "That wasn't Tony! It couldn't be!"

Agony lined Dan's face as he reached for his daughter. "Olivia, honey." She turned into his arms, and he hugged her tight. "You're safe now. Everything is going to be all right."

"I'm sorry, Daddy," she said between jerky sobs. Photographers circled around, snapping pictures until a police officer finally blocked their path and told them to move on. The other officer began questioning Dan and Olivia.

Jonas joined Janelle and gathered her in for a hug.

Tears burned her eyes. "You were right. I should've listened to you and warned Maggie and Dan."

"It's okay. We made it in time." His voice sounded heavy with emotion.

She drew in a shaky breath. "If I'd said something, we could've prevented this."

He tightened his hold on her. "Olivia's safe now. That's what matters."

~

The next morning, Janelle and Olivia boarded the tube on their way to the museum. Janelle glanced at her young friend, recalling the frightening events of the previous afternoon, and offered up another prayer of thanks.

Across from them, a man opened his newspaper. Olivia cringed and lowered her head. She wore a baggy hooded sweatshirt, dark sunglasses, and a ball cap with her hair tucked up underneath. When Janelle had first seen her that morning, she'd been surprised and asked why she'd chosen that outfit.

Olivia had lowered her sunglasses and sent Janelle a pained look. "I don't want anyone to recognize me."

Olivia's near-abduction at the Royal Opera House, just minutes before the arrival of the Prince and Princess of Wales, had been featured on several evening news programs. The story had also been printed in the *London Times*, with a warning to parents and teens. A photo of Dan hugging Olivia, with Jonas and Janelle in the background, had been included with the story. Fortunately, Olivia's face had been turned away from the camera, and the reporter had not included her name since she was under eighteen, but they had given her father's name.

The announcement for their stop sounded, the car slowed, and the door slid open. Janelle rose and wove between passengers toward the exit. Olivia followed. Once they were up on the street, Janelle turned to her. "So, how would you like to handle things at the museum?"

Olivia tugged down the brim of her ball cap. "What do you mean?"

"Some of the staff may have watched the news last night or read the paper this morning. You might want to think through how you'll respond if they ask you about it. I'll support you however you think is best."

Olivia walked along silently for a few seconds. "I don't mind if you tell Lisa and the other interns, but I'd rather you didn't say anything to the rest of the staff unless they ask."

Janelle's eyebrows lifted. "You want *me* to tell the interns, rather than you?"

Olivia's cheeks flushed below her sunglasses. "I don't know what to say. I feel like such a dope for believing everything Tony told me."

Janelle shook her head. "You heard what the police said last night. Tony—though that's likely not his real name—is probably a professional trafficker. He used every trick in the book to lure you into a relationship and make you believe he truly cared for you."

Olivia heaved a sigh. "And I did believe him." She scrunched up her face. "He's such a jerk!"

Janelle couldn't deny she held the same opinion of the man who'd spent weeks appealing to Olivia's weaknesses and setting her up for an abduction. "I hope the description you gave, plus the information from your phone, will help the police catch him."

"Yeah. He needs to be put in jail so he can't try that on any other girl."

Janelle looked her way. "You're right, and that's why I think you might want to tell the other interns and volunteers what happened."

Olivia grimaced.

They turned the corner, and the museum came into view. She slowed to a stop and glanced up at the three-story brick building. "You really think I should tell them?"

"Yes, but it's up to you."

Olivia crossed her arms and looked down for a few seconds. Finally, she released a deep sigh. "I guess I can tell Lisa when we eat lunch together, and then I can tell the others if it comes up."

Janelle nodded, certain telling Lisa was a good first step.

Olivia brushed the hair from her eyes. "It'll be embarrassing, but I wouldn't want this to happen to Lisa or anyone else."

Janelle slipped her arm around Olivia's shoulders. "I'm proud of you for being willing to warn your friend. That takes courage."

Olivia slipped off her sunglasses. "Thanks. You want to eat lunch with us today?"

Janelle smiled. "Sure. I'll be there."

27

1885

Matthew knocked on Lillian's door, feeling so happy he could hardly keep from singing. In one hand, he held a bouquet of red roses, and in the other, a large bag of girls' clothing. Nancy and Jane, the two young girls who had worked with Ellen at the Golden Swan, stood with him on the front steps.

Nancy looked up at the house with a wide-eyed gaze. "This is a real nice place."

Matthew grinned. "Yes, and it's even nicer inside."

Jane brushed a lock of blond hair over her shoulder. "Ellen lives here?"

"That's right, and I'm sure she's going to be very happy to see you."

The door opened, and Stanford looked out. His gaze dropped to the two girls. Surprise flashed in his eyes, then he resumed his formal expression. "Good morning, Mr. McGivern."

"Morning, Stanford. We'd like to see Mrs. Freemont."

"Of course, sir. Please come in." He pulled the door open wider.

Matthew and the girls walked into the entry hall, and both girls looked around with amazed expressions.

"Mrs. Freemont is on the terrace. If you'll follow me." Stanford led the way through the sitting room and dining room and stopped at the French doors. "Mr. McGivern and . . . two young ladies," he announced.

Lillian turned with a welcoming smile. "Matthew, please join us."

He stepped out, followed by Nancy and Jane.

Ellen squealed, then hopped up from her chair and ran toward the girls, pulling them into a tight hug.

Lillian and Serena exchanged delighted looks.

Ellen's eyes shone. "These are my friends." She slipped an arm around each girl. "This is Nancy and Jane."

Serena crossed toward them. "Welcome, girls. We're glad you've come."

Lillian joined her. "Yes, we're very happy to see you at last."

Ellen turned to Jane. "This is Miss Lillian and Miss Serena. They're ever so nice. I know you'll like them." She looked up at Lillian. "May I show them around the house?"

Lillian smiled. "Yes. But first, why don't you introduce them to the other girls?"

Ellen nodded and led her friends across the terrace to meet Cathy, Daisy, and Mary. When she finished introductions, Serena ushered all six girls into the house, and their cheerful chatter faded as they passed through the dining room.

Matthew held out the bouquet of roses. "These are for you."

Lillian accepted them with a sweet smile. "Thank you, Matthew. They're beautiful." She raised the roses to her nose. "And they have a lovely fragrance."

He held out the bag. "Reverend Howell sent these clothes for the girls."

Lillian set the flowers on the table and peeked in the bag. "That was very kind." She glanced toward the door. "How did you manage to get the girls out of the Golden Swan?"

"Reverend Howell and I have been to the police station twice, appealing for their release. Each time, they told us they were working on it. This morning, we finally received word we could come and collect them at the station."

"I'm sure the righteous uproar from your articles prompted them to follow through and do their duty."

He dipped his head, humbled by her words. She always built him up and offered such encouraging words. It was one of her many fine qualities he appreciated. "I'm thankful they're free." He glanced toward the house. "There will be some papers to sign so you can become their legal guardian. Reverend Howell will bring those by when they're ready."

She nodded. "I'm so glad. We've been praying for them every night, usually at Ellen's prompting."

"Caring for six girls will be a big responsibility."

"True, but it's such an important task." She gazed toward the garden for a moment, then looked back at him. "I certainly wouldn't attempt it without Serena, Mrs. Pringle, and Bessie."

"You're giving them a chance for a new life." He reached for her hand. "I admire you, Lillian. I don't know anyone else who would open their home and help these girls recover from all they've been through."

"So, you don't mind?"

"Mind? Why would I mind?"

She hesitated. "I intend to keep my commitment to care for the girls. And if you and I continue on the path we're on now, that would mean . . ." She lifted her lashes and looked up at him.

"That would mean I might have a role in their lives one day."

Her cheeks flushed. "Is that something you would consider?"

He laughed softly. "Lillian Freemont, are you proposing to me?"

She gasped. "No! I just—I just want to know how you feel about—"

He lifted his finger and touched her lips. "I understand what you're saying, and I'm fully on board with the idea of partnering with you to guide and raise these girls."

"You are?" She gazed up at him with such an endearing expression it made his heart catch.

"Yes, I am." He drew her closer and wrapped his arms around her. "I love you, Lillian."

She leaned back just enough so their gazes could meet. Sweet sincerity glowed in her luminous brown eyes as she looked up at him. "And I love you, Matthew."

A wave of joy washed over him, and he leaned down and kissed her tenderly. Her loving response filled him with delight. Lillian Freemont was a valuable treasure, and he would do everything in his power to care for her and cherish her all the days of his life.

Three months later, Lillian totaled the cost of their monthly bills and released a resigned sigh. Feeding and clothing six girls, Serena, and herself, as well as paying their staff, had increased her expenses more than she'd expected. She was thankful the police had finally returned the money Matthew had given Mr. Parker. Those funds, along with the investments she had made after inheriting her late husband's shipping business, were needed now, and she would put them to good use.

Last week, Matthew had proposed after a candlelight dinner, with Serena and the girls present. Her heart warmed at the precious memory. Just thinking of him and the future they would share eased her concerns. Next June, he would come and live with them, help with the parenting responsibilities, and add his salary from the *Gazette* to help cover some of the needs of their family. And that was what they were becoming—a family.

The girls had settled into a good routine. Lessons, reading

aloud, sewing, prayers, songs, games, and walks to the park filled their days. Soon, some of them would begin attending school.

On a quiet evening two weeks after Mary Alice had arrived, Serena took her out to the terrace and explained their true connection. Mary Alice had sent her a shy smile and said the first time she saw Matthew at the Lady's Slipper, he'd told her he knew her aunt and mum. She'd wondered what he'd meant and who they might be. Serena hugged her then, and Mary Alice had wrapped her arms around her mum's neck and clung to her for a long time.

Lillian smiled at the memory. Since that day, Serena and Mary Alice's connection had grown even stronger, and that brought much joy to Lillian's heart.

Serena and Mary Alice walked into the library and crossed toward the desk where Lillian was seated. Serena placed her hand on her daughter's shoulder. "Mary Alice has written something, and I wanted her to read it to you."

Lillian smiled and nodded to her niece. "I'd love to hear it."

Mary Alice returned a shy smile and looked down at her paper. "'I always wanted a sister, but I never had one, until I came home to live with my mother and my aunt, and they gave me five sisters.'"

Lillian and Serena exchanged heartfelt looks.

"'These girls were not born into our family,'" Mary Alice continued, "'but they live with us, and we love each other just like we were born to the same mum and dad. Sometimes we fuss, but that doesn't last long. Soon we are playing together and doing our lessons just like we never said a cross word. I am glad I have sisters.'"

Serena bit her lip, obviously touched by what her daughter had written.

"'I hope I can always live with my sisters and my mum and

my aunt. I don't want to go anywhere else. This is home for me, and I am glad.'" Mary Alice looked up at Lillian with an expectant expression.

"That is excellent writing. I can tell you're a gifted storyteller. Perhaps one day you'll write a book."

A look of wonder filled Mary Alice's face. "Do you really think I could write a book?"

Lillian nodded. "Of course. As you continue your studies, you can develop the skills you need to become a good writer. And I'm sure Matthew would be glad to help. He's a very skilled writer."

Mary Alice hugged her paper to her chest. "I'm going to tell Cathy. Wait until she hears I am going to write a book." She spun and dashed out of the room.

Serena laughed as she watched her go, joy and pride filling her expression. "She has really bloomed, hasn't she?"

"Yes, it's been wonderful to see how much she's changed in just a few months."

"She does seem to have a gift with words. Her studies come so easily to her. She would spend all day with her nose in a book if I didn't call her away to do something else."

"I can't wait to see where that gift takes her." Lillian thought of each girl who had come into their care. "They all have unique talents and interests. The future is an open door for them now."

"Yes, it is—thanks to you," Serena added.

Lillian rose and came around her desk. "We both have an important role in their lives. I could never do this without you, and I wouldn't want to. I'm so glad you came home."

"So am I." Serena reached for Lillian and pulled her close for a hug. "The Lord has His hand of blessing on us and our dear girls. He'll guide us through the days to come."

Lillian lifted her misty gaze and looked into her sister's eyes. "Yes, I'm sure He will."

28

The next two weeks passed in a blur as Janelle balanced managing her role at the museum and spending time with Jonas. He continued filming at the museum, then went to a few historical sites related to the Foundling Hospital for more filming. She and Jonas shared takeout dinners and long conversations most evenings, drawing her heart even closer to his. They'd attended Hope Church last Sunday and enjoyed lunch at an Italian restaurant that afternoon.

Earlier that week, they'd dressed more than a dozen children in costumes to act out scenes for the gala film. The level of excitement in the room had been electrifying. It had been a memorable day for the children and for the parents who were on hand to watch the filming.

Olivia had toted equipment, set up lights, and made sure Jonas and Howie had plenty of snacks and water. She also helped with costumes and kept the children quiet while they waited for their turn in front of the camera. Janelle could tell it had been a meaningful time for Olivia and given her a positive focus as she recovered from her near-abduction. Maggie and Dan had taken time off so they could see Olivia and the boys playing their parts.

Janelle smiled, recalling the way Jonas had worked patiently with the children and how they'd responded to his directions and soaked up his words of praise. He was not only a gifted filmmaker, but he was great with people of all ages.

Jonas walked into her office. "Hey, Janelle."

A wave of happiness filled her. "Hi. I didn't expect to see you until later."

"We finished filming at the archives. I think we got everything I wanted there."

"That's great."

"We only need a couple more days outdoors, and I'll be done filming."

"Wow. I can't wait to see how it comes together. When can I have a preview?"

Jonas met her halfway across the office, and she stepped into his arms for a hug. "There's still a lot to do before I'll have something to show you."

She wrapped her arms around his waist. "I thought you said you were almost done."

"What I have right now is a lot of scenes and images that are out of order—and way more footage than we need for a fifteen-minute film."

"Can you save some of that for the documentary?"

"Yes, I've got some scenes that might work, and some still shots."

"That's good."

"Now I've got to go through it all and put it in order. While I'm working on that, I'll be auditioning narrators. When the rough-cut film is ready, the narrator will record his part, and we'll add that. Then it goes to a music scorer, who finds or composes the background music to set the right mood."

She looked up at him. "I didn't realize there was so much involved."

"It's a process." He leaned down and kissed her nose.

She laughed and stepped back. "Well, I'll be very excited to see the finished project."

He grinned. "You and me both."

⌒

Jonas leaned back in his desk chair and rubbed his eyes. The hum of his flat's air conditioner matched the buzzing in his brain. Man, he was tired. He'd been editing the film ten hours a day for the last five days.

Knowing Janelle was counting on him was pushing him to get it right. He couldn't let her down. Plus, there were lots of important people who would be attending the gala—people with connections to other organizations and nonprofits. If they were impressed with his work, it might open the door for future projects.

Howie took a sip of his iced coffee. "I think that last round of changes gives the film a better flow."

Jonas's thoughts spun back through the scenes he'd rearranged. They'd expanded the historical portion of the film and used most of what they'd filmed at the museum with the kids in costume. Those scenes were key to tapping into viewers' emotions. At least he hoped they would be effective and bring in needed donations. But after viewing the film so many times during the editing process, it was hard to know if he'd hit the mark or not.

Howie looked his way. "What do you think? Is it ready?"

Jonas glanced at the final scene on his computer screen, pulled in a deep breath, and nodded. "I think we're done. I'll send it over to the narrator in the morning."

"How much time does he need?"

"He said he'd have it back to us by the end of the week."

Howie frowned. "It takes him that long to read a fifteen-minute script?"

"That's what he said."

"But that doesn't give Ben much time to work on the music."

"I know, but we don't have a choice at this point."

Howie crossed his arms. "Maybe we should get someone else to do the narration."

Jonas shook his head. "He's got the right voice."

"Okay." Howie glanced at his phone. "Yikes! I'd better get going. I told Lauren I'd be home by six for dinner."

Jonas watched Howie collect his iPad and papers and put them in his backpack. It would be nice to have someone cooking dinner and waiting for him after he finished his work. Thoughts of Janelle rose in his mind, as they did so often. He hadn't seen her since he'd started editing. Five days was too long. He missed her.

Howie slung his backpack over his shoulder. "I'll check in with you in the morning."

"Thanks, Howie." Jonas followed him into the living room. "I'll see you tomorrow."

Howie grinned as he reached for the doorknob. "Have a good night." He pulled open the door and stopped.

Janelle stood on the other side, her hand raised to knock. She laughed. "Hey, Howie."

Howie grinned. "I'm going, and you're coming. That will make Jonas happy." He chuckled as he strode past her and continued down the hall.

Jonas smiled, and his heart thumped a quick rhythm. "Hi, Janelle."

Her cheeks flushed as she lifted the bag in her hand. "Have you had dinner yet?"

"No, but I'm starving. What's in there?"

"I stopped at Crown of India and picked up chicken tikka masala."

"Oh, wow. That sounds great. My mouth is already watering."

They headed to the kitchen for plates and silverware, then they settled on his small balcony to enjoy dinner and a view of Soho. They talked about the museum and the upcoming gala while they enjoyed the spicy chicken in creamy tomato sauce, along with fragrant jasmine rice and soft naan bread.

Jonas swallowed his last bite, then wiped his mouth and sat back. "That was so good. Thanks for coming over and bringing dinner."

"So . . . it was okay that I surprised you?"

Was that a hint of uncertainty in her voice?

"Sure. I get so caught up in the editing process that I don't always stop to make a meal. I usually just grab whatever I have on hand and end up eating way too much junk food."

Something flickered in her eyes, and she glanced away.

He watched her a moment more, trying to understand what was behind her pensive expression. "Hey, is something wrong?"

"No, it's just . . . I haven't heard from you for a few days, so I thought . . . oh, never mind."

"I've been focused on finishing the film so I can get it to the narrator. The schedule is tight. And the gala is only a few days away."

She nodded, tore off a piece of bread, and popped it in her mouth.

Was she stressed about work or upset about something else?

She chewed for a few more seconds, then looked up. "Our time working on the film is coming to an end."

"Yeah, it's been great. I've really learned a lot. It's been a good experience."

She searched his face. "I've enjoyed it too." But there was hesitation in her voice that didn't match her words.

A wave of weariness washed over him, and he rubbed his eyes. His throat felt dry and scratchy, and now that he thought about it, his head hurt too. "Man, I'm beat. We better call it a night."

Janelle rose, took their plates, and walked back toward the kitchen.

He picked up the leftover food. Something was up with Janelle, but he didn't have the energy to figure it out tonight. They could talk tomorrow, after he got a good night's sleep. Maybe he'd feel better and be able to think straight.

～

Janelle glanced at the clock on her office wall, then picked up her phone and checked the screen to be sure she hadn't missed a text from Jonas. She'd phoned him twice that morning and left messages both times, but he hadn't phoned back. Maybe she should text him. She grimaced and shook her head. He knew how to get hold of her if he wanted to talk.

Sadness wrapped around her heart and squeezed tight. Jonas seemed to be pulling away. Memories of how Marcus had gone silent several times rose and filled her mind. She should have realized what was happening, but she'd let several months pass before she'd discovered the heartbreaking truth. He didn't love her. He wasn't committed. He'd been seeing someone else the whole time.

She closed her eyes, pushing those thoughts away. *Lord, I know Jonas is nothing like Marcus, but this is so confusing. Why hasn't he been in touch? What do you want me to do?*

A knock sounded at her open door, and her eyes popped open.

Amanda walked in. "Good morning, Janelle."

Janelle rose. "Hi, Amanda. This is a surprise."

"I know. I should've called to let you know I was coming."

"No. It's always good to see you."

"My mum came to the hospital this morning. She said she'd stay with Wes and suggested I take a break." She held out her hand and wiggled her fingers. "I went for a manicure."

315

"That looks nice."

"Thanks. I was only a short distance from the museum, so I thought I'd stop in and see how everything is going."

Janelle motioned to the chair in front of her desk. "Please, sit down."

Amanda took a seat and glanced around Janelle's office. "How are things coming for the gala?"

"Our number is up to one ninety-two. I spoke to the event coordinator at the venue and confirmed the details."

Amanda nodded, looking pleased. "How about the film? Have you seen it yet?"

"Not yet. I believe they're still working on the narration and background music."

Amanda frowned. "That's cutting it awfully close. I thought they'd be finished by now."

Janelle shifted in her chair. She was about to reassure Amanda that Jonas would have the film ready on time, but something held her back. She had aligned herself with Jonas and persuaded Amanda to trust him with the gala film and the documentary to follow. What if she was wrong about him?

"When I spoke to you two at the hospital," Amanda continued, "Jonas said everything was on track. That film is the focal point of the program. If he doesn't come through for us, we'll have spent our entire promotional budget and have nothing to show for it."

Janelle's stomach twisted. The gala was only two days away. She wanted to believe Jonas would fulfill his promise, finish the film, and make that part of the evening a success, but questions and doubts tugged at her heart.

29

Janelle slowly circled the venue's elegant great hall, checking the place settings, floral centerpieces, and flickering votives on each table. Everything looked perfect. Overhead, gold-and-crystal chandeliers sparkled with shimmering light that reflected off the corniced ceiling and paintings on the walls.

She shifted her gaze to the stage, where the podium and microphone waited for her to introduce the evening and welcome everyone to the gala. The large screen had been lowered in preparation to show the film.

Everything was ready . . . except Jonas had not arrived, and the gala was due to start in forty-five minutes.

She pulled in a deep breath, trying to calm her fluttering stomach. The future of the museum hung in the balance tonight. If they were going to maintain their staff and continue offering programs and classes for vulnerable children and families, they had to strengthen their donor base. Amanda, the board of governors, and the staff were all counting on her.

And she was counting on Jonas.

After three days of silence, he'd finally responded to her texts and explained he'd had the flu. But those texts had been brief and businesslike. He'd said nothing about their relationship. When she'd asked about the film, he'd said he was putting the final touches on the project, and he'd see her at the gala. She wanted to trust him and believe what he said was true, but now that he was fifteen minutes late, the unsettled and anxious feelings were back.

She crossed toward the entrance, hoping to catch Jonas as soon as he arrived. Lisa and Olivia were stationed by the door to greet guests and hand out place cards. A few people had come early and gathered in small groups for conversation or were picking up a beverage at the drink station.

Olivia looked up as Janelle approached. She wore a cocktail-length teal dress and had put her hair up in an attractive style, with tendrils around her face. Rhinestone earrings dangled from her ears, making her look older than sixteen.

Janelle sent her a warm smile. "You look very pretty, Olivia."

"Thanks. Lisa fixed my hair." She sent her friend a grateful look.

Lisa grinned and patted Olivia's back. "I told her a dress like that deserves a special hairstyle." Lisa wore a bright pink ruffled top, a pink-and-orange flowered skirt, and large gold hoop earrings. She'd taken out her usual crown of braids and let her wavy blond hair flow over her shoulders.

Maggie and Dan walked in and greeted Janelle. Olivia handed them their place cards. "You're sitting at table number three, with Lisa and me." She pointed to the table in the center of the first row. "Janelle and Jonas are sitting with us too."

Janelle swallowed. If Jonas showed up.

"Thanks." Dan studied Olivia for a moment. "Your hair looks nice."

Olivia brushed her hair from her eyes. "Thanks, Dad."

Maggie turned to Janelle. "You look great too. Royal blue is your color!" She glanced around the room. "Wow, this is a beautiful venue."

Janelle nodded as her gaze darted from Maggie to the door. If only Jonas would arrive and put her worries to rest.

Maggie stepped closer. "Is everything okay?"

"Jonas isn't here yet," Janelle whispered.

Maggie's eyebrows shot up. "Where is he?"

"I don't know. He was supposed to be here at six to set up the film."

Maggie glanced at her watch. "He's only a few minutes late. I wouldn't worry—at least not yet."

"What am I going to do if he doesn't come?"

Maggie shook her head. "Jonas is not going to leave you high and dry. Have a little faith!"

Janelle pulled in a shuddering breath and let Maggie's words sink in. She needed to believe the best about Jonas, not jump to conclusions. He said he'd be here. She would choose to hold on to that.

"Why don't you text him and see what's going on?"

Janelle nodded and glanced at the table where she'd left her handbag and phone. Just then, Howie and Lauren walked in. Janelle made a beeline for them. "Howie, have you heard from Jonas? I asked him to be here by six to get the film ready before the guests arrive."

Howie frowned and glanced toward the door. "I talked to him about an hour ago. He should be here soon."

She sensed there was more he wasn't telling her. "Howie, is everything okay with the film?"

Howie pulled in a deep breath. "I don't want you to worry, but there was a slight hitch."

Janelle's eyes widened. "What kind of hitch?"

"The narrator didn't finish his work, and we had to send the film to the guy who scores the music to give him time to record his part . . . so Jonas is finishing the narration."

Janelle stared at Howie, trying to process his words. "What?"

"Everything is going to be fine. Jonas knows what he's doing." Howie gave a confident nod. "I'm sure he'll be here by seven." He took Lauren's hand and headed toward the drink station.

A dizzy wave flowed through Janelle as she watched them walk away. *Please, Lord, have mercy on us. Help Jonas finish and get here soon.*

Maggie returned to Janelle's side. "What's going on?"

"Jonas had an issue with the film, and he had to finish the narration himself."

"Well . . ." Maggie blinked rapidly, obviously trying to think of something positive to say. "He does have a great voice."

Dan joined them, and Maggie hooked her arm through his. "Come on, honey. We need to give Janelle a moment."

Dan sent his wife a confused look as they started toward their table.

Several more guests entered, including Amanda and Wesley. Janelle forced a smile and greeted them.

Amanda scanned the room. "Everything looks good."

Janelle nodded. "The event coordinator has been very accommodating. She arranged everything just as I asked."

"How about the program? Are we all set to show the film?"

Janelle hesitated, debating her answer. It was time to exercise her faith—in the Lord and in Jonas. She nodded. "We'll be ready."

Wesley approached. "Nice to see you, Janelle. It looks like you've got everything under control." He smiled. "You know, it's been hard for Amanda to step back and let go of things at the museum, but it's clear you've handled those responsibilities well."

Janelle's cheeks warmed. "Thanks. Taking on Amanda's role has been a real learning experience. I know everyone will be happy to have her back when she's ready."

Wesley and Amanda exchanged a glance, and Amanda turned to Janelle. "That's something I want to discuss with you."

Did Amanda want to talk about the date of her return, or was she hinting that she wasn't coming back to work at the museum? "Of course. Whenever you're ready."

Amanda took Wesley's arm. "We'll talk more later. I see some of our key donors. I want to make the rounds." They turned to an older couple who had just picked up their place cards.

The next half hour passed quickly as she greeted guests and then touched base with Sydney, the event coordinator, about one guest's special request for their meal. She returned to the entrance and glanced at her watch. Ten minutes to seven. Where was Jonas?

Sydney strode across the room toward her. "The tech crew has the background slides ready, but they're wondering about the film you want to show after dinner. They need a link to the film file or a portable drive. Do you have either of those?"

Janelle's mind spun, and her tongue stuck to the roof of her mouth. What should she say? Movement to the left caught her eye.

Jonas hustled through the door and headed straight toward her.

Relief poured through Janelle. "The man overseeing the film just arrived."

"Great. He can speak to our team in the sound booth, and they can set it up during dinner."

"Thanks."

Sydney strode away as Jonas approached. The concern and sincerity in his expression flew straight to her heart, and she reached for him. "Jonas."

He pulled her in for a hug. "I'm sorry I'm late."

She swallowed past her tight throat and nodded. "I'm just glad you're here."

"Me too. What a week! I've missed you so much."

Janelle's heart swelled, and relief rushed through her. "I've missed you too." She stepped back. "Now, come with me. We've got to talk to the tech guys and get everything set up for the film." She walked across the room, and he matched her quick pace.

They entered the sound booth, and Jonas handed over the SSD portable drive and thanked the two men handling the lights, sound, and video. Then he and Janelle crossed to their table and took a seat.

The lights came down, and Janelle leaned toward Jonas. "That's my cue." She rose, stepped up on the stage, and walked to the podium. "Good evening, and welcome to the Foundling Museum's Annual Gala. We're delighted you could be with us tonight. My name is Janelle Spencer. I am the acting director of the museum while Amanda Preston, our executive director, is enjoying time with her twin daughters during their first few months of life."

The audience clapped politely.

"Tonight, we hope to give you a clear and inspiring picture of the Foundling Museum's past, our present, and what we hope to accomplish in the future. We invite you to sit back, relax, and enjoy the delicious meal that has been prepared for you. After dinner, we have a very special presentation that I know you'll enjoy." She motioned for Pastor Brown to come on stage. "I've asked Pastor Scott Brown from St. Mark's to offer a blessing before we enjoy our meal." She noted the flash of surprise on Amanda's face and quickly shifted her gaze to Jonas, who sent her an approving nod.

Pastor Scott mounted the steps and invited everyone to join him in prayer.

Janelle bowed her head and slowly pulled in a deep breath as she listened. The pastor's sincere tone and kind words soothed her jumbled emotions. Pastor Brown finished his prayer, and he and Janelle returned to their seats. The waiters appeared, carrying trays, and began serving the guests.

Laughter rose from the next table, where Amanda and Wesley were seated with some of the museum's top donors. Janelle and Jonas exchanged a smile. The efficient service and contented guests eased the tension in Janelle's shoulders. Now, if only the film and Amanda's appeal would result in a new wave of generous donations, Janelle could go home and sleep soundly for at least twelve hours.

The waiter lowered a full dinner plate in front of her, then served Jonas.

Jonas glanced her way. "You're eyeing my dinner. Did you want to try something?"

She laughed softly. "No, I was just checking to be sure they're serving what we agreed on."

He took a bite. "I don't know if it's what you asked for, but it tastes great."

She smiled. "Glad you like it."

Pleasant conversation continued around their table for the next half hour while everyone enjoyed their dinner. The waiters returned and cleared their plates. Then they served coffee and tea and offered a choice of puddings.

Sydney approached and leaned down between Janelle and Jonas. "There seems to be a problem with the film file on the portable drive."

Janelle's stomach dropped, and she shot a glance at Jonas.

"Don't worry. I'll take care of it." He rose and followed Sydney to the back of the room.

Janelle closed her eyes. *Please, Lord.* No other words would come. Her emotions had been on such a roller coaster. Her stomach knotted, and she pushed away her half-eaten lemon tart.

The waiters cleared the dessert plates. She glanced at her watch. It was time for her to return to the stage and introduce the film. Her gaze darted to the closed door of the sound booth. Where was Jonas? What was happening? Should she stay seated and wait for him to return or . . .

She glanced across the table at Maggie, caught her friend's eye, and mouthed the word *pray*.

Maggie's eyes flashed. She nodded and gripped Dan's hand. He turned to his wife with a questioning look.

The lights came down, and the spotlight shone on the podium. Janelle pulled in a sharp breath, then she slowly rose and climbed the steps to the stage.

Forcing strength into her voice, she looked out over the audience. "Tonight, we want to take you on a journey to share the Foundling Hospital's rich history, then shine a light on our present work and what we dream of doing in the future. We hope you'll enjoy this inspiring film created for us by Jonas Conrad and the team at Vision Impact Films."

Janelle stepped away from the podium. As soon as she reached her seat, the spotlight switched off, and the room was plunged into darkness. Her heartbeat pounded in her ears, and her hands and arms tingled.

Soft music began to play, the screen came to life, and the image of an infant wrapped in a blanket and held in a woman's arms came into focus. Jonas's voice rose above the music.

"She was only three months old the day her life changed forever—the day her mother surrendered her into the care of the Foundling Hospital. She was one of the twenty-five thousand children who was given an opportunity for a better life and a future."

As the film continued, highlighting the museum's history and impact, hot tears flooded Janelle's eyes. The images were beautiful, and the narration and music added just what was needed to make the story come alive. Jonas had done it—he'd taken everything he'd learned and crafted it into a film that showed all she loved about the museum's past and present. She brushed a tear from her cheek and sent off a prayer of thanks.

～

Jonas leaned back in the sound booth chair and pinched the bridge of his nose, fighting off the flood of emotion washing over him. After almost three months of intense researching, writing, and filming, and then countless hours editing, revising, and narrating, the film was finally rolling for the intended audience.

His thoughts shifted back through the last few weeks and the race to complete the project before the deadline. The schedule had already been tight, and then he'd been knocked out with a bad case of the flu for several days. He'd been so ill, he hadn't checked with the narrator until last Wednesday.

The narrator's lame excuse for not being able to complete his work had angered Jonas. After a few desperate calls to Howie and prayers for direction, the answer became clear. The only way to finish the film on time was to narrate it himself.

Though he was still feeling the effects of the flu, he practiced and ran through the narration several times while working with Ben on the music. Scene by scene, they fit the words and music together. With only ninety minutes before the gala was set to begin, they'd finished the last scene. He'd been so relieved he nearly lost it. But there was no time for that. He jumped in the shower, changed into his best suit, and hailed a taxi to drive him to the venue.

Jonas released a deep breath. *Thank you, Lord. I never could've done this without your help and guidance. Please use this film as you intended and let it help the museum continue their important work. Show Janelle I'm a man of my word, a man she can trust and love.*

The technician seated next to him glanced his way. "Hey, don't worry. Everything's good."

Jonas swallowed. "Yeah, thanks."

"No problem." The technician settled back in his chair, crossed his arms, and watched the film play on the big screen while the other man raised the sound just a bit.

Jonas's gaze traveled past the window and through the crowd until he found Janelle. Her back was to him, but he could tell she was focused on the screen, taking in the film along with the rest of the audience. They had no idea how hard he'd worked on this project or how tough it had been to convey the message he wanted to portray, but Janelle knew. She understood. And that made it all worthwhile.

He wished he could join her and see her reaction as the film showed the museum's exhibits, programs, and kids who took part in the programs. But he didn't want to distract her or anyone else by walking in at this point. He would wait and let the film tell the story that had come through his heart, mind, and camera.

⁓

Fifteen minutes later, Janelle watched the closing scenes of the film through misty eyes. Happy children holding up their finished art projects filled the screen and brought a smile to her lips. Memories of her own experiences, and the pride and confidence she'd gained attending those classes and meeting other children in care, came to her mind. The Lord had used those museum programs to teach her much more than how to mix colors, follow directions, and create unique designs. In the company of those friends, she'd sensed she was not alone or abandoned. She was unique and talented, with gifts she could share.

That solid truth had settled in her heart, and though her birth parents had not been able to care for her, others had stepped up to meet her need for love and belonging. The Lord had taken care of her. She was blessed.

The music rose, and a beautiful sunset appeared on the screen, along with the words: *The mission of the Foundling Museum is to continue to tell the story of the UK's first children's charity and its first public art gallery—the outcome of a centuries-old project designed to care for and educate London's most vulnerable citizens. We ask you to partner with us in this worthy cause by supporting the ongoing work of the Foundling Museum. Thank you.*

The credits rolled with the names of those who had been interviewed and acted in the film. The final image showed the logo of the museum next to the Vision Impact Films' logo.

Janelle's smile spread wider, and her heart felt like it would burst with love and gratitude for Jonas and the creativity, skill, and heart he had poured into the film.

The lights came up, and the audience applauded. Wesley rose to his feet, and others soon stood and joined him, expressing their enthusiastic approval.

Janelle rose and glanced to the left as Jonas strode forward and appeared at her side. She sent him a tearful smile and gave him a quick side-hug while the applause continued. "The film was amazing! Thank you!"

He released her, grinning and looking at a loss for words.

The audience settled back in their chairs, and Amanda took the stage. She sniffed and touched her nose with a tissue. "Well . . . that was my first time seeing the film, and I'm so impressed.

"I want to thank Janelle Spencer and all the museum staff for planning this wonderful event and for carrying on the work of the museum while I've been at the hospital with my twin daughters. They were born two months early, and we're grateful to say, after some challenges, they're doing very well and due to come home soon."

The audience clapped, and Amanda smiled her appreciation. She shifted her gaze to Jonas. "Our special thanks go to Jonas

Conrad of Vision Impact Films for creating such a powerful film to portray the vital mission of the Foundling Museum."

Janelle squeezed Jonas's hand, and he returned the gesture.

Amanda continued, "At the museum, we are committed to inspiring and educating visitors, as well as serving vulnerable children, young adults, and their caregivers who take part in our programs and events. As you saw in the film, those programs strengthen and enrich the lives of all those who participate. Many of these children have grown up in care and need the connection and support provided through our many classes and programs. So, tonight, we ask you to partner with us to honor the history of the Foundling Hospital and give generously so we can continue the important work of the Foundling Museum.

"You'll find contribution cards and envelopes in the center of your table. You may fill them out now and leave them on the table, or you can give online through the link on the screen." She motioned over her shoulder toward the final slide. "One-time gifts and monthly donations are both welcome and appreciated. Thank you for joining us tonight, and thank you for your interest in and generous support of the Foundling Museum. Good night."

Janelle and Jonas spent the next thirty minutes speaking to guests and thanking them for coming. Several people shook Jonas's hand and praised the film. A few gave him their business cards and asked for more information. Janelle was thrilled Jonas had made contacts that could lead to future film projects.

The crowd thinned, and Maggie, Dan, Olivia, and Lisa collected the donation cards and envelopes that had been left by the guests.

Janelle turned to Jonas. "I need to take down the display."

"I'll give you a hand."

They crossed to the side of the room, where several photos from the museum's exhibits had been arranged on a long, cloth-covered table. Mary Alice's book and token sat in the middle, surrounded by other tokens and artifacts.

A delightful shiver of anticipation traveled through Janelle as she thought of the documentary Jonas planned to make. After seeing tonight's film, she felt confident he was the right one to tell Mary Alice's story. He would handle it with honesty and sensitivity that would honor her life and support their work at the museum.

Janelle picked up the token and gently ran her finger over the words *Remember My Love*. That phrase had taken on a deeper meaning as she'd worked on this project with Jonas. Mary Alice's mother, aunt, and uncle had demonstrated their love and commitment by never giving up their search for Mary Alice until she'd been rescued and brought safely home. Their example had made a deep impression on Janelle. She would take that lesson to heart, seek to keep her commitments and treasure those she loved.

Jonas stepped up beside her. "What are you thinking?"

She held the token out to him. "This token represents the bond of love between Mary Alice and her mother . . . and so much more."

He gave a thoughtful nod.

"After all we've learned about Mary Alice and her family, I feel like I know them. I'm so glad we're going to tell her story. Children are not for sale. They need to be protected and cared for in loving families."

He took her hand. "Tonight's film gave the big picture, but there's so much more to tell. People need to know what happened to Mary Alice is still happening to countless other children today." His earnest gaze met hers. "You can show them through a new exhibit, and I'll tell them through a documentary."

She nodded, love for him warming her heart. "I'd say we've got our work cut out for us."

He grinned. "You're right about that."

She added the token, book, and other artifacts to the case and closed the lid.

Maggie and Dan approached and handed Janelle a stack of envelopes. Maggie gave Janelle a hug. "I'd say the evening was a wonderful success."

"Yes, and I'm so relieved."

Jonas touched Janelle's arm. "I'm going to get the film drive from the tech crew." He and Dan walked toward the sound booth.

Maggie's eyes twinkled, and she leaned closer. "Jonas did an amazing job on that film."

Gratitude washed over her again. "Yes. It was wonderful."

Maggie grinned. "See, I told you he'd come through for you. All you needed was a little faith."

Janelle's heart lifted. "You're right."

Jonas returned to Janelle's side and slipped his arm around her waist.

Maggie glanced between Jonas and Janelle. "Do you want a ride home?"

Before Janelle could answer, Jonas said, "I'll see that she gets home safe." He looked her way. "If that's okay with you."

She smiled. "It is. Thanks."

Lisa and Olivia joined them, and Janelle turned to Olivia. "Thank you for your help tonight and with the film."

"It was fun." Olivia hesitated a moment, then met Janelle's gaze. "School starts next week, so I'm going back to my mom's tomorrow. Do you think if I come back next summer, I could be an intern?"

Lisa's eyes lit up. "That's a great idea!"

"You usually need to be eighteen," Janelle said, "but since you volunteered this summer and did such a great job, we might be able to make an exception. Stay in touch, and you can fill out the application after the first of the year."

Olivia smiled and nodded. "Thanks. I will."

Janelle gave her a hug. "Take care. I'll miss you."

"I'll miss you too."

Dan, Maggie, Olivia, and Lisa said good night and walked out the door.

Jonas turned to Janelle. "There's a great view of the city from the balcony. Want to take a look?"

Her heartbeat fluttered, and she nodded. "I'd love that."

He took her hand as they walked upstairs and stepped out on the balcony. The twinkling lights of the city spread out before them. In the distance, she could see the illuminated clockface of Big Ben and the lights on the London Eye. A cool breeze carrying a hint of autumn ruffled her dress. Jonas slipped his arm around her shoulders, and she leaned into his side.

"It's beautiful," she said softly.

"Yes, it is." He was quiet for moment, then said, "Janelle . . . I'm sorry these last couple of weeks have been so crazy. Trying to finish the film and then catching the flu really threw me for a loop. But I know I should've made more of an effort to stay in touch."

"I was worried about you . . . and about us."

He released a deep breath. "I could kick myself now. I really need to learn some better communication skills."

She looked up at him. "Let's learn them together."

He leaned down and kissed her cheek. "I like the sound of that."

"So . . . even though we're done with the film . . . you still want to spend time together?"

He pulled back with a stunned look. "Yes, of course. Now that I've found you, I'm not letting you go."

Her heart lifted. "Really? That's how you feel?"

He turned and took both of her hands in his. "Janelle, you are a beautiful, caring, smart, and amazing woman, and I want

331

to spend more time with you and give our relationship time to grow."

A warm glow of happiness wrapped around her. "I'd like that too."

He leaned closer. She tilted her face up, breathing in the clean, spicy scent that was Jonas, and kissed him. That kiss carried her away in a whirl of hope and pleasure. Jonas Conrad was the man she had been waiting for—not a perfect man, but the perfect man for her.

A joyful prayer of thanks rose from her heart. Together they would chase after all the dreams the Lord gave them and see where the journey would take them . . . and she would always treasure and remember their love.

EPILOGUE

On a sunny afternoon in early June, Jonas slipped his hand into Janelle's as they walked through the Queen Elizabeth Gate into Hyde Park. She glanced up at him, and a sense of peace and contentment filled her. They'd decided to celebrate the one-year anniversary of the day they'd first met by taking a stroll through the park and going out to dinner.

What a journey they'd traveled together in the last year.

In October, Amanda had resigned so she could stay home with her twins, and Janelle accepted the promotion to executive director. From the contacts Jonas made at the gala, he'd contracted five more projects.

In May, his documentary of Mary Alice's story, *A Foundling's Tale—Lost, Sold, and Redeemed*, had been shown at the festival and won the prestigious British Independent Film Award for Best Historical Documentary.

Janelle smiled as she recalled the last few images in the film. Mary Alice stood in a garden setting, surrounded by her husband, mother, aunt, uncle, and four sons. The caption listed their names and said the year was 1910, when Mary Alice was in her early thirties.

Another photo showed her in midlife, seated at a table with five other women. The caption stated the six women had been raised together as sisters after they were rescued from brothels. What an amazing family! How kind and caring Mary Alice's relatives were to bring all those girls into their home and help them heal from what they'd experienced.

The final photo showed Mary Alice in later life, wearing a cloche hat and 1920s-style dress. In her hands she held a copy of her life story and the round golden token her mother had left with her when she'd been given into the care of the Foundling Hospital.

Viewing that film with Jonas and seeing him win the prize had been a joyful night she would never forget.

That same month, they had opened a new exhibit at the museum featuring Mary Alice's story and including portions of the film as part of the display. The exhibit had received extensive media coverage, drawing attention to the history of human trafficking in London and challenging viewers to consider the ongoing impact on women and girls.

It had been a busy and exciting twelve months, and sharing all those changes and events had drawn Janelle and Jonas even closer.

Janelle pulled in a deep breath, thankful they could escape the bustle of the city and soak in the tranquility of the peaceful park. She glanced at Jonas as they continued down the path. "This was a wonderful idea. I'm glad you suggested coming here."

Affection shone in his eyes as he looked her way. "I filmed some scenes here last week. I know how much you love flowers, so I thought you'd like to see this special spot I found."

Her heart danced, knowing she'd been on his mind and that he wanted to share what he'd found with her.

They turned left and walked through an intricate wrought-iron gate with a delicate rose design and followed the path toward a circular fountain with a statue of a boy and a dolphin. The gentle sound of splashing water and the light fragrance of flowers sent a soothing wave through her. "This is beautiful."

He nodded, a twinkle in his eye. "It's nice, but this isn't the spot I had in mind."

She tipped her head and sent him a questioning look, then scanned the path ahead. Lush flower beds came into view, filled with colorful roses—vibrant reds, soft pinks, sunny yellows, and pure whites. Their fragrance wafted toward her, delighting her senses. "I've never seen so many lovely roses."

"I knew you'd like it . . . but there's more." They stepped off the path and into the shade of several tall trees beyond the flower beds.

"Where are we going?"

He grinned. "You'll see."

They took one more turn and walked onto a circular lawn surrounded by arches of climbing roses. Janelle's gaze traveled around the secluded garden. "Oh my . . . this is lovely."

He took her hand again and led her toward a small round table with two folding chairs. Janelle blinked. The table was covered with a white cloth and set with pretty china plates and sparkling silverware. A small bouquet of roses and two flickering votive candles sat in the center.

She turned to Jonas. "What is this?"

He motioned toward the table. "Dinner for two. I thought this would be a great place to celebrate our one-year anniversary."

She laughed softly. "How did you do this?"

He lifted his eyebrows. "I have my connections." He pulled

out the chair for her, and she took a seat. Then he reached down on the other side of the table and lifted a tray with two covered plates. "Your dinner, my lady."

"Thank you, kind sir." She took her plate and placed it on the table, then she set his across from her.

He turned away and reached down for something else.

She smiled, pleased by his thoughtful planning.

Jonas turned around, then knelt in front of her. In his hand he held an open black velvet box with a sparkling diamond ring.

Janelle gasped, and she lifted her hand to cover her mouth.

Tender vulnerability filled his expression as he reached for her hand. "Janelle, you've won my heart. I love you more than I ever realized was possible. I think we are stronger and better together, and I can't imagine a future without you. Will you marry me?"

Her heartbeat raced, and her spirit soared. "Yes! Oh yes!" She rose and reached for him, and they held each other close. Joy spiraled through her. Jonas loved her. He wanted to marry her. They would be a family and spend their lives together. It was almost too wonderful, too much to take in. Happy tears filled her eyes.

He kissed her and slipped the ring on her finger, then he turned toward the trees. "She said yes!" he announced in a loud voice.

Janelle's eyes widened as Howie, carrying a camera, stepped out of the bushes and walked toward them. Lauren followed, beaming and carrying Liam in her arms.

"Congratulations!" Howie called, lowering the camera and grinning from ear to ear.

Maggie, Dan, Olivia, Cole, and Caleb stepped out from behind the trees. The boys jogged toward them, laughing and dancing. Dan grabbed hold of Jonas's hand and pumped it vigorously. "Great job! Congratulations!"

Maggie hugged Janelle. "Oh, I'm so glad he finally proposed! I've known about his plans for three weeks, and it was killing me to keep it a secret!"

Janelle laughed and hugged her back. "So, you helped set this up?"

Maggie nodded, her eyes shining. "Olivia and I arrived about an hour ago. It was so fun."

Olivia grinned. "You should have seen us carrying in the table and chairs, and then guarding everything until you two arrived."

Maggie nodded to her husband. "Dan picked up the food, Lauren arranged the flowers, and of course Howie filmed it, so you'll always have this memory to treasure."

Janelle's smile spread wide, and her eyes misted as she looked around the group. "Thank you! This is so, so special."

The circle of smiling friends gathered in closer, patting Jonas on the back and hugging Janelle.

Jonas slipped his arm around Janelle's shoulder. "So, you liked your proposal?"

She looked up at him. "Liked it? I loved it!" Then she wrapped her arms around his neck. "But I love you even more." She kissed him then, with the happy chorus of cheers and applause from their friends playing in the background.

Author's Note

Dear Friend,

I hope you enjoyed reading *A Token of Love* and were touched and encouraged by the story. Life in Victorian England was quite different than it is today, yet women and girls still face some of the same challenges and need protection from those who would take advantage of them. The research for this story impressed me deeply, especially learning how Christian believers confronted troubling social issues and worked for changes that would protect women and girls.

Readers often ask which parts of a story are true and which are fictional, and I'd like to tell you a little about my research and how the story was born to answer that question.

One day, I was scrolling through Pinterest and saw a heart-rending painting of a woman handing over her baby. It linked back to information about London's Foundling Hospital, the first children's charity home in England. The Foundling Hospital cared for approximately twenty-five thousand children between the years of 1741 and 1953. The Foundling Museum, and their partner organization, Coram, continue the work today by sharing the history of the Foundling Hospital and offering exhibits and programs for families and vulnerable children.

I was especially intrigued by the Foundling Museum's display of tokens that mothers left with their children in the hope they would be able to return and reclaim them. That idea sparked the beginning of the story in my imagination.

The descriptions of the museum's exhibits, programs, and rooms are true. But selling young girls to brothels is not a part of the Foundling Hospital's history. That idea was taken from the 1885 *Pall Mall Gazette* series *The Maiden Tribute to Modern Babylon*, which was written by the editor, W. T. Stead. He is considered the father of investigative journalism and was a crusader for social change. After writing the series, he was jailed for buying a girl to prove it was possible to obtain them. Those articles caused a huge outcry, which prompted a change in the laws to raise the age of consent and protect girls.

With each book, I look for ways that my fictional characters can meet real people in history who lived out their faith in their daily lives. I was delighted to discover Josephine Butler and include her in the story. She was a courageous woman of deep faith who spoke publicly and wrote articles to protect women and girls and improve their lives. Her speeches inspired the ones in this novel. She and W. T. Stead knew each other and worked together for this cause and others.

All the other characters are fictional, but they became very real to me as I wrote their story.

The topic of human trafficking, and missing and abducted children, is not an easy topic to research or write about, and I suspect it may have been a challenge for some of my readers. But understanding those dangers in the past and how they continue today is important for all of us.

If you'd like to learn more about this topic, I suggest you visit the International Justice Mission website at ijm.org, and the

International Centre for Missing and Exploited Children website at icmec.org. You can learn more about the Foundling Hospital and the Foundling Museum at FoundlingMuseum.org.uk.

I enjoy using Pinterest to collect images that inspire my story. I hope you'll visit my Pinterest board to see the characters, setting, and images of Victorian England: pinterest.com/carrieturansky/loves-token/

If you enjoyed *A Token of Love* and you're looking for other books filled with family drama, romance, and inspiration, please stop by my website, CarrieTuransky.com, and peruse my other novels. I'd love to stay in touch via my email newsletter. You can sign up at my website, and if you do, I'll send you a free short story.

Until next time . . .
blessings and happy reading!
Carrie

Acknowledgments

I am very grateful for all those who have given me their support and encouragement and provided information in the process of writing this book. Without your help, it never would have been written! I'd like to say thank you to the following people:

My husband, Scott, who always provides great feedback and constant encouragement when I talk about my characters, the plot, the editing process, and what happens next. Your love and support have allowed me to follow my dreams and write the books of my heart. I will be forever grateful for you and our love and partnership in life!

Steve Laube, my literary agent, for his patience, guidance, and wise counsel. You have been a good advocate who has represented me well. I feel blessed to be your client, and I appreciate you!

Jessica Sharpe, Jennifer Veilleux, Bethany Lenderink—my gifted editors—who helped me shape and reshape this story so readers will be able to truly enjoy it. I appreciate your thoughtful questions and insight, and your gracious way of collaborating!

Kathleen Lynch of Black Kat Design, for the lovely cover and for allowing me to give some input in the final stages.

Raela Schoenherr, Anne Van Solkema, Rachael Betz, and all the marketing, publicity, sales, and other teams at Bethany House for publishing and promoting my books and helping me share my stories with readers.

Cathy Gohlke, Cher Gatto, Terri MacAdoo, Stacy Ladyman, and my friends in the ACFW NY/NJ group for your encouragement and support. We have more adventures ahead on this writing journey!

Debb Hackett, my British friend and fellow author, for helping me spot phrases that were "too American" and suggesting British words and phrases to replace them.

My dear readers, especially those who are members of Carrie's Reading Friends on Facebook, who offer their kind reviews and help me spread the word about my books. Your thoughtful posts and encouraging words keep me going! I can't wait to write more new stories for you!

Most of all, I thank my Lord and Savior, Jesus Christ, for His great love, wonderful grace, and faithful provision. I am grateful for the gifts and talents you have given me, and I hope to always use them in ways that bless you and bring honor and glory to your name.

Questions for Readers

1. How does Lillian Freemont's character evolve throughout the story in terms of her personal growth and her relationships with other characters?

2. The novel explores the themes of love and justice across two different time periods. How are these themes shown in the characters' lives and actions in both 1885 and the present day?

3. Discuss the role of mystery and suspense in the narrative. How does the author build tension, and were there moments where you were surprised by the plot twists or revelations?

4. How does the author use the settings of 1885 London and present-day London to create atmosphere and enhance the reading experience? How does the historical context influence the characters and their decisions?

5. Explore the relationships between Lillian and Matthew in the 1885 timeline and Janelle and Jonas in the present day. How do these partnerships contribute to the

overall storyline, and what challenges do the characters face in working together toward a common goal?

6. The novel touches on social issues such as the treatment of foundlings and the challenges faced by women in the past. How are these issues portrayed in the story?

7. Discuss the significance of the Foundling Museum in both timelines. How does it serve as a central element in connecting the characters and the overarching plot?

8. Characters in the story are often faced with difficult choices and must make sacrifices. Identify key moments where characters had to decide between conflicting priorities. How do these choices shape the plot?

9. Romance plays a significant role in the novel. Analyze the romantic relationships in both timelines. How do the characters navigate love, and do you find the romantic elements satisfying or surprising?

10. Carrie Turansky is known for incorporating faith elements into her stories. How is faith explored and portrayed in *A Token of Love*? How does it influence the characters' decisions and perspectives on love and justice?

For more from Carrie Turansky,
read on
for an excerpt from

The

LEGACY

of

LONGDALE

MANOR

Art historian Gwen Morris is evaluating paintings at a British estate when she uncovers a connection to the father she never knew through a one-hundred-year-old journal. In 1912, Charlotte Harper struggles with a painful family secret that she can only confess in her journal, which shatters her faith and leaves her wondering if she can ever trust in love again.

Available now wherever books are sold.

One

2012
LONDON, ENGLAND

The lift door slid open, and Gwen Morris stepped into the third-floor offices of Hill and Morris, one of the most prestigious art and antique auction houses in London. She still felt a thrill each time she walked down the dark-paneled hallway toward her new office and took in the beautiful paintings, jewelry, and antiques on display.

The receptionist looked up as Gwen approached. The young woman's eyes widened, and she quickly looked down at her desk and shuffled some papers.

Gwen's steps slowed. "Good morning, MaryAnn."

"Morning." MaryAnn slowly lifted her eyes to meet Gwen's. "Your grandfather—I mean, Mr. Morris—would like you to come to his office right away."

A prickle of unease traveled through Gwen, but she quickly dismissed it. He probably wanted to discuss some new acquisitions, or perhaps give her feedback on her first month as junior specialist for art history and antiques.

"Thank you." She started down the hall and glanced through Charlene's open office doorway. As the older woman met her gaze, her expression hardened, and she turned toward the windows.

That was odd. Charlene usually offered a "Good morning," or at least a nod as Gwen passed.

She continued down the hall and received chilly looks from three other colleagues. What was going on? Certainly, the weather was gloomy, and they all had a heavy workload, but she couldn't imagine why everyone seemed to be in such a dark mood this morning.

She approached her grandfather's outer office, and Mrs. Huntington, her grandfather's fiftyish administrative assistant, lifted her head, her face impassive. "Mr. Morris said you are to go right in."

Gwen's stomach tensed. This did not bode well. She straightened her shoulders, stepped into her grandfather's office, and closed the door.

Her grandfather looked up, his gray eyes cool and assessing. He sat behind his large wooden desk, with his back to the tall windows behind him. Dark gray clouds draped the buildings on the opposite side of St. James Street, and rivulets raced down the glass in a dizzy dance. The downpour outside seemed a perfect reflection of her grandfather's shadowed expression.

He nodded to the chair in front of his desk. "Have a seat, Gwen."

A shiver raced down her back as she lowered herself into the chair. She should ask what was wrong, but she couldn't seem to force out the words.

"We have a situation . . . a very serious situation, I might add." His gray eyebrows drew down into a deep *V*. "One of the Impressionist paintings we auctioned last Saturday"—he glanced at his computer—"*Avenue of the Allies*, which you listed as a copy of Childe Hassam's painting by the same name . . ."

Gwen nodded, remembering the painting clearly. Hassam was an American Impressionist who painted in Britain and

France as well as the US. His work was copied by many artists in the late 1800s and early 1900s.

He focused on her again. "It was an original."

A shock wave jolted Gwen, and she sucked in a sharp breath.

"The buyer is thrilled to have purchased an original Hassam at one-tenth of its true value," her grandfather continued. "But the seller, Ivan Saunders, is irate. He's threatening a lawsuit and promising to spread the story of our incompetence far and wide."

She stared at her grandfather and tried to swallow, but her throat seemed blocked by a huge boulder. How could she have made such a terrible mistake?

Her thoughts raced back to the last week of February, when she'd started in her new position. After one year as an intern, stepping into the role of junior specialist had been a huge transition. That same week, she'd gone through a painful breakup with her boyfriend, Oliver St. Charles. She'd lost hours of sleep over that heartache, and her mind had been in a fog. Was that why she'd failed to realize she was evaluating an original Hassam?

"Well, Gwen, what do you have to say for yourself?"

"I . . . I don't know what happened. I checked the painting's provenance. Then I compared it to other paintings by Hassam, looking at the style and brushstrokes, the color choice, and size of the work. They all seemed so different from his other paintings, and there was no signature, so I assumed—"

"His signature was revealed when the frame was removed. It's been verified as the original." Her grandfather steepled his fingers, his serious gaze drilling into her. "Why didn't you remove the frame and look for the signature?"

"The frame was beautiful. I thought it might possibly be worth more than the painting, and I didn't want to damage it. And the fact that there was no visible signature made it seem most likely it was a copy."

"Did you check the catalogue raisonné?"

"Yes. It said the original was part of a private collection owned by . . . someone. I don't remember the name, but it wasn't Ivan Saunders."

"If you had any question, you should have spoken to Charlene, or run your findings past others who have more experience before you catalogued it."

The burning sensation in her stomach rose, singeing her throat. "Charlene was unwell that week and not in the office."

He gave a brief nod. "Charlene and a few others are looking at the pieces you've evaluated since then. Nothing else glaring has come up, but that doesn't excuse the mistake you made with the Hassam."

Gwen lowered her chin, wishing she could melt into the floor. She had seriously disappointed her grandfather. Worse than that, she'd confirmed what she'd always suspected: She wasn't good enough. She wasn't ready. She might never be. This position had only been given to her because she was Lionel Morris's granddaughter. And now that she'd made this colossal error, she faced losing the position she'd worked so hard to attain.

She looked across at her grandfather, pain and regret squeezing her heart. "You're right. There's no excuse. I should've done more research and consulted with others, rather than trying to handle it on my own."

"I imagine you were trying to prove yourself, but I'm afraid that was a very costly error in judgment. You've tarnished your reputation in the art community and with your colleagues at Hill and Morris."

He didn't add *and with me*, but she could feel the weight of those silent words. "I'm sorry." Her voice came out a rough whisper.

"This is a very difficult way to start your career."

That went without saying. "What will happen now . . . about the painting?"

"I've spoken to our legal department."

Gwen's heart clenched. Oliver worked in the legal department. Now he had even more reasons to be glad he'd broken up with her. Everyone at Hill and Morris would consider her a foolish upstart who'd proven she didn't deserve the position she'd been given.

"They'll work out a settlement with Ivan Saunders," her grandfather continued, "but it will be costly and not soon forgotten by anyone."

Gwen acknowledged his words with a slow nod. How could she have let this happen? Was it her pride or lack of experience that had taken her down that path . . . or both?

She looked up and met her grandfather's gaze. "What can I do? How can I make this up to you?"

He tapped his index fingers together for a few seconds as he studied the rain-washed windows to his left. "I have an old friend, Lilly Benderly. She wants to sell some of the art and antiques in her home, Longdale Manor, near Keswick. She can't afford our usual fees, but there's the possibility of a future investment there, and I'd like to help her." He shifted his gaze back to Gwen. "I want you to go to Longdale, evaluate the pieces she's interested in selling, and make the arrangements to have them shipped to London and prepared for auction."

Hope surged in her chest. "Of course. I'd be glad to go." She had no idea where Keswick was located, but she didn't want to admit that to her grandfather. She'd look it up later. "Did she say how many pieces she wants evaluated?"

"No, she didn't. But this will give you time away from London until the storm blows over. I think that is the best way to avoid embarrassment."

His embarrassment, or hers? She closed her eyes and suppressed a sigh. Why hadn't she been more careful? Couldn't she do anything right? She pushed those questions down, opened her eyes, and focused on her grandfather again. "When did you want me to go?"

"As soon as we can make the arrangements."

Gwen nodded, but questions swirled in her mind. What type of art and antiques did her grandfather's friend want to sell? If she handled this project well, could she regain her grandfather's trust?

"Take your time, and be sure you evaluate each piece correctly," he said. "Lilly is a recent widow, and a bit eccentric. But I want her to receive the best sale price possible. Can you do that, Gwen?"

She gave a firm nod. "I'll do my best and run all my work by you and Charlene."

"Good. Mrs. Huntington will give you Lilly Benderly's contact information. Let her know you're coming. Stay in Keswick as long as needed to do a thorough job." He paused and looked toward the door, indicating the meeting was over.

She rose on wobbly legs, then willed strength into them and faced her grandfather. "I know my mistake has put you in a difficult position. I'm truly sorry for that. It won't happen again. I promise."

His stern expression softened. "We all make mistakes, Gwen. It's what we learn from those mistakes and how we recover that's important. I hope you'll take this lesson to heart."

His gentle words sent new courage flowing through her. "Yes, sir. I will."

"You've been given a great opportunity at Hill and Morris. I hope you'll do all you can to make the most of it."

⌒

Gwen lifted her suitcase onto the bed in her small London flat, pulled the zipper around, and flipped open the top. Her hand stilled, and she looked out her bedroom window as the painful events of the morning replayed through her mind. She'd let her grandfather down in the worst way and made a costly mistake that was going to follow her for years to come.

She blinked and tried to shake off the dazed, disappointed feeling coursing through her. This was not the end of her career. It couldn't be. Somehow, she would find a way to rebuild. She crossed to the dresser and took a shirt from the top drawer.

The front door opened, and footsteps sounded on the wooden floor. Lindsey Winters, her roommate, looked in from the hallway. "Gwen, what are you doing home?" Her gaze darted to the suitcase on the bed. "What's going on?"

Gwen sighed. "It's a long story. You might want to sit down."

Lindsey lowered herself into the chair next to Gwen's bed. "What happened?"

Gwen sank down on her bed. "I made a huge mistake evaluating a painting, and my grandfather is sending me away until the dust settles."

"What kind of mistake?"

Gwen poured out the story, her eyes burning as she repeated what she'd done and the response of her grandfather and co-workers.

"Oh, Gwen, I'm so sorry. It's no wonder you're upset. But he didn't sack you. He's giving you a chance to show him you can do the work." That was just like Lindsey, always looking for the positive side in any hard situation.

Gwen gave a reluctant nod. Lindsey was right. Her grandfather had offered her the opportunity to redeem herself and prove she was worthy of her position at Hill and Morris.

"Where's he sending you?"

"He wants me to evaluate some pieces for an old friend who lives in Keswick, wherever that is."

Lindsey's eyes lit up. "That's in the Lake District."

A distant memory stirred Gwen's mind at those words. "The Lake District?"

"Yes, up north. Oh, it's so lovely this time of year." Lindsey smiled. "Mum and Dad took me to Windermere on holiday when I was sixteen. That's not far from Keswick. We went hiking in the hills. They call them *fells* up there. And we took a boat ride across Lake Windermere and visited Beatrix Potter's Hill Top Farm."

The Lake District . . . Gwen rose and crossed to her closet. Her mum had mentioned painting in the Lake District when she was younger. She reached up to the top shelf, pulled out a large round hatbox, and carried it back to her bed.

"What's in there?" Lindsey asked as Gwen lifted the lid.

"Everything that was in my mum's desk." She glanced at the papers and photographs that nearly filled the box, and her throat tightened. "It's hard to believe she's been gone almost two years."

"I'm sorry, Gwen." Lindsey's voice softened. "I wish I'd known your mum. From what you've told me, she sounds like a very special person."

"She was. I still miss her every day." Gwen blew out a breath and pushed the first few papers aside. "I think my parents met in the Lake District."

"Really?" Lindsey scooted closer. "I've never heard you say much about your father."

Gwen's throat tightened, and she tried to force down the jumbled feelings coursing through her. "That's because I've never met him. He left my mum before I was born."

Lindsey's eyes widened. "Oh, Gwen. I didn't know."

"It was a long time ago." She tried to sound as though it

didn't bother her, but that wasn't the truth. She'd asked Mum about her father several times. But Mum only gave brief replies that left Gwen with more questions than answers. Finally, when she was eighteen, she'd begged to know why her father hadn't been a part of their lives. Did he even know she existed? And if he did know, why didn't he care he had a daughter?

Mum said she had her reasons and made Gwen promise she would not go searching for him on her own. Mum said she would explain more when Gwen graduated from university, so Gwen had reluctantly agreed. But Mum had died in a terrible car accident only three weeks before Gwen's graduation, taking the story with her to her grave.

Gwen lifted a stack of photos and sorted through them. A few seconds later, she found the one she'd been looking for. A young couple stood arm in arm on the shore of a lake with high hills in the background. Her mother looked as though she was in her early twenties. Her long brown hair cascaded over her shoulders, and her bright blue eyes shone with a hopeful light. The tall man standing beside her looked ruggedly handsome, with light brown hair, deep-set gray eyes, and a strong, square chin. Gwen guessed he was also in his twenties, but older than Mum. His arms were muscular and suntanned, and he held what looked like a tall wooden stick that curved at the top and had a carved head.

Lindsey leaned closer. "Is that your parents?"

"Yes." Her voice quavered as she stared at the father she'd never met.

Lindsey tipped her head. "It looks like there's something written on the back of the photo."

Gwen turned it over and read, *Jessica and Landon on our wedding day, 10 June 1985, Keswick.* She blinked and stared at the words. Her parents were married in Keswick.

She studied her father's image, considering the possibilities.

Did he still live in or near Keswick? The thought of meeting him after all these years sent a shiver down her back. She'd promised her mum she wouldn't search for him, but that was before her mum died. Surely her mum's death released her from that promise.

But doubts rose and clouded her thoughts. Something very painful must have happened to make her mum keep that part of her life a secret. Was she ready to learn the truth about her father and discover why he'd never been a part of their lives?

She'd always longed to know her father and sense that true father-daughter connection. This was her chance. It would take courage to begin her search. But if she did find him, would he welcome her into his life, or would he break her heart as he'd broken Mum's?

~

David Bradford gripped the sides of the old folding ladder and climbed toward the top. He pushed open Longdale's attic door, and cool musty air rushed out, along with an odd scent he couldn't name. Squinting into the darkness, he pointed his torch toward the eaves and scanned the dusty timbers. Something moved, and he gripped the ladder.

"What do you see?" his grandmother called from the bottom of the ladder.

David scrolled the beam of light over the squirming black mass between the wooden eaves and suppressed a shudder. "I'm afraid you've got bats, Nana."

"Bats! Good heavens!" His grandmother tugged on his pant leg. "Come down at once! Bats carry rabies."

David doubted the bats in Longdale's attic had the disease, but he'd rather not personally test that theory. Gritting his teeth, he backed down the steps. Bats! One more problem to add to the growing list of things he needed to address before they could move ahead with his plan to convert Longdale into a luxury hotel.

"This is dreadful!" His grandmother looked up, her soft gray eyes filled with worry. "We have to be rid of them."

"It won't be easy, Nana." He stepped down beside her and raised the ladder into the ceiling. "Bats are protected. It's against the law to disturb their roosts."

Her silver eyebrows rose. "Protected?" Her stunned expression quickly changed to steely resolve. "They must go! I won't stand for an attic full of bats!"

David kept his voice even, hoping to calm her. "We might be able to get permission to move them. If not, we'll probably have to enclose the area so they can continue living there undisturbed."

"We can't open Longdale to paying guests with bats roosting in the attic!"

He laid his hand on her shoulder. This kind of upsetting news wasn't good for her heart. "Don't worry, Nana. I'll make some calls and take care of it." He guided her down the hallway, away from the soft rustling sounds coming from the attic.

She looked back at him. "Oh, you are a dear. I'm so glad you've come. Arthur always took care of things like this, but now that he's gone . . ." Her voice choked off, and she shook her head. "I need some tea. Let's go down to the kitchen."

He agreed, and they took the back servants' stairs down two flights to the bottom level and followed the long, arched hallway to Longdale's cavernous kitchen.

Mrs. Galloway, or Mrs. G., as his grandmother liked to call her, stood by the stove, stirring a pot of something that smelled delicious. He sniffed again and determined it must be chicken soup.

Mrs. G. greeted them with pink cheeks and a cheery smile. Then she noticed his grandmother's worried look, and her smile melted away.

"We're in need of some tea." Nana crossed to the large work-table in the center of the kitchen. "David has discovered what's making those strange noises in the attic."

Mrs. G. turned from filling the electric teakettle. "What is it?"

"Bats!" Nana's chin quivered. "We've been invaded by a colony of bloodsucking creatures!"

Mrs. G.'s hand flew to cover her heart. "Saints above! They can't get out of the attic, can they?"

"No," David quickly replied. "I'm sure they won't bother us. I faced a similar situation last summer when we converted an estate in Berkshire into a spa." He didn't add it had taken more than a month to get permission to remove the bats, and it had cost several hundred pounds to remedy the problem. His grandmother's income didn't match the needs of maintaining the estate, and he didn't want to add to her financial worries. He'd figure this out. He had to if he was going to help her save Longdale.

A bell buzzed behind him. He turned toward the bell board to see where the summon originated. "Someone is at the front door."

"Nancy is cleaning upstairs," Mrs. G. said. "She'll answer it for you."

David turned to his grandmother. "Are you expecting some-one?"

She blinked a few times, then her eyes widened. "I am. We better go up."

He held back a chuckle. His grandmother's memory was not as sharp as it used to be.

His grandmother started toward the kitchen doorway, then looked back. "Mrs. G., will you please bring our tea up to the library, along with some cinnamon biscuits and an extra cup for our guest?"

Mrs. G. nodded. "I'll be up as soon as it's ready."

David followed his grandmother up the stone stairs. "Who's joining us for tea?"

"Gwen Morris. She's the granddaughter of an old friend from London."

He'd never heard his grandmother mention someone by that name. "Is she in the area on holiday?"

"No, dear. She works at Hill and Morris."

His steps stalled. "The auction house?"

"Yes. Her grandfather, Lionel Morris, has been a dear friend for many years."

He stared at his grandmother. "*The* Lionel Morris of Hill and Morris?"

"Yes, dear. That's what I said. His granddaughter is going to look at the paintings and antiques and help us decide what to prepare for auction."

He grinned and shook his head. Lilly Benderly was always full of surprises. He'd mentioned the idea of selling some of the paintings and furnishings a few days ago, as that seemed like a logical way to raise the funds needed for the repairs and renovations. At the time, she hadn't seemed in favor of the idea. He supposed she'd changed her mind and forgotten to tell him. He followed her into the large entrance hall.

Nancy, the middle-aged woman who helped with cleaning twice a week, stood by the front door, blocking his view of the woman waiting there. Nancy turned to his grandmother. "This is Miss Gwen Morris to see you, ma'am." She stepped aside.

"Welcome to Longdale." Nana crossed toward her with an outstretched hand and warm smile. "I'm Lilly Benderly."

Gwen returned his grandmother's greeting and smile, and David did a double take. She was young and attractive, with long golden-brown hair that fell over her shoulders in soft waves. Her eyes were an unusual shade of blue green, like the lake on a summer day. She wore a fashionable green wool coat and brown leather boots and . . . she towed a rolling suitcase.

Had his grandmother invited her to stay at Longdale?

"I'm pleased to meet you." Gwen lifted her gaze, taking in the dark woodwork and elaborately carved staircase and mantel over the marble fireplace. "Longdale is a beautiful home."

"Thank you. We're very fond of it." She motioned toward David. "This is my grandson, David Bradford. He's the one I told you about."

He shot his grandmother a questioning glance. What had she told her?

Gwen looked his way and held out her hand. "It's good to meet you, Mr. Bradford. I'm looking forward to assisting you and Mrs. Benderly."

He took her hand. It was soft and warm, matching the look in her eyes.

"There's no need to be formal." His grandmother looked from Gwen to David. "You must call us Lilly and David."

Gwen nodded. "Thank you. Please, call me Gwen."

David studied her. She couldn't be more than twenty-five, and she looked more like an actress or model than an art and antique appraiser. Why had Lionel Morris sent her instead of someone older and more experienced? "What is your position at Hill and Morris?"

"I'm a junior specialist for art history and antiques."

"A junior specialist . . . as opposed to a senior specialist?"

She lifted her chin and met his challenge with a steady look. "Yes. I have an undergraduate degree in art history and a master's in art business. I finished a one-year internship at Hill and Morris in February. That's when I started my current position."

His grandmother sent him a puzzled look. "David, there's no need to question Gwen's credentials. She traveled all the way from London to help us. We want her to know how much we appreciate her coming."

Chastised, he nodded. "You're right." He turned to Gwen. "We're glad you're here. No offense meant."

"None taken." But her cheeks glowed bright pink, and her words sounded a bit forced. She turned back to his grandmother. "I appreciate your invitation to stay at Longdale, but if that's not convenient, I'd be glad to find accommodations in Keswick."

His grandmother shook her head. "Oh no. You must stay with us. What would your grandfather think if I sent you off alone?"

Gwen sent David a quick glance before she looked back at his grandmother. "If you're sure it's all right. It would make my job easier."

"We're positive, aren't we, David?" His grandmother turned to him with a lifted brow.

"Yes, of course. It makes sense for you to stay here. We have plenty of room."

His grandmother gave an approving smile. "Good. Now that's settled, let's go into the library. Tea is on the way, and we can have a chat."

Gwen sent an uncertain glance toward her suitcase.

David stepped forward. "I'll take that for you." Without waiting for her reply, he rolled it over to the bottom of the staircase, then he followed Gwen and his grandmother into the library.

He watched Gwen as she took a seat next to his grandmother. Her earlier prickly response to his questions had faded. She seemed more relaxed now, smiling and nodding as his grandmother regaled her with the history of Longdale.

His chest tightened as he watched his grandmother's delighted expression. She loved every beam and window of this crumbling old house. If he was going to save it for her, he would need to build an alliance with Gwen Morris.

But did she have enough experience to appraise his grandmother's treasures for their true value? And even if she did, would the sale provide the funds needed to take care of the repairs and renovations, or would he and his grandmother lose the home that had been in the family for generations—the home that one day should be his?

Two

1912
LONDON

The low murmur of the crowd filling the Fairweather Music Hall drifted past the closed velvet curtain, sending a thrill through Charlotte Harper. She turned to her father with a wide smile. "It sounds like a full house."

Her father nodded, his dark eyes glowing. "I believe you're right. The committee was wise to move the meeting here so we could accommodate a larger audience."

Charlotte's heart lifted. How proud she was of her father and his rise to prominence in the Higher Life Movement. As keynote speaker for this series of four meetings, his messages about pursuing a deeper commitment to God and gaining total victory over sin had captured the hearts and minds of devoted Christians all over London. The church sanctuary had been filled the last three nights, and hundreds of people had to be turned away. That had prompted the committee to change the venue to this new location for the fourth and final meeting.

Her mum, Rose Harper, stepped forward and brushed a piece of lint from the lapel of Father's new black suit, affection shining in her soft brown eyes. "You look quite handsome, Henry."

He sent her a brief glance, then looked away with a slight frown. "I'm sure the audience is more concerned about the content of my message than my appearance."

A flash of hurt crossed Mum's face, and she stepped back. "Of course, dear. I simply meant the new suit was a good choice." The black fabric with the pale gray pinstripe was an unusual choice for her father, but the tailor insisted it was quite appropriate for a speaker of his standing. Charlotte hoped the more conservative members of the audience wouldn't criticize him for his appearance.

Father's gaze darted to the men working backstage, then he grimaced and ran his finger around the inside of his collar.

Mum's brow creased. "You look flushed, Henry. Are you feeling ill?"

"I'm fine. This collar is simply too tight. You'll have to order me a larger one tomorrow."

Mum nodded. "Yes, dear. I'll take care of it."

Charlotte studied her father's glistening forehead and hoped he wasn't coming down with an illness. She pushed that thought away. He was in perfect health. It was probably just the excitement of tonight's events or the warmth of the backstage lights that was making him uncomfortable.

Charlotte's twelve-year-old sister, Alice, pulled the curtain back an inch and peeked out. "Oh, look at all the people!"

Charlotte reached for her sister's arm. "Alice, step back."

"They won't see me." A delighted smile lit up her sister's face. "There must be at least a thousand people out there."

Charlotte stepped behind Alice and looked around the edge of the curtain. Her breath caught, and her heart soared. Almost every seat on the main floor was filled, and the balconies swarmed with more people eager to find a seat . . . and they had all come to hear her father give his message.

She glanced back at her parents, intending to tell them what she'd seen, but Sir Anthony Fitzhugh, the head of the Higher Life Spring Series Committee, approached.

"Good evening." Sir Anthony nodded to Mum, then reached out and shook Father's hand. He was taller than her father and had a silver moustache, full beard, and kind blue eyes that gave him a distinguished appearance. He and her father had been good friends for several years.

Father smiled. "Good to see you, Anthony."

"Glad to be here with you. It's almost seven o'clock. Are you ready?"

Father nodded. "I'm looking forward to it."

Sir Anthony's expression radiated warmth and approval. "So am I, my friend. So am I." He turned to Mum and motioned to the right. "I've reserved seats for you and your daughters in the first row. If you go down those steps and into the hallway, you'll see the side entrance to the auditorium to your left. An usher will help you find your way."

Mum smiled. "Thank you, Sir Anthony. That's very kind."

"You're most welcome." He cocked his eyebrows. "If I hadn't reserved them, I'm afraid you'd be left standing."

Charlotte and Alice exchanged a smile. How wonderful that their father was receiving the respect and acclaim he so well deserved. He spent hours preparing, consulting commentaries and various books to add depth and insight to his messages. In the last few months, invitations had been pouring in from congregations and groups all over England. One had even arrived from New York. Her father's eyes had glowed when he'd read the letter and announced the news to the family. He hadn't accepted the invitation yet, but if he agreed, they would all be sailing to America in a few months, and Charlotte was delighted at the prospect.

Mum rose on tiptoe and kissed Father's cheek. "We'll see you after."

He accepted her kiss but turned away without answering.

Mum hesitated a moment, then she shifted her gaze to Charlotte and Alice. "Come along, girls." She took Alice's hand and started down the backstage steps.

Charlotte squeezed her father's hand. "I'll be praying for you."

He took his handkerchief from his jacket pocket and blotted his forehead. "Thank you." But he didn't meet her gaze. Instead, he glanced toward the curtain, as though he was already engaged with the audience.

Her hand slipped from his, and she turned and followed her mother and Alice into the hallway. Mum gave her name to the usher, and he opened the door to the auditorium and led them to the three reserved seats in the center of the first row.

Charlotte took the third seat. Mum sat in the middle, with Alice on her left. As Charlotte settled in and looked around, the lights came down and the crowd hushed. All around them a sense of excitement and anticipation filled the air.

Sir Anthony stepped from behind the curtain, strode to the pulpit in the center, and faced the audience. "Good evening, ladies and gentlemen. It is my great pleasure to welcome you to the fourth meeting in our Higher Life Spring Series." The audience responded with polite applause.

Charlotte glanced at Mum. Her cheeks were slightly pink and her expression expectant as she looked up at Sir Anthony.

When the applause died down, Sir Anthony's gaze traveled across the audience. "The Lord is doing powerful work among us, calling us all to full surrender and total commitment to Him. Our hope and prayer are that tonight's message will bring deep conviction and holy consecration to each one present. May we all dedicate ourselves fully to pressing on to God's higher calling.

"And now I encourage you to give your full attention to Henry

Harper, our dear brother and deeply devoted fellow sojourner on the road to the higher life." Sir Anthony swept his hand to the right.

Her father stepped out from behind the curtain and crossed to center stage as hearty applause filled the auditorium. The two men shook hands, and Sir Anthony walked offstage. Her father placed his Bible on the pulpit and looked out at the audience, his dark eyes bright and intense.

Love for him surged in Charlotte's chest. His dedication to God, his powerful preaching, and his handsome appearance made her proud to call him her father. There was no one she loved and admired more.

He opened his Bible and raised his gaze. "Tonight, we will look at the words of Jesus and His call to enter through the narrow gate. We will ask the question, Are you following the Savior through that narrow gate and down the road that leads to eternal life? Or have you, like so many others, lost your way and wandered to the wide and rocky path that leads to destruction?"

Charlotte clasped her hands in her lap, stirred once again by her father's words. Ever since she was a little girl, she'd heard him speak about that narrow gate. He and Mum had modeled a life of devotion and commitment, and she tried to follow their example. But she had to admit there were times she resisted the Spirit's promptings and stubbornly chose to go her own way. That thought niggled her conscience. She pushed it away and focused on her father's words once more.

He lifted his hand as his gaze swept the audience. "There are many trials . . . and temptations that come our way. The enemy of our soul is always on the prowl, looking for an opportunity to steal, kill, and destroy those who follow the Lord. He tries to . . . pull us off that narrow path." Her father's voice faltered. He looked down and gripped the sides of the pulpit.

Confusion wound through Charlotte. Had he paused for emphasis, or was something wrong? She glanced at her mum, hoping for reassurance. But concern lined her mum's face as she looked up at him.

Her father slowly lifted his head, his eyes searching the crowd. His face had gone deathly pale, and his chin quivered. "I'm sorry. I can't seem . . . to catch my . . ." He swayed, then he slumped and crashed to the floor behind the pulpit.

The crowd gasped. Charlotte's hands flew to cover her mouth, and she sprang from her seat.

"Father!" Alice cried and grabbed hold of Mum's arm.

Mum pulled away and strode toward the stage. Charlotte gripped Alice's hand and hurried after her. Sir Anthony rushed out from the side of the stage. Two other men followed and circled around Father, hiding him from Charlotte's view.

A man pushed through the gathering crowd behind Charlotte. "Let me through! I'm a doctor!" He climbed onto the stage and knelt beside Father.

Charlotte's heart pounded, and fearful thoughts raced through her mind. Voices rose around them, and the crowd pushed in closer. Mum bowed her head and clasped her shaking hands in front of her mouth, her lips moving in silent prayer.

Alice looked up at Charlotte with tear-filled eyes. "What happened? What's wrong with Father?"

"I don't know." Charlotte's voice trembled. She leaned to the left, trying to see past the men surrounding Father, but it was impossible.

"Stand back. Give him air," the doctor commanded, and the men moved back, widening their circle.

All around her, voices rose in prayer, some crying out, others murmuring softly.

Sir Anthony rose and looked their way. "Mrs. Harper, Henry is asking for you."

Mum opened her eyes and started for the side stairs. She looked over her shoulder, pain etched across her pale face. "Come with me, girls."

Charlotte took Alice's hand and followed Mum. When they reached center stage, the men surrounding her father parted and let them through. Charlotte's stomach dropped, and dizziness washed over her. Her father's face had gone pasty white, and his eyes were clouded. They had loosened his collar and unbuttoned his shirt at the neck.

Mum knelt and reached for Father's hand.

"Rose," he whispered.

"Yes, I'm here," she said softly.

"I'm sorry. I . . . never meant . . . this to happen." Anguish twisted his pale, glistening face.

"It's all right, Henry." Tears gathered in Mum's eyes. "Please, be calm. You don't have to speak."

"But . . . I . . ." His gaze shifted to Charlotte, heartbreaking emotion flickering across his face. "Forgive me."

Charlotte's throat swelled, and she knelt next to Mum. "There is nothing to forgive," she said, forcing out her words.

Father shook his head and closed his eyes. "If this is the end . . . know that I am truly sorry. I love you all very much."

"And we love you." Mum raised their clasped hands and kissed his fingers.

A man ran in and leaned toward the doctor. "The ambulance is here."

The doctor laid his hand on Mum's arm. "We're taking him to St. Luke's."

Mum nodded and swiped a tear from her cheek. "We'll follow." Her voice faltered, and her gaze traveled around the circle of men.

Four men strode in, carrying a canvas stretcher. Sir Anthony and the doctor moved everyone back. The men lowered the stretcher and transferred Father into place, then they grabbed the handles and lifted him.

Gasps and voices rose from the crush of people gathered in front of the stage.

"Henry!" a woman's voice cried out.

Charlotte turned and scanned the crowd. A blond woman stood at the edge of the stage, a handkerchief clutched to her mouth and tears flooding her blue eyes. Her gaze connected with Charlotte's, and her features twisted painfully. She spun away, pushed through the crowd, and strode up the aisle.

Sir Anthony turned to Mum. "I can take you and your daughters to the hospital in my motorcar."

"Thank you." Mum's voice barely rose above a whisper. Sir Anthony offered her his arm. Mum slipped her hand through, and they followed the men carrying Father's stretcher offstage.

Charlotte took Alice's hand and hurried after them, her mind spinning in frantic circles. Would Father recover, or was this the last time she would see him? A chill traveled through her, and she closed her eyes against that dreadful thought. She had to hold on to hope.

But hope seemed like a distant dream as more unsettling thoughts filled her mind. She'd always been taught God watched over and protected those who loved Him. Her father was at the height of his ministry and having a profound impact on many people. How could God strike down such a devoted and faithful servant? Her frightened heart couldn't make sense of it.

⁓

Charlotte carried the tray of used teacups into the kitchen and let the door swing closed behind her. She set the tray on the table, released a deep sigh, and rubbed her gritty eyes. Bone-weary and numb with grief, she could hardly connect one thought to the next, but she had to keep going.

Hundreds of people had come to her father's funeral that morning at the church, and Mum said it was only proper they invite their closest friends back to their home for a reception after. Now, Charlotte was stepping in as hostess to give Mum a short break.

She closed her eyes and leaned against the kitchen counter. If only she didn't have to return to the sitting room where a crowd of guests waited. They'd come to express their condolences and try to offer comfort. But it had been a long, painful day. Surely they would leave soon so the family could grieve in private.

Her eighteen-year-old brother, Daniel, walked into the kitchen. His wavy, dark brown hair was mussed, and his brown eyes shadowed. He looked almost as weary as she felt. He had been away at Oxford when Father collapsed. They'd sent him a telegram, and he'd raced home in time to see Father in the hospital. But Father had been unconscious by the time he arrived. Daniel hadn't been able to say good-bye, and that added to his grief.

He met her gaze. "Where's Mum? Sir Anthony and Mr. Walker want to speak to her before they leave."

Charlotte glanced toward the back stairs. "She went up to her room for a few minutes."

He nodded, lines creasing his forehead. "I'll go up and get her."

"No, I'll go. Could you tell them she'll be down shortly?"

He nodded, then searched her face, and his anxious expression eased. "I know this is hard, Charlotte, but we'll get through it."

She gave a slow nod, but she wasn't sure how. Father had been like the sun, the center of their universe. And they'd been like planets rotating around him, soaking in his powerful energy and light. How could they go on without him?

She forced those painful thoughts aside and climbed the back stairs. She found Mum in her bedroom, standing in front of her dressing table mirror, pressing a washcloth to her face.

Charlotte kept her voice soft, hoping not to add to Mum's pain. "Mr. Walker and Sir Anthony want to speak to you."

Mum turned and looked her way with a dazed expression. "What do they want?"

"I don't know. Daniel said they're preparing to leave and are asking for you."

Mum sighed. She dried her pale face and looked in the mirror once more. Her eyes were red-rimmed from weeping, and gray shadows beneath her eyes gave evidence of her lack of sleep.

Charlotte stepped closer and laid her hand on Mum's back. "I'll go down with you."

Mum met her gaze in the mirror, then turned and touched Charlotte's cheek. "Thank you, my dear. I don't know how I would've survived this week without you and your brother. Even Alice has been a sweet comfort."

Charlotte's eyes stung. She pressed her lips together and nodded. Mum was always gentle and ladylike, qualities Charlotte admired but often lacked. She'd been closer to her father and more like him with her love of reading and spending time outdoors. But Father was gone now. She and Mum would have to look out for each other if they were to survive this great loss.

Mum pulled in a deep breath and lifted her sagging shoulders. "I'm ready."

Charlotte forced a brief smile, then followed her mum down the stairs and into the sitting room.

Sir Anthony and Mr. Walker stood together by the fireplace. They both looked up as Mum and Charlotte crossed the room toward them.

Mum nodded to the men. "Thank you for coming. It's a comfort to have friends with us at a time like this."

Sir Anthony reached into his jacket pocket and pulled out a

white envelope. He held it out to Mum. "This is the honorarium
we'd planned to give Henry. I wish it were more."

Mum took the envelope and looked down for a moment.
When she raised her head, her eyes shimmered. "Thank you."

Sympathy filled Sir Anthony's face. "Please let me know if
there is anything I can do to help. I'd count it a privilege to
assist you with any practical matters or spiritual counsel. Just
send word, and I'll come."

Mum bit her lip and glanced away. "I appreciate that."

"Very well, then. I'll take my leave." Sir Anthony nodded
to her and walked toward the door, where his wife waited for
him.

Mr. Walker stepped forward. "I want to echo Sir Anthony's
words and offer my assistance as well. I can return to go over
your husband's will and his other business affairs whenever
you're ready."

Mum's eyebrows lifted. "His will?"

"Yes. As his solicitor, I prepared his will just a few months ago."

"I see." But confusion filled Mum's face.

"I'll help you take care of those matters, Mrs. Harper. That's
what Henry would want."

"Yes. Of course." Mum glanced at Charlotte, and then back
at Mr. Walker. "Can you come tomorrow?"

His eyes widened for a moment. "That soon?"

"Yes. I think it's best if we understand Henry's wishes."

Mr. Walker shifted his weight to the other foot, looking uncomfortable. "Very well. I can return tomorrow afternoon, if
that's agreeable."

"That will be fine. Thank you."

Charlotte's gaze followed Mr. Walker as he left the sitting
room. What had Father stated in his will? Her parents owned
their home. That would go to Mum, but Charlotte knew little
else about their financial situation. Surely Father had made

plans to provide for them. He loved them and would've made certain their futures were secure, wouldn't he?

∽

Charlotte stared across the dining room table at Mr. Walker, and her throat constricted. How could what he was saying be true?

Confusion filled Mum's face. "So, Henry left the house and all our belongings to me, but that's all? There is no life insurance?"

Mr. Walker shifted in his chair. "I'm afraid that's correct." He flipped through the papers in the open file on the table. "I spoke to Mr. Harper's banker this morning. He told me there are one hundred forty-two pounds in the account. As soon as I have the death certificate, I can withdraw those funds for you."

Mum gaped at the man. "One hundred forty-two pounds? I don't understand. Is there another account? Where is the money he received from his tutoring and speaking engagements?"

Mr. Walker shifted his gaze away. "I'm not aware of any other account."

"But Henry always led me to believe we had sufficient income and savings. He never mentioned a shortage of funds."

Daniel shot a worried glance at Charlotte, and she returned an uncertain look. Was that truly all that was left to them?

"I suppose Mr. Harper expected to live a long time and continue adding to his savings."

Mum sat back, looking stunned. "I had no idea we had so little money." She focused on Mr. Walker again. "Well, at least we have our home."

Mr. Walker grimaced. "Were you aware the house is mortgaged?"

Mum shook her head. "You must be mistaken. The mortgage on the house has been paid off for several years."

"That may have been the case, but the banker said Mr. Harper took out a loan against the house last year."

Mum blinked. "How much is the loan?"

He gave the amount, and Charlotte stifled a gasp. She shot another quick glance at her brother, trying to make sense of Mr. Walker's words.

Daniel turned to Mum. "Why would Father take out a loan?"

"I have no idea. He always gave me a generous monthly household allowance, but he took care of everything else. We rarely discussed finances."

Daniel's dark eyebrows dipped. "Do you think he took out the loan to pay my expenses at Oxford?"

Mum looked back at him. "He told me your school expenses were taken care of. Perhaps that is what he meant."

Mr. Walker closed the file and looked across the table at Mum. "I'm sorry, Mrs. Harper. I realize this puts you in a rather difficult position."

She lowered her gaze. "Yes . . . yes, it does."

Charlotte clasped her hands in her lap. With no funds coming from life insurance, they would have a difficult time providing for themselves. Daniel might have to quit Oxford and find a position. But who would hire him without a proper education?

Mum pressed her lips together for a few seconds, then looked across at Mr. Walker. "This is all quite overwhelming. I'm not sure what to do."

"I understand. I wish I had better news." Mr. Walker slipped the folder into his leather case. "Is it possible you have some other source of income I'm not aware of?"

Mum sighed. "No, we have no other income."

Mr. Walker leaned forward. "You might want to consider selling the house to pay off the loan and any other outstanding accounts. That would settle your debts, and you'd be free to make a fresh start."

Mum's eyes widened. "Sell the house? Do you really think that's necessary?"

"I'm not sure what other course to suggest."

Charlotte's stomach dropped.

"Do you have family members who would . . . take you in? That would lessen your expenses."

Mum's cheeks flushed. "My mother and brother have both passed away. And my father and I are . . . not closely connected."

Mr. Walker nodded. "I see. Well then, perhaps you have friends who might open their home to you?"

Mum lifted her hand to her forehead, shielding her eyes. "I'm afraid most of our friends live in modest homes. Taking in all four of us would be a great imposition."

Mr. Walker's expression turned grim. "I'm afraid, madam, you may have no other choice."

Mum's chin trembled as she rose. "Thank you for coming. You've given us much to consider."

"Of course. I'll be in touch when I have the death certificate and the funds from the bank." Mr. Walker reached for his leather case and stood. "I'll let myself out."

Charlotte's stunned gaze followed him as he passed under the archway and left the room. This was the only home she'd ever known. Where would they live if it had to be sold?

Mum turned toward Charlotte and Daniel, new resolve in her expression. "Well, my dears, it seems we have only one course of action. I'll have to write to my father at Longdale and try to repair the breach."

Carrie Turansky has loved reading since she first visited the library as a young child and checked out a tall stack of picture books. Her love for writing began when she penned her first novel at age twelve. She is now the award-winning author of twenty-three inspirational romance novels and novellas.

Carrie and her husband, Scott—who is a pastor, author, and speaker—have been married for forty-five years and make their home in New Jersey. They often travel together on ministry trips and to visit their five adult children and eleven grandchildren.

Carrie is active in the women's ministry at her church, and she enjoys leading women's Bible studies and mentoring younger women. When she's not writing, she enjoys working in her flower gardens, walking around the lake near their home, and cooking healthy meals for family and friends.

She loves to connect with reading friends through her website, CarrieTuransky.com, and via Facebook, Instagram, and Pinterest.

Sign Up for Carrie's Newsletter

Keep up to date with Carrie's latest news
on book releases and events by signing up
for her email list at the link below.

CarrieTuransky.com

FOLLOW CARRIE ON SOCIAL MEDIA

Carrie Turansky   @CarrieTuransky   @CarrieTuransky

More from Carrie Turansky

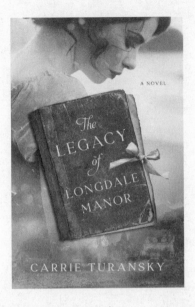

Art historian Gwen Morris is evaluating paintings at a British estate when she uncovers a connection to the father she never knew through a one-hundred-year-old journal. In 1912, Charlotte Harper struggles with a painful family secret that she can only confess in her journal, which shatters her faith and leaves her wondering if she can ever trust in love again.

The Legacy of Longdale Manor